POWDERED GOLD

TEMPLARS AND THE AMERICAN ARK OF THE COVENANT

A Novel by
David S. Brody

Eyes That See Publishing
Westford, Massachusetts

Powdered Gold
Templars and the American Ark of the Covenant

Eyes That See Publishing
Westford, Massachusetts

ISBN 978-0-985-83307-7
1st edition

Cover Art by Kimberly Scott
Printed in USA

POWDERED GOLD

TEMPLARS AND THE AMERICAN ARK OF THE COVENANT

David S. Brody

Praise for David S. Brody's Books

"Brody does a terrific job of wrapping his research in a fast-paced thrill ride that will feel far more like an action film than an academic paper."
— PUBLISHERS WEEKLY (*Cabal of the Westford Knight*)

"Strongly recommended for all collections."
— LIBRARY JOURNAL (*The Wrong Abraham*)

"Will keep you up even after you've put it down."
— Hallie Ephron, BOSTON GLOBE (*Blood of the Tribe*)
"A riveting, fascinating read."
— MIDWEST BOOK REVIEW (*The Wrong Abraham*)

"Best of the Coming Season."
— BOSTON MAGAZINE (*Unlawful Deeds*)

"A compelling suspense story and a searing murder mystery."
— THE BOSTON PHOENIX (*Blood of the Tribe*)

"A comparison to *The Da Vinci Code* and *National Treasure* is inevitable....The story rips the reader into a fast-paced adventure."
— FRESH FICTION (*Cabal of the Westford Knight*)

"An excellent historical conspiracy thriller. It builds on its most famous predecessor, *The Da Vinci Code*, and takes it one step farther—and across the Atlantic."
— MYSTERY BOOK NEWS (*Cabal of the Westford Knight*)

"The action and danger are non-stop, leaving you breathless. It is one hell of a read."
— ABOUT.COM Book Reviews (*Unlawful Deeds*)

"The year is early, but this book will be hard to beat; it's already on my 'Best of 2009' list."
　　—BARYON REVIEW (*Cabal of the Westford Knight*)

"Five Stars."
　　—Harriet Klausner, AMAZON (*The Wrong Abraham*)

"An enormously fun read, exceedingly hard to put down."
　　—The BOOKBROWSER (*Unlawful Deeds*)

"Fantastic book. I can't wait until the next book is released."
　　—GOODREADS (*Thief on the Cross*)

"A feast."
　　—ARTS AROUND BOSTON (*Unlawful Deeds*)

About the Author

David S. Brody is a *Boston Globe* bestselling fiction writer recently named Boston's "Best Local Author" by the *Boston Phoenix* newspaper. He serves as a Director of the Westford Historic Society and is a former Director of the New England Antiquities Research Association (NEARA). A graduate of Tufts University and Georgetown Law School, he is an avid researcher in the subject of pre-Columbian exploration of America. His *Cabal of the Westford Knight* novel was recently made into a full-length feature film entitled, "The American Templars."

For more information, please visit
DavidBrodyBooks.com

Also by the Author

Unlawful Deeds

Blood of the Tribe

The Wrong Abraham

*Cabal of the Westford Knight: Templars at the
Newport Tower*

Thief on the Cross: Templar Secrets in America

Preface

This novel is a continuation of the themes I first explored in *Cabal of the Westford Knight* and continued exploring in *Thief on the Cross*. Specifically, did ancient explorers visit the shores of North America, and if so, why? Readers of *Cabal* and *Thief* will recognize the protagonists, Cameron and Amanda (and also young Astarte), as well as the Knights Templar themes. However, *Powdered Gold* is not a sequel to *Cabal* and *Thief* and readers who have not read the earlier novels should feel free to jump right in.

As in *Cabal* and *Thief,* the artifacts and sites pictured in this story are real, actual objects. If it is pictured in the book, it exists in the real world. (See the Author's Note at the end of this book for a more detailed discussion covering the issue of artifact authenticity.)

I venture outside of New England in this story, which takes place largely in the American Southwest. The story features artifacts such as the Tucson Lead Artifacts, the Mustang Mountain Rune Stone and the Los Lunas Decalogue Stone—do these objects somehow tie back to the Knights Templar or their French forbearers? Readers may enjoy learning about a strange, seemingly-magical substance called White Powdered Gold, or ORME, derived from the desert sands of Arizona. I was intrigued by the similarities between this substance and *manna*, the miraculous food that nourished the Israelites while they wandered in the desert. Is it possible, I wondered, that White Powdered Gold is the key to understanding the mysteries of, and power behind, the sacred Ark of the Covenant?

These musings result in me (through my characters) exploring and offering up some rather unorthodox interpretations of Biblical stories and religious history. **Please therefore be forewarned that this book contains themes that may be offensive to readers with strong Christian, Jewish or other religious beliefs.**

Every present-day story must be set against a modern backdrop; the plot turns in this novel are triggered by a

Survivalist community attempting to go "off grid" in the Arizona desert. I found learning about the beliefs and practices of these Survivalists to be almost as compelling as researching the ancient artifacts themselves. Note that I said "almost."

I remain fascinated by the hidden history of North America and the very real possibility that waves of European explorers visited our shores long before Columbus. It is my hope that readers share this fascination.

David S. Brody, October, 2013
Westford, Massachusetts

PROLOGUE

[AD 1214, Present-day Arizona]

Climb the mountain of snakes. Find the priest with the milky eyes. Trading for the information had cost Hurech his best dagger—a trade well worth it if the intelligence was correct. But why did quests like this always seem to end amidst snakes and strange oracles? Couldn't just once the secret be safeguarded by buxom maidens frolicking on the banks of a cool stream?

After wandering in this strange, arid land for almost two years, Hurech welcomed the portending closure—even if it meant a milky-eyed priest who would no doubt speak in riddles. Three of his fellow knights had died and another made lame. Only he and Geoffrey remained of the expedition that had left a ship and its crew two thousand miles to the southeast. Hurech turned to his young compatriot. Perhaps not so young anymore—the fuzzy-chinned monk who had left Staffordshire with him three years earlier was now a man. Not as solid yet as Hurech, but already a bit taller. "Be wary of the snakes," Hurech said.

Geoffrey nodded. He rarely spoke, perhaps a product of the years spent in silence in a Cistercian abbey before training as a soldier monk at Hurech's preceptory. Geoffrey's sword did most of his talking.

If Geoffrey was now a man, Hurech mused, surely gangly Elizabeth had flowered as well—had she grown into a willowy beauty like her mother? And the twins were now old enough to begin training with wooden swords. Hurech stopped and turned to the eastern horizon. Perhaps five thousand miles of desert and mountains and ocean separated him from his family. But sometimes their faces were so real he felt he could reach out and tousle their hair....

The cursed cactus bushes intruded on his thoughts, clawing at his legs like angry house cats as he climbed. Between the snakes on the trails, the scorpions in their bedding and these needle-like plants bloodying their skin, Hurech would not miss this land. He wiped the sweat from his brow and sipped from his water skin. Not to mention the dust and cursed desert heat.

After an hour climb they reached the ridgeline and, as instructed, followed a narrow descending path. Despite the heat, a smoky campfire smoldered at the base of a cliff face, serving as their beacon.

They approached the fire, Hurech in the lead. He exhaled and straightened himself. An elderly priest sat cross-legged in front of a cave, facing them as if awaiting their arrival. His gnarled skin was caked with dirt and his nose, unlike the flat features of the natives, protruded beaklike off his narrow face.

The priest sniffed the air as they closed to within five body lengths. "You have come," the priest sang out in Latin, his cloud-white eyes somehow focusing on Hurech's face. His reddish-brown hair and beard, streaked with gray, were long and unkempt, and he wore a dark vest over a dirty white robe. Based on the way the vest hung, Hurech guessed it was made of some kind of heavy metal.

"How do you know it is I?" Hurech asked.

The priest chanted his response, as if following the cadence of some ancient prayer. "Our people different smell than people of this land."

Hurech nodded. He didn't ascribe to his Order's prohibition on bathing, but the reality was that there was little fresh water in this desert land and he and Geoffrey no doubt reeked. "*Our* people?"

"Yes. My ancestors from Gaul fourteen generations came to this land. But already that you know. That is why here you are." In addition to the chanting, the priest formed his words slowly and arranged them oddly, as if he rarely used them. Which made sense—how much Latin would be spoken here, half a world away from Rome?

"So the French legends are true."

The priest nodded. "It is good you now came. Of my people I am last."

"The last? There are no others?" So much for the maidens.

The priest shook his head slowly. "God wills it not."

Hurech looked past the priest, into the cave. "The legends also state you possess the *Aron Habrit*. Can this be so?"

The priest turned up his palms and smiled, showing a mouth empty of teeth. "You must determine. Merely I am caretaker."

The priest angled his head toward the cave opening, inviting Hurech inside. Hurech sighed. He lit a torch from the campfire and peered deeper into the cave, allowing his eyes to adjust after the midday glare of the desert. Propped against the cave walls stood a dozen swords and crosses fashioned out of a dark metal.

Hurech bent and lifted one of the swords. "Too heavy even for the strongest man," he said to Geoffrey. "Lead, I think. Probably ceremonial."

Geoffrey dropped to one knee in front of one of the crosses as Hurech held the torch. "I see writing," Geoffrey said. "Latin, and also some Hebrew."

"As the legends suggest. We will decipher it later."

Hurech moved deeper in, following the cave as it angled to the left. His torch illuminated a large rectangular object resting inside a cavity in the back of the cave. *Could it be?*

"Geoffrey, stay back. The legends speak of grave danger to those who approach too close." He wondered if the metal vestment the priest wore was a necessary precaution. But precaution against what?

Hurech took two small steps. Then another. He held the torch forward as far as he could, straining to make out the details of the relic in the niche. The flame reflected off the object, dancing as the torch flickered. Hurech had spent his adult life searching for this sacred artifact, not only in Europe and the Holy Land but now far across the western ocean. He took a deep breath and moved closer still.

Suddenly the object glowed and crackled. Before Hurech could back away a bolt of lightning shot out, striking him in the chest and catapulting him backwards. He had been thrown from a horse a few times, and clubbed across the back by a battle ax, but nothing had ever incapacitated him like this. His entire body felt like it was afire, and he could not force air into his lungs. A crushing pain spread through his chest. *So this is it. This is God's will.* He fought to meet death with honor.

"Geoffrey," he whispered, "you must bury my body and mark the spot. Just as we discussed. Then you must find the ship and return home to tell of what we have found." He gasped, forcing the words out with his last breath. "Do not try to retrieve the relic. God has decreed it is not yet time to do so."

CHAPTER 1

Willum Smoot peered out the window of his two-passenger helicopter as he banked toward the winter sun rising over the Arizona foothills. Below, just cresting a ridgeline, a cluster of hikers scampered for cover. Willum made out a handful of kids and a few adults—probably a family of illegals hoping for a better life than the one they had just abandoned in Mexico. *Good luck with that.*

Circling back, he swooped in lower for a better look. Yup, Mexicans. Nine of them, their entire lives stuffed into plastic bags and vinyl suitcases. If they died out here, or were killed, nobody would miss them. They looked up, fearful, the copter now barreling toward them on the mountain ridge. A man, probably the father, shouted instructions. Willum steered the copter directly at him.

The Mexican knew nothing about Willum—his time in prison, his belief in the pending collapse of society, his decision to move to a fortified desert compound. Five minutes ago Willum never existed, and after today—assuming he made it out of the desert alive—the man would never see Willum again. But now, at this moment, the copter plunging toward him and the bearded, crazy-eyed pilot in its cockpit were the very center of his universe.

The man took a deep breath and raised himself up, ready to accept the full brunt of whatever Willum intended to throw at him. Down the slope, crouched behind a boulder, a dark-haired woman reached out to her man, fingers clawing at the air.

Shifting his bulk as best he could in the tight confines, Willum reached behind his seat and grabbed one of the half-dozen tightly-bundled canvas packs he kept on board. Aiming carefully, now only fifty feet above the ground, he tossed the bag out the open doorway. "Welcome to America," he mouthed, knowing his voice would be drowned out by the sound of the copter. The pack thumped to the ground, bounced and came to rest a few yards from the man.

The Mexican's first reaction was to recoil from the balding hulk of a man tossing things from the sky. But Willum knew the man's curiosity, and perhaps desperation, would win out and he would cautiously approach the pack. He would probably probe it with a stick, perhaps nudge it with his toe. But, eventually, hands shaking, he would reach down, unclasp the buckle and slowly fold back the flap...

Willum wished he could stick around to see his reaction, see his eyes grow wide. He would look skyward, find the retreating copter on the horizon and wonder about the crazy copter pilot who delivered care packages from the heavens—water, trail mix, a couple of blankets, even a few hundred bucks in cash.

Everyone deserved a chance at a better life. And shame on his government for treating these people like criminals.

Good deed done, Willum turned his attention back to his mission. He banked the copter to his right, using the morning sun as a spotlight to illuminate the crags and nooks along the east-facing peaks. Was it possible that hidden in these hills rested a golden chest, presumably filled with some kind of treasure?

Common sense told him it was unlikely. And it was even more unlikely that an aging, overweight ex-con who happened to be a whiz in chemistry would be the one to find it. Yet Willum couldn't shake from his memory the dying words of his jailhouse cellmate.

"It's up there, Willum," Boone had said. "Up in the Mustang Mountains. My great-granddaddy used to prospect in those hills, and he swears he saw it. He and another fellow. He drew a picture of it." Boone had lifted a shaky hand up to the narrow shelf above his bed, removed a manila envelope from a cigar box, pulled out a brownish and crinkly piece of paper and handed it to Willum. Other than its age, there was nothing remarkable about the drawing—a simple rectangular chest with a pair of long poles passing through eyelets on either side of the chest, apparently to carry it.

Boone had continued. "When my great-granddaddy's buddy reached out to open it, it electrocuted him. Killed him dead.

Almost like magic." The old man had sat up a little. "My great-granddaddy said God was protecting it, didn't want anyone to take it from the mountains. I tell you what: If I get to heaven, I'll ask the Good Lord. If he says it's okay, I'll come back and guide you to it." Boone had smiled, probably for the last time in his life. "And I get half."

Willum had bunked with Boone for almost two years, and he was pretty sure the old con man wasn't going to heaven. But the dying Boone had nothing to gain by sending Willum on a quixotic quest. Boone really believed the golden chest was up in those hills. Was he right? Well, a treasure chest was not the kind of thing one could just walk away from. At least Willum couldn't. And, fortunately, he was at a time in his life where he could indulge in some harmless treasure-hunting. The government had taken a huge chunk of his fortune, but not all of it, and he had more time on his hands than he knew what to do with.

And Willum had found one tantalizing clue. He glanced down at the photograph of the engraved stone he had found a year ago while exploring these hills. The stone sat in front of one of the caves pock-marking the cliff face of the range's highest peak.

MUSTANG MOUNTAIN RUNE STONE

The inscription was written in an alphabet called runic. Willum had had it translated by an expert who opined this style of runes dated to medieval times and was of Anglo-Saxon, rather than Scandinavian, origin:

> *The body of rough Hurech lays here.*
> *He enjoyed merriment.*
> *The secret is near rough Hurech's body.*
> *Fame and glory await.*
> *The body turns to dust and goes to Eden's temple.*

Willum had reached the obvious conclusion that the carving served as a grave marker, a eulogy for a man named Hurech, an apparently rough fellow who enjoyed merriment, was entrusted with an important secret and was buried inside the cave

Willum had returned the next day with a shovel to dig up Hurech, rough fellow or not. A bit uncomfortable with his task, and trying to add some levity to the exhumation, Willum called out as he dug, "Alas, poor Hurech!"—a clumsy nod to the speech Hamlet gave after Yorick's bones had themselves been exhumed.

Six inches below the surface, near the mouth of the cave, Willum had found bones in a shallow grave. But the skeleton had been disturbed—perhaps by animals—and the skull and other bones were missing. He removed a rib, dropped a wad of tobacco in the grave as payment to the spirit of rough Hurech, and re-covered the grave. He also looked around the cave for some kind of hidden secret but found nothing. He sent the rib to a lab in Cleveland owned by an old college classmate. A week later the friend phoned to report the bone likely belonged to a northern European male eight or nine hundred years old. This result was consistent with the runic analysis.

When Willum found English land records showing a man named Hurech in Staffordshire around the year 1200, the story seemed to hold together. Unless there were a bunch of runic-speaking Indians running around the hills of Arizona carrying 800-year-old European bones, there was only one rational explanation: At least two Europeans (rough Hurech plus the fellow who carved the eulogy and buried him) had been exploring Arizona well before Christopher Columbus. And if they were here, they were here for a reason—probably the secret rough Hurech was guarding. Which brought Willum full circle back to old Boone's dying words about some kind of treasure chest.

Willum decided to make one more pass with the copter. Other than illegal aliens navigating their way inland from the Mexican border twenty miles to the south, not many people climbed these mountains anymore. But in the late 1800s they had been teeming with silver miners. Men like Boone's great-grandfather. Willum was pretty sure none of the other prospectors had found the chest—it was not the type of thing that would have gone unnoticed in a frontier mining town. Which was why he was staying away from the old mining sites and focusing instead on areas that had been left undisturbed.

The sound of his chopper caught the attention of a team of border patrol agents patrolling on horseback. Willum slapped his thigh. Time to call it a day. He angled the copter away from the illegal Mexicans, hoping to draw the agents away.

It was just bad luck that southern Arizona had so many military installations—Willum would have much preferred to be hundreds of miles away from anyone working for the federal government. At least so far, the feds hadn't seemed to take any interest in the desert compound Willum recently bought and fortified.

Of course, that's probably what the good folks in Waco and Ruby Ridge thought not long before the government assassinated them.

Astarte swung as they walked along a path bisecting the college academic quad, one hand grasping Cam's and the other Amanda's. "Don't let me step on the cracks," the girl said. "It will break my mother's back." She glanced up at Amanda. "I guess that would be you, Amanda, since you're my mother now."

Amanda stopped and cocked her head, green eyes wide and glistening. Going through the foster-parenting process with a nine-year-old had been harder than they thought—Cam knew that Astarte referring to Amanda as her mother was a big step. "I'm happy to be your mum, Astarte, but what's this about broken backs?"

"It's a game kids play," Cam said, chuckling. "You didn't have that superstition in England?"

Amanda laughed. "No. But you Americans don't think twice about passing someone on the stairs, and you think a black cat is unlucky, so what do you know?"

Astarte looked up. "Wait, so a black cat is *lucky*?"

"Very much so." Amanda smiled. "Unless, apparently, it steps on a sidewalk crack." She resumed walking. "Is there something special about the cracks in Arizona, or is it everywhere?"

"It's everywhere," Astarte said. "But at home there's too much snow on the ground, so it doesn't matter." They had flown out of Boston during a February snowstorm.

"I see. Well, I'd not fancy a broken back, so up we go." Amanda hoisted the girl skyward as Astarte giggled and kicked her feet, her dark braids swinging around her almond-colored face. The girl's dark coloring contrasted with Amanda's flaxen hair and fair complexion—creamy skin highlighted by emerald eyes and wine-red lips, like a lightly-decorated Christmas sugar cookie.

Cam smiled. Astarte was a decent-sized kid, yet Amanda lifted her effortlessly. Cam stayed in good shape for a guy pushing forty, but Amanda regularly beat him in tennis; only with the greatest effort—and perhaps her silent understanding of the fragility of the male ego—did he keep up with her on their mountain-biking expeditions. Yet she managed to look willowy.

"That's the building," Cam said. He pointed at a sprawling, windowless, two-story white stucco structure with 'Arizona Historical Society' inscribed across the front. They had passed beyond the academic quad, emerging onto a side street rimming the University of Arizona's Tucson campus.

"Are we all going in?" Astarte asked.

"Not to start with," Amanda said. "We'll let Cameron get set up and begin to examine the artifacts. You and I will get some breakfast and join him later."

"How old did you say the artifacts were, Cameron?" Her cobalt eyes, large and expressive, stared up at him.

Good question. "Well, some people think they are over a thousand years old. And some people think they are only about a hundred. I'm here to see if we can solve the mystery."

"Well, I'm not very good at remembering all the dates, but I bet whoever it was came here after the Phoenicians," Astarte said. "The Phoenicians had bigger boats than Christopher Columbus and the Pilgrims. They came to America to get copper." Astarte had previously been home-schooled by her uncle, and obviously had learned a different version of American history than was taught in the public schools. Her uncle had been a researcher of early American exploration who shared his research with Cam before he died. A Mormon, he had spent a lifetime trying to prove that the history recounted in the Book of Mormon—that of white explorers traveling to America beginning approximately 2500 years ago—was correct. Cam was intrigued by his research, though both he and Amanda rejected the patriarchal teachings of the Mormon faith. Astarte continued to cling—understandably—to the religion that had played such a prominent part in her upbringing, and Cam and Amanda weren't sure what to do about it. They didn't want her growing up believing that she couldn't go to heaven unless she was married, and that her primary job in life was to have babies, and that her husband was also her master—not that all Mormons believed these things, but Amanda had a friend from New Hampshire who had been raised with these precepts as a child.

"Yes, Astarte," Amanda said. "We are learning that many people came across, over many centuries. People need to start thinking of the Atlantic Ocean as a highway, not a hurdle."

The girl nodded. "Mormon people already think that way. We learned about it from the Book of Mormon."

We. Cam and Amanda shared a glance. Now was not the time to get into it again. Cam kissed Amanda, gave Astarte a hug and said goodbye. "After I'm done we'll go horseback riding, okay?"

As he turned one last time to watch them go, Cam noticed a gangly man sipping a cup of coffee while leaning against a bike rack across the street. He wouldn't have given it a second thought had it not been for the old Montreal Expos insignia on the baseball cap the man wore—Cam had rooted for the Expos as a kid, though of course the Red Sox were his favorite. And he had seen that hat in the hotel lobby this morning. Could there really be two Expos hats within a few blocks of each other in Tucson, Arizona?

Trying to appear casual, he yelled to Amanda and began jogging toward her. "Hey, you forgot your key." And as he got closer. "Play along. I think that guy is following us." A cab turned the corner and headed toward them. "I'd feel better if you got into this cab and got out of here." He waved at the taxi.

Amanda glanced over. "Bloody hell. You're right. I think I saw him in the hotel elevator last night. The hat makes his ears flare out."

Cam smiled, trying not to alarm Astarte. "Well, I'll say this for him. He's not very good at his job if we both recognize him." He kissed them again as they got into the taxi. "Don't come back until I call you, okay?"

Amanda nodded. "What are you going to do?"

"For now, nothing. But if he's still here when I come back out…"

Astarte interrupted, tugging on the sleeve of his coat through the open window. "I just took his picture. He didn't see me through the window."

"Good job." In some ways Astarte was nine going on nineteen. "Can you text it to us?"

Cam jogged back to the stucco building, one eye on the Expos hat. Why would someone be following them? He knew it was a stupid question even as it formed in his brain. A few months earlier he and Amanda had uncovered religious artifacts that called into question some of Christianity's basic teachings. In doing so they had foiled the plans of a group of religious fanatics hoping to usher in a new messiah; the group had been aided by a team of rogue federal agents. So their list of enemies included the Catholic Church, some federal intelligence operatives and a violent religious sect. Other than that, most people liked them.

Cam pushed through the door, taking a second to use the darkened glass as a mirror to see behind him. The man was watching him but had not moved. Cam shrugged and allowed the door to close behind him.

It was just before nine; he was scheduled to meet a geology professor from the nearby University of Arizona campus in the front lobby and together they would find the archivist. They would be examining lead artifacts that had been found buried in the desert outside Tucson in the 1920s. The artifacts, numbering about thirty, were inscribed in both Hebrew and Latin and purported to tell the tale of a colony of Christianized Jews from France exploring the area in the ninth century AD. The items caused quite a stir when first found—the New York Times ran a series of front-page stories chronicling the discovery. But within a few years the sheer outlandishness of the story swung public opinion—more specifically, the academics who studied the artifacts—into concluding the artifacts must be fake. So the lead pieces had been boxed, archived and largely forgotten for almost ninety years.

Cam thought it might be time to take a fresh look.

A fifty-something man wearing wire-rim glasses and long grayish hair pulled back in a ponytail stood up from a bench as Cam entered the building. "You Cameron Thorne?" He spoke softly, almost in a whisper.

Cam smiled and stuck out his hand. "Nice to meet you. Thanks for coming, Professor Schneider."

"You can call me Max." The geology professor wore a wrinkled gray blazer over a blue button-down and a pair of jeans. He carried a silver, suitcase-like container.

"Is that your microscope?"

"Yes." He smiled. "I'm not much use without it." They followed signs to the archivist's office. As they walked, the aroma of pipe smoke wafted from the professor's blazer. "So you've never seen these artifacts before?" Cam asked.

"Never even heard of them until we got your call. But I spoke to a couple of the old-timers in the department. They think you're wasting your time." He shrugged. "The artifacts are fake."

"Have they examined them?"

Max smiled and shrugged again. "I don't think so."

Cam came across this often. "It's amazing how so many people, even those in academia, jump to conclusions."

"Well, I'm here with an open mind."

Ten minutes later the archivist ushered Cam and the professor into a small conference room. "Nobody has looked at these things in almost fifty years," she said, smiling. The lead artifacts were displayed on three multi-shelved metal display carts. She handed the men each a pair of white cotton gloves. "Please wear these when you handle them. There are thirty-two objects in total. Take all the time you need."

Yanking the gloves on as he crossed the room, Cam made a beeline for the most elaborate objects. He had seen pictures of most of the artifacts before, but two crosses that contained both Hebrew and Latin writing were the ones that most intrigued him. Each was about eighteen inches long and intricately decorated. One of the crosses had a snake entwining the four arms of the cross, and the top of the cross had been shaped into a sharp arrowhead. The other cross had been shaped so that the lower end of the cross resembled the hilt of a battle sword.

TUCSON LEAD ARTIFACTS

Using two hands, Cam lifted the snake cross. Despite the arrowed point, it was much too heavy to be used as any kind of weapon. These were obviously ceremonial objects. Peering closer, he noticed that parts of the artifact were engraved in Latin and parts in Hebrew.

TUCSON LEAD ARTIFACTS

"If you want to bring one of those over, I'll take a look at it," the professor said. Cam was so enthralled with the artifacts that he had almost forgotten about Max setting up his microscope.

Cam handed him the snake cross. He knew a little about forensic geology, but obviously not as much as a trained geologist. "It seems to me, there are only two possibilities for these artifacts. Either they're authentic, or they were planted there as a hoax or a scheme by the guy who found them—maybe as a way to make money or garner publicity."

"Sounds fair. As I understand it, these were found on the outskirts of the city, out in the desert. I can't imagine how else they would have gotten there."

"So is there anything you can tell microscopically about how long they may have been buried? Mineral growth or weathering or something like that? The guy who found them had only lived in Tucson for three years. So if they were in the ground longer than three years that would help rebut the hoax possibility."

The professor took the object and placed it under the scope. He moved it around, finally settling on the area where the Hebrew letters had been carved. "Interesting," he said after a few minutes.

"What?"

"Here. Take a look."

Cam peered into the scope. "I assume that grooved area is one of the Hebrew letters?"

"Yes."

"So what's the white stuff inside?" It looked like some kind of buildup, almost like cholesterol forming on the inside of artery walls.

"That's calcite. It often accumulates in lead pipes."

"How long does it take?"

"Well, in pipes it can build up in a couple of years."

Cam felt his shoulders slump. He had hoped to be able to prove the artifacts were authentic. "So that's not going to help us. Our guy could have planted the artifacts and waited a couple of years to discover them."

"Not necessarily." The professor turned to face him. "It only takes a couple of years for calcite to form in pipes because pipes have a constant supply of water. But you said this cross was buried in the desert, right? Was it near the surface?"

"No. Six feet down."

"So only rarely would it have been covered in water. I can't see how the calcite would have built up in less than, say, many decades. Probably much longer."

"Really?"

The professor shrugged. "The science doesn't lie."

Cam tried to stay focused. If the geologist was correct, then the artifacts were almost certainly authentic. He wanted to call Amanda right away and share the news, but he also wanted to maintain an air of professionalism in front of the professor. "Do you see anything else?"

"Not on this artifact." He pointed to a thick lead cross on one of the display carts. "But what about that one? It has some green growth I'd like to take a look at."

TUCSON LEAD ARTIFACTS

Cam retrieved the cross, which was unadorned but freckled with blotches of green. Using two hands, he carried it over and gently rested it on the microscope. This time he stood by while the professor examined the object.

"Well, I think my estimate of many decades is actually incorrect."

Cam's stomach tightened. "Why?" He tried to be objective when studying these artifacts, but his passion for the subject always made him hope they were authentic.

The professor moved aside again. "Take a look. See that green build-up? It's called malachite. And there's a blue deposit called azurite also. Both of these are formed from the copper ore that is present within the lead. Essentially what happens is, over many centuries, the malachite and azurite seep to the surface."

"Did you say over many centuries?"

The professor pulled a pipe from the inside of his jacket pocket, sat back and chewed on the end. "Yes, Mr. Thorne, I did. It seems you have at least two very old artifacts here. I'll leave it up to you to explain how they found their way to Arizona."

It was the type of thing that made Ellis Kincaid realize how anachronistic many members of the nation's intelligence community were. A meeting in a bathroom stall at a highway rest area? Really? Would the Cone of Silence be used while Maxwell Smart talked into his shoe?

Ellis had received the text on his cell the night before. "Tuesday, 18:00. Meet in men's room stall at state liquor store on Interstate 93, Hooksett, NH." But the idiot hadn't specified whether it was the northbound or the southbound rest area. And the text had come in from a dummy phone, so Ellis couldn't reply. Worse still, it was rush hour in New Hampshire, to the extent such a thing really existed, and it was snowing, so traffic was creeping along at about half speed. So it's not like Ellis could circle around, exit to exit, checking out both the northbound and southbound stalls, comparing flatulence levels. Would the fart of a senior Defense Department intelligence operative smell better or worse than some poor slob on his way home from work?

So what to do? Ellis put on his analyst hat which, after all, is what the U.S. taxpayers had been paying him for since his tour in Afghanistan ended. Unlike most Navy SEALs or other elite force members, his specialty was a non-physical one: Ellis was trained in forensic psychology and psychological profiling—he figured out what people were going to do and when they might do it. In his job, 'people' meant terrorists or others who might threaten the interests of the United States. Most notably, he had used his skills to evaluate the intelligence regarding Osama bin Laden's hideout in Pakistan—was it consistent with the psychological profile of the man? Ellis had concluded it was, and that correct bet had earned him a post-deployment job in the DIA, the Defense Intelligence Agency. The DIA was the military's version of the CIA and operated out of a military installation in downtown Washington, D.C.

Ellis had been in Washington when he received the text. But since he had been summoned to New Hampshire, that meant whoever he was meeting was senior to him and already up in the area—why make Mr. Important travel when you can put the young grunt on a plane just as easily? The rest area was only fifty miles north of Boston, so maybe the senior agent was in Boston. But if so, why not meet in the city? It was more likely the agent was in one of two places: at a ski resort in the northern mountains or at Dartmouth, probably consulting with one of the many intelligence community operatives with ties to the college. Either way, Ellis's bathroom buddy would be traveling south on Route 93 to Hooksett. Probably.

At 5:55 Ellis kicked the slush off his boots and entered the southbound rest stop's men's room. He stopped at the sink to eye himself in the mirror—his stylist had lightened his hair and given him what she called a 'Brit-rock indie' cut, sweeping all his hair forward so that thick waves of his blond-tinged orange locks kissed his eyebrows. Not bad. And it screamed slacker rather than soldier, so it made for a good cover.

He kicked open both stall doors. Leaning against the wall of the stall closest to the door, he killed time playing *Words With Friends* on his iPhone. If Mr. Important were in the northbound rather than the southbound stalls, well, it might just cost Ellis that promotion he had been waiting on.

Ten minutes later a large pair of duck boots approached and trudged into the end stall. The man cleared his throat. "You a Patriots fan?" Deep voice, New York accent. And a bit of a wheeze. So probably not a skier.

"Yup. Also the Redskins."

"Me too." A lie. Probably a Giants fan. But they both understand the Washington reference. Duck Boots coughed. "First things first: This meeting never happened."

"Understood." Great. That meant if he fucked up, he would take the fall. Alone. But the opposite was also probably true—this was an important assignment, success at which would likely advance his career.

"We need Smoot to produce that fuel cell. He's a goddamn Einstein when it comes to this stuff. I'm talking decades ahead of everyone else."

Ellis had been assigned the case a year ago—from what he'd read in the file, the government had harassed Smoot, put him in jail, even convinced a judge to keep his kid away from him. Smoot simply didn't want to help. "With all due respect, I think Smoot is unreachable. He's living in some desert compound. The last thing he wants to do is help the government. I think he'd rather take it down."

"Kid, listen to me: The damn Chinese are close to figuring this out themselves. This is bigger than putting the first man on the moon. Almost as big as getting the A-bomb. Whoever perfects this technology can cut their oil needs in half, maybe more. And then patent and sell the technology to the rest of the world. Right now China has the people and the Arabs have the oil. But if China figures out this fuel cell first, all that money that goes to the Towel Heads now ends up in the pockets of the Chinks." He coughed again. "You combine all that money with all those people, well, it's only a matter of time before we're eating apple pie with chopsticks and washing *their* laundry."

Ellis didn't know much about fuel cell technology other than the cells, unlike batteries, needed a constant source of energy. But unlike batteries they could, with this energy source, run forever. The key was to find a fuel source that was both economical and practical. Hydrogen was one promising possibility as a fuel source, but nobody had been able to make it work in the real world. "So what do you want me to do?"

"Son, let me be clear here: You are to do whatever the fuck it is you need to do to get Smoot to build that fuel cell. Blow him, bribe him, brainwash him, boil him in a vat of hot oil—I don't give a shit." Duck Boots hit the flush lever. "There are no rules on this one, understand?"

"Yes, sir. No rules."

"And no excuses, either."

The professor left to go teach a class, but not before Cam elicited a promise that he would email a short report summarizing his findings later that morning. Cam wanted to lock down the professor's conclusions as soon as possible, knowing that at some point the professor would be pressured to reconsider his findings by those who refused to entertain the possibility of Europeans in America before Columbus.

Cam phoned Amanda. "You're going to want to see this. Take a cab. Text when you get close—I'll meet you out front." In the meantime he examined the other artifacts. Many of them were unadorned spears and knives, but a half dozen others contained Roman and Hebrew inscriptions along with various Jewish symbols such as menorahs and Jewish stars. Thankfully he didn't have to resort to his rudimentary knowledge of either Latin or Hebrew—a manuscript summarizing the history of the artifacts, complete with photos and maps, lay on one of the carts. It had probably taken some graduate student an entire semester to compile, and from the way the pages stuck together there hadn't been more than a handful of eyes that had ever seen the inside of it. Cam thumbed through and found the translation of each of the artifacts and summarized them in his notebook.

Essentially, the inscriptions carved onto the artifacts related the history of a group of Roman Jews who relocated to the Gaul region of France around AD 400 and later, in approximately AD 775, journeyed to a land they called 'Calalus'—maps carved on the artifacts identified Calalus as the American southwest. As was the case with many Jews of this period, they had begun to become Christianized as a way to assimilate and avoid persecution, but also maintained many of their Jewish traditions. They fought many wars with the local people, whom they called the Toltecs, eventually defeating them and ruling for more than 100 years. Finally, in AD 880, their leader named Israel III freed the Toltecs, a decision which caused his people to condemn and eventually ostracize him. The now-free Toltecs, on the other hand, venerated Israel III for liberating them. When Israel III died, war again broke out, this time catastrophically for the French Jews who were defeated and presumably killed and/or enslaved. The last record, telling of this final battle, was dated AD 895.

When Cam finished writing his summary, he glanced through other sections of the bound manuscript, focusing on the reports written in the 1920s. Amanda texted, interrupting him. "We're about five minutes away."

Instead of going directly to the lobby, Cam found an empty office overlooking the street. He peered through the window. Expos hat had moved to a park bench and was now reading a newspaper; every few seconds he glanced up at the front door of the building. Cam studied him—fifty-something, tall and lanky, prominent Adam's apple to go along with the big ears Amanda had noticed, probably not military or law enforcement based on his slouched posture and slovenly appearance. Cam eyed him for a few more seconds, sighed and made his way to the lobby. Trying to act nonchalant, he exited the building as the taxi pulled up, greeted his family and escorted them to the conference room. Expos hat watched them but didn't budge.

Feeling safer once inside the building, Cam showed them the artifacts and explained the geology.

"Extraordinary," Amanda said. "You'd have to be loony to argue against this kind of hard science."

Astarte crossed her arms. "Why would anyone argue? Uncle Jefferson knows about this already. He says the Native Americans told him the white men have been coming here for thousands of years." She often referred to her uncle in the present tense, as if he were still alive. It made Cam want to lift her in his arms and hug her.

Cam nodded. "Isn't there a legend about it?" he asked. Astarte was part Native American herself. "Something about a white god arriving from across the Atlantic?" Cam wanted to get back to the artifacts, but he also wanted to let Astarte have her say.

The girl nodded. "I think his name was Gloop-cat."

"Is it Glooscap?" Amanda asked.

"Yes. Glooscap. He had fire-colored hair and rode a giant bird with one white wing. Uncle Jefferson says that was his sailboat." She swallowed. "Glooscap taught the Native Americans how to fish with nets. My uncle thinks he was really Prince Henry." Some historians believed Prince Henry Sinclair led an expedition from Scotland to eastern Canada and New England in 1398, leaving in his wake the Westford Knight carving and other evidence Cam and Amanda had studied.

"Did he come as far as Arizona?" Amanda asked.

"No, but others did. Before him. All the Native Americans know about it. So do the Mormons."

"Fascinating," Amanda said. "Good job remembering all that, Astarte."

The girl grinned. "Uncle Jefferson says if I'm going to be princess, I need to remember all the stories." According to Astarte's uncle, the girl carried the blood lines of King David, Jesus, Isis, the prophet Mohammed and Mormon founder Joseph Smith in her veins. And he claimed to have ancient artifacts and documents to prove it. The uncle had told Astarte she carried more holy blood than anyone in the world, and that her destiny was to unite the world under one religion. Not too much pressure.

Amanda squeezed Astarte's shoulder and turned to Cam. "So what is it that caused everyone to say these artifacts were a hoax in the first place?"

"You know, when they were first found, most of the scientists and academics who examined the site believed the artifacts were authentic. The dean of the University of Arizona was convinced, and so was the guy the Smithsonian sent out here. They were on site when pieces were being dug out of the desert, six feet deep. The artifacts were imbedded in thick desert crust called caliche, which takes decades to form and is almost as hard as concrete."

"So what changed their minds?"

"For the dean, I think it was just simple expediency. The two local papers took opposing positions on the artifacts, and one of them was beating him up pretty good about being gullible. Plus all the Ivy League guys were treating him like a country bumpkin for believing that Dark Age Europeans were exploring Arizona, of all places. So finally he just said nobody could prove it either way and stopped talking about it."

"And that was it?"

"Yup. People moved on and the artifacts were put in storage."

Amanda smiled. "Until you popped in for a visit."

CHAPTER 2

Using Interstate 10 as a directional marker, and cruising at about twice the speed of the cars below, Willum flew northwest out of Tucson. He couldn't let his mind wander too much—the Interstate 10 corridor was infamous for its desert wind microbursts and resulting dust clouds. From his high vantage point Willum could usually see the burst coming in the form of tumbleweeds racing across the desert, like something out of the old *Roadrunner* cartoon. Today, for now, all seemed serene and he covered the sixty miles in a half hour.

He had made the trip dozens of times but always grinned like a thirteen-year-old spying his uncle's stash of *Playboy* magazines at the sight of his domed compound rising out of the desert in Casa Grande. And it wasn't just one breast—the compound consisted of a series of massive interconnected domes. Five domes were strung together like a caterpillar in the rear of the complex. An underground tunnel connected this group of domes to another set of four domes which in turn linked to a final set of four more domes. At the front of the complex, abutting a rural highway and partially hiding the thirteen domes from view, sat a flying-saucer-like structure.

The compound had originally been built as an electronic assembly plant—the domes housed the production lines and the saucer the corporate offices. The plant had never been finished, and the domes and saucer had sat unused for decades save for teenagers drinking beer and telling ghost stories. Many locals believed the place was haunted. Willum had purchased the complex almost three years ago, paying a half million dollars for what had become a run-down and obsolete set of buildings sitting on sixteen acres in the middle of nowhere.

He could have negotiated a better deal, but it was perfect for his needs and he had more money than he knew what to do with—besides, it probably wouldn't be long before society imploded and money would be worthless. Gold would retain its value, as of course would food and water and the means to produce them. Otherwise those who survived would need two things: weapons and the ability to produce electricity. So after sinking a deep well for water and installing a massive generator and the solar panels needed to power it, Willum loaded one of the domes with truckloads full of bottled water, military meals known as MRE's and other non-perishables. Another dome he stocked with a few dozen assault rifles, a hundred handguns and enough ammunition for both, along with machetes, gasmasks and first aid supplies, including potassium iodide anti-radiation pills. He then surrounded the compound with a thick, twenty-foot high concrete wall along the street side, an iron gate and guardhouse at the entrance, and an electrified fence around the remaining perimeter. Finally, he converted the rest of his money to gold bullion, set up a satellite dish so he could watch live sports and keep abreast of the news, and waited.

Not that this was how he had planned to live his life. He had expected his mid-life crisis to be like most others—a sports car, maybe a new job, perhaps even a young girlfriend. But a fortified, armed compound in the middle of the desert while waiting for society to collapse? No.

It never had to come to this. Or perhaps it was inevitable. Working in a small lab outside Cleveland, he had invented a sophisticated fuel cell that he sold to General Electric. The Department of Defense, convinced the technology had some invaluable military applications, invited him to work with them. Willum considered the offer and passed. But apparently the request from DOD was more like a summons—when Willum didn't respond he got a terse letter from the IRS. He had paid capital gains taxes of approximately six million dollars on the twenty-six million dollar profit from the GE deal. One would think that would have been enough. But the IRS demanded more, Willum refused to pay while also refusing to work for DOD, the IRS took him to court, some judge ruled against him, Willum stubbornly continued to refuse to pay ... and found himself in jail.

Before he could even file an appeal, his wife divorced him and took his son and half his money; the government grabbed another four million for itself. He was left with a decent nest egg of about six million, a criminal record and a giant chip on his shoulder. All because he refused to work for a government that as a child he had pledged allegiance to, as a Marine had fought for, as a young adult had begun to question, as a businessman had come to dislike, and finally as a middle-age man had grown to abhor.

While in jail he did a lot of reading, and a lot of thinking. Without the distractions of everyday life, he came to see the corruption of the federal government and its inevitable collapse. Government in America no longer served the populace but rather had become a living, voracious being itself—it existed to serve the vast numbers of people who worked for it. And to ensure that the electorate never turned on it, it handed out entitlement payments—bribes, really—to a huge percentage of the population. Life in America had become an Ayn Rand novel.

Like Rome, the greatness of America had passed. And like Rome, the fallout from its inevitable collapse would probably usher in a Dark Ages-like period of lawlessness, poverty and general regression.

So Willum began to plan for the ugliness looming around the corner. It might be three years, it might be thirteen, it might be thirty. But collapse would come. He hoped it would be later rather than sooner—he wanted his nine-year-old son Gregory to have as normal a childhood as possible. Not that Willum had been allowed to play much part in it. He was entitled to one day of visitation every two weeks, his ex-wife having convinced the Family Court judge that a felon living in an armed desert compound was an inappropriate role model for Gregory. Of all the things the feds had done to him, this was the most ... inhumane. Taking a child away from a parent, influencing that child to see the parent as some kind of monster—it was beyond wicked. His ex-wife had allowed him one hour of trick-or-treating this year with Gregory—the boy dressed as Harry Potter and Willum as the hulking, bearded, kind-hearted Hagrid. But only one hour?

When the collapse came, Willum would swoop into Phoenix with his copter, take the boy and never look back—he had secretly imbedded a GPS microchip in a medical bracelet

Gregory wore so he could track him when the time came. That's what all this was really for.

Willum landed the copter on what once served as the plant's parking lot. Clarisse, a straight-haired, hard-bodied brunette in her early forties, jogged out to meet him. An ex-ballet instructor from Phoenix, she had been one of the first to join him at the compound and had become his chief lieutenant. At one point their relationship had been a romantic one, but it was hard for either of them to commit to anything serious when they both believed some kind of apocalypse was imminent—so their bond had evolved into one based on mutual respect and affection, with an occasional sexual liaison mixed in.

"They came back," Clarisse announced.

"Sheriff?"

"Yup. Said we needed an occupancy permit to live here. Said we would have to clear out until we comply with the building code. Same old shit."

"What did you say?"

"I told him to be fruitful and multiply … but not in those exact words."

Willum smiled. Clarisse had an edge to her. "Nice."

When he had first hunkered down in the compound, he never expected people like Clarisse would seek him out and want to join him. Perhaps they came because he did not recruit. Or perhaps because they just understood at a fundamental level the same things he understood—that the federal government was corrupt, and that all corrupt entities eventually collapse from within. It was simply a law of nature. The termites and maggots that controlled Washington, DC had gnawed away the foundation of American society; the next strong wind would blow it away.

Whatever the reason, there were now eighty-five people camped out in the domed pods, while Willum lived in the front saucer building. Two domes housed men, one housed women, another served as a dormitory for married couples and families and a fourth was a communal area containing kitchen facilities, some tables for dining, a small library and a couple of television sets. Most residents lived in tents scattered within the domes and cooked their meals on hot plates or charcoal grills or sun ovens surrounding the pods. The domes had been coated with three inches of concrete when they were built, which was one of the things that attracted Willum to the compound in the first place. Recently he had added armored snipers' nests to the peaks of a few of the domes, from which compound residents could survey the surrounding desert lands for miles in every direction. Combined with the electrified perimeter security fence, it would take an army to breach their defenses.

Willum didn't think the sheriff or local authorities cared one way or another who lived at the compound or what they did. But the feds still had it in for him, so they were pressuring the locals to harass him. Once a week the sheriff drove out and, rather unenthusiastically, informed them they had to vacate. But the sheriff didn't push it. He knew how heavily armed they were, and he had come to believe—no doubt because the feds had told him so—that Willum was a trigger-happy anarchist just looking for a gun battle. Willum had in fact hung a couple of anarchist banners and flags, figuring it wasn't such a bad reputation to have. He had also converted a desert area in the rear of the complex into a shooting range, so all the residents were proficient in handling an AK-47 and other weaponry, including the rocket-propelled grenade launchers he had recently added to their arsenal. When the sheriff arrived someone always went out to practice at the shooting range, just so whatever conversation the sheriff might be having would be accompanied by a background ballistic orchestra.

"Find anything?" Clarisse asked as they walked side-by-side back to the saucer dome.

"Afraid not. On a map it doesn't look like too big an area, but it's like looking for a needle inside a farm full of haystacks. Every range has a bunch of peaks, and every peak has a bunch of caves and nooks." Talking about the problem, especially to Clarisse, seemed to help him work through it. "I think the problem I'm having is that I don't know how these people think. Whoever it was that hid the chest—let's just say it was the Knights Templar—I don't know enough about them to get inside their heads, to think like they thought." From what he had read, the Templars were the most likely group to have been dragging treasure chests across the Atlantic eight hundred years ago.

"Speaking of which, you might want to check this out." She handed him a notice of an upcoming lecture. "This guy is an expert on the Templars. You should go hear him speak. It's tonight."

He glanced at the title of the lecture and smiled: *Templars in America*. "I'm one step ahead of you; I'm driving down later today."

"Good. In the meantime, I have something interesting to show you."

She detoured him away from the saucer, toward some of the vacant acreage in the rear of the property. Clarisse and a couple of other residents had been experimenting with growing crops—it would obviously help to have fresh produce after a collapse. They had also begun raising chickens; they used the chicken waste to fertilize the crops. In fact, they had more shit than they knew what to do with. The compound's growing population convinced Willum to install a private sewage treatment plant along with a bath house on one corner of the property. It wasn't ideal to have the latrines, shower and washing facilities separate from the living areas, but he didn't doubt that the feds had slipped a couple of undercover agents in among the construction workers and he wanted to keep them far from the nerve center of the compound. Willum didn't have to take the same risk with the compound's residents: He subjected each new prospective resident to questioning under sodium pentothal, or truth serum.

"So remember how we told you the high sodium content in the soil made it hard to grow stuff back here?" Clarisse asked.

"Yeah. The sodium makes the soil crunchy and impenetrable to water."

"You told us to try adding sulfuric acid."

"Right," he said. "That would convert the sodium to sodium sulfate, which would be more water soluble."

"Okay. So we've been doing that. And some weird shit is happening."

He knew Clarisse well enough to know she wanted to show him, not tell him. So he followed dutifully, their shoulders and elbows sometimes brushing against each other. She always seemed to smell good. A combination of clean and flowery and the yeasty smell of private parts. A chemist friend who worked in the perfume industry told him he was describing the smell of musk. Whatever it was, Willum was happy to follow along in its wake.

Following an irrigation pipe running from the main compound, they skirted the shooting range and descended into one of the few areas of the property where a handful of low trees had managed to take root. Startled, a flock of sparrows took flight—Willum had installed bird feeders near the perimeter of the entire compound, the birds providing a low-tech but fail-safe intruder-alert system.

The irrigation pipe terminated at a rectangle of darkened sand about the size of a tennis court that had been marked out and tilled. The smell of poultry droppings replaced the smell of Clarisse. From what Willum could see, nothing was growing. "Glad I'm not a huge fan of salad."

She cuffed him playfully. "We're just starting out. Give us some time." She pulled a magnifying glass from her pocket. "Besides, I didn't bring you down here to show you my black thumb." She kicked up a small clod of soil with her sneaker. "This is one of the areas we added the sulfuric acid. Which, by the way, should be part of any well-balanced diet."

He smiled, appreciative of her wit. "The plants won't absorb it, don't worry."

"That's not what we're worried about." She crouched and, using the magnifying glass, directed the sunlight onto the clod of earth she had kicked up. "I don't even need to use the glass— what I'm going to show you happens just from the sun heating the soil. But this will make it faster." She held the glass for fifteen seconds, using her free hand to shield her face.

Suddenly the clod of earth began to smoke. Clarisse scampered to Willum's side. "Watch carefully."

After a few seconds the clod burst into a blaze of light before quickly burning out. "Huh?" Willum said. "That shouldn't happen." He moved closer. Nothing remained of the soil clod. Somehow it had vaporized.

Amanda grinned as Cam and Astarte, clad in bathing suits and flip-flops, raced out the door of their hotel room. "It's my turn to push the elevator button," Cam shouted as he chased the giggling girl down the hall. Amanda had been concerned that it might be difficult for the two of them to bond—after all, what did Cam know about tea parties and Barbie dolls and ponytails? Most fathers had the benefit of bonding with their children from birth; Cam had only known Astarte for a few days when they decided to take in the young orphan. But he worked hard to find intersecting points in their lives. And Amanda made a point—like now—of allowing the two of them to spend time together without her.

Ironically, and unexpectedly, Amanda was the cause of much of the tension in their new family. She had been raised by a mother who viewed herself as nothing more than a chattel for whatever man happened to take an interest in her—and was treated accordingly. As a result, Amanda had little patience for male chauvinists or sexists or curmudgeons. She had moved to Boston largely because of its progressive attitudes, had fallen for Cam largely because he treated her as an intellectual and physical equal, had become enthralled with the Templars largely because they secretly believed God was equal parts woman and man, and had been anxious to foster-parent Astarte largely because she believed the bright child would shatter whatever glass ceiling the world might erect to impede her. Instead she found herself with a nine-year-old daughter inexplicably bound to a Mormon religion that viewed women, in some kind of cruel irony, as little more than chattel.

How had this happened? She wanted to scream.

She dead-bolted the hotel door. Expos hat guy had been hanging around the hotel lobby when they returned from horseback riding. Cam could take care of himself but she'd never be able to concentrate with the door unlocked. And she wanted to dive full-body into the Tucson lead artifacts mystery.

Cam's translation of the inscriptions on the artifacts mentioned interaction with a people called the Toltecs. She knew the Toltecs were the predecessors to the Aztecs, but she didn't know if the dates matched up with the inscriptions on the artifacts. A quick internet search revealed that they did: The Toltecs thrived in the AD 800-1100 era, ruling much of what we now call Mexico. So it was entirely possible, even likely, that any Europeans making their way from the Gulf of Mexico to southern Arizona would have encountered the Toltecs; in fact, it would have been almost impossible not to. Like the Aztec, the Toltecs worshiped as their primary god a feathered, serpent-like male known as Quetzalcoatl. The legend of Quetzalcoatl, which was passed on by the Toltecs to both the Aztec and the Mayans, told of a great priest-king who, to avoid ensnaring his people in a long war, chose to banish himself. He departed on a raft, promising to return one day via the eastern sea. Because of his selflessness the Toltecs elevated Quetzalcoatl to the status of their greatest god. What Amanda found especially intriguing about Quetzalcoatl was that, like the god Glooscap whom Astarte had told them about, Quetzalcoatl featured white skin and a long beard, attributes that would—or at least should—have been unknown to the people of Mesoamerica at that time. Amanda found a number of images that portrayed him with a long, Semitic-looking, nose. In many cases, but for his feathers and serpentine appendages, Quetzalcoatl looked like something out of an illustrated book about King Arthur. A mural of him— fair-skinned and surrounded by many dark-skinned natives— which hung in the Mexican Presidential Palace was particularly striking:

MURAL OF QUETZALCOATL
NATIONAL PALACE, MEXICO CITY

The mural image matched a carving in the wall of a temple appropriately called "The Temple of the Bearded White God" in the Yucatan Peninsula. Not only did the carving clearly show a beard, but the profile also portrayed a classic Semitic nose.

TEMPLE CARVING OF BEARDED WHITE GOD CHICHEN ITZA, MEXICO

Amanda continued her research. Apparently when the Spanish conquistadors first arrived in Mexico in the 16th century, the Aztecs welcomed Cortés, believing the white-skinned, bearded Spaniard to be their returning, long-awaited god Quetzalcoatl.

She reread Cam's summary of the inscriptions on the artifacts. After the French Jews had been in America for about a hundred years, one of their leaders, named Israel III, freed the Toltec peoples from bondage, apparently to avoid a costly war—later he was ostracized by his people for doing so. Clearly Israel III was fair-skinned, and most likely as a Jew he was bearded as well. After having freed the Toltecs, he would have been revered by the native peoples. And could the banishment of Israel III have included him being sent away by raft or small boat? A striking number of similarities existed here. Amanda looked again at the image of Quetzalcoatl in the National Palace mural. Was Israel III the historical inspiration for the priest-king Quetzalcoatl?

Willum and Clarisse entered the saucer. Now he had two mysteries to chew on: Had the Templars hidden a treasure chest in the Arizona foothills? And what was up with the vaporizing desert soil?

Though the mid-afternoon temperature outside approached eighty, the dome remained cave-cool. Willum had put down a carpet and filled the space with some basic furniture—no telling how many years he would be here. But it was still a cave, and Clarisse's voice echoed off the walls as she spoke. "I suck at science so I can't help you with the vaporization problem." She always seemed to sense what he was thinking. "But I might be able to help with the Templar stuff; I've been doing a lot of reading about them." She pinched his ass. "Did you know they were celibate?"

"I'll pass on that, thanks. And they didn't bathe. I'll pass on that part of it also."

"Maybe the celibacy thing wasn't their choice; maybe it had to do with not bathing."

He smiled. "Good point. And they were also religious. Celibate, smelly and sanctimonious—tough way to go through life."

She turned toward him. "From what I've read the Templars were not religious in the way we think of it today. They didn't subscribe to the woman-is-the-root-of-all-evil doctrine that the Church preached back then. They may have seen things differently. May have actually worshipped Mother Nature—what they called the Sacred Feminine."

"Really?" He hadn't known that. He stepped toward her. Again, that intoxicating scent. "Nobody worships the Sacred Feminine more than I do. I pray to her as often as I can."

Clarisse smiled. She had straight, cotton-white teeth and an olive-tinged complexion which made her look healthy no matter what the season. And she had kept her dancer's figure. He breathed her in as she widened her eyes, brushed the back of her hand against his cheek and shook her dark thick hair out of its hair elastic. She put her lips against his ear. "Do you get down on your knees when you pray?"

Clarisse turned away from Willum's low-pitched snoring. A mattress on the floor of a saucer-shaped cavern in the desert was hardly the fairy-tale castle of her childhood fantasies. But it was a hell of a lot better than her previous life teaching runny-nosed six-year-olds how to *plie* and pirouette, only to come home to find her slob of a husband asleep on the couch in front of the TV. When she finally left him, her Mormon parents—who had helped arrange the marriage when she was only seventeen— almost disowned her, the bonds of parenthood only barely holding under the weight of the shame of divorce.

Some women may not have found Willum attractive, but she liked big, burly men. And he kept himself clean and well-groomed. Plus he made her laugh. Her only criticism was that he lacked ambition. He had brains and common sense and even charisma. And more to the point, he controlled this compound and a small army of followers devoted to him. In the coming Armageddon, Willum could emerge as a Moses-like figure in the deserts of the southwest. Could she take on the wife-like role of Zipporah? Or if not Willum's wife, perhaps a sister-like advisor in the mold of Miriam? Either way she would be considered royalty.

But only if she could first push Willum to become that modern-day Moses.

Willum normally did not allow Clarisse to cook or perform other domestic tasks for him, but by the time he woke from his post-coital nap she had already put a fresh salad and a couple of cold beers on the table. Through the open door to the saucer he could see her at the grill, flipping burgers. The aroma of beef fat and charcoal wafted over him—somehow Clarisse seemed to know exactly what he craved.

She turned and smiled. "Nice nap?"

"Yes. Thanks. And thanks for making lunch." He looked at his watch. "Or maybe it's dinner. Whatever, thanks."

She shrugged. "Once in a while the king should not have to cook his own meal in his castle. So my pleasure."

"How did you know I'd want a burger and a beer?"

She grinned. "Um, let's see. You just had sex. And you're a guy. Not that hard to figure out."

He smiled. "And the salad?"

"Actually, what you really want is potato chips. But you know if you want me to keep having sex with you, you need to maintain some of that manly figure of yours."

He patted his belly and smiled. "Wow, you're pretty good at this."

She brought the burgers in and clicked her Corona against his. "And I also know you want to go to that lecture in Tucson. And after that you'll no doubt go to your lab and try to figure out the vaporizing soil mystery. So eat up, and then I'll be on my way."

Cam was pleased to see a large crowd gathering in the high school auditorium that the Tucson Historical Society secured for his lecture. He had been a bit surprised to receive the invitation to speak—Amanda's and his research on the Knights Templar and other early explorations of America didn't in any way involve Arizona or its history. When he accepted the invitation, he was concerned that only a few people would turn out for the event. But ten minutes before his talk more than half of the hundred or so seats had filled. And with his discovery of earlier today, he had some exciting—and locally relevant—information to share.

Amanda didn't attend all of Cam's lectures, but when she did Cam liked her to sit off to one side and observe the audience's body language. Much of their research not only challenged conventional wisdom about American history, but called into question many mainstream religious beliefs as well. Some groups were open to these possibilities—the Freemasons, for example. And groups like the Sons of Norway were, for obvious reasons, receptive to suggestions the Norse did more than just touch their toes on the North American continent during the centuries before Columbus. Amanda not only observed, she also had begun to teach Astarte how to judge an audience's reaction—a person with crossed legs and arms folded across the chest indicated a defensive, uncomfortable posture while an audience member leaning forward and making constant eye contact with Cam reflected enthusiasm for the information being delivered. Cam had himself been studying body language since his days in law school, where reading a jury was a crucial skill. But having a second—and even third—set of eyes helped him refine and improve his presentations.

After being introduced, Cam began his lecture. "Anyone know any good archeologist jokes?" He scanned the room, eyebrows raised. "No?" He shook his head. "Me neither. And I'm surprised by that. Because if you look at their record, they're not much better than weathermen and economists."

Cam paused. "Here's what I mean: A generation or two ago the archeologists told us that the Clovis culture was the original Native American culture, dating back about ten thousand years. And they also told us that civilization as we know it today begin in the Middle East approximately six thousand years ago, in Mesopotamia. Well, we now know the Solutrean and other coastal migration peoples preceded the Clovis culture. And we also know from the Gobekli Tepe dig in Turkey that civilization began earlier than what we were taught. But here's the amazing thing: The dates we were taught aren't just wrong, they're wrong by a factor of two. It wasn't ten thousand years ago that people came to America, it was twenty thousand. And it wasn't six thousand years ago that civilization began, it was twelve thousand. Think of that. The archeologists weren't even close."

Cam scanned the room. If there were any archeologists in the crowd—or mothers of archeologists for that matter—they wouldn't be too happy. But at least he had everyone's attention. "In light of that, I'm here to tell you that the historians—who often rely on the archeologists for their information—are also wrong. Christopher Columbus wasn't first. In fact, he was a few hundred years late to the North American party."

This was always a tricky part of his presentation. Nobody liked a know-it-all and—even though he was about to explain why every history book in America was wrong—Cam didn't want to appear to be one. It was like talking to people who recently discovered religion, who seemed to respond to every question or comment with a smug look that said, 'Well, that may be the case, but I will be spending eternity in heaven while you alternate between needles being poked in your eyes and fire ants crawling into your ears.' He didn't want to *tell* his audience about this hidden history, he wanted them to see it for themselves.

One by one he projected images of artifacts and sites evidencing medieval exploration of America. Rhode Island's

Newport Tower and Narragansett Rune Stone, Minnesota's Kensington Rune Stone, Maine's Spirit Pond Rune Stones, Massachusetts' Westford Knight carving and Westford Boat Stone—Cam explained how all of these objects had been studied and, in most cases, scientifically shown to date back to the medieval era.

"We shouldn't be surprised by this," Cam said. "We know the Vikings were in North America in the early years of the 11th Century. So why wouldn't they, or their Norse descendants, continue to island-hop their way across the North Atlantic over future decades and centuries?" It was just common sense—they would have been drawn by the abundance of fish, timber and fur. "In fact, Vatican records tell us the bishop from Iceland set off for the Vinland settlement in the early 12th Century. We can debate where Vinland was specifically—Newfoundland, Maine, Cape Cod, Narragansett Bay—but everyone agrees it is on the east coast of North America. Why would the Vatican send a bishop to Vinland?" He scanned the room. "Well, presumably, because there were Christian souls to minister to."

Cam stole a glance at Amanda. She nodded. So far, so good. He would plow on. The next part was a bit more controversial. "So, who were these explorers and why did they come? Putting aside the obvious economic reasons, I think we have one possible answer."

He displayed an image of Bernard de Clairvaux, a French cleric later elevated to sainthood. "In the early part of the 12th Century, Bernard became the leader of the Cistercian order of monks. A few years later, he created a sister order to the Cistercians called the Poor Fellow-Soldiers of Christ and of the Temple of Solomon, more commonly known as the Knights Templar. While the Cistercians prayed and farmed, the Templars fought and traveled and engaged in commerce. For approximately 200 years, the Templars were the most powerful force in Europe, second only perhaps to the Church itself."

Cam flashed an image of the Kensington Rune Stone and explained how various clues in the carving indicated it was carved by Cistercian monks. "Because of similarities between the Kensington stone and the rune stones in Maine and Rhode

Island, we think all the stones were carved by the same men or group of men: the Cistercians. And if the Cistercians were here, the Templars could not have been far behind. So, again, why?"

Cam hesitated for a second before clicking to the next image. This one often single-handedly changed the dynamic of his lectures. "We believe Saint Bernard—along with the Cistercians and the Templars—was engaged in a secret battle with the Catholic Church. It was a simple battle, as old as religion itself: The Church wanted God to be viewed as a strong, masculine deity while Bernard and his groups believed in a god who shared feminine characteristics as well as masculine. In short, Bernard worshiped the Sacred Feminine." He finally displayed the image.

BERNARD DE CLAIRVAUX AND THE VIRGIN MARY

"This is a medieval painting showing Saint Bernard, drinking from the breast of the lactating Virgin Mary while the baby Jesus looks on." Cam paused. "As you might imagine, this teaching was not part of the orthodoxy of the medieval Church. In fact, a century later thousands of French Christians who followed

Bernard in venerating the Sacred Feminine were murdered by the Church in the Albigensian Crusade."

Cam paused for some water, allowing his audience to digest his message for a few seconds. He stole another glance at Amanda. She shrugged this time rather than nodded. This could go either way.

"So," he continued, "what was up with Saint Bernard? To answer that we need to go back to the time of Jesus. After his crucifixion, the legend is that Mary Magdalene fled Jerusalem and ended up in the Provence region of France; even today, many churches in that area are dedicated to her. And many people in that area believe, and believed, that when she arrived she was carrying Jesus' child. Most of us just learned of this from *The Da Vinci Code* book and movie, but this legend has been floating around Europe for two thousand years. And for two thousand years the Church has been trying to quash it. But if you know where to look, and you have eyes that see, you can find the clues." This was the part of his research that Cam found so compelling—ferreting out fresh clues from ancient fragments of parchment and in dingy corners of churches. Even the Catholic Church could not scrub the historical record completely clean.

Cam clicked to the next image.

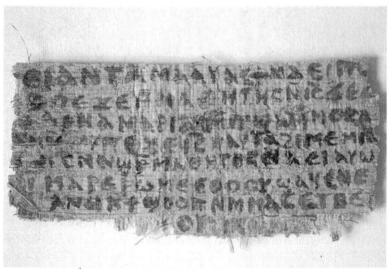

4th CENTURY COPTIC CHRISTIAN FRAGMENT

"This is a fragment from a 4th Century Coptic Christian writing. It makes a specific reference to the 'wife of Jesus.' That reference tells us that Christians in the 4th Century believed that Jesus had a wife."

He clicked again.

14th CENTURY PAINTING
CISTERCIAN MONASTERY, TARRAGONA, SPAIN

"This is a 14th Century painting from a Cistercian monastery in Tarragona, Spain. I've cropped it, but we can see Mary Magdalene at the foot of Jesus' cross. To my eye she is clearly pregnant. If so, this tells us that at least some Cistercian monks in the 14th Century believed in the marriage of Jesus and Mary Magdalene."

He was about to click again when a movement in the back of the room caught his eye. A man had stood up and was edging toward the rear exit—not a big deal, as sometimes people walked out on Cam as he started getting into sensitive religious subjects. But this guy was wearing an Expos cap. Cam shifted his eyes to Amanda and pointed his chin toward the back of the room. She blanched and reached her arm around Astarte. Cam waited until the door swung closed, took a breath and clicked to the next image.

KILMORE CHURCH STAINED GLASS, SCOTLAND

"This…" He coughed and cleared his throat before sipping at his water again. "This is Jesus and Mary Magdalene on a stained glass window in a church in Scotland. Their right hands are clasped in the universal sign of matrimony and, again, she pretty clearly is pregnant. Once more, this tells us that at least some people in Scotland believed in the Jesus and Mary Magdalene marriage."

One eye still on the back door, Cam clicked yet again. As he did so he searched the front and side of the auditorium for other egress points. There was a fire door leading outside on both sides, but presumably they were locked from the outside. So at least Expos man could not sneak back into the room. But he and Amanda and Astarte would still need to leave the auditorium at some point....

BASILICA OF NOTRE DAME, MONTREAL

He refocused on the lecture. "This is a mural from the Basilica of Notre Dame, in Montreal. The Basilica was first built in the late 1600s by a group called the Sulpicians, who were descendants of the French Templar families. Most people who look at this think it is the Virgin Mary with the baby Jesus. But the Virgin Mary is never depicted with her hair down—I challenge you all to go home tonight, get on the internet and try to prove me wrong on this. And she's almost always wearing a blue gown, not orange. In fact, orange is the color of Mary Magdalene. And look at that long hair." He paused again to let the image sink in. "More to the point, if this is the Virgin Mary holding Jesus, why is she wearing a crown and yet Jesus isn't?"

He glanced up at the projection; even after years of studying it, the painting still fascinated him. How many people looked at it every day and immediately assumed it was the Virgin Mary, their preconceptions tricking their brains into seeing what they expected to see? "I would suggest it is not the baby Jesus we are looking at in this mural. It is the baby *of* Jesus."

A number of people nodded. "I could show you more," Cam continued, "but you get the idea. What these images tell us is that, over the centuries, many different groups in Europe *believed* Mary Magdalene was the wife of Jesus and bore his child. Whether this is true or not is not really relevant. Because it is beliefs that motivate behavior."

Cam clicked back to the stained glass window of Jesus and Mary Magdalene with their hands clasped, leaving the image up for a few extra seconds. There really was no other way to interpret it, and sometimes images like this swayed even the staunchest skeptics. He took the opportunity to again check the back door. He guessed that Expos man was waiting for them in the school lobby, or perhaps the parking lot. "So let's go back to southern France for a minute. Like I said, this is the area where Mary Magdalene supposedly ended up after the Crucifixion, and it is the Provence region that historically has been most open to the idea of a Jesus bloodline. In fact, in the 5th and 6th centuries, France was ruled by a series of kings known as the Merovingians. The Merovingians believed themselves to be descended from Mary Magdalene. The name itself tells us all we need to know: Etymologically, the word 'Merovingian' means 'Vine of Mary.'"

He had made it through the toughest part of the talk. "So, not surprisingly, we find that most of the key champions of the Jesus bloodline are from southern France and are descended from the Merovingians: not just Bernard de Clairvaux, but also the nine French noblemen who first founded the Knights Templar and most of the Templar Grand Masters as well. Also the Sinclair/St. Clair family, who eventually immigrated to Scotland and built Rosslyn Chapel."

Cam took a step closer to his audience. "It is these people who fought to have Mary Magdalene recognized as the wife of Jesus. It is these people who were massacred by the medieval Church in the Albigensian Crusade. It is these people who were eventually arrested and tortured when the Church outlawed the Knights Templar in 1307. And it is these people who looked to America as a haven from religious persecution."

He paused. "And, believe it or not, it is these people who found their way to Tucson approximately twelve hundred years ago."

He displayed an image of two of the more ornate lead crosses. "I just examined these artifacts today." He described the collection's history and the geological testing. "They are authentic. The science doesn't lie. So, the obvious question is, what were French Christianized Jews doing in the Arizona desert in the 8th century? Well, I think I've just explained it to you. These families were part of the Merovingian line. They knew at some point the Church would turn on them. They came to America for the same reason so many millions of others have done so: They came looking for religious freedom."

Amanda watched as Cam took questions. She knew as much about this research as did Cam—in fact, she had first introduced Cam to the Templars and their role in the hidden history of America. But she was happy to watch Cam, trained as a lawyer, give the lectures and interviews.

A burly, bearded man in the back, near where the Expos hat had been sitting, raised his hand. "The argument we most often hear to rebut the idea of explorers being here before Columbus is that there is no archeological evidence supporting it. Even if we don't totally trust the archeologists, shouldn't we expect to see archeological remnants of these visitors?"

"You mean no archeological evidence other than the artifacts themselves?" Cam asked. "I would argue the artifacts are strong evidence in their own right."

The man bowed his head. "Fair point. I'm talking about pottery shards and stuff like that."

Amanda knew this was an easy question for Cam. "There are a number of problems with this premise," Cam said. "First, in this case, let's assume our European friends here in Arizona were on the move, fleeing or trying to escape as the natives turned on them. At some point they would have abandoned their 300 pounds of lead artifacts in an effort to survive. In that case, there would be no evidence of a settlement or village—they were on the run. Any evidence—things like campfires and bones of animals eaten—would have long since disappeared and in any event be undistinguishable from native campsites. Second, even if there had been a small settlement at the Tucson site, why should we think the settlers would have left things behind? Even today people who are out camping typically don't leave behind their tools and weapons and utensils—they need them, so they take them with them. Today we call it 'carry in, carry out.' In the old days they called it survival—you leave your knife or your flint behind and you're likely to die. Archeologists are good at finding large villages, but bad at finding explorers and temporary settlements."

Cam waited for the bearded man to nod before continuing. "Thirdly, and this is probably the most fundamental reason: Less than one-tenth of one percent of these areas has been excavated." He smiled, the same confident, kind smile Amanda had been captivated by when she first met him. "So they tell us there is no archeological evidence to support the theory of pre-Columbian exploration. But why should we expect there to be? Do we expect this evidence to just magically bubble its way to the surface? Most areas have never been excavated. Digs are expensive, and there are very few of them. But then the archeologists say, 'Aha, no evidence!' Well, that's silly. The absence of proof is not proof itself—it just means we haven't looked in the right places yet."

Willum shook his head. Whoever this Cameron Thorne fellow was, Willum liked his passion and intellect. Most of all he appreciated his willingness to fly into the wind, to question the establishment, to live outside the comfort zone. His answer to Willum's question about the absence of archeological evidence had been both well-argued and persuasive. Thorne was an independent, contrarian thinker—this nation needed more men and women like that.

Willum sat, waiting for the crowd to clear after the lecture— a few people had approached Thorne to question him. Willum reflected on Thorne's findings. He had placed Templar forbearers here in Arizona over a thousand years ago. There were still many missing pieces to the puzzle, but Thorne's research offered at least a plausible explanation for why the Templars, and their treasure, might have been in Arizona. Maybe old Boone really was onto something.

As the last of the audience members left, Willum ambled down the auditorium stairs. Before he could greet Thorne, Willum's phone buzzed. Boonie. Boonie was old Boone's grandson. He was a bit of an outcast—a quiet, harmless fellow with some learning disabilities—but he had been one of the first to move to the compound with Willum. He came and went sporadically, sometimes disappearing for a few days to camp in the mountains or hitchhike to Las Vegas to play the slots with whatever money he scrounged. When he was around Willum paid him to do odd jobs, such as driving Willum to tonight's lecture. "I'm still here. Sure, come on in if you want."

Willum greeted Thorne, introduced himself and shook his hand. "Great lecture, and thanks for answering my question. Do you have a few minutes?"

Thorne glanced at an attractive woman with sparkling green eyes and a young girl; they all seemed a bit ... unsettled. "A few, I guess."

"Well, then, I'll get right to it. I'm an ex-Marine. After that I started my own company; I'm a chemist. Now I live in a compound out in the desert because I fear that our society is on the verge of toppling. That makes me a Survivalist." He smiled. "How's that for an introduction?" Willum normally would not have been so candid or blunt, but he sensed Thorne would appreciate a direct approach.

Thorne smiled. "I must say, I've never heard that one before." He introduced Willum to his fiancée and the girl.

"The reason I'm interested in all this is I have reason to believe an ancient golden chest is hidden in the desert south of Tucson. I think the Templars may have brought it here."

Thorne smiled politely. "The Templar treasure disappeared in the early 1300s and has never been found. It has to be somewhere, so why not Arizona?"

Amanda spoke, surprising Willum with her British accent. "That would be a remarkable find. And you know, it's not just their treasure that disappeared. They were rumored to have all sorts of religious artifacts as well. Your chest may not be a treasure chest at all." She smiled, her teeth white and even. "At least not in the conventional sense."

Willum nodded. A golden chest filled with ancient religious artifacts would be fine with him. "I don't expect you to just take my word for it." He handed Thorne a photocopy of the drawing Boone's great-grandfather made. "Some old prospector drew this in the late 1800s. Claimed they found it up in the foothills just north of the Mexican border. Said when his buddy went to open it, it zapped him with some electrical charge. Killed him. Like the thing was booby-trapped."

Thorne and Amanda glanced at the drawing and handed it back. "You can keep it," Willum said.

Thorne placed it in a folder, noncommittal.

Willum plowed on. "Here's what makes me think the story might be true." He offered Thorne a picture of the Mustang Mountain rune stone. "This stone is a grave marker for a guy named Hurech buried in a nearby cave; it also talks about some secret Hurech was buried with. I dug up the body and we did DNA testing and carbon-dating on a rib bone: It looks to be an 800-year-old European male."

Thorne's eyes widened. "Really? Eight hundred years old?"

"That's a tough one to explain away," Amanda said.

"Right," Willum said. He exhaled. "So I was wondering if you'd like to come take a look at the rune stone and cave. It's a

Powdered Gold   51

bit of a hike, but this is the time of year to do it. Temperatures are cooler and the snakes are mostly hibernating."

Thorne and Amanda exchanged looks. As they did so a door opened from the back of the auditorium. Boonie called down to them. "I'm here, boss." He began jogging down the stairs to them, his Adam's apple bobbing as he bounced.

Thorne and Amanda froze. They looked alarmed, even afraid. Thorne moved in front of the girl. "He's with you?"

Willum didn't understand. "Yes. He lives at my compound."

Thorne's jaw pulsated. "He's been following us since yesterday."

So that was it. Willum stepped back so as not to appear threatening. "Yes, he has. Not really following you, but just checking up on you. But he's not a threat in any way." It hadn't been hard to find their hotel—Willum simply called the major Tucson hotels seeking to "confirm" a reservation for Cameron Thorne until he hit pay dirt. Then he sent Boonie down to wait in the lobby with a picture of Thorne that Willum had pulled off the internet.

Amanda responded. "Why would you need to check up on us?"

"Just to make sure you were who you said you were—you know, a family out here on vacation while Cameron gave a lecture."

"Well," she said, "we're not fond of strangers stalking us."

"Hold on, he wasn't stalking you. That's a bit paranoid."

"Don't tell us about paranoid," Thorne said, his voice rising. "You're the one who's having *us* followed. And you're the one who thinks society is on the verge of collapse."

This was not going well. Willum held up his hands. "Fair point. Paranoid was the wrong word. And I'm sorry for having you followed. I just need to be very careful." He turned to Boonie. "Can you wait for me in the car?" And back to Thorne. "Again, I'm sorry. But I hope you are still interested in seeing the rune stone."

Amanda spoke before Thorne had a chance. "Not bloody likely."

CHAPTER 3

Unable to sleep after the lecture and the disappointing encounter with Cameron Thorne afterward, Willum had done some preliminary work on the soil sample last night in his lab. Today he woke up at eight, which was early for him, anxious to dive in and solve the mystery of the vaporizing desert soil.

One of the unintended benefits of life at the compound was that it gave Willum the chance to return to his first love—chemistry. Without the demands of running a company, he was able to spend many hours a day experimenting like a kid with his first chemistry set. He had converted the basement of his saucer into a sophisticated laboratory and reinforced it to survive an attack; the only access to it was from his saucer.

After eating a quick breakfast, he locked the saucer door from the inside, took the plastic bag of soil samples he had collected with Clarisse the day before and lifted a skylight-like hatch protruding above the concrete floor in a corner of the saucer. He flicked a light switch and descended a metal ladder—it reminded him of a submarine companionway—into a well-lit concrete-walled passageway. Willum was used to underground spaces like this being dank and musty, but other than an occasional scorpion, which seemed to fear him as much as he did them, the dry air of the desert kept the passage almost sterile.

Willum followed the passageway past a utility room and into his lab. The area was a U-shaped span of flat surfaces, cabinets, shelves, a sink and a refrigerator. Were it not for the microscopes, vacuum hood, and other pieces of instrumentation sitting atop many of the work areas, the space would have looked like a kitchen in a school cafeteria. The lab was one of the few things he had kept from his previous life, salvaging the equipment when he had liquidated his company.

Sitting on a raised lab stool, he first examined the soil under a microscope. Nothing out of the ordinary—just basic dirt. He then dragged the stool to a machine called an Arc Emission Spectrometer. The machine looked like an office photocopier, except for the polished metal podium protruding from the front. Willum put on goggles, placed the soil sample on the flat surface of the podium and flicked a switch. An electric spark shot through the sample, heating it to a high temperature to excite the atoms within. Excited atoms emit light at characteristic wavelengths that can be detected and identified—in this case the instrumentation showed that the soil sample was comprised of iron, silica and aluminum. Pretty typical for inland desert sand. But something wasn't right.

The entire test was supposed to last no more than fifteen seconds, during which time the sample would burn away. With this soil, however, after fifteen seconds a glowing white bead comprising most of the sample's original mass remained on the podium. Yet the spectrometer indicated that all of the components of the sample had burned away—there was nothing left to read. Willum's eyes told him the substance remained largely intact, yet the instruments told him all of the elements had burned away. How could this be? What was this strange soil which, with the addition of sulfuric acid, both burst into flame when heated by the dessert sun and seemed to defy scientific analysis?

After repeating the test and getting the same results, Willum wrestled with the seemingly scientific impossibility for the rest of the morning, scouring his old reference books and searching the internet for clues. Finally he read about a device the Soviets had invented which used the same technology but extended the test time from fifteen seconds to five minutes. Apparently certain hard metals only began to register in the lab tests after many minutes of its atoms being excited. Overriding the fifteen second timer on his spectrometer, Willum took a fresh soil sample and zapped it for the full three hundred seconds. Sure enough, after a few minutes the sample revealed its secret—the glowing white bead, which eventually crumbled into a pile of white powder during the process, was comprised of the platinum group metals—palladium, platinum, ruthenium, rhodium, iridium and osmium.

Platinum? From normal soil and sulfuric acid? Willum rubbed his hand over his face. Was Clarisse playing some kind of elaborate practical joke on him? These metals were invaluable to the industrial sector, some of them worth more than gold.

Willum repeated the experiment using a different soil sample, his hand unsteady as he removed the soil from the bag. He worked a wad of chewing gum, keeping time with the digital clock's flashing countdown from three hundred. Again, one by one, the spectrometer identified platinum group metals. Again, Willum rubbed his face. Had he stumbled upon a simple way to extract precious metals from desert sand? A decade ago the businessman in him would have turned the discovery into a small fortune. Or maybe a large one. Yet money would soon be meaningless and these types of precious metals would be of little use in an unindustrialized, post-collapse society. Still, the sheer mystery of this discovery enthralled him. What was going on here?

He checked his watch. One in the afternoon. Normally he would break for lunch, but a wave of nausea washed away any desire for food. He sipped a Diet Coke, hoping the bubbles would settle his stomach. Steadying himself with his free hand, he pulled out another soil sample from the sealed plastic bag. This time he alternately heated and cooled the samples, weighing and analyzing them as he did so. "What the…" he whispered. He checked his figures again. Somehow the weight of the sample seemed to rise and fall as he heated and cooled it. This made no sense whatsoever.

Still fighting the queasiness, Willum walked over to the sink and splashed cold water on his face. He removed another soil sample and again repeated his experiment. This time he heated the soil more gradually, carefully weighing the sample at close, regular intervals. *There.* At the moment the sample changed from its original dullness to a bright white bead and subsequent powder, its weight fell to 56% of the original. The other 44% had disappeared.

How could something change weight just from being heated? This was scientifically impossible, except under one condition: when being suspended within some kind of magnetic field. But there were no magnets around.

He paced the lab again, this time stopping to fill a shot glass with Jack Daniels. To hell with the nausea. He downed the whiskey quickly, stared at the empty glass, took a second shot and spoke to the walls. "Okay then. They told me this place was haunted when I bought it."

He tottered back to the Spectrometer, plopped onto his stool and stared at the white powder. *Once you eliminate the impossible, whatever remains, no matter how improbable, must be the truth.* Willum couldn't see it with the naked eye, but his experiments led to only a single rational explanation: Somehow the white powder was partially levitating.

Cam knew Amanda was happy to be leaving Tucson. The guy with the Expos cap creeped her out. As had the Willum fellow with all his paranoia. Even though both men turned out to be harmless, this was not the way she wanted to be spending their vacation. The trip was supposed to be their time to bond with Astarte, to continue the process of becoming a family. And what better American family vacation than the Grand Canyon?

They packed up their rented Ford Explorer and began the five-hour drive north across the state of Arizona. The desert of the south slowly gave way first to foothills and then to piney, snow-covered mountains of Flagstaff. The temperature dropped as well, though it was still a balmy (by Massachusetts standards) 45 degrees when they checked into their Flagstaff hotel mid-afternoon.

"Can we go swimming again?" Astarte asked.

"I'd fancy a swim, Astarte. How about you, Cam?"

"I'd actually like to head over to the town library. If there really were Europeans in the area in prehistoric times, chances are they would have found their way to the Grand Canyon. I mean, it's a hard thing to ignore."

Cam found a helpful reference librarian, a mousy, older woman who seemed to share his love of history. "So, any legends of Europeans visiting the area before the Spaniards arrived in the 1500s?" he asked.

"Not unless you consider Egyptians to be European."

She smiled at his surprise. "Egyptians?" he asked.

"Take a look at this." She clicked on her computer keyboard and turned the monitor toward him, displaying a blurry image of a hundred-year-old newspaper clipping.

ARIZONA GAZETTE, APRIL 15, 1909, FRONT PAGE

Cam scanned the article from the front page of the Arizona Gazette in 1909. The article recounted how a Smithsonian archeologist stumbled upon a massive cave system full of Egyptian artifacts and hieroglyphs in the Grand Canyon. The Egyptians regularly employed Phoenician navigators and sea-captains to lead their sea voyages, and as Astarte had pointed out there was strong evidence that the ancient Phoenicians had explored North America, so the idea of Egyptians in Arizona was certainly a possibility.

"Other than the article, nothing has ever been reported," the librarian said.

"Well, what does the Smithsonian say about it?"

She smiled. "I actually sent an inquiry. The Smithsonian denies any knowledge."

Cam was not a conspiracy theorist, but the Smithsonian had a reputation for "misplacing" or "misfiling" objects and information that its caretakers believed should be hidden from the public. This practice had its roots in the 19th Century, when the country was spreading westward in what later was labeled as Manifest Destiny—the belief that white European settlers had been ordained by God to discover and then populate the North American continent. Well, that argument fell on its face if the reality was that the continent had already been "discovered," hundreds or even thousands of years earlier. "So," Cam asked, "has anyone found this cave?"

She clicked to another image. "This is believed to be the cave entrance."

GRAND CANYON CAVE ENTRANCE

"So has anyone gone in there?"

She smiled again. "That area of the Grand Canyon is now off-limits. Even park rangers are not allowed there."

"How convenient." Cam thanked her and began to turn away.

"Oh," she said, "and a curious mind might want to take a look at a map of the Grand Canyon."

Cam stopped and furrowed his brow. "Sorry, a map?"

She nodded and waited until he met her glance. "Isis Temple. Osiris Temple. Tower of Ra. Tower of Set. The rock formations near the off-limits area have some pretty remarkable names, if you ask me."

Clarisse clinked her Corona against Willum's. He had spent the past thirty-six hours in his lab—two days and a night—wrestling with the white powder and its mysteries. Clarisse had not interrupted, but when she saw the lights on in his saucer Thursday evening she came over with a six-pack. According to what she had told him, when she had left her husband, the Mormon Church refused to grant her a formal divorce until she had lassoed herself a new husband. So she left the Church as well. And then discovered alcohol. A win-win.

"Hey, what's that on your face?"

He looked up. "What?"

"It looks like some kind of rash."

"I don't know. I've been feeling sick the past couple of days. Like I have the flu or something." Even the beer didn't agree with him.

"So you kept working."

"It's not like I was running a marathon."

She shrugged. "So talk to me. What's happening with this mysterious white powder?" She smiled. "After I didn't see you yesterday, I thought maybe it was cocaine."

He had conducted a number of experiments, and consulted as many reference books and online sources as he could find. And he seemed to have finally figured it out. In simple terms, heating and cooling the platinum metals in the soil sample converted them to a monatomic altered state. It not only worked for the platinum metals, but for gold and silver also. For all these so-called "heavy" metals, the alteration of the chemical state yielded the same levitating, white powder substance. Other researchers had stumbled upon the phenomenon also—they had labeled the substance 'white powder of gold.'

He explained this to Clarisse. But he was not sure she grasped it. In fact, he was not sure even *he* grasped it. "The irony of all this is that this white powder is the secret to making the perfect fuel cell. Which is what the Department of Defense was trying to get me to do for them six years ago." He tried to keep it simple for her. "Do you know what a superconductor is?"

"Um, not really."

"Basically it's an energy source that, once it's activated, it never shuts down."

"Okay."

"And within a superconductor, all magnetic fields are excluded. So things around the superconductor can levitate. That is what is happening with the white powder of gold."

"I think I'm following you." She smiled. "But maybe I shouldn't have had that beer."

"Look. The science doesn't really matter. What matters is, like I said, this powder can be used to create the perfect fuel cell. Once you start it up, it never stops. No waste, no pollution, no need for a power source to keep it going. The fighter jet takes off and never needs refueling."

"All that from desert sand and sulfuric acid."

He waved toward the door. "Our desert sand, at least."

"So, what, you'd just put sand in your gas tank? Every three hundred miles, just fill 'er up?"

"It's even better than that. Once you start the engine, it runs forever. No need to fill up, at least hypothetically. And if it does need more fuel for some reason, like you said we just throw more sand in." He paused. "This is exactly what the Department of Defense wanted me to help them create. Now I seem to have stumbled upon the perfect solution to the problem. And it doesn't really matter any more."

Clarisse looked off into the distance. "Why not? Wouldn't having this kind of technology be crucial when the grid goes down?"

It was an obvious comment, but for some reason—the fog of research or perhaps his nausea—this possible use of the technology hadn't occurred to him. He had been thinking of the fuel cell's application to military usage, since it was the Department of Defense that had been pushing him to work with them. But obviously the technology could be applied to domestic use as well. It wouldn't be cheap—it wasn't as simple as just packing some desert sand inside a metal tube and flicking a switch. And not many people in the world could design a superconducting fuel cell from scratch. But he could do it if he set his mind to it. He could do it.

This was the kind of conversation that exasperated Clarisse. How could Willum not see the potential strategic benefits behind building a fuel cell powered by desert sand? When the collapse came, this kind of technology would make its holder almost god-like.

"I'm going to hit the ladies' room." Actually, she just wanted a minute to calm down. It would do no good to snap at Willum; she had gained much by never letting him see that side of her. And, though he exasperated her, he no longer surprised her. His brilliance manifested itself in many ways—his knowledge of chemistry, obviously. And also his ability to envision this compound and then make it come to life. But he also had many blind spots in which he simply lacked common sense. She took a deep breath and let it out slowly. Well, that's what she was for, what made her so valuable to him. After all, a man with perfect vision didn't need a seeing-eye dog.

She strolled around the compound, listening to fragments of the various post-dinnertime conversations. Most people nodded and smiled as she passed; her status as Willum's lieutenant gave her some cachet among the residents. But mostly she had won their respect and admiration through her hard work and contributions to the well-being of the compound. In the end, these people wanted to survive the inevitable collapse. And they knew their best chance to do so was to surround themselves with other competent, like-minded neighbors.

Once an applicant passed the truth serum test, the rules for life at the compound were simple: Come and go as you please, pray to whatever god you choose, bring your own food in and carry your trash out, and live by the Golden Rule. Willum had had to kick a few people out, but for the most part adults behaved like adults and life in the compound was not much different than living in a dormitory or military barracks. Clarisse assigned each resident a chore, which kept the compound relatively clean and self-policing. Many of the residents commuted to jobs in Phoenix or Tucson, and some even maintained homes in the area, but they made it a point never to be more than an hour drive away from the compound and were ready to leave their outside lives behind at a moment's notice. When the collapse came, they would be ready.

Clarisse herself believed the collapse would be sparked by social and political unrest. Society worked fine when ninety percent of the people took care of the neediest ten percent. But when the able-bodied began to feel an entitlement that they, too, should be taken care of, and when the ratios began to change so that half the people were producing and the other half leeching, this became an unsustainable model. Clarisse had seen it herself all over Arizona—immigrants here illegally, not to fulfill the American dream but to feast at the trough of government handouts. What kind government gave money to the poor to pay for things like manicures and jewelry and lottery tickets? And it infuriated her that Willum distributed those survival packs to illegals coming across the border. But he was in the minority. At some point the workers and producers—the real Americans— would rise up and just say no more. And then it would get ugly.

In fact, one of the projects Clarisse had been working on was building a mutual assistance network involving other Survivalist groups in the event of civil unrest. A single group standing up to the federal government could easily be squashed—witness Ruby Ridge and the Branch Davidian compound. But a network of dozens of compounds acting collectively, across the country, would be impossible to put down absent a nationwide military offensive. Would the American people stand by and allow this? Clarisse thought not. A confederation of like-minded Survivalist groups, pledging to rise up collectively if any one of them was in danger, was their best strategy. Since the policy required effective communication to be successful, she was working to link all the groups via a ham radio network.

Not everyone in the compound agreed with Clarisse that social and/or political unrest would spark the coming societal meltdown. There were almost as many theories as to what would bring about the apocalypse as there were residents in the compound. Some believed God would bring down his wrath in a series of natural disasters as punishment for the immorality of the time. Others expected a massive solar flare to short-circuit all technology, sending society back to the days of candles and plow-horses. Still others forecasted a massive volcanic eruption in Yellowstone National Park that would cover the continent in thick ash and bring about food shortages, pestilence and perhaps another Ice Age. Others predicted nuclear war or global pandemic or terrorist attacks or even alien invasion. Whatever the cause, they all had taken refuge in Willum's compound. They would all follow his lead. And he would follow his seeing-eye dog.

They had spent the day hiking along the South Rim of the Grand Canyon. From the skywalk viewing area, the enormity of the chasm and its breathtaking beauty humbled Amanda almost to the extent of making her weak-kneed—she felt like she was looking down at the very skeleton of the earth, the skin and connective tissue having been pulled aside to allow for a privileged few to view the planet in its raw, unimproved form. In the distance, the snow-capped peaks ringing the canyon looked like white-frosted cupcakes. Or perhaps helmeted sentries, surrounding the sacred site and guarding it from afar.

Astarte, exhausted from the miles they had trudged, now slept in the back of the SUV as they drove back to Flagstaff. Or maybe not—a giggle came from the back seat as they passed a billboard for the Santa's Workshop tourist site. Amanda turned. "Good morning, sunshine. What's so funny?"

"The sign made me think of Secret Santa with Cameron's family."

Amanda chuckled. "Yes, that was a memorable folly."

Amanda stared out the window, the hours on the highway a good opportunity for reminiscing:

Some members of Cam's extended family celebrated Christmas, while others celebrated Chanukah, so they had come up with a tradition of having a family dinner the weekend before Christmas. The children all received toys, of course, while the adults arranged a Secret Santa—at Thanksgiving all the names were put in a hat and drawn randomly with each adult assigned to give a small gift to another.

"I think Astarte should be in charge of the Secret Santa this year," Cam had announced. "It will be a good way for her to get to know everyone. I'll write everyone's name on a slip of paper and put them in the hat. Then Astarte can go around and everyone can pick them out and maybe have a little chat with her. And remember, everything has to be a secret." Everyone had agreed, of course, as they wanted to make Astarte feel welcome.

When they gathered at Cam's parents' house a month later to exchange gifts, the children, as was customary, each took one of the gifts from the gift table and unfolded the gift label.

"Okay little elves," Cam's mother called out, "deliver your gifts."

Cam had plopped down in an oversized easy chair, a smug look on his face that Amanda could not figure out. But she soon realized what he had orchestrated as one-by-one the children delivered their gifts to Cam.

"Well," he grinned, a stack of a dozen gifts piled on his lap, "I guess we know who's been naughty and who's been nice this year."

"Cameron," Astarte blurted out. "You wrote your name on every slip of paper!"

Cam had made up for it by renting a ski chalet for the entire family in New Hampshire for New Year's weekend. But Amanda still smiled as she pictured him, smirking, tears of laughter pooling in his eyes, as the family cursed and his cousins wrestled him to the ground. Amanda hoped it would be just one of many fond memories Astarte would have of her new life. This trip was another. They should make the most of it....

"You know, we're not so far from New Mexico," Amanda said.

"And?" Cam asked.

"And it's only three o'clock. And our flight doesn't leave until tomorrow night."

Cam smiled. "You thinking the Los Lunas Decalogue Stone?"

They had discussed the possibility earlier. "It's a five hour drive to Los Lunas from Flagstaff—we could check out of our hotel and do the drive tonight. Hike up and see the stone tomorrow morning, then fly out of Albuquerque rather than Tucson."

Cam nodded. "Sounds good. We're here, and it's worth seeing. If it costs a few bucks to change flights, it's still worth it."

"What's the Los Lunas Stone?" Astarte asked.

"It's a boulder that is covered with ancient writing that some people think is the Ten Commandments."

Astarte nodded. "Well then, I think we should go see it. It sounds important."

"This is your exit. Route 6," Amanda said. "Go west fifteen miles. When we cross a small river, that's our spot."

Cam drove the Explorer, his back beginning to ache from the many highway hours they had logged. But the weather was cooperating—clear and dry and already up to forty degrees even though the sun had barely crested over the horizon. They had checked out of their Albuquerque hotel early so they would have plenty of time to see the stone and still make their Friday evening flight. The landscape differed little from that in southern Arizona—low-growing, prickly shrubs and brownish grass poking through a hard-baked desert soil.

"Before we talk about the Los Lunas stone," Amanda said, "I wanted to show you this coin. It's Roman, dating back to AD 320. One just like it was found in northwest Arizona. So it's another piece of evidence of ancient exploration of this area."

ROMAN COIN, AD 320

"Or someone dropped their coin collection in the woods," Cam said, smiling.

"I know you're only playing devil's advocate, but whenever some bloke finds an ancient coin in America, the so-called experts always say some collector must have dropped it. If you had a collection of ancient coins, would you bring them out into the wilderness with you on your camping trips? And then just carelessly scatter them about? I mean, these are valuable items." She sat back. "It's just patently ridiculous."

"Tell me how you really feel," Cam teased.

"I feel like I have horrid taste in men," she said, sticking out her tongue.

A minute later she pulled out her iPad and read from an article she had copied to it. "The Los Lunas stone was found around 1880. The Native Americans showed it to some early settlers. It's at the foot of a hill called Mystery Mountain. The Natives insist they didn't carve it."

"They didn't," Astarte said.

"How can you be sure?" Amanda asked.

"Native Americans remembered things by telling stories, not writing them down," Astarte said matter-of-factly. "That way the people could remember the stories even if the writings got lost."

Cam nodded. Give Astarte's uncle credit—he made sure to teach her about her Native American culture as well has her Mormon one. Cam took a left onto a single lane road after crossing the narrow river and followed it for a quarter of a mile. "Pull over there." Amanda pointed to a squat, flat-topped foothill out Cam's window. "That's Mystery Mountain. We walk from here." A twenty minute walk along a narrow, rising path through clumps of small trees and high grass and even a few patches of shaded snow brought them partway up the hill and around the other side. In this part of the country, even a hundred feet of elevation changed the landscape from barren to almost lush.

"Stay on the path," Cam said. "And be careful of snakes—they like to come out and sun-bathe even in the cold." He was glad they had taken the time to stop at a convenience store to buy a snake-bite kit.

They crested a small ridge and Amanda stopped. "There it is," Amanda said, pointing to a boulder the size of a one-car garage.

Near the bottom of the boulder someone—either Mother Nature or a patient human—had created a flat, smooth, vertical face.

Amanda said, "Most people think the boulder was on the top of the mountain at some point and then skidded down the slope. That's why the writing is cockeyed."

LOS LUNAS DECALOGUE STONE

Cam knelt in front of it. There were maybe ten lines of writing, each about an inch-and-a-half tall, covering a surface the size of a desktop. "So these are the Ten Commandments."

"Almost exactly," Amanda said. She pulled out her iPad. "Here is the exact translation:

"I am Yahweh your God who has taken you out of the land of Egypt, from the house of slaves. There must be no other gods before my face. You must not make any idol. You must not take the name of Yahweh in vain. Remember the Sabbath day and keep it holy. Honor your father and your mother so that your days may be long in the land that Yahweh your God has given to you. You must not murder. You must not commit adultery. You must not steal. You must not give a false witness against your neighbor. You must not desire the wife of your neighbor nor anything that is his."

"Wow," Cam said, "who knew God had a British accent?"

"You're surprised by that?" she smiled.

"Anyway, that's a pretty accurate version of what we learned in Sunday school."

Astarte nodded. "It sounds like the Ten Commandments in the Book of Mormon also."

"But it's not exact," Amanda said. "The last commandment usually says not to covet your neighbor's house and servants and donkeys in addition to his wife."

Cam nodded. "Which in some ways makes it more compelling. If it were exact, I would be more willing to think it's a hoax." The mainstream historians' standard reaction to these artifacts claim was to claim they are hoaxes. Cam could name probably fifty sites and artifacts that evidenced early exploration of America, every one of which the so-called experts claimed was a hoax or prank or folly. Not to say there might not be a few hoaxes mixed in, but to dismiss every artifact, without any actual evidence of inauthenticity, was ludicrous—most people had better things to do with their time than to climb mountains or wade into oceans with hammers, chisels and ancient foreign-language dictionaries.

Cam took out a jeweler's loupe and examined the carved letters. "Has a geologist ever looked at this?"

"Many times. But unfortunately the carving has been cleaned and polished and scored so many times that any chance to do any science on it is lost."

"I recognize some Hebrew letters," he said.

"And there is some Greek as well," Amanda said.

"Uncle Jefferson has stones with this kind of writing," Astarte said, using the present tense again. At what point would she stop thinking of her uncle as still alive? "He says it's Phoenician."

Amanda nodded. "Interesting observation, Astarte. I believe the Phoenician language borrowed letters from both Hebrew and Greek. From what I was able to learn last night, the writing is similar to the writing on something called the Moabite Stone, which was found in Jordan not far from Israel. It dates back to around 800 BC."

"Was this Moabite Stone carved by Jews?" Cam asked.

"No, but close cousins. The Moabites descended from Lot, who was Abraham's nephew. At that time they were paying tribute to King David, almost like a colony. Their writing was very similar to ancient Hebrew."

Cam looked around. "So unless this is a hoax, we have ancient Jews out here in the desert sometime around 800 BC. Also around that time, maybe a few centuries earlier, we have Egyptians and Phoenicians at the Grand Canyon. And then another group of Christianized Jews comes over in AD 765 and leaves the Tucson artifacts. And, if Willum can be believed, we have the Templars here around AD 1200 carving that rune stone he found." Cam turned up his palms. "I get the whole dry heat thing. But there seems to be an awful lot of people coming halfway around the world to go traipsing through the desert for no apparent reason." He scanned the horizon. "What the hell were they doing here?"

Willum sat in a director's chair outside his dome and stared at the sky as he gulped a cold Corona. He still had the rash on his face but he had slept for sixteen hours and felt better—at least physically. He rubbed his hand through his hair, surprised to see a few dozen strands intertwined in his fingers. Great. As if middle age wasn't hard enough.

The hair in his hand only contributed to the malaise that had settled over him. Nobody else at the compound understood enough about chemistry to help him work with the white powder of gold, and there was still much about it he didn't understand. At times like this people needed to bounce ideas off one-another, to collaborate, to brainstorm. And here he was secluded in a desert compound.

Not only that, he had missed a great opportunity to connect with Cameron Thorne two nights ago. Just as he could use some help on the white powder mystery, he couldn't figure all this Templar stuff out himself. Willum was a chemist, not a historian. What did he know about the Templars and their treasures? It was just bad luck that Thorne and his fiancée had been so spooked by Boonie.

He counted the empties—nine of them. And he was just getting started. In retrospect, he should have anticipated that Thorne would be jumpy. Willum hadn't been able to get all the details, but based on a few things Thorne had said in interviews Willum had dug up, the federal government had treated Thorne and his fiancée as badly as it had treated Willum. Maybe even worse. Apparently the spooks at Langley had been willing to let the young couple be killed by some rogue agent in order to keep potentially inflammatory information about the Catholic Church from coming to light. Willum swigged the last few ounces of his beer. Can't be having the truth come out.

He popped open a fresh bottle. Big Brother. Deciding what the people should know and not know, think and not think. How had America come to this?

A knock on the door of his saucer woke Willum. "Who is it?"

"Clarisse."

"There a problem?" He checked his watch. Ten o'clock. Please, please, please don't be that the sheriff came back. His head hurt and his pillow smelled like a frat house. Plus it was covered with more strands of his kinky black hair.

"Just that it's a beautiful day in the desert and you're acting like a mopey child. Get dressed and get your ass out here. And bring a Frisbee."

Willum sat up. She was right. He took an alternating hot and cold shower and swigged some pickle juice. Twenty minutes later he shuffled out of his saucer to a clearing they called the quad, a rectangular area that once served as a parking lot but had since been reclaimed by the desert sands. He flicked the Frisbee to her and sipped a Gatorade. "Good morning." He kept his back to the sun—looking into it made his brain throb.

She snapped the disk out of the air and sent it soaring back to him. Three disks arced against the blue sky; he tried to focus on the middle one. "So when you were in high school, and you liked a girl, and you asked her out, and she said no—what did you do?"

"I'm sorry, what?" Even his hair hurt.

"You heard me. If the girl said no, what did you do?"

He shrugged. "Nothing. Or I looked for another girl."

"See, that's your problem. You know I adore you, but sometimes you don't have enough ambition. Why not fight for her, why not try to change her mind?"

He got out of bed for this? Hell, he had an ex-wife for these kinds of conversations. "Well, okay, but that was thirty years ago."

"What I'm talking about is this Thorne guy. You scared him off. I get that. But don't give up. If you think he can help you find your golden chest, stay after it. How hard can it be to find his email address? Apologize, send him more info on the rune stone, get him to take another nibble on the worm." She smiled. "You seduced me, you can seduce him."

He threw the Frisbee again. "Actually, you seduced me."

"That's my point." She reached around her back and caught the disk behind her hip. "You should have come after me from the beginning."

"Well, it worked out okay my way."

"Maybe so. But Cameron Thorne's not as desperate as I was."

His head throbbed. But that didn't change the fact that she had a point.

Just as Willum's head began to stop throbbing a bigger headache arrived at the front gate of the compound. "Sheriff is back," the sentry reported via cell phone, "and this time he brought friends."

Willum glanced at the sun. High noon; how appropriate. "I'll be right there." He made sure a couple of guys had manned the sniper's nests above the domes, found Clarisse and jogged the hundred yards to the far corner of the compound. Four police cars, lights flashing, idled along the shoulder of the rural highway in front of the compound's front gate.

Willum walked the last fifty feet; he didn't want to be out of breath when he arrived. He pushed the gate open and stood in the open so the security camera in the guard house could capture the scene. "Sheriff Vaca," he said. "What can I do for you?"

"Mr. Smoot," the sheriff nodded. But for their skin tone and Willum's thick beard, the men were almost mirror-images of one another: late forties, just over six feet, husky. The sheriff wasn't a bad guy. But he was in a bad spot.

Behind him stood five uniformed deputies and a handful of men and women in business suits carrying briefcases. County officials and maybe a lawyer or two, Willum guessed. Plus no doubt a soulless bureaucrat from the feds. "Surprised to see you all on a Saturday. What can I do for you?"

The sheriff took a step closer, his hands behind his back to appear non-threatening. He lowered his voice. "Mr. Smoot, we need to get in there to do an inspection. You've got people living in there but you don't have an occupancy permit." He gestured behind him. "The Building Inspector needs to check for health and safety violations."

"I promise you, Sheriff, that we have everything under control. I just changed the smoke detector batteries myself." Willum smiled.

"Glad to hear it. But I'm talking about structural issues. Are those domes of yours safe? Is the electrical up to code?"

Willum had studied the Ruby Ridge disaster. The feds fabricated some bullshit minor charges against Randy Weaver, and then when he refused to leave his compound to defend himself in court they issued a warrant for his arrest. The largest law firm in Phoenix, more than happy to take Willum's money, had devised a careful legal strategy for him. "We only use the domes and other buildings for storage," he said. "Everyone in the compound lives in tents." He smiled again, knowing every word was being recorded. "Just like Boy Scouts on a camping trip. So we don't need occupancy permits—we're not occupying the buildings."

The sheriff, in turn, smiled. "Once we verify that, we can be on our way."

"I have no problem with that. But you're going to have to verify it from outside the fence. This is private property, and I'm not inviting you in."

"What if I have a warrant?"

"Well, I suppose that would be a problem for both of us. Since this is Saturday, there is no way my lawyers can go to court and obtain a protective order." Willum glanced back at the snipers atop the dome roofs. "So that means my options would be limited."

The sheriff nodded, turned and began to walk away. He hesitated and turned back to Willum. He stuck out his hand. "It seems fate has determined we are to be *adversarios* for some reason. I think in different circumstances we would have been amigos instead. I regret that."

Willum clasped the sheriff's hand. Willum suspected that at some point the sheriff knew he would be pressured to force the same hand that currently held his. Willum was just relieved it wasn't today. "As do I," Willum said. "As do I."

Ellis watched Sheriff Vaca and Smoot talk and interact. Ellis had never met Smoot, though he knew him intimately. But you never really knew someone until you saw them in person, in three dimensions. Otherwise it was like falling in love with a centerfold or movie star after having learned all about them from the gossip magazines. Yet even this, standing ten feet away, wasn't enough. Ellis wanted to smell Smoot's breath, see the hairs growing inside his nostrils, count the number of times he blinked or licked his lips or swallowed. But this would have to do for now.

The hard-bodied woman, Clarisse was her name, was his lieutenant. Earlier, when they approached, Smoot had whispered something to her. Most people when they whisper do so into the ear so as not to offend with their breath or invade personal space. But Smoot whispered directly into her face. Interesting.

Ellis had edged close enough to hear Smoot's conversation with the sheriff. Instead of fanning Smoot's paranoia Vaca was placating him. It would have been preferable if Vaca were more of a hot-head—what were the odds of some country sheriff in rural America being a reasonable guy? It probably was unrealistic to expect them all to be like the redneck played by Jackie Gleason in *Smokey and the Bandit*, but that's really what Ellis needed here. Some prick to do something stupid to raise the stakes and get everyone's blood boiling. It wasn't essential that bullets begin to fly. Though that wouldn't necessarily be a bad thing either.

CHAPTER 4

Cam sensed something was bothering Astarte even before she slid into the back seat of his Subaru Forester. "Why would God command Abraham to kill Isaac?" she asked, a pink ski hat framing her face.

The girl had been living with them for only a few months, but Cam knew better than to talk down to her. "Good question. I think God was wrong to do that."

"But how could God be wrong about anything. Shouldn't he always be right?"

They wanted Astarte to have some kind of religious education so they had enrolled her in Sunday school at Westford's white-steepled Unitarian church. During their car rides home her questions often forced Cam to reexamine his own religious beliefs. Which was probably a healthy thing. "First of all, didn't we agree God might be a woman not a man?"

"No. You and Amanda said that. But the Book of Mormon says he's a man. And I've seen pictures."

"Well, isn't it possible the Book of Mormon is wrong? Women give life to the world, so couldn't a woman have created life in the first place?"

"Well, either way why would God tell Abraham to kill his own son?" Her cobalt eyes narrowed in anger.

"I think God was just testing Abraham—he … I mean she … wouldn't have let him actually kill Isaac."

Astarte chewed on her lip and stared out the window. Cam glanced in the rearview mirror and waited, the traffic steady around the town's snow-covered Colonial common. They had flown back on the red eye Friday night, landed Saturday morning in Boston, driven to their Westford home 30 miles north of the city and spent the rest of Saturday unpacking and shaking their jet lag. "Well," she said, "Abraham was still a bad father. He didn't know the angel would tell him to stop." She brushed at her eyes with the back of her hand and sniffled. "He probably scared Isaac."

That was it then. The psychologists had warned that Astarte might have issues with trust after the death of her uncle, who himself had taken custody of her as a toddler after the death of her mother. Still only nine years old, she was already on her third set of parents—the last thing she needed was to hear about parents slitting the throats of their children. Cam looked into the mirror again and waited for Astarte to meet his gaze. "You're right, Astarte. Amanda and I would never do anything to harm you." He smiled. "Even if God told us to."

She sat up. "So you wouldn't do what God says?"

"Not in that case, no."

She looked out the window again. "Well then why do we call Abraham the father of our people? He wasn't a very good father, it seems to me."

"Again, I think you're right. I'm guessing Sarah was very angry with him when she learned what he almost did to Isaac."

"She shouldn't argue with him. Her job is to obey her husband."

Cam pursed his lips. He had read that the Mormon Church required women to swear obedience to their husbands. "Do you think Amanda always obeys me?"

Astarte shrugged. "Well, she should."

"We don't believe that. We believe we are equal partners."

She didn't respond for a few seconds. "Well, maybe Abraham should have at least told Sarah before taking Isaac up the mountain. She was probably worried." She chewed her lip again. "I think what the Bible is trying to tell us is that women need to be careful who they pick for their husband. They don't want to get someone mean like Abraham."

Cam started to respond but instead just nodded. Astarte's interpretation was clearly not the one the religious school teacher was trying to impart. But it was a pretty damn good one compared to some of the other things the Bible taught.

Cam turned into the driveway, making a wide turn around a dark sedan wedged tight against a snow bank in front of their home. He hoped whoever it was wouldn't be staying long— already the frozen lake behind their house had begun to fill with ice skaters, dog walkers and cross-country skiers; he planned to have a quick lunch and join them. It was one of the best things about living on a lake—they were only thirty miles from Boston, but most winter weekends unfolded in a scene straight out of a Norman Rockwell print. Astarte, Amanda and he would skate for a bit and when Astarte got tired their dog Venus would pull her in the sled. At some point they would end up at a neighbor's bonfire where the children would build a snow fort and the adults would sip schnapps-laced hot chocolate. Cam hoped that whoever was visiting brought warm clothes.

Amanda met them at the door, crouching to embrace Astarte before standing and tilting her neck to kiss Cam on the mouth. Venus, tail wagging, nosed at Cam's thigh.

"Sorry to interrupt your Sunday, Cameron."

Cam recognized the slight Southern drawl immediately. "Georgia? What are you doing here?"

A full-figured, sixty-something woman seated at the kitchen table pushed back her chair, stood and smiled. Cam ambled over and greeted her with a hug. Georgia Johnston wasn't the most touchy-feely person, and neither was Cam, but they had— literally—gone to battle and almost died together. So a handshake didn't seem to cut it.

Astarte also hugged her, which Georgia accepted more comfortably.

"How's the little princess?"

Astarte swallowed and looked the older woman in the eye. "Very well, thank you. I like living with Amanda and Cameron."

"I knew you would."

"But nobody here in Westford calls me the princess. They just call me Astarte."

Georgia smiled. "Good. It will be hard enough to be a princess when you get older. For now, just enjoy being a girl."

They chatted over sandwiches. "So when are you two getting married?"

"We've been a trifle busy," Amanda laughed.

"But you're right, Georgia," Cam said. "If I don't pin her down soon, she might change her mind."

When Astarte ran off to change her clothes, Georgia lowered her voice. "Astarte seems happy. How's it going?"

Cam deferred to Amanda. "Pretty well. The hardest thing is the religious question. She has some really strong bonds to her Mormon faith—she's angry we don't let her go to the local Mormon prayer house. And of course she always argues with her Sunday school teachers at the Unitarian Church. But I can't stomach raising a girl in a religion that is so patriarchal." She paused. "Do you know they teach that, in heaven, a man can take as many wives as he wants and his job is to keep all of them pregnant?"

Georgia nodded. "And there are no female religious leaders—I agree, it's not a great message to send to little girls."

Cam weighed in. "Well, to be fair, there are no female Catholic priests either. Or Orthodox Jewish rabbis. Or Muslim imams, except in all-female congregations." Cam didn't totally agree with Amanda that they needed to yank Astarte away from her religion. Eventually, yes. But perhaps not so quickly. "And don't forget, her uncle convinced Astarte that her destiny was to be some kind of worldwide spiritual leader. So it's not like she was being groomed just to make babies."

Amanda turned, pink rising on her cheeks. "Yes. But he also told her she could only be the princess or queen or whatever if she married some guy to be king and legitimize her. Astarte won't be taught she's anything special in the Mormon Church. She'll just be taught to wear those high-neck dresses and hope for a husband who doesn't beat her."

Cam didn't press it. Mostly because Amanda was probably right, though she was probably overstating things. He smiled at Georgia. "So basically we know we don't want to raise her Mormon, Catholic, Muslim or Orthodox Jewish. There's an old Woody Allen joke where he says he's an atheist and his wife is an agnostic and they always fight about what religion *not* to raise the children in. That's sort of us right now."

"Well, I'm sure you guys will figure it out." Georgia sipped from her coffee and got to the point of her visit. "Cam, we need your help."

"When you say *we*, who you mean?"

"ODNI." The Office of the Director of National Intelligence was created in response to 9/11 to oversee and coordinate the nation's various intelligence communities, most of whom historically didn't talk to each other.

"It's bad enough that you are still working for them, Georgia. But why would we want to help them?"

Amanda chimed in. "Cam is right. They tried to kill us. And you." Religious zealots had infiltrated ODNI and abducted Astarte, planning to use her unique bloodlines as a way to unite the country under the rule of religious extremists. Cam and Amanda, with Georgia's help, had eventually stopped them. But not before Astarte's uncle was dead. Amanda had suffered cracked ribs and Cam a torn-up knee and a concussion as well. And who knew what emotional scars Astarte carried.

"That's not totally fair, but I do see your point," Georgia responded. "To answer your question, the reason I'm still working for them is that there are still people out there trying to attack our country, our values, our way of life. I'm trying to prevent them from succeeding. Simple as that." And she was in a position to do so, recently having been promoted to deputy director.

Cam took Amanda's hand—what he really wanted to be doing was leading her around the lake by it. And after Astarte went to bed, they would cuddle in front of the fireplace and watch an old movie or read or play a board game. But it seemed Georgia had other ideas.

"So what do you need from me?" Maybe he could answer a few questions for Georgia about the Templars or some artifact and she would be on her way. But if that was the case, why did she fly all the way up from Washington....

She leaned forward in her chair. "I need you to go undercover."

Amanda spat out a response. "Not to be rude, but are you daffy? Cam's a lawyer and a historian, not an operative."

Cam was tempted to point out that he—and Amanda—had been put in more dicey situations over the past two years than some operatives had experienced in a lifetime, but he bit his tongue.

"I wouldn't ask if it weren't important."

"Okay, I'm listening." Amanda shot him a look. She was still peeved about the Mormon conversation. But it couldn't hurt to listen.

Georgia sipped her coffee. "There's a group of Survivalists down in Arizona who have us concerned. They're starting to get a bit ornery."

Cam sighed. "Let me guess. Willum Smoot."

"Exactly. We know he came to your lecture. Like I said, we've been watching him."

"What do you mean by ornery?"

"They're heavily armed, and they've begun to cause trouble with the local authorities."

"How so?"

"Nothing overtly aggressive. Yet. But that's how these things start."

Amanda chimed in. "I'm sorry, but get to the point, Georgia. You didn't come up here to ask Cam to put on a sheriff's badge and play John Wayne."

The older woman sighed. "Sorry, you're right. The other thing Smoot's been doing is traipsing around the mountains south of Tucson. He's convinced something is hidden up there. And I'm convinced he would welcome your help in finding it."

"Let me guess again," Cam said. "A golden treasure chest."

Amanda broke the silence. "Look, we met this Willum Smoot chap. He's loony. You don't really think the Templars buried their treasure in some cave in Arizona?"

"I don't." Georgia shrugged. "But who really knows where it is? Nobody's seen it in seven hundred years." One of the main reasons the King of France outlawed the Templars in 1307 was to procure their treasure. But when his soldiers stormed the Templar headquarters in Paris, the storerooms had been emptied. Apparently the Templars had been forewarned and the treasure secreted to some safe haven.

"Come on, Georgia," Cam said.

"I didn't say he found it. I just said Smoot believes he will find it."

"He also believes the end of the world is near," Amanda said. "Like I said, those people are loony." Amanda loved Cam, and was fond of Georgia, and she had made many other friends in the States, but there was a current of paranoia and distrust that seemed to run through the American psyche—why couldn't they just sit back and enjoy life rather than always being terrified that Armageddon was just around the corner?

"Yes, they're loony," Georgia said. "But they believe what they believe. And we all know beliefs—rational or not—dictate behavior. And Willum Smoot believes he's hot on the trail of the Templar treasure."

"Sounds to me like he's watched too many Indiana Jones movies," Amanda said.

"Even so, Smoot concerns us. He's brilliant—a retired chemical engineer who made a ton of money inventing some kind of fuel cell technology. Then he spent three years in jail for tax evasion. Ever since he got out he's been building up and arming this Survivalist group. They're not just Survivalists, they're also a private militia—they have assault rifles, rocket launchers, maybe even chemical weapons. And they no longer recognize the authority of the local, state or federal government—Smoot won't pay taxes, won't let authorities in to inspect for safety. There are kids in there, and we don't know if they are being abused or neglected." She paused. "The biggest issue is that our experts feel the group might turn cultish, with Smoot some kind of god-like personality. Sort of like David Koresh and the Branch Davidians. But Smoot is much smarter than Koresh." She lowered her voice. "Look, seventy-six people died in the Waco siege. And twenty-three of them were children. Innocent children, like Astarte."

Cam took Amanda's hand. "So, again, what does this have to do with me?" he asked.

"I've got a bunch of trigger-happy yahoos who think we need to storm Smoot's compound before he fortifies it even more. I can persuade them to wait, but only if we can use the time to get some useful intelligence. But Smoot's group is very secretive and very insular. We've been trying to infiltrate them for a year now, but we can't break through. What we need is someone they will recruit, rather than someone looking to join. And he's already reached out to you." She looked from Cam to Amanda and back to Cam. "I'm afraid you're the only one we know who can get in there."

Georgia knew better than to push Cam for an answer right away. She hugged Astarte again and said her goodbyes. "I'll leave you to your day on the lake. But Cam, please call me tomorrow. We may have waited too long on this as it is."

An hour later Cam had the ice skates and sled out and the three of them, along with Venus, squinted as the midday sun reflected off the snow-covered lake. Shoveled paths wound their way across the lake's surface; occasionally these paths terminated in larger clearings swept clean for pond hockey.

The temperature was in the mid-thirties with little breeze. Astarte, normally fearless, gazed tentatively across the frozen expanse. She knew that mid-thirties was above the freezing point. "Cameron, how can you be sure the ice is safe?"

"Well, once people have been skating on it for a few hours and nobody has fallen in, I figure it must be okay."

"Cameron!" Amanda chided.

"Sorry." Apparently an attempt at morbid humor was not the correct way to respond to a frightened nine-year-old. It was tough enough to take a child into your home virtually unknown; they should at least provide some kind of owner's manual. "Usually after a week of really cold temperatures, it starts to get thick enough. Then the ice fishermen go out in the shallow areas and drill a hole. Once the ice is five inches thick, it's safe. We don't have any currents on this lake, so the thickness is pretty much the same all the way across. And even if it gets up to 35 or even 40 degrees for a day or two, it's still safe as long as it stays cold overnight."

They skated along one of the paths paralleling the shoreline of the lake. Cam and Astarte held hands; Amanda held Venus' leash, sometimes urging the dog to run and allowing herself to be pulled behind like a water-skier. "You want to try this, Astarte?" Amanda asked.

"No thanks. I'm not ready to go that fast." The girl, like Amanda, had just learned to skate. She smiled up at Cam. "And Cameron is too big. Venus wouldn't be able to pull him."

Nothing like a nine year-old to be brutally honest. Cam had, indeed, gained a few pounds this winter. Now that his knee was almost back to normal after surgery he'd begin to jog again. It felt pretty good today, though he wore a thick brace to help keep the ligaments stable. And the bright sun wasn't giving him a headache, which meant his concussion symptoms had faded.

At the far end of the lake a few guys had cleared a rink and were playing pond hockey. Amanda noticed Cam eyeing them. "You want to go play?"

He smiled. "How could you tell?"

"You had the same look that Venus has when I'm grilling steaks." She smacked his butt. "Go. Just be careful. And be home by dinner."

He circled back to grab a hockey stick he kept in a shed by the lake and, lengthening his strides, sprinted the few hundred yards to the end of the lake. As he approached he watched the game—four young teenagers, plus a red-haired guy about his age. Good, an odd number.

The man smiled a welcome. "Thank God. Somebody my own age. These kids never get tired." He stuck out his hand. "My name's Ellis." Not a big guy—a few inches under six feet, like Cam.

"I'm Cam. You live around here?"

"No. I'm visiting my sister—she lives a few blocks over. But I was driving by and I saw the game. These are my brother-in-law's skates; they're two sizes too big." He smiled again. "But, hey, can't beat pond hockey."

Cam introduced himself to the boys, a couple of whom he recognized from the neighborhood. The oldest youth divided the teams three versus three and threw a puck down. Cam played tentatively at first, not trusting his knee, but after ten minutes his adrenaline kicked in and his instincts took over. The kids were decent players, as was Ellis, and the puck moved crisply from stick to stick as the teams traded goals.

Each player took a turn as goalie. Since the rules were that the puck had to remain on the ice to count as a goal, playing goalie really meant blocking what you could with your stick and skates and then chasing pucks that you missed. At one point Ellis broke in and fired a puck high and far wide of the net. Cam raised an eyebrow. "Sorry," Ellis said. "I didn't mean to lift that. The puck bounced just as I was shooting. You want me to get it?"

Cam shrugged. "No problem, I got it." He skated to the edge of the rink and trudged through the crusted snow, perhaps six inches deep, toward where the puck lay buried fifty feet from the rink. A few feet from the puck the snow turned fluffy, almost as if it had been disturbed. Odd.

A split-second too late Cam realized there was indeed something odd. And also nothing beneath his right skate. Forward he tumbled. A moment of panic, just enough time to gasp for some air. And then heart-stopping, numbing, almost deadening cold engulfed him. He forced his eyes open and kicked, fighting to stay directly beneath the break in the ice—the only way out of a frozen lake was the way you came in. Every second or so the beat of his heart concussed in his ears. *Look for light. Find the hole.* His left skate touched the soft bottom of the lake and he steadied himself. Using his hockey stick, he probed the ceiling of his icy tomb, his movements slow and awkward as his saturated clothes bound his limbs and his muscles spasmed. *Why was there no light, no opening?* He thrashed his head around, searching for an escape. The movement forced cold water up his nose, the ice-water like a sledge hammer to the inside of his skull. His eyes closed in an involuntary reaction to the pain. A heavy weight settled in his chest and Cam felt thick, numb, almost peaceful. *No.* He ripped his eyes open again, the view of his icy dungeon a reminder he was still alive. He thrust his stick upward once more, wildly probing the surface, the stick moving in underwater slow motion. On the fifth thrust the stick impacted something flexible and soft. Cam shoved upwards—a tarp-like sheet billowed away to expose the opening. Even in his desperation to survive, Cam understood what had happened: Someone had cut a hole in the ice, covered it with a tarp, and piled snow on top to hide the break. A trap.

As if on cue, something grabbed the end of his stick and pulled upward. Cam braced himself—was he being pulled up just to be clubbed unconscious and shoved back down? He released his right hand from the stick, ready to block a blow or throw a punch. He thought about letting go of the stick altogether, but no matter what awaited him at the surface it was preferable to an icy drowning.

As he broke through the surface, missile-like, Ellis leered down at him. Cam swung his arm out, trying to upend his adversary-turned-rescuer. Ellis danced away from the sluggish thrust, grabbed Cam by the back of his soaking jacket and yanked him out of the hole. Cam flopped on the snow, gasping and shivering. Ellis leaned in and whispered, his warm, acrid breath actually welcome on Cam's face. "You were never going to die, Mr. Thorne. I would have jumped in to get you if it came to that—it's what I'm trained to do. But when your government asks you to do a favor, you shouldn't need to think about it." He showed a row of straight white teeth in what was supposed to pass for a smile. "This country is at war, Mr. Thorne. You have a unique set of skills we need. And the way we look at it is if you're not with us, you're against us. I'm just saying."

The first thing Willum did when he awoke late Sunday morning was check his pillow. A few strands of hair, but nothing like the past two days. And his nausea had abated.

Many residents left the compound on Sundays to visit relatives or do errands. Willum was planning to take his son

Gregory to a spring training game this evening in Scottsdale. He would use the block of time beforehand to research the mysterious white powder of gold.

He turned on his computer and sipped his coffee. A couple of days ago while on the internet he had stumbled upon a report of an archeological expedition to Egypt back in the early 1900s— it was one of many pages he had bookmarked with plans to revisit.

According to the report, a British Egyptologist named Petrie led an expedition in 1904 to Egypt's Sinai desert, to a mountain called *Serabit el Khadim*. At the top of the mountain they discovered a ruined temple of ancient Egyptian origin whose design and structure seemed more to resemble a massive workshop. In stone containers they found large quantities of a fine white powder whose nature they could not identify. The existence of an unknown white powder in the desert of Egypt is, of course, what intrigued Willum.

He clicked on links and followed threads. Eventually he stumbled upon a modern-day author by the name of Laurence Gardner who theorized that this white powder was in reality the ancient substance known as *mfkzt*, a mystical substance that ancient priests molded into conical-shaped bread-cakes and fed to both the Pharaohs and the Egyptian gods. Willum quickly found a number of engravings from Karnak and other ancient religious sites showing the priests offering these cakes to the Pharaohs and the Pharaohs in turn offering them to Egyptian deities.

PHARAOH OFFERING CONICAL LOAF OF *MFKZT*
TO ANUBIS, FROM THE TEMPLE OF ABYDOS

Willum continued to read. The *mfkzt*, which most people pronounced 'mufkizit,' apparently expanded the consciousness of the Pharaohs and heightened their senses. Gardner believed that the priests of *Serabit el Khadim* were the caretakers of an ancient technology, as manifested by the workshop, which allowed them to transform gold into a powdered monatomic state which was the essential ingredient in the *mfkzt* bread-cakes fed to Egyptian royalty. As proof of this, Gardner pointed out that the Egyptian afterlife was a place called the *Field of Mfkzt.*

Willum sat back in his chair. Could it be possible that the monatomic white powder derived from the desert sand also was some kind of hallucinogen or mind-expander? He shook his head. What didn't the desert sand do? It burst into flames for no reason; it levitated; it yielded precious metals; and now it seemed to be the key ingredient used to feed and drug the ancient Pharaohs. Did it also cure cancer?

Willum still had a couple of hours before he needed to leave to pick up Gregory. So he continued to surf the internet. Surprisingly, a few individuals claimed to have figured out how to produce white powder of gold. They claimed the substance heightened their senses, gave them boundless energy and made them telepathic—well, that would explain why the Pharaohs ate it. And, yes, these people claimed the powder even cured cancer.

Willum laughed and clicked off the computer. It was time to grab a bite and then go watch some baseball with his boy.

Cam had refused medical care, instead opting for a long hot shower. He downplayed the incident to Astarte, telling her he had fallen through a hole made by an ice fisherman. "There was a flag right there marking the spot, but I was looking for the puck and didn't see it."

Amanda sensed there was more to the story, and now that Astarte was in bed Cam related the incident. They sat in an oversized chair by the fireplace, Cam wrapped in a thick blanket, sharing a mug of hot apple cider mixed with cinnamon and rum. A bonfire across the lake danced in the distance, a miniature partner to the flames popping beyond their outstretched toes. "That guy Ellis—assuming that's really his name—set the whole thing up, guessing we would come out to skate."

Amanda's eyes grew large. "Wait. Someone did this on purpose? Someone working with Georgia?"

Cam nodded. "He said he was trained in cold water rescue, ex-Navy SEAL or something, so I wasn't really in danger. Asshole."

"Beyond asshole, Cam. Criminal asshole. Dangerous asshole."

"Federal agent asshole."

"So he just gets away with it? Bullshit." She pulled her phone from her pocket and scrolled through her list of contacts.

"Who you calling?" Cam asked.

Amanda glared as her call connected. "Georgia!" she spat into the phone. "What the hell is wrong with you people?"

"I made sure Thorne went for a little swim," Ellis said. He sat sideways, taking up two seats on a Green Line train in Boston. He had time to kill—waiting for the call he knew would come from Georgia—and loved to people-watch on the nation's subways. "Just to let him know we were serious."

"Just to let him know we were serious?" Georgia spat into the phone. Ellis pictured her leaning forward in her seat, teeth grinding, as her plane taxied to the terminal at Reagan National. He imagined her thoughts, wondering if she had been saddled with some kind of whack job. Maybe even something harsher, along the lines of, *This Ellis guy is supposed to be some kind of expert in psychology; it sounds like he needs to be on a couch himself.* "If that doesn't work, should we water-board him?" she asked, interrupting the conversation he was imagining in his head.

"He's fine. Maybe a bit wet and cold. But I wouldn't have let him drown." A goth, college-aged girl opposite him checked her watch, checked the subway map on the wall of the train, then checked her breath by breathing into her hands. Next stop, first date. She wasn't bad-looking despite the nose ring; maybe Ellis would circle back later and try to find her again. Just in case she needed some cheering up.

"Weren't there kids out there also? What if one of them had fallen in?"

"Hey, I had it under control. I was trained in cold water rescues. And I made sure the kids stayed away after I marked the hole with a flag." What, did she think he was incompetent? It was like when he was a SEAL. He wasn't as strong and big as the other elite soldiers, and his specialty kept him at base more than out in the field, so the other men had given him the nickname 'Snapper,' which was a play both on his red coloring and the fact that he was smaller than his SEAL brethren. It wouldn't have been so bad if they actually treated him with some respect. Well, that would change when he stepped on their heads climbing the promotional ladder in the intelligence community.

Georgia interrupted his musings. "And you think almost drowning him is going to persuade Cameron to want to help us?"

Even though Georgia was the senior member assigned to the mission, she didn't know what he knew, didn't know what was at stake here. As far as she knew they were trying to prevent another Ruby Ridge. Ellis had been assigned to the team from the DIA. That's how ODNI worked: Agents from various governmental departments were assigned to work a case together so that the various branches of government knew what the others were doing. No one agent was in charge, which made for some interesting group dynamics and turf battles. Anyway, Georgia knew nothing about the fuel cell.

"Look," Ellis said, "I like your idea of using Thorne to get to Smoot. It's a good plan. But it's only going to work if Thorne is all in." And it was precisely because Georgia told him Thorne would be hesitant to help that Ellis had thought to prepare the little swimming hole for Thorne—he and his fiancée had been out skating pretty much every weekend this winter, so it was a safe bet he'd be on the lake that day as well. It wasn't an ideal plan, and it was a bit clumsier than Ellis would have preferred, but out in the field no plan was perfect. Or even close to it. "Well, the way to get someone to be all in is to find a way for them to convince themselves that what they are doing is really important. If Thorne agreed to do this just as a favor to you, he wouldn't be fully committed. But now look what's happened: He felt the numbing cold." What Ellis wanted to say was, *Thorne spent time in the dark, icy dungeon,* but that sounded too much like something out of a Hitchcock movie. Aloud, he continued. "Thorne *knows* at a core, base level what the stakes are. Plus he despises me, but is considering looking past that to do the right thing. Classic cognitive dissonance—he'll convince himself that if he's willing to work with assholes like me, it must be really important. Bottom line: If he does this now, he'll do it right."

"And if he doesn't? If he decides he'd rather not deal with lunatics?"

"Then he wasn't the right person for the job in the first place, was he?"

Amanda snuggled into the far corner of the couch. "So you're still considering it."

Cam shifted so that he could look at her. Her pale skin had flushed from the day on the lake, and her green eyes shone in the yellow glow of the fire. She was chewing on her bottom lip, a sure sign she was concerned.

"Well, yeah. Considering."

Amanda nodded silently.

"Georgia didn't know anything about that guy."

"So she says."

"You don't believe her?"

She leaned forward, elbows on her knees. "I don't know, Cam. How many times do we have to get … ambushed … by her colleagues before we accept that maybe she's just not trustworthy?"

"No." Cam shook his head. "No, I don't believe that. We've been through too much with her. She's proven herself time and again." He softened his voice. "But if you feel really strongly about it I won't do it." He understood her concern. Once they decided to take on the job of parenting Astarte, they forfeited the right to do stupid and dangerous things.

"I appreciate that, but that doesn't seem fair either." She sighed. "And part of me is really quite curious."

Cam brightened. "Me too. If it was just about getting Georgia her information I wouldn't be so tempted, but if there's even the possibility that a Templar treasure is hidden out there, well," he fixed his eyes on her, "we have to look for it. Don't we?" Their research had shown that the Templars traveled to North America in the centuries before Columbus—Amanda and he had always suspected one of the things they were doing was hiding their treasures from the Church.

Amanda rubbed her hands over her face. "Oh, bloody hell."

"So yes?" Cam grinned. "Yes, you agree?"

She smirked. "I agree we should sleep on it and discuss it more tomorrow." She paused. "I suppose the only other way to learn the truth is to sneak into the Vatican archives, which would probably be even more dangerous."

Cam smiled. "I used to fantasize about sneaking into the Vatican archives."

Amanda leaned forward and rubbed his thigh. "That's some fantasy."

He smiled. "I don't have the kind of fantasies other guys have." He leaned in and kissed her. "For that I have you."

Willum rolled to a stop along the curb in front of a sprawling, stucco-coated ranch home on a quiet side street in Scottsdale. A new BMW convertible sat in the driveway. His ex-wife lived pretty good on his dime.

In the fading daylight he strolled to the front door and rang the bell.

The door opened a crack, the chain still latched. His ex-wife's voice, tight and tense, squeezed through the crack. He was just as happy not to have to look at her face. "What are you doing here?"

Shit. "Taking Gregory to the ballgame."

"You didn't get the papers?"

He fought to control his voice. "What papers?"

"The court papers."

"No." He had been dodging the sheriff for weeks, figuring it had to do with the building code crap.

"Well, that's not my problem." She steeled her voice. "I don't want you seeing Gregory."

"You don't get to make that decision."

"No. But the judge does. And he did. Now leave or I'm going to call the police."

Astarte's comment about him being too heavy for Venus to pull still ringing in his ears, Cam woke up at the first hint of sunlight the next day, found his running shoes in the back of his closet, bundled up, put Venus on a leash, and charged into the gray morning chill before he could talk himself out of it. As a diabetic since childhood, he knew staying fit was almost as important as eating healthy. It took the better part of a mile of gasping and wheezing before his breathing turned regular and he settled into a steady pace. He kept to the side roads, running down the middle of them so Venus could avoid the pockets of rock salt which had mostly been kicked to the sides by the traffic.

As he ran, he allowed his mind to drift, bouncing from thought to thought like an AM radio scanning through the talk shows. Not surprisingly, his thoughts settled on Georgia's visit and her request. Military service was something of a tradition in Cam's family, though he had never served. He had wanted to enlist after 9/11, but his diabetes disqualified him. He was approaching forty—this might be the only chance to serve his country. It wasn't exactly an armed conflict, but there was something ... honorable ... about the thought of putting himself in harm's way to serve his country.

And of course he was curious. Was it really possible a Templar treasure was hidden someplace in the deserts of the southwest? Smoot must have had some reason to think so. And the Las Lunas Decalogue Stone and Grand Canyon mystery and the Tucson lead artifacts and Smoot's rune stone seemed to confirm that something had been going on there in the centuries before Europeans were believed to have first arrived in North America....

He liked to joke to Amanda that he refused to die until he had figured out the truth behind the hidden history of America, the stuff buried beneath a mountain of mistake-filled history textbooks written by a cadre of myopic academics. Uncovering this truth had become his passion. Amanda would understand it because she understood him. And because she shared that passion herself.

He sprinted the final fifty yards, stopping where Georgia's car had been parked the day before. The car was gone, but the journey which it portended was soon to begin.

Amanda sat at the kitchen table with a cup of tea and a sliced apple, glancing through the newspaper while Cam and Venus walked Astarte to the bus stop. He had showered after his run and, his face still flush, threw on a fleece jacket. Astarte—she of boundless energy—had waited impatiently for him, anxious to get to the bus stop to help build a snow fort before the bus arrived. Snow rarely fell in England, and Amanda had been wary of relocating to Westford and facing the winters. But Cam and now Astarte had taught her to welcome the season, embracing the cold and snow and diving into a full range of winter recreation. Today, however, her thoughts were on desert sand, not New England snow.

Just before he left, Cam had kissed her quickly and said, "I thought about it on my run. I want to do this Arizona thing."

She had spent the last twenty minutes stewing. She waited until he removed his jacket. "I'm not sure about Arizona."

He gave her a puzzled look. "Okay, why?"

Amanda tried to modulate her voice, tried not to sound shrill. She knew she was not being totally rational—but that was only making her more frustrated. "It's just that I thought we were going to sleep on it and then talk about it."

"Okay." He paused. "I'm listening."

"Well, with Astarte and everything...."

He sat down across from her at the table and waited for her to look up at him. "If you don't want me to go, just say so. But please also tell me why."

"Of course I want you to go, Cam. This is what you *do*." Actually, it was what *they* did. Or used to do.

"So what's your hesitancy? Do you think it's too dangerous?"

"That's partly it." But Cam could take care of himself, and Georgia had proved in the past that she would do her best to ensure he wasn't in too much danger. "It's just, well, we've always done this research together." Why should he get to jump on a plane for a new adventure while she stayed home with Astarte? Was this what married life would be like for them? Hadn't they agreed to raise Astarte together? They were supposed to be partners, sharing their lives together. She didn't want to be selfish, but it was how she felt.

He nodded. "Yeah..."

"And now you're going off alone. And I'm stuck here."

He raised an eyebrow, paused and chuckled. "Who said anything about leaving you here? Don't you want to come?"

"*Of course* I want to come."

"Well of course I expected you would. And Astarte also; I assume she'll want to come. She's nine—who cares if she misses a week of school?"

She took his hand and sighed. "I was worried you were going to go alone."

"Um, I don't think Georgia would be too happy with that. I think she wants the 'A' team."

"Well, she asked you."

"Only because I'm the one Willum thinks is the Templar expert. He reached out to me, not you."

She smiled. "You're right. I guess I was feeling a bit sorry for myself. Maybe unappreciated."

"Yeah, it was very inconsiderate of that Ellis fellow not to drop you in the lake also."

Later that afternoon they reached Georgia on her cell. Again sitting at their kitchen table, Cam put her on speaker.

"Of course I want Amanda's help." Georgia chuckled. "I'm not sure I've ever been accused of being sexist before."

"Sorry, Georgia," Amanda said.

"Don't worry, honey. I've seen you in action. I'd take you over most of the men in the Agency. I just didn't think, with Astarte and all, that you'd be available."

Amanda responded. They wanted to get some concessions from Georgia before agreeing. "We're not sure either one of us is available. First of all, you'd said it'd be safe—but this Ellis guy almost drowned Cam in our own back yard. Can you get rid of him?"

Georgia grunted. "I wish I could. But don't worry about Ellis. I'll rip his pretty hair out if he tries a stunt like that again."

They had discussed the Ellis situation already, and had expected Georgia's hands would be tied. It was not a deal-killer for them.

"Okay," Amanda said, "putting Ellis aside for the moment. Smoot met me, and he even met Astarte. How realistic would it be for Cameron to move into the compound and leave his fiancée and child in a hotel?"

"The way I see this working is that you go out there and Cam takes Smoot up on his offer to see the rune stone. One thing leads to another, and hopefully eventually Cam gets invited back to the compound. But Cam can't show up with his bags packed. Smoot would never believe it."

Cam and Amanda glanced at each other and nodded. Seemed reasonable.

"So what next?" Cam asked.

"You'll need an excuse to go back to Arizona, first off," Georgia said.

"That's easy. Smoot already sent me an email over the weekend with pictures and more info on the rune stone. I can tell him something about it resonated or made me think it was connected to the Templars."

"Perfect. Even better that he contacted you first."

Amanda spoke. "It's still going to be hard to justify flying across the country again just to look at the rune stone."

"I agree," Georgia said. "What if I could arrange an invitation for you to speak at a Masonic lodge out there? Maybe someone heard your first lecture and invited you back. Then you could hook up with Smoot."

"Guys, you're making this too complicated," Cam said. "As far as Smoot knows, we never left Arizona. We don't need an excuse to go back. I'll email him now—we can get on a plane tomorrow and I'll call him when we land."

"Hmm," Georgia murmured. "That might work. You can tell him you went to New Mexico, which you did, and then came back to Tucson. And I can make sure you get the same rental car just in case he made a note of the license plate."

"At some point," Amanda said, "he'll be expecting us to return home."

"But you can make up some excuse to extend your stay when we get to that point." Georgia exhaled. "So it's agreed. Book your flights and hotel, and I'll make sure you get reimbursed. I'll meet you out there."

"Great," Amanda said. "You can watch Astarte while Cam and I go out for a nice dinner."

Willum had spent most of Sunday evening and night in some dive bar on the outskirts of Phoenix, alternately shooting tequila and pool. He lost a few hundred bucks at the table, blew another few hundred on booze, and was probably lucky not to get rolled for his watch and wallet. At midnight he at least had the good sense to call Boonie to come get him and take him home. The last thing he remembered was crying himself to sleep.

And all he wanted to do was take his boy to see a ballgame.

A little before noon he rolled out of bed and staggered into the shower before forcing down a glass of juice and a dry bagel. He left a message for his lawyer, not that he had much hope of overturning the judge's order—the feds seemed to have the judge in their back pocket. Now what? He could mope around all day, but that wouldn't help him see Gregory.

He turned on his computer. He had sent the email to Thorne on Saturday night. No reply yesterday. Willum stared at the screen, feeling a bit like a teenager waiting by the phone for some girl to call. Ding. Thorne's email flashed him a greeting.

Clarisse stuck her head in as Willum finished reading the message. "It smells like a distillery in here."

"Yeah, tough night."

"You okay?"

He shrugged. "No. But listen to this, from Cam Thorne: 'The connection between Hurech and Staffordshire is intriguing. There is a heavy Templar presence in that region. And the fact that Hurech is from the village of Kinver is even more intriguing—the rock houses in Kinver are remarkably similar to the Anasazi cliff dwellings I've been seeing here in the Southwest. Is this just a coincidence, or is there some kind of other connection between Hurech's village of Kinver and the Arizona area? I, for one, don't believe in coincidences.'"

Willum turned the laptop toward her. "So look at these images. The first one is a rock house from this Kinver village in England, and the second an Anasazi cliff house. As far as I know, these are the only two places in the world that have rock houses like this."

KINVER ROCK HOUSE, STAFFORDSHIRE, ENGLAND

ANASAZI CLIFF HOUSE, MESA VERDE, COLORADO

"Wow, they're pretty similar," Clarisse said.

"More important, Thorne thinks so. He's interested in visiting the rune stone site on Wednesday." At least it would keep his mind off of the Gregory situation.

"Excellent." She smiled. "You can thank me later. Corona Light. Ice cold. With nachos."

While Cam booked flights and did a couple of loads of laundry, Amanda busied herself researching the lost Templar treasure. What was it? A better question might be, what *wasn't* it? Curled up in an oversized chair looking out over the lake, the midday sun reflecting off the frozen surface as clouds of snow swirled in the wind, she surfed the internet on her laptop, jotting down possibilities on a legal pad:

- gold and silver (lots of it)
- lost gospels telling the "true" story of Jesus and the early Church
- the Ark of the Covenant
- the Holy Grail (whatever that was)
- the Philosopher's Stone (turns lead into gold)

She sat back. Which of these might fit in a golden chest in Arizona? Gold and silver obviously would, though it would seem that the Templars would have had scores of these chests, not just one; perhaps they spread them out, stashing them in remote corners of the world. A lost gospel would fit inside the chest, but why such a large chest for a book or codex? The Ark of the Covenant would fit inside a large chest—but why put a golden chest inside a golden chest? For kicks she searched for images of the Ark to see how large it was. Dozens of images appeared, most of them showing not only the golden Ark but the long poles used to carry the holy relic.

ARK OF THE COVENANT

Something about the image rang a bell.

She unfolded her legs and stood. "Cam," she yelled. "You down in the basement?"

"Coming up."

She met him at the top of the stairs, her laptop open. "This look familiar at all?"

"Sure. Ark of the Covenant."

"What about the poles."

He nodded. "I see where you're going with this. Same kind of poles as on Willum's golden chest."

"Spot on."

He shrugged. "My guess is that's the way people used to carry heavy objects."

"Well what about this. Do you remember what the Ark did in the Indiana Jones movie?" She hoped he wouldn't laugh at her.

"It zapped the Nazis with some creepy energy bolt."

"Again, sound familiar?"

"Okay … You're thinking Willum's chest zapped one of the prospectors."

"Yes. Doesn't that seem odd?"

"I guess so. But you can't think Willum's chest is the Ark of the Covenant."

"I don't think it is, no. But I don't think we can totally eliminate the possibility. And from what I've read the sizes match up also."

He sighed. "I guess you might as well research it more." He smiled. "Just don't tell Willum."

Amanda returned to her easy chair overlooking the lake.

After an hour of research, two things had become clear: First, the Ark disappeared about 2,500 years ago; and second, the Arizona desert was one of the few places in the world where the Ark was *not* believed to be hidden.

According to the Book of Exodus, the Ark was built in accordance with detailed instructions given by God to Moses on Mount Sinai. The Ark—approximately the size of a blanket chest—was constructed of wood and plated with pure gold. A pair of golden angels sat at either end of the Ark's cover, their outstretched wings nearly touching at the center of the chest. A pair of gold rings was attached to each side of the Ark; as she had already learned, through each pair of rings a wooden pole was inserted to carry the Ark. Once constructed, the Ark contained and transported the Ten Commandment tablets.

The Old Testament prominently featured the Ark in the early history of the Jewish people. Often they carried it into battle, where its seemingly-supernatural powers made the Israelites almost invincible. Sometimes the power of the Ark turned on its Jewish caretakers, killing priests or others who approached or touched it. In 586 BC, the Babylonians captured Jerusalem and destroyed King Solomon's temple, which had housed the Ark—after that date there is no further mention of the holy relic. The Ark was either destroyed with the Temple or had been removed and hidden prior to the destruction.

Amanda sat back and stared at the lake. So had the Ark been destroyed? It seemed unlikely—the Babylonian siege lasted some thirty months, during which time the caretakers of the Ark would surely have foreseen Jerusalem's imminent collapse and had time to save Judaism's most holy relic from destruction. So where was it?

The leading theory postulated that the Templars learned of the hiding place of the Ark while searching for treasures and fighting infidels in the Middle East and, sometime in the 12th Century, brought the relic back to Europe. Later, when the Church turned on the Templars, they would have either hidden the Ark in Europe or removed it to some safe haven—perhaps North America. Oak Island in Nova Scotia was frequently mentioned as a North American hiding place, while Rosslyn Chapel in Scotland, Warwickshire in England and Chartres Cathedral in France were the locations most often mentioned in Europe.

Of course, there was no certainty the Templars ever found the Ark in the first place. If not, the Ark might remain hidden in the hills of Jordan, where many believed the prophet Jeremiah secreted it during the Babylonian invasion. However, still other authorities believed the Ark had been removed from Jerusalem in the centuries prior to the Babylonian invasion—one popular theory held that Solomon's son Menelik, the product of an illicit rendezvous between the Jewish king and the legendary Queen of Sheba, stole the relic and brought it home to his mother in what is today Ethiopia.

Amanda let her mind wander, trying to make a pattern out of the whirlwind of information. The writing on the Los Lunas Stone in New Mexico matched the script on the Moabite Stone, which was dated 800 BC or about the time the Ark may have first gone missing. Similarly, the rune stone Smoot found was dated about 1200 or about the time the Templars may have found the Ark and brought it out of the Middle East. Unless, of course, their French ancestors—many of whom descended from Jewish royalty and who may have known where the Ark was hidden—had somehow obtained the Ark before then and brought it across the Atlantic for use as the centerpiece of a new Jewish colony, a New Jerusalem....

Amanda sat back and stared out over the lake. She was just wildly speculating. Was it likely the Ark was in Arizona? No. But on the off chance someone had dragged the relic to the deserts of the Southwest, there must have been a compelling reason to do so. And the first step to figuring out that reason would be to learn as much as she could about the mysterious relic.

She spent another ninety minutes on the Internet, jotting down dozens of theories and observations regarding the Ark. Even after discounting many of the most outlandish claims, she easily filled up three pages of a legal pad. Cam joined her in the living room just as she finished up.

He sat on the arm of her easy chair. "What you working on?"

"Ark of the Covenant."

"Still?" He smiled. "Did you find it?"

"All I can say for certain is that it's not in our basement." She scooched over. "Sit."

He slid next to her and slipped his arm over her shoulder. "Before we get into this stuff, did you get a chance to look at the images I sent to Smoot last night?"

"Not yet. I'm deep into the Ark, probably too deep. I could use a break; talk to me."

"I was just looking for a reason to justify my renewed interest in seeing his rune stone—after we blew him off it would seem strange if suddenly I did a one-eighty. Funny thing is, there are actually some pretty interesting connections between his artifact and some Templar stuff in Europe. You should come with me when we hike up to look at it—Astarte can stay with Georgia for the day."

Amanda smiled. "Did you think I would let you go without me? I was ready to hide in the trunk if necessary."

"Good. You can protect me from the snakes."

"How very Eve-like of me."

He looked at her questioningly.

"I took a comparative religion class at university. There's one version of the Adam and Eve story which says Eve slept with the snake to prevent it from killing Adam." Before Cam responded she leaned over and kissed him on the mouth, lingering for a few seconds against the warmth of his mouth. "A shame we don't have time for me to play temptress at the moment."

She kissed him again quickly and sat up. "So here's what I've learned. First, there's a lot of evidence that the Ark was some kind of energy-producing device. Like a giant battery or capacitor."

"You mean God didn't live inside?"

"Negative. But I can see why ancient peoples believed He did. The Ark was pretty frightening." She turned back to the first page of her list. "Okay, fancy this. First, it seems the Ark was some kind of weapon. The Israelites brought it into battle, it knocked down the walls of Jericho and it somehow smote their enemies." She smiled. "For those who don't speak the Queen's English, that means killed."

"Thanks. Does the Queen know where the Ark is?"

"Also negative. Anyway, anyone who got too close to the Ark was zapped or burned, just like our Arizona prospector. I counted four different passages in the Old Testament describing people suffering 'blasts of Heavenly displeasure.' Only the priests, who wore special gold vestments and carried the Ark using poles, knew how to handle it. Even then there are stories of tying a rope around the ankle of any priest who went near the Ark so they could pull him away if it zapped him."

"I can think of some priests I wouldn't mind seeing get zapped."

Amanda smiled and looked at her notes. "Second, many people who went near the Ark were disfigured by it. Did you know Moses wore a veil after overseeing the building of the Ark?"

"No."

"The Old Testament says he wore the veil because his face radiated after speaking with God. I think he got burned by the Ark and wanted to cover his scars."

"Interesting."

"And the same thing happened to Miriam, his sister. Supposedly God afflicted her with leprosy because she spoke out against Moses. Later the leprosy was cured. But leprosy was incurable back then. I think rather she suffered facial burns like Moses." She looked down at her notes. "And get this: There is always one priest in Ethiopia whose job it is to guard the Ark, or at least what they claim is the Ark—that's all he does for his entire life. And for some reason he always ends up going blind from cataracts. They call it milk-eye."

"So Moses had a radiant face, Miriam had something like leprosy, and our Ethiopian priests have cataracts. Sounds more like radiation than normal burns."

"Are cataracts caused by radiation?"

"Can be."

"Interesting theory. In fact, it ties in with my third point. During one battle the Philistines captured the Ark and brought it home with them. But anyone who came near the Ark suffered from skin rashes and boils and tumors and fingernails falling off." She paused. "And get this, also hemorrhoids."

"Hemorrhoids?" Cam chuckled.

"Yes. The Hebrew word is *emerods*. All this comes straight from the Old Testament. "

"Count me out then. The Ark—if that's what it is—can stay up in that cave."

"My brave hero," she smiled.

"But seriously, all those ailments can all be caused by radiation. Even hemorrhoids. My uncle went through radiation treatment for cancer a few years ago."

"So why would the Ark be radioactive?"

"The Ten Commandments were inside the Ark, right? Maybe they were carved on some kind of meteorite?"

"Good theory, but meteorites are not radioactive—despite what people think."

"Maybe uranium then?"

"Perhaps."

Cam leaned back and closed his eyes. "So the Ark is some kind of power source, almost like a giant battery. And it also seems to be radioactive."

"Which would explain why Solomon finally built a temple around it and kept it deep inside. It was the only safe way to handle it."

"Let's go back to the battery idea. I read about something a few months ago—can you Google 'Baghdad Battery'?"

Amanda did so. Apparently a 2000-year-old working battery was unearthed in Iraq back in the 1930s. A cylinder of copper had been rolled around an iron rod and placed inside a terracotta jug. "Here's a drawing posted on the internet," she said.

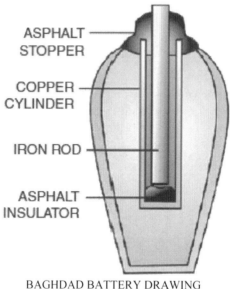

ASPHALT
STOPPER

COPPER
CYLINDER

IRON ROD

ASPHALT
INSULATOR

BAGHDAD BATTERY DRAWING

Experiments on the battery showed that when vinegar was added to the jug, the device produced an electric charge. "They built a replica for a TV show and it almost knocked the host unconscious when they hooked him up to it," Amanda said, "So, if batteries existed 2000 years ago, who's to say they didn't exist even earlier?"

"And think about the design of the Ark. It was built of acacia wood, which would be a good insulator. And the pure gold which covered the Ark is an excellent conductor."

"I read the Ark was never to be placed on the ground." The pieces were beginning to fit together. "Presumably grounding it would cause it to lose its charge."

"Right. And on the top of the Ark are the two winged angels, leaning over the cover toward each other—that would be a perfect arrangement for a spark gap."

Amanda turned in the chair. "Spark gap?"

"Sorry. When I was a kid I was a bit of a science geek. Picture a lightning bolt moving from a cloud to a tree—the air between them is a spark gap. If the Ark was some kind of battery or capacitor, the electricity would jump from angel to angel in the form of a bolt of electricity. It would, as you said, zap anyone standing close by."

"And it says here some author in 1999 built an Ark replica and proved it was an electromagnetic accumulator, whatever that is."

"I think that just means it stored power, like a battery."

"Geek is right," she smiled. "Would it be possible to redirect that electricity?"

"I suppose so. Maybe with a bronze disk of some kind, mounted between the two angels."

"So they could turn those sparks into a weapon?"

Cam nodded. "I suppose so, sure."

"*And the walls came tumbling down.*" Amanda sighed. "All very interesting. But it still doesn't explain how the Ark might have ended up in Arizona."

CHAPTER 5

Normally there would be no way Clarisse would miss out on tomorrow's hike up Mustang Mountain. Not only did it promise to be an interesting adventure, but she didn't totally trust Willum's new associates and it would be a good chance to get a better sense of them. But with them occupying Willum's time she would be able to focus on something far more promising than a treasure chest. This white powder of gold Willum had discovered, or rediscovered, could be exactly what she needed.

Willum had gone into town for supplies; as soon as he left the compound she slipped into his saucer with the spare key she held for him. She locked the door behind her and flicked on a floor lamp. Careful not to disturb anything, she opened the floor hatch, descended the metal stairs and followed the passageway to Willum's lab.

She had never been in the lab before, and she didn't know exactly what the white powder of gold substance would look like, but she did know Willum tended not to clean up after himself. So it only took a few seconds to find a plastic bag filled with a powdery substance resting next to a scale. She lifted the bag and held it up to the light—it looked like corn starch.

Did the powder really have the miraculous powers the ancient Pharaohs believed it had? She emptied half the contents into a plastic bag of her own, turned off the lights and left the lab. For some reason the witches' spell from *Macbeth* popped into her head. "Double, double toil and trouble; fire burn, and cauldron bubble." She laughed aloud, hoping it didn't sound too much like a cackle.

Whistling, Willum parked his Land Cruiser in front of the saucer and unloaded the supplies. Most of them were for tomorrow's hike—water, energy bars, a flashlight, a first aid kit.

Clarisse strolled out to greet him, as she often did. He remembered how Gregory, as a toddler, used to stand behind the screen door, bouncing with joy, when Willum pulled into the driveway. Clarisse didn't exactly bounce but she always seemed pleased to see him. "I have an idea," she said, smiling.

"Uh-oh."

"One of the compounds up in Montana is doing a two-day fast, nothing but water."

"Why?"

"They want to see how the residents react to it. Are the defense posts manned? Does the chain of command break down? Can people tough it out? You were in the military so you understand what this is like. But most of our people are civilians."

Willum nodded. "Okay. When should we do it?"

"No time like the present. Let's start after dinner tonight, and we'll end it Thursday dinner."

He smiled. "Just in time for my hike."

"It's only an hour-and-a-half." She patted his belly. "You'll be fine. Lots of water is all you need."

Following Smoot's directions, Cam and Amanda found the gas station south of Tucson. Their flight had landed without incident the night before; as promised, Georgia had arranged for the same Ford Explorer to be waiting for them at the car rental lot.

"You know," Amanda said, "this is the first time we've left Astarte since she's been with us." Georgia planned to take her to the zoo.

"Really?"

"I'm certain. Three months."

"Well, she needed some stability after what she's been through."

A text came in on Cam's phone. "It's from Willum," Cam said. "He's a mile away." Cam unloaded their packs. "Last chance for the bathroom."

"I'm good. Do you need to check your blood sugar level?"

"Just did. You have enough sunscreen?" Amanda was extra-sensitive to the sun and burned easily; a desert hike would be a challenge for her.

"Yes. And a hat." She smiled. "We sound like an old married couple."

Cam kissed her lips. "Good."

When Cam had first met Smoot, he knew nothing about the man. Now, at their second meeting, Cam knew about his Survivalist activities along with, according to Georgia, his rabid militancy. But the man who stepped out of the Land Cruiser looked more like a 1960s peace activist than a trigger-happy radical.

Wearing a yellow Grateful Dead t-shirt, a straw cowboy hat and a pair of jeans, the burly Smoot smiled and ambled over. A patchy pink rash discolored his cheeks and forehead. "Thanks for coming." He shook his head. "I wouldn't have blamed you if my paranoia scared you off."

Cam shrugged and shook Smoot's hand. "No harm done."

"I'm guessing you might be a bit nervous." He smiled. "Or maybe I'm projecting my paranoia onto you. But if you want to inspect my pack, you'll see that I'm not armed. Other than a pocket knife, that is."

Cam shook his head. "No need."

Amanda looked at Cam, who nodded. "I hope you don't mind if I tag along," she said. They had wanted to meet Willum again before making the final decision on Amanda joining them.

"Not at all." Smoot motioned toward the gas station. "Do you guys have enough water and food?"

Cam nodded. They had stocked up after landing yesterday. "We should be good."

"Just one more thing then." Smoot handed Cam a piece of paper. "This is a confidentiality agreement. You agree not to tell anyone about the site, and also agree anything we find belongs to me." He shrugged. "Sorry if it sounds paranoid."

Cam glanced through it. "Fair enough." He signed it and handed it to Amanda to do the same.

"Okay then," Smoot said. "We can leave your car here."

Smoot turned off Highway 82 about a mile from the gas station and bounced south along what would have been called a logging road in New England. Here, apparently, ranchers used the rutted paths to access their herds. Periodically, Cam got out of the front seat to unlatch a gate so they could pass.

"Make sure it closes tight," Willum said. "The ranchers get pretty pissed off when their cattle go missing." He lowered his voice. "Plus sometimes the animals wander out onto the highway."

As they drove, Amanda explained what they had learned about the Ark of the Covenant.

"Do you really think that's what this chest is?" Willum asked.

"Probably not," she replied. "Especially because your chest doesn't seem to have the angels on the top. Or at least the drawing doesn't show it. But we just wanted to fill you in on our research."

Occasionally they passed a dusty pick-up truck or SUV coming the other way. Each time Willum pulled off to the shoulder, lifted his hat and allowed the vehicles to pass. "This is their land. We're just visitors."

About twenty minutes into the bumpy ride a black pick-up angled toward them on an intersecting road. Two men rode in it, both wearing sunglasses and cowboy hats like Willum. The driver, his left elbow resting on the window, raised his arm in a half-wave as they passed. It was the sunburn that first caught Cam's attention—a red area framed a white blotch on the man's wrist, as if he had been out in the sun wearing a wristwatch and the skin around the watch burned. A local rancher would not have a sunburned arm in February. But a federal agent who flew in yesterday and sat in the sun while waiting to check into his hotel room would. Sloppy.

Cam pulled out his phone and texted Georgia, careful that Willum couldn't read the message. "I just made your agents. Black Dodge Ram 1500. Tell them to back off. Willum's not stupid." Cam hadn't gotten a good look at the man in the passenger seat, but the red hair peaking out from beneath his hat and the fact the man kept his head turned made Cam guess it was Ellis Kincaid. Hopefully so—Cam owed him some payback. Not that embarrassing him in front of his cohorts would make them even close to even. Once the message transmitted, Cam deleted it from the sent folder just in case Smoot ever accessed his phone.

Smoot veered off the rutted road and angled toward a pair of jagged peaks. "That peak on the right is where we're going" He drove off-road for another five minutes, the Land Cruiser bouncing along, before he stopped in a pasture-like area at the foot of a rocky incline. "We walk from here." He gestured toward a path they had passed a few hundred yards back. "We'll follow the streambed." Moisture from the stream made the area bordering it alive with growth—from the distance the path looked like a green ribbon running up the mountainside.

"Not a big deal," Cam said, "but why not just park at the bottom of the path?"

Smoot nodded. "I did that the first time I came here, but I couldn't see the Land Cruiser from the cave and I got lost on the way down. I was lucky I had a key fob that made the horn go off—it was almost dark by the time I staggered back to the car."

Maybe that made sense for the first time. But by now Smoot should know the way down. "That the only reason?"

Smoot stared at Cam for a few seconds and smiled. "Very perceptive, Mr. Thorne. You're right. I parked the car in an open area so I could see it from the cave at the top. I don't trust the feds to not sneak over and hide a listening device in it."

Cam sized up the hike. Not a huge mountain, but fairly steep especially near the top. If it were a ski trail it would be a medium-length black diamond. The landscape was varied, with desert ferns, cacti, wildflowers and a few scraggly trees pushing their way through the rocky soil. Smoot pulled three walking sticks out of the back of the SUV. "They help, especially on the hike back down. Plus, I like to poke mine ahead of me just to make sure I don't step on a rattler."

"Based on that, I'm happy to march in the rear of the pack," Amanda said.

They applied sunscreen, put on their packs and gulped some water. "The more we can drink now, the less we'll have to carry with us," Smoot said. "The dry heat makes you feel like you're not sweating, but what is really happening is it's evaporating before you can feel it. It'll climb into the eighties soon and we're all wearing thick jeans." He smiled. "And one of us is forty pounds overweight. We're going to sweat."

They hiked in silence for the first few minutes. "So why don't you practice law anymore?" Smoot asked as they settled into their climb up the rocky incline.

Cam knew the question was meant to draw him out, to help Smoot get a feel for him. Which was fine. "Long story."

"It's an hour-and-a-half climb," Smoot smiled.

"Okay, as long as you don't mind me gasping for breath once in a while." The peak rose to over six thousand feet, which put them at the elevation of Denver; Cam already noticed the air was thinning. "When I got out of law school I took a job at a big firm in Boston. That was in 1999. I was doing okay, working my way up the partnership track. Then in 2005 our firm took a case helping the state Attorney General sue the company that was overseeing a massive construction project—the main highway going through Boston was being torn down and rebuilt underground. The cost ballooned from, like, two billion dollars to sixteen billion."

"The Big Dig," Smoot said. "I remember that."

"Even I heard about it in London," Amanda said.

"I actually helped bring the case in—one of the guys at the Attorney General's office was an old friend of mine from law school. It was a pretty big deal for me, a really big client for an associate to bring in. Anyway, we were suing the company because they did such a shitty job managing the project. It was a fascinating case, involving all sorts of unique legal questions. Plus it was high profile. The partner in charge was a guy name Chas Hansen, one of the firm's big rainmakers and an ex-quarterback from Dartmouth. Big guy, square-jawed, but also really bright. Juries ate him up. You know the type—women want him, men want to be like him."

"Just like you, honey." Amanda grinned.

"Yes, thanks for that." The trail steepened and they climbed single file, Cam in the middle. On either side of the narrow, rocky incline cacti and other needle-pointed plants clawed at them as they ascended. Cam was glad they had worn leather gloves, even in the heat.

Before Cam could continue his story Willum stopped and picked something up from the trail. He turned and showed them a tattered book. "It's a Bible, written in Spanish. Probably dropped by some illegals sneaking across the border." He scanned the mountainside. "Hopefully this book was the only casualty." He placed the Bible in his pack, wiped his face with the sleeve of his shirt, swigged some water and smiled. "Reminds me of a joke. A cowboy lost his Bible in the desert. A couple of months later a cow wanders over with a book in its mouth. The cowboy takes the book—it's his lost Bible. 'What a miracle; praise the Lord!' the cowboy exclaims. 'Not really,' says the cow. 'Your name is on the inside cover.'"

Cam and Amanda laughed, Willum chuckled to himself, and the three of them turned back up the trail. "Continue your story, Mr. Thorne."

The burly man was sweating through his shirt and breathing heavily; he was probably happy to let Cam do the talking. "So I did most of the research and case management and strategizing for the Big Dig case. This went on for a couple of years and Chas Hansen and I got really close; he took me under his wing and I spent a lot of time with him and his family. But in the meantime the economy tanked and the firm announced they wouldn't be making any new partners for the next year. Plus they elected a new managing partner, a guy named Rolando. He and I never got along—one year at our Christmas party I saw him make a drunken pass at one of the firm's secretaries; I think he was always worried I would blackmail him or something. Anyway, at about the same time I got a call from a buddy who worked at a law firm in New York. They were opening a satellite office in Boston and needed someone to chair the litigation department. One thing led to another and the New York firm offered me the job along with a promotion to partner and a pretty big raise."

"I never heard this part of the story," Amanda said.

Cam shrugged. "So I was pretty psyched. This was a big deal for me professionally. So the first thing I did was go tell Chas Hansen. I expected him to be happy for me—he knew Rolando didn't like me and it would be tough for me to make partner. But instead he laid a guilt trip on me about being a team player, how he needed me on the Big Dig case, how it would be hard for him to train a new associate to help him. Well, I told him my first preference had always been to stay put, but not if it was a dead end for me. He told me to wait, walked out of the office and came back a half hour later. 'I just spoke to Rolando,' he said. 'I told him if you weren't made partner next year I'd quit the firm. I've got your back, buddy.'"

"So you stayed?" Smoot asked.

"I stayed. Even though it was less money and no guarantee about making partner. About three months later I got an email from Rolando. He was pulling me off the Big Dig case and putting me on a case where the firm was defending the Boston Archdiocese in a bunch of priest sex abuse cases. I wanted nothing to do with that—my best friend growing up committed suicide after being abused by a priest."

Amanda touched his arm. "So what happened next?"

"I went to see Chas Hansen, of course. He was pissed that Rolando pulled me off the case—he hadn't known. And he promised he'd make it right. But when push came to shove he just caved. I think he was afraid to stand up to Rolando—he had a good thing going and didn't want to risk it. Turns out he had a strong jaw but a weak spine."

"What happened to having your back?" Amanda asked.

"I think in the end having a corner office and having a fat bonus and having a ski chalet in Vermont was more important than having my back."

"And that's when you went to the press," Amanda said.

"That was a few months later. It was bad enough representing these priests who abused kids, but the partner in charge was a real scumbag. He kept trying to demonize the victims. Finally I got sick of it and leaked some internal memos to the press."

Smoot turned and looked at Cam. "I'm sorry to hear about that. It doesn't sound like Chas Hansen was a bad guy. Just a bad friend."

Cam nodded. "That's a good way to put it."

"Mind if I tell another joke?" Smoot asked.

"Please do."

He stopped and faced them. "What do you throw to a drowning lawyer?"

Cam shrugged.

Smoot smiled. "His partners." He stared at Cam. "I'm glad to see you're a different kind of lawyer, Mr. Thorne." He resumed the hike. "So, did you get disbarred?"

"No, but I was suspended for a few months. After that I went to work for my uncle's firm out in the suburbs." Cam smiled. "I still do real estate closings and stuff for him when I'm not out looking for Templar treasure."

Smoot glanced back over his shoulder and returned the smile. "Well, I'll make sure we find the treasure chest soon. I wouldn't want to keep you away from anything *really* important."

Of course Amanda was curious to see the rune stone. But more so she wanted to study Willum Smoot. As Cam had told the story of his ill-fated law career and Willum listened, Amanda observed their host.

He listened more than he spoke, which Amanda's grandfather had always told her was a good way to go through life. "God gave you two ears and one mouth; employ them in that proportion." He also seemed to have a good sense of appropriate behavior, which Amanda had always thought was one of the best tests of a person—the cowboy and lawyer jokes were cliché but at least they were appropriate for the occasion. And his commentary on Chas Hansen—that he was not a bad guy, just a bad friend—was both insightful and spot on. But more telling was his seeming concern about the illegal immigrants and the care he showed in placing the Bible in his pack rather than discarding it on the trail. Often the little gestures spoke more loudly than the grand ones. As for his paranoia with worrying the Land Cruiser might be bugged, well, maybe the paranoia was justified—Cam had whispered that he had spotted Georgia's men tracking them. And at least Willum had been honest about it.

They hiked in silence now, the ridge line only a hundred feet ahead, angling to the right. The late-morning sun beat on them and the cool desert morning had turned to a warm desert day. Amanda knew to keep her skin shaded from the sun, but she wondered about Willum. "Willum, do you want some sunscreen? I notice you already have a burn."

He turned. "It's actually not a burn. It's a rash. Not sure what brought it on but it seems to be getting better." He looked back up the trail. "Once we reach the ridge line, we circle back toward the left again. We actually go back down a bit, to a saddle between the two peaks."

"So you said you dug up the body," Cam said.

"Yeah," he shrugged. "I'm not too proud of that, but really how could I not?"

"I guess you could have called the authorities," Cam responded. Amanda knew he was just testing Willum; no way would Cam have trusted the so-called experts with this type of find.

Willum smiled. "I think we both know how that would have gone."

They followed the ridge line before descending into the saddle between the two peaks. "Was there anything else in the cave?" Cam asked.

"Actually, yes." Willum pointed. "The cave's up there. You can see for yourselves."

To their right the rocky cliff-face of the peak rose up another few hundred feet; to the left the mountain fell steeply to the brownish-green valley perhaps a thousand feet below. "Straight that way," Willum said, "is Mexico. Maybe 20 miles."

"So the cave faces due south?" Cam asked.

"Yes. Exactly."

"Hmm," Cam responded. "That may not be a coincidence."

Another twenty strides and Willum stopped. "Here we are."

Cam crouched in front of a flat, orange-tinted, coffee-table-sized boulder that sat just outside the opening to the cave. He ran his fingers across the blackened runes carved into the stone. "Can you translate this for me again?" Cam asked. Willum had sent it by email but Cam wanted the exact translation again.

"Sure." Smoot read from a piece of paper he pulled from his pocket.

> *The body of rough Hurech lays here.*
> *He enjoyed merriment.*
> *The secret is near rough Hurech's body.*
> *Fame and glory await.*
> *The body turns to dust and goes to Eden's temple.*

While Cam examined the inscription Amanda clicked on her flashlight and approached the cave.

"Hold on one second," Willum said. "Sometimes there are mountain lions or other animals in these caves. Let's at least give them an easy way out." He shined his light in and tossed a rock against the back wall as he gently pulled Amanda aside. The stone echoed but roused no hidden animal. "Coast is clear. Just be careful of snakes—if they're in here they'll be sleeping. But they'll wake up if you step on them."

Amanda entered the cave, which approximated the size of a one-car garage with an arched entryway. "Look on your right," Willum said. "There are more carvings." Four runic letters, each four inches tall, had been carved neatly on the wall of the cave. Willum approached. "Those four letters match the first four letters of the inscription on the boulder outside."

"Really?" Amanda pondered this. And the cave faced due south. "What do the first four letters say?"

"It's the guy's name, Hurech," Willum responded.

She glanced at the cave opening. The midday sun did not penetrate the cave, being too high in the sky. But it was late February, two months later than the winter solstice. "I wonder." She took her cell phone out of her pocket—she had downloaded an astronomy app which allowed the phone, when in camera mode, to project the path of the sun across the horizon at any given date of the year. She entered December 21, held the phone up against the runic inscription on the cave wall, pointed it out the cave opening and waited for the program to project the path of the sun. After a few seconds a blue arc-shaped line appeared across the top of the camera display. "Bloody perfect," she whispered. At high noon on December 21 the sun, moving across the horizon, passed just below the top of the cave opening, shining its beam into the cave and illuminating the 'Hurech' inscription carved on the wall. Only once per year, on the winter solstice, would the sun be low enough in the sky to shine on the inscription.

"What?" Willum asked.

Amanda ignored him and instead called Cam over and showed him the display. "What do you think, Cam?"

MUSTANG MOUNTAIN CAVE ENTRANCE
WINTER SOLSTICE SUN PATH PROJECTION

He grinned. "It's exactly what the Templars would do. It's a perfect allegory." Cam turned to Willum, "I think it's safe to say the Templars were here."

"I don't get it," Willum said.

Amanda turned. "Okay. In ancient times the days before the winter solstice were the most frightening time of the year—the sun was dropping lower and lower in the sky and the days getting shorter and shorter, not to mention colder and colder. If the sun continued its descent, life would end. The people truly feared this. But by the twenty-fifth or so of December they would have been able to ascertain that the days were getting longer again, that the sun was ascending. That's what the original Christmas celebration was for—the earth had been saved, or reborn, for another year." She paused. "Life would go on."

"I get that, but what does it have to do with Hurech?" Willum asked.

"The Templars observed many of the ancient pagan rituals, which really were just a way to worship Mother Earth, or what some people call the Sacred Feminine. You may recall Cameron discussing this in his lecture."

"Okay."

"That's what we have here. Hurech's mates wanted Hurech to go to heaven. To be reborn. The sun shining on his name on the winter solstice is a way for the fallen Knight to be reborn, just like the earth." She bowed her head. "It's really quite a beautiful allegory."

Willum stared off at the horizon before shifting his gaze to the runic letters on the cave wall. "I guess I was smart to bring you guys up here."

Ellis chuckled at his reflection in the hotel bathroom mirror as he washed his face. Thorne had spotted him in the pick-up truck out in the desert. Of course he had—Ellis had wanted him to. If he hadn't, he would have made a point of covering or dying his red hair. But Ellis wanted Thorne to think he was smarter than the agent, to give him confidence he was not in over his head. Maybe even make him over-confident.

Ironically, it might be harder to manipulate the little girl. Ellis understood adults, knew which buttons to push. But it had been quite a while since he was in the third grade. And Astarte seemed like a bright kid.

Georgia and the girl had just returned to the hotel from the zoo and were headed to the pool. Thorne and Amanda wouldn't be home for a couple of hours. Ellis threw on his swim trunks, grabbed a paperback and sauntered down the hall toward the smell of chlorine.

He greeted Georgia, dove in and swam a few laps. After floating on his back for a few minutes, he ambled over toward Astarte. Georgia had one eye on the girl as she talked on her phone.

"My friends call me Ellis, but my real name is Geronimo," he said, smiling. "I work with Georgia." Kids tended to trust him because he had a small face with delicate features which made him look, well, like a kid. He sat on the edge of the shallow end, feet dangling in the water, while the girl played with a dark-skinned doll in a bathing suit.

"No it's not." She didn't look up.

"Okay, you're right. But I am part Native-American. I belong to the Cherokee tribe. My Indian name is Flying Fox. Probably because of my hair color." He held his smile. "But I can't really fly, just like real foxes."

"A flying fox isn't a fox, it's a big bat with a face like a fox," she said, still looking at her doll.

Oops. He should have researched that better—the girl was sharp. "Well, anyway, I know a lot about your Uncle Jefferson's research. He was a very smart man." Ellis had spent most of the night going through the man's file and studying his research. Essentially her uncle believed that Astarte carried the bloodlines of King David, Jesus, Isis, Mohammad and Mormon founder Joseph Smith—a neat trick made possible by direct descendants of these dynastic rulers having voyaged to America per the teachings of the Book of Mormon and adding their bloodlines to a Native American royal family, of which Astarte was the latest issue. It was Astarte's destiny, her uncle believed, to unite the world's religions.

The girl swam the doll in a circle. Ellis continued. "And I think he was right. I think lots of people were here before Columbus."

She nodded. "He lets me help him with his research."

Interesting use of verb tenses. And the opening he needed. He switched tenses himself. "I'm sure you are a big help; you seem very smart. And of course he wants you to know all about it—as the princess you would need to possess this knowledge." He paused. "So why didn't Cam and Amanda bring you with them today?"

She shrugged. "I don't know."

"I heard them say they didn't think you could make it all the way up the mountain. But I bet you could."

She looked up, her cobalt-blue eyes flashing. "I've climbed lots of mountains."

He shrugged. "Well, maybe they didn't think you were old enough to know the truth."

She crossed her arms, the doll now upside-down and dripping water. "What truth?"

"Well, if they find the Templar treasure up there, then that will prove your Uncle Jefferson is wrong. He thinks the Nephites and Lamanites and other people written about in the Book of Mormon came to America and left all the artifacts. But if it was the Templars or other French families who were here, then he must be mistaken. And I guess that would mean you're not the princess." Ellis kicked at the water. "Maybe your uncle isn't such a smart man after all. Or maybe his research is just wrong."

Astarte gazed deep into the pool. Droplets of water dripped down her face, some just below her eyes. Her eyes locked onto Ellis's. "He's *very* smart." She swallowed. "Smarter than you."

Willum dropped his guests off at their car mid-afternoon, shook their hands and said goodbye. "Thanks for your help," he said. "Do you mind if we stay in touch? I feel like you guys can really help with this search."

Cam nodded. "Sure thing. Thanks for showing us the carving."

As he drove away, Amanda asked, "So, what do you think?"

"I think I want a shower and a cold beer."

"You're getting predictable, Cameron," she smiled.

"Sorry. I liked him. Not at all what I expected. Hard to believe the feds think he might start some kind of armed insurrection."

"I agree. I liked him also. But that does not mean he is not paranoid. And does not mean he is not dangerous. He truly believes the feds are out to get him."

"What's that saying? 'It's not paranoid if it's true.' Maybe he's right; maybe they are out to get him."

"Well, I think there is little doubt that he would welcome you into the compound."

"Thanks to you. That was amazing, how you figured out the winter solstice alignment. Smoot was blown away by it."

"So was I," she laughed. "Imagine how difficult it must have been to find just the right cave."

"Or maybe they found almost the right cave and then hacked away at the opening to make it work."

"Either way, it wasn't a coincidence." She smiled. "Yes, I know, you don't believe in coincidences."

"I think Einstein was the one who said coincidences were God's way of remaining anonymous. Well, since I don't really believe in God—at least not in the sense of some puppet-master up in the heavens pulling our strings—I guess I can't believe in coincidences either."

Cam and Amanda returned to their hotel in Tucson, retrieved Astarte and took a much-needed shower. Over dinner at the hotel grill, Astarte seemed morose. Or maybe just tired. After some prodding, she told them about the zoo. "They had alpacas, just like at America's Stonehenge." The New Hampshire America's Stonehenge site contained both stone chambers and astronomically-aligned standing stones evidencing habitation by an ancient culture approximately 3500 years ago. Carbon-dating had confirmed this date, and a carved stone dedicated to 'Baal of the Canaanites' indicated the ancient inhabitants were probably the seafaring, Baal-worshiping Phoenicians who lived in what is today Lebanon. The alpacas kept the kids entertained while their parents explored the stone ruins. Most kids, that is—Astarte had been fascinated by the ancient history as well as the friendly, llama-like animals when they had visited during the recent winter solstice.

"Did they eat your bagel again?" Amanda asked, recalling how one of the alpacas had snuck up on Astarte.

"No," she said, playing with her food.

"Speaking of America's Stonehenge," Cam said, "check out this email I just got. The son of the owners of the site has been researching the alignments and playing with them on Google Earth, trying to see if they tie in with any other ancient sites. So here's the summer solstice sunset alignment." He turned his iPad so Amanda and Astarte could see.

AMERICA'S STONEHENGE
SUMMER SOLSTICE SUNSET ALIGNMENT

Cam explained to Astarte. "This is how the ancient people knew when the seasons were changing. When the sun rose just over the tip of this boulder, they knew it was the summer solstice. Other boulders—they call them standing stones—marked the winter solstice and the spring and fall equinoxes."

"Like a calendar?" Astarte asked, perking up a bit.

"Exactly," Amanda responded. "In ancient times people needed to know when to plant their crops and when to sail their ships and when to hunker down for the winter."

Astarte tilted her head to the side. "It's a little crooked," she said.

Cam smiled. "You're right." The sun did not rest precisely over the peak of the standing stone. "And that actually helps us date the site. Over the centuries the earth actually tilts a bit on its axis. Three or four thousand years ago, the sun would have been perfectly centered."

"Okay," the girl said as she chewed a french fry.

Cam clicked at the keypad for a few seconds. "Google Earth will show you the sun on any given day. So here is June 21. This is an overhead view of America's Stonehenge, with a line extending from the center of the site, over the standing stone and to the rising sun."

AMERICA'S STONEHENGE
SUMMER SOLSTICE SUNRISE
(LINE FROM CENTER OF SITE TO HORIZON)

"I'm guessing the image is dark because it's dawn?" Amanda said.

"Right." Cam smiled. Amanda could tell he was loving this. "So if you extend this line all the way across the Atlantic Ocean, what do you think you hit?"

Astarte cocked her head again. "Well, the sun rises in the east. Is it Jerusalem?"

"Nice guess, but no." Cam turned his iPad again. "Here's a hint."

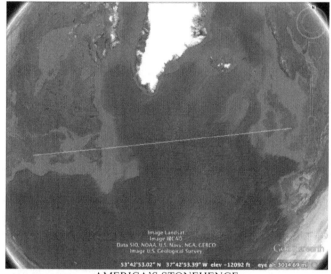

AMERICA'S STONEHENGE
SUMMER SOLSTICE SUNRISE ALIGNMENT PROJECTION

Amanda's eyes widened. "That looks like it passes near Stonehenge in England."

"Not just near. You're not going to believe this." He clicked to the next image.

AMERICA'S STONEHENGE
SUMMER SOLSTICE SUNRISE ALIGNMENT PROJECTION TO
STONEHENGE, ENGLAND

"This is the same line that began at America's Stonehenge. It passes straight through the main arch," Cam said.

Amanda leaned closer. "Unbelievable. Like threading a needle from across the ocean," she breathed. She felt the hair on the back of her neck bristle—she wasn't frightened in the traditional sense, but there was something astonishingly eerie about the cross-Atlantic connection. "How could they possible have done this?"

"You mean you don't think it's a coincidence?" Cam smiled.

"Not bloody likely."

"Somehow they reverse-engineered it. Probably by using the stars. And then they built America's Stonehenge right on the alignment projection. Obviously it had some kind of religious significance."

"Of course it did," Amanda said. "These people were sun-worshipers. On the summer solstice the sun is at its maximum strength, so this would have been a crucial day. Building the sites so they aligned to each other on the summer solstice sunrise makes perfect sense." If this research was accurate, it was truly a stunning discovery.

"Does that mean the Phoenicians built Stonehenge in England?" Astarte asked.

"Maybe not built it, but at least worshiped there," Cam said. "Otherwise why would there be a connection between the two sites?"

Amanda nodded. "Yes, it all fits together nicely. A few years ago they found a body at Stonehenge—they did DNA testing and determined the man was Middle-Eastern, not European. This baffled researchers until somebody remembered that the Phoenicians were making regular trips to Cornwall in southern England to trade for tin during that period—they needed tin to make bronze. So one of the theories was that the Phoenicians recognized the religious significance of Stonehenge—all the celestial alignments and such—and used it as a place to worship while far from home."

"And then they continued on from Cornwall to North America to mine or trade for copper," Cam said. "The tin needed to be added to copper to make bronze, and there wasn't enough copper in Europe or Africa."

"And in North America they erected another Stonehenge—aligned to the original—to worship at while across the Atlantic," Amanda concluded. Numerous reports from early settlers of the Great Lakes region and southern Quebec described gaping voids where copper had been mined in ancient times; according to Native American oral history, these miners were white-skinned men who came from the east. A worship site near the Atlantic coast, aligned with Stonehenge England, made perfect sense.

They sat back and stared at Cam's screen for a few seconds. "So," Cam said, "to try to tie this all together: Is it possible the Phoenicians could have brought the Ark of the Covenant to America? Do the dates work?" The possibility of the Ark making its way to America, as far-fetched as it seemed, was still on the table.

Amanda did the arithmetic. America's Stonehenge was built around 1500 BC. The Phoenicians, though their empire gradually faded, continued as a maritime trading power until about 300 BC.

And there would have been a demand for copper from North America until around 600 BC, when the Bronze Age gave way to the Iron Age. So, yes, the dates worked. "I would say if the Ark disappeared between 800 BC and 600 BC, the dates are spot on. The Phoenicians would have been still sailing to North America during that period."

"And don't forget, the Phoenicians are the ones who Solomon hired to build the original temple in Jerusalem, where the Ark was housed. So they knew about the Ark, and maybe knew how to handle it."

"How far is Phoenicia from Jerusalem?"

Amanda shrugged. "Phoenicia is basically what we know today as Lebanon. So not far—maybe fifty miles."

Cam nodded. "Okay, so maybe the Phoenicians brought the Ark to North America. But how did it get to Arizona?"

Amanda smiled. "Hey, I just tracked it across the Atlantic for you. You can figure out the rest yourself. Astarte and I are going to get some ice cream." She stood, grinned and kissed him. "See you in an hour."

"Then you should call him, Willum," Clarisse said.

Willum had resisted picking up a bucket of chicken on the way home from Mustang Mountain and, having showered, was describing the climb to Clarisse as they sat across from one another at one of the dozen round picnic tables arranged in a sheltered area between two of the sets of domes. A handful of kids ran by playing flashlight tag in the dwindling daylight and the smell of a bonfire wafted over them. Sometimes the compound felt more like summer camp than an armed safe-haven. Willum drank a Gatorade, wishing he was on his way to finger-licking-good heaven—he had burnt enough calories on the climb to deserve the treat but he couldn't very well indulge while the other residents were fasting. "Now?" he asked. "Shouldn't I wait?"

She smiled. "We're not in middle school. You said they figured out the winter solstice thing right away. And you trusted them, right?" She paused and waited for him to meet her gaze. "Look, this is important stuff." She gestured generally to the compound around them. "People are counting on you. And right now you are being distracted by this quest of yours." She held up her hand. "I'm not blaming you, I'm just stating a fact. So if you think Thorne and his fiancée can help find the treasure chest, you have to call them. For all you know, they are getting on a plane and flying back to Boston soon. Then it'll be too late."

"So I should just call him now."

She nodded. "That's what I said. Be brave."

"We brought you mint chocolate-chip," Astarte said, handing Cam a plastic bowl half-filled with a pair of sludgy greenish orbs. He was sitting in a leather easy chair in the lobby of the hotel sipping a Diet Coke and playing with the America's Stonehenge alignments on Google Earth.

"Thanks, honey," Cam said, kissing Astarte on the cheek.

Amanda smiled and shrugged as Cam eyed the semi-frozen mound. "I reckon the ice cream is better in Boston."

"So," he said, "I just got a call from Smoot. He wants us to come out to his compound tomorrow. He wants to brainstorm about finding the chest. You in?"

"For a bit, yes, but I'll probably cut it short to come back and spend some time with Astarte."

"Okay." He turned his laptop toward her. "Care to guess where the summer solstice sunrise alignment line extends to?"

"Going from North America to England, or the other way?"

"West to east, after it passes through the Stonehenge arch."

"The line was angling north a bit, so someplace in Scandinavia?"

"It's actually tough to wrap your brain around this. But because the earth is round, the line actually bends south."

She gave him a funny look.

"Look at it this way. If you go due north, what do you hit?"

"The North Pole."

"And if you continue on, what direction are you now heading?"

She nodded. "I see. South."

"Okay, it's the same with this solstice line." He pulled a globe from the floor next to him. "I borrowed this from the front desk so you could see what I mean. Here, hold this string on America's Stonehenge. Now, extend it to Stonehenge England. Here's some tape."

Amanda placed the globe on the coffee table and dropped to one knee. "Done."

"Now keep it going. Where does it hit?"

"Looks like the Middle East someplace." She taped the string in place.

"Here it is on Google Earth. It's a little more accurate than the string."

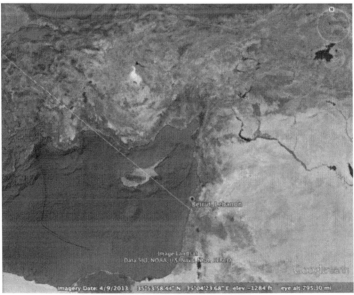

AMERICA'S STONEHENGE
SUMMER SOLSTICE SUNRISE ALIGNMENT PROJECTION TO
STONEHENGE, ENGLAND, FURTHER EXTENDED TO MIDDLE EAST

Amanda gasped. "Brilliant. Right into southern Lebanon."

Cam grinned. "I don't know how they did it, but Stonehenge England and Stonehenge America align straight back to the heart of ancient Phoenicia."

"No doubt the Phoenicians had a stone temple to honor Baal as well."

They both stared at the image for a few seconds. Cam broke the silence. "Well, it doesn't prove the Ark is here in America. But it sure says a lot about the Phoenicians navigating the globe."

"And it also hints that the Phoenicians may have been involved with building Stonehenge England—the experts have never suggested that."

"Well, the experts might have to change their minds."

"Not bloody likely. You know how most of them are. The only evidence they look at is the stuff that fits their theories. It's amazing that archeologists call themselves scientists—a scientist would never disregard evidence that didn't fit her theory. But these duffers think it's okay to toss artifacts aside if they don't fit their premise. They call them anomalies. The whole lot of them are blinkered."

"Blinkered?" Cam could always tell when Amanda got worked up because she used more British slang.

"You know, like a horse wearing blinders."

Cam smiled. "So back to Smoot. We'll drive out there in the morning, do our little brainstorm session, and then I'll either come back with you or hang out at the compound. Georgia wants me to spend as much time there as I can. To look around, un-blinkered."

"Very funny." Amanda exhaled slowly. "Okay, but I'll want regular updates after I leave. And if you start dressing in camouflage and talking about the world coming to an end, don't bother to come home."

Since Astarte loved how Georgia doted on her it was a simple matter to leave the two of them together at the hotel for the morning. Cam drove while Amanda navigated—the ride from

Tucson to the compound in Casa Grande should take about an hour against morning traffic.

"Wow," Cam said, "car thermometer says 67. A cold snap."

"Yes. Yesterday was 68 at this time."

"I like the sun and warmth, but it's actually getting old already."

"I agree. I'm having trouble keeping the sun from turning me into a swamp monster." Amanda was allergic to the sun, which if she wasn't careful caused her face to blister and pus. "Speaking of which, did you notice the rash on Willum's face?"

"What of it?"

She shrugged. "We had just been talking about face rashes with Moses and Miriam. It just struck me as an odd coincidence." She smiled. "And we know how you feel about them."

As Cam drove, Amanda used her phone to bounce around the internet, looking for clues as to where the Templars may have hidden their golden chest. "I think we need to think allegorically. The Templars were big into the concept of duality and balance: the male and the female, the king and the priest, the dark and the light, the heavens and the earth."

"Sort of like the Chinese with their yin and yang."

"Yes. The obvious spot to hide the chest is in the cave with Hurech. But that's too easy, too simple."

"So you think the opposite."

"Perhaps. If Hurech's cave marks the winter solstice, perhaps the chest is in a cave marked by the summer solstice."

Cam nodded. "I like it." He pointed to a series of dome-like buildings on the horizon ahead. "There's the compound. You can run your theory by Willum yourself."

Amanda and Cameron had left for the day, and Georgia was up getting fruit from the hotel breakfast buffet. Astarte pushed the cereal around in her bowl, the milk splashing over the edges. Normally she didn't like to make a mess—she would clean it up later so the waitress didn't have to do it but for now she was too busy thinking.

Maybe the Flying Fox man was right. Cameron and Amanda believed explorers came here before Columbus, but they didn't seem to agree with the rest of Uncle Jefferson's research. And if they didn't believe that, they probably didn't believe she was the true princess. She thought about the talk Cameron gave earlier in the week—he never once mentioned the Nephites or Lamanites or the Book of Mormon or the Burrows Cave artifacts or the Michigan Tablets or any of the research Uncle Jefferson spent so much time on. Uncle Jefferson may have a few details wrong, but is it possible he is wrong about *everything*?

Uncle Jefferson had warned her that many people would disagree with his research because of what he called 'religious blinders.' Maybe it was true. Maybe that was why they wouldn't let her go to the Mormon Church. When Amanda told Cameron about Quetzalcoatl, they both acted like the only way to explain the white god with a beard was that he was one of the Roman Jews from France. But Uncle Jefferson and other Mormons who studied Quetzalcoatl think he might be one of the prophets from the Book of Mormon—maybe the prophet Lehi, who came to Mexico in a boat across the Atlantic Ocean. Either one might be true, so why had Cameron ignored Lehi? In fact, couldn't Lehi or his descendants have made the lead crosses and swords?

She sighed. Even though he was in heaven watching over her, and sometimes even talking to her, she missed Uncle Jefferson. Why did God let him die? She was happy to have found a new home, and she liked Amanda and Cameron. But that didn't mean she could just forget about Uncle Jefferson. Or forget about being a princess.

"So, are you going to make them take the sodium pentothal?" Clarisse asked.

Willum's brow furrowed. "Cam and Amanda? Of course not. They're my guests." It came out with more of an edge than he intended. "Sorry, this fast is getting to me a bit." They were walking the three-quarter-mile perimeter of the sixteen-acre compound, a morning ritual they undertook both for exercise and as a security check.

"That doesn't mean they aren't spies." She sipped from a water bottle.

He waved the comment away. "I'm the one who's supposed to be paranoid."

"You going to tell them about the white powder of gold?"

"Probably not. It doesn't really have anything to do with the chest." They reached the main gate; Willum checked his watch. "They should be here soon. You want to wait with me?"

"No thanks. I'll catch you guys later." She smiled. "Somebody has to run this place. I think the natives are about ready to storm the kitchen." She stood on her tiptoes and kissed him on the cheek. "Good luck."

Ten minutes later, the musty, floral scent of Clarisse still swimming in Willum's nostrils, a maroon SUV approached from the south and slowed in front of the iron gate. Willum smiled and waved, motioned for the guard to open the gate, and moved aside to allow Cam to drive in. They exchanged pleasantries as Willum gave them a quick tour and explained the original use of the compound.

"And everyone here honestly believes society is on the verge of collapse?" Amanda asked.

Willum smiled—somehow blunt questions like that always seemed less offensive when delivered with a British accent. Especially when the accent came from such a pretty face. "Actually, no. I would say only about ten percent of the people believe that. The other ninety percent believe it is a possibility and want to be prepared just in case. You know, very few people think they are going to die before their kids grow up, but almost all of them buy life insurance." He shrugged. "So this is sort of like insurance. If we don't need it, so much the better."

He led them into the saucer. He had brought in a couple of folding tables and spread a number of topographic maps across them. "I've tried to make my search as methodical as possible." He had placed pins on peaks he had explored. "But there are probably a couple of hundred peaks in the area, and each has at least a few caves. Sometimes I feel like Sisyphus, forever rolling a boulder uphill."

They sat, and Amanda explained her theory about how the Templars believed in duality. "I don't think they would have hidden the chest with Hurech. Not only is it too obvious—anyone finding the rune stone would investigate—it is also too … simple. Or inelegant. The Templars loved allegory, and they loved codes and puzzles."

Cam continued. "So we thought the winter solstice alignment might be a clue. Again, using the duality concept, what might they have paired with the winter solstice?"

Willum shrugged. "Maybe the summer solstice?"

Cam nodded. "Exactly. In fact, we see this today with the modern Freemasons. Their two most important dates of the year are the winter and summer solstices. Light and dark, hot and cold, life and death."

"So we need to find a cave that has a summer solstice alignment?" Willum asked. "That might narrow it down some, but we're still talking scores of mountain peaks."

Amanda said, "I think we can narrow it down further." She asked him to translate the runic inscription again. "That's what I remembered. So here are the clues from that. First, it says the secret lies near Hurech's body. Second, it says Hurech's body turns to dust and goes to Eden's temple. Let's take the second one first."

"Hurech's body turning to dust," Cam repeated. He looked at Willum. "Did you tell me some of the bones were missing?"

"Yes."

"And how deep was the body buried?"

"Actually, not very deep at all. I was surprised." Why hadn't he figured out the clues on the rune stone himself?

Cam continued. "And you said there was no skull, right?" Willum nodded. "So how about this for a theory? Hurech's buddy buries him in a very shallow grave. But he keeps the skull and thigh bones to bring back to Europe—that's what the Templars did when knights died in battle, they brought home the skull and crossbones. The bones that are left in the cave turn to dust, right?"

Willum nodded again. "That makes sense. I don't remember seeing any thigh bones either."

"Wait," Amanda interjected. "Which way does the wind blow in those mountains?"

As a helicopter pilot, Willum needed to know this type of stuff. "Almost always west to east. Other areas of Arizona are different, but in those hills it's pretty consistent."

Amanda's face flushed. "Okay then. Let's put Cam's theory on hold for a second and focus on the rest of the clue, about the body going to Eden's temple. We know Eden is always associated with the east. So if the body turned to dust, and the wind blew from the west, the dust would blow to the east, right?"

"To some kind of temple," Cam said.

"The Templars often used caves as religious sites," Amanda said. "They worshiped Mother Earth; the cave symbolized being in her womb. Royston Cave in England is just one example."

Willum wanted to make sure he was keeping up. "So you think the inscription tells us that Hurech's bones turned to dust and were blown in an easterly direction, to some cave."

Amanda nodded. "And let's not forget the first clue: The secret is buried near Hurech's body."

"Which has now been blown to the east," Cam said.

"So that's where the chest is buried," Willum said.

Amanda stood and looked down at Willum's maps. "Willum, can you show me where the rune stone cave is?" Willum pointed it out. "So to the east of it is the saddle we climbed up, and to the east of that is another peak?"

"Yes."

"And are there any caves on that peak that face, say, in a northerly direction?"

"I'm sure there are; that whole ridgeline is pockmarked with fissures. But why specify northerly caves?"

"Because if I'm right, if the cave is marked by some kind of summer solstice illumination, then we are looking for a cave where a sunbeam penetrates the opening only when the sun is at its most northerly point on the horizon." She scratched out a drawing. "I'm guessing at this latitude the sun gets pretty far north at the summer solstice." She turned the drawing to the men. "So we're looking for a cave that opens to the north, but is actually angled a bit to the west."

Cam nodded. "And, ideally, it'd be sort of a straight shot from one cave to the other. That's how the dust would blow over."

Willum looked down at his maps. "Well, that sure narrows it down." He pointed with a pencil tip. "If you're right, there's only a few caves that fit the bill." He tried to check his excitement. "You guys up for another climb?"

"Today?" Cam asked.

"Why not?"

Ellis finished connecting the wires and wiped the greasy residue off his hands with a paper towel before answering his cell phone. "Hello Georgia."

"Cam and Amanda are at the compound."

Ellis knew that, but Georgia didn't know he knew, so he acted surprised. "Excellent. So your plan is working?"

"Yes." She paused. "You know, Thorne recognized you yesterday when you were tailing them."

Good. Thorne was bragging about matching wits with the pros. If this was going to work, Ellis needed Thorne to bring his A-game. "Really? That was sloppy of us."

"No harm done," she said.

"So what's the plan now?" he asked. Georgia wasn't in charge but Ellis didn't mind making her think she was.

"We'll give Cam a few days to poke around inside the compound. So sit tight for now."

Fat chance of that. Just like he needed Thorne on his A-game, he needed a better effort from Willum as well, needed him to stop focusing on his treasure chest and instead get back into his lab. At first Ellis had not agreed with Duck Boots' opinion that Willum was the best bet for figuring out the fuel cell technology. Surely the government had hundreds of scientists in dozens of labs for this kind of stuff. And no doubt they were hard at work as well. But what could be more American than some guy in his garage or basement or armed compound tinkering with his chemistry set and inventing the next great thing? Ben Franklin, Eli Whitney, Thomas Edison, the Wright Brothers, Steve Jobs—but for their lack of paranoia they were no different than Smoot. All Smoot needed was a gentle kick in the ass.

In the end they decided to survey the site by helicopter first, and wait until the next morning to do the climb. Willum's canary-yellow Robinson R22 was only a two-seater, so Amanda returned to Tucson while Cam joined Willum for the copter ride south.

"I just follow the highway down past Tucson," Willum said.

"How'd you learn to fly?" Cam asked, shouting above the sound of the rotor.

"I was trained in the Marines. Then I kept my license. When I bought the compound I also bought this copter."

"Can I ask how much they go for?"

"Sure. A quarter-million, new. I got a used one for about half that." He shrugged. "But if I'm right and society collapses, money won't really mean anything. And if I'm wrong, well, I still have the copter."

"How will you fly it if you can't find fuel?"

"I salvaged an underground tank from a gas station going out of business and buried it in the back of the compound. So I have about three thousand gallons of aviation gasoline in reserve. The copter tank holds thirty gallons, which gives me a couple hours flight time. So I would be able to take about a hundred trips like this before I ran out of fuel. If I'm wrong about the collapse, I still have the gas to use in my SUV."

"Will it work in a car?"

"With a few modifications. Lots of guys with muscle cars use it even though it's more expensive."

Cam nodded. He had expected Willum to be more of a nut-job. But really all he was doing was taking the Boy Scout motto of 'Be Prepared' to the next level. And who was to say he was wrong?

"There's the range," Willum pointed. "We'll only have about forty-five minutes to look around; we're carrying a full load with both of us, and we'll need gas to get back to the compound."

"If Amanda is right about the clues, my guess is we won't need that long. We'll either see a cave that fits or we won't."

"I'll hover over the rune stone cave first, okay?"

Cam nodded again. That way they could get their bearings. If Amanda was right, the cave would be east of that with its opening oriented to the north-northwest. A few minutes later Willum slowed and pointed down to the cliff-face. Cam recognized the cave. He looked east—as shown on the maps, a second peak rose up above the saddle.

Willum climbed and circled to the shaded, northern side of the eastern peak. Peering through binoculars Cam examined the crevices, looking for an appropriate hiding spot. "The prospectors were crawling all over these hills. So I'm guessing it's not that accessible, otherwise somebody besides Boone's great-great-grandfather would have stumbled upon it," Willum said.

"Boone was your cellmate?"

"Yes. Boonie's uncle."

Cam pointed. "Can you get a little closer? That cave is pretty high up the cliff-face so it would be hard to get to."

"And it's oriented to the northwest."

Willum flew closer. "Look down below," he said. "See all those boulders? Part of the cliff fell away. Centuries ago, maybe there was a better path to get up to that cave."

Cam nodded. They had surveyed the entire northern face. "That's definitely our best possibility." He scanned the rock face with the binoculars. "But it's going to be a bear of a climb to get there."

Cam and Willum flew back to the compound. They discussed the research Cam and Amanda had been doing on the Ark of the Covenant; intermittently Cam texted with Amanda, describing the cave they had found and making plans for tomorrow. Tonight Cam would sleep in the compound; in the morning Amanda would drive back to the gas station where the three of them would gather again for another hike. In the meantime, no doubt, Georgia would debrief Amanda.

"After we land, we'll need to go out and get some rock-climbing gear," Willum said. "We're going to need to lower someone down that cliff-face; I don't think there's any other way to get to the cave."

Cam nodded. "I'm sure Amanda will be up for it." He didn't love the idea but he knew there was no way he could talk her out of it. She was the lightest, and she had done some rock-climbing, so she was the obvious choice. Given her gymnastics background she would have little trouble rappelling down the cliff-face.

Willum swallowed. "Um, I know you were a little spooked by Boonie. But we could use another strong back up there. He knows those mountains, and he really is harmless. And it was his grandfather who told me about it in the first place."

"Okay."

Neither asked the obvious question: If they found the chest, how would they get it down even with Boonie's help?

A bright-smiled Clarisse jogged out to meet them at the landing pad. Willum introduced her to Cam. "She runs this place," he said.

"I thought we could do a group dinner tonight to break the fast," she said. "Give Cameron a chance to meet everyone."

"Sounds good," Willum said. "Will you make your chili?"

"Nope. New England clam chowder, in honor of Cameron. Already on the stove."

Willum described the cave they had found. "We need to go out and get supplies for tomorrow. After that I want to show Cam our special desert sand."

Willum thought he detected a look of displeasure from Clarisse. "Oh. All right. I thought we would be concentrating on finding the chest."

"You know, I'm beginning to wonder if the two things might be connected."

"How so?" she asked.

"Well, Cam was telling me more about the Ark of the Covenant. Did you know it may have been a power source, some kind of capacitor? That got me thinking: Maybe the desert sand in the Middle East is similar to the sand here. And if so, maybe they somehow used the sand to energize the Ark?"

"Are you talking about that fuel cell stuff again?"

"Exactly. The Ark might have been an ancient fuel cell, energized by the desert sand."

She shrugged. "Well, okay. I suppose it's no more whacky than some of the other theories we've had around here."

"Hey," Cam said. "Can I see this desert sand before we go into town to shop? That way we can talk about it in the car."

"Sure." Willum brought him to the compound's garden area and, using the magnifying glass, vaporized a clod of dirt. Then he brought him into the lab and demonstrated how the white powder seemed to transform itself and levitate. Finally, as they walked to the Land Cruiser he summarized the research he had done involving the feeding of this substance to the Pharaohs. "Some English archeologist found a bunch of this powder at a place called *Serabit el Khadim* in the Sinai desert. It was in a temple that looked more like a workshop. Almost like they were producing the stuff there."

"A temple in the Sinai? I wonder…" Cam stopped walking, pulled out his smart phone and punched at the keys.

"What?"

Cam held up his hand. "Give me a second." He continued punching at the key. "Okay. You said the name of the place was *Serabit el Khadim?*"

"Yes, why?"

He grinned. "Okay, so you know the story of Moses, how he killed a foreman who was beating a Jewish slave?"

"I think so. Wasn't he exiled for it?"

"Exactly. For forty years. Later he came back and led the Jews out of Egypt—that's the story of the Exodus we all know. While in exile he lived in a place called Midian, in present day Saudi Arabia. But he also lived near Mount Sinai for a while—that's where he witnessed the burning bush miracle. Many scholars believe Moses was training to be a priest while in exile—his brother Aaron was a high priest. In fact, Freud believed Moses was actually a pharaoh, so he definitely would have had religious training."

"Wait. Freud, as in Sigmund Freud?"

Cam nodded.

"But how could Moses be a pharaoh?" Willum tried to picture Charlton Heston in a braided beard and kilt.

"Look, pharaoh or not, what's important is that Moses trained to be a priest. And when you mentioned a temple in the Sinai, I played a hunch." Cam lifted his phone so Willum could see it. "According to this web site, Moses received his training at a place called *Serabit el Khadim*."

Willum felt his eyebrows lift. This could not be a coincidence. "Are you sure?" All those names tended to sound the same.

Cam held the screen closer. Sure enough—same place.

"So Moses lived in the temple where they made the white powder of gold," Willum breathed.

"Not just a temple—inside the temple was a workshop. Moses was an initiate, learning the ancient secrets of alchemy. That's what priests did back then." Cam paused and waited for Willum to look him in the eye. "If Moses lived at *Serabit el Khadim*, he would have learned how to make white powder of gold. The stuff you call *mfkzt*."

Clarisse stood over the massive pot, stirring and adding spices to the mix of clams, cream, potatoes and onions—she was making clam chowder for sixty. The irony was that her ex-husband used to complain she didn't cook enough.

Boonie pushed open the curtain separating the kitchen from the eating area. "Would you die to protect Willum?" he asked. He never really made eye contact with her from under the brim of his baseball cap, but this time his glance made it as high as her chin.

Interesting question. "Die, as in take a bullet for him?"

"Yes." He swallowed, his Adam's apple dipping and rising. "Like a body guard."

"I don't know."

"I definitely would. We all should."

Boonie had a limited I.Q.—when Clarisse was a kid they would have called him a retard—plus Willum treated him like a son, so his feelings may not be representative of the group. But he was beginning to adopt just the selfless attitude she was hoping all the compound residents would adopt.

Humming to herself, she stirred the pot.

Willum remembered everyone gathering around the picnic tables for dinner, and he remembered getting a large bowl of clam chowder and a hunk of bread. He also remembered thinking he shouldn't have more than one beer since he hadn't eaten in two days. But apparently even the one beer was a lot because here he was, four hours later, and he still had the perfect buzz.

And buzz was the right word. A distant, constant, vibrating hum—as if someone turned on an electric razor and followed Willum around with it in his back pocket. But it didn't bother him. It sounded more as if the universe was singing background harmony to whatever happy thoughts swam inside Willum's head.

He stood on the bench of the picnic table. "Can I have everyone's attention," he said. He was pretty sure he wasn't slurring; in fact, his voice resonated like a Shakespearean actor. "I want to publicly thank Clarisse not only for this dinner but for all the things she does to make this compound function." He looked around, somehow able to make eye contact with scores of people at the same time.

Someone in the back began a refrain of 'For She's a Jolly Good Fellow.' Willum had never realized how many strong singing voices resided in the compound; maybe they should form a chorus; maybe even he would join.

Clarisse stood on a bench of her own. "Thank you for that spirited rendition." She smiled. "But we all know that we should be thanking Willum, not me. It is he who provides for us, he who has given us hope for the future."

The night air echoed with applause and shouts of support; amid the cacophony, Willum heard each voice individually. But he didn't want this, didn't want the attention. These people were his brothers and sisters, not his minions. Clarisse continued nonetheless.

"We all know the sheriff has been making regular visits. And we expect this will continue, and continue in a peaceful manner. But we also know how these things can get out of hand." She raised her voice. "We need to be prepared. We need to be ready to fight. We need to trust Willum to lead us through the difficult days ahead." She paused and scanned the silent crowd; all eyes had shifted from her to Willum. He suddenly felt uncomfortably hot, as if he had stepped too close to the bonfire. "We need to trust Willum to lead us out of this desert and eventually to a Promised Land of our own."

Cam slipped away after Clarisse's speech and walked to the parking lot. He felt wired, as if he had had too much caffeine. And there was something about the nighttime desert air that sharpened his vision—it was like the first time he had watched a football game in high definition. He saw every individual star, noticed the freckles on every face. And not just his sight—he heard every insect, smelled every marshmallow toasting, felt every grain of sand beneath his foot.

He phoned Amanda.

"It's weird here," he said after exchanging pleasantries.

"How so?"

"It's almost cult-like. They almost worship Willum. And this Clarisse woman just gave a speech about Willum leading them to the Promised Land."

"I didn't notice that earlier today."

"I didn't either. But it's different tonight."

"I wonder if the sheriff visits are getting to them. It must be tough knowing that at any point police might storm your home."

"Georgia doesn't think that's going to happen."

"That's her opinion, but nobody knows for sure—least of all the residents. It's their paranoia that brought them to the compound in the first place. It's only natural in this situation to rally together."

Cam had never been in battle, but he had heard accounts of men blindly following their leaders to a certain death. Was that we he was witnessing tonight, a group of individuals being transformed by fervor and danger and shared purpose into a single cohesive entity? "Like I said, it's almost like a cult."

"Well, please resist the urge to shave your head, put on an orange robe and chant *Hare Krishna.*"

Normally Cam appreciated Amanda's flippancy. But tonight he saw clearly into a future that was anything but laughable. If push came to shove, these people would follow Willum to their death.

Willum had put in a couple of long days without much nourishment; he should have been exhausted. But midnight had turned to one o'clock and then to two and nobody seemed to want to call it a night. Someone had broken out a harmonica and a couple of dozen adults and a few of the older kids sat by the bonfire singing and counting the stars.

Finally at two-thirty Willum told everyone to go to bed. But when his head hit the pillow ten minutes later the buzzing in his ear and the rapid-firing of the synapses in his brain made sleep impossible. He threw on a t-shirt, sweatpants and sneakers and went to his lab.

At some point over the past few days, without even thinking about it consciously, his mind had been working on how to build a fuel cell using the desert sand as a power source. Working almost mechanically, like a puppet being controlled by unseen strings, Willum opened a closet and pulled out a half-dozen prototypes of various fuel cells he had designed or modified over the years. Connecting wires, cables, tubes and magnets to metal plates and gaskets, he tinkered and experimented, the hidden hand of some Muse inspiring and guiding him. Hours passed, Willum barely aware of the passage of time, until a banging on the locked door of the underground lab startled him back to reality.

"What is it?"

"It's Clarisse. Cam's ready. You guys are supposed to climb today."

He looked at his watch and shook his head. Seven o'clock already. But that wasn't nearly as startling as the prototype of a next generation fuel cell staring back at him from his work bench.

CHAPTER 6

Amanda nestled against Cam in the back of the Land Cruiser while the Expos hat guy sat up front with Willum. She and Cam had spent only a few nights apart in their year-and-a-half together. She was glad to hear he slept poorly.

"I had strange dreams," he whispered. "I was wandering through the desert surrounded by robed, chanting automatons."

"What were they chanting?"

"It wasn't even words. More like a melodic hum."

"Well, I missed you."

"You guys want some bread?" Willum asked. "Clarisse made it."

"I ate already, thanks," Cam said. Amanda had brought him a fruit salad and multi-grain bagel—as a diabetic he needed to be especially careful about what he ate for breakfast.

"Me, too," said Amanda. She noticed the rash on Willum's face had returned.

Willum tore at the crust and handed Boonie a chunk. "It's really good," Willum said, crumbs dropping into his lap.

Boonie took the offering with a dirty hand and picked at the crust, his cap pulled low on his forehead. He reminded Amanda of an abused dog, skittish and submissive and mangy. Hard to believe they had felt threatened by him.

They had at least twenty minutes, so Amanda took the opportunity to update Cam on some research. "You remember that one of the theories is the Ark ended up in Warwickshire?"

"Yeah. You Brits are pretty sticky-fingered."

She rolled her eyes. "Well, you're going to like this. The theory is that it was brought there by a Templar commander by the name of Ralph de Sudeley."

"*Our* Ralph de Sudeley?"

"The same." One of the documents Astarte's uncle had obtained was an ancient Templar travel log recounting a journey made by the Templars to the Catskill Mountains in New York in the late 1100s. Cam and Amanda had confirmed this journey when, following clues left in the travel log, they found ancient artifacts hidden in those mountains. One of the five Templars on the expedition was named Ralph de Sudeley.

"So you think he found the Ark of the Covenant in the Catskills and brought it back to England?"

"Actually, no, though I suppose it is possible. I think he came here after he already found it. In the 1180s he captained a Templar fortress called Petra, in the hills of southern Jordan."

"Let me guess. Near where the prophet Jeremiah hid the Ark before the Babylonian invasion."

"Spot on. He purportedly returned to England with many religious treasures—the exact term in the tax rolls, written in French, was *objets sacrés* or sacred artifacts. And he returned a very rich man."

Cam nodded slowly as he peered out the window. "Okay, I'm with you so far. But you think the fact our boy Ralph also came to the Catskills is just a coincidence?"

She looked at him. She didn't need to say what they were both thinking. They would file away the information for now and hope it fit into the puzzle once more pieces had been put into place.

Amanda leaned forward in her seat. "So what's the plan?" Amanda asked Willum.

He spoke with his mouth full. "We'll climb up the same way we did the other day. Except this time we'll cross the saddle and go up the other ridge. The only way to get to the opening is from above."

"So I get to play Spiderwoman," Amanda said. Cam looked at her, obviously wondering if she was nervous or scared. She squeezed his hand. "I'll be fine. I've done a bit of rock-climbing." And who could pass on the chance to be the person who found the Templar treasure?

After another bumpy ride they parked the Land Cruiser and began trudging up Mustang Mountain. "Same temperature, same sunshine, same topography, pretty much same day," Cam said

"Welcome to the desert," Willum responded. "It's either this or a massive thunderstorm." He stopped and scanned the rocky crags rising above them. "But it sure is beautiful."

Boonie led the way, ears forced outward by his cap, often stopping to offer Willum a hand or knock a prickly plant aside for him. Amanda couldn't get a feel for him, mostly because he rarely spoke. But it was obvious from his behavior that he doted on Willum. Again, like a loyal dog. About halfway up they angled to the left and Cam pointed to an opening in the cliff wall. "That's our cave."

"Yup," Willum said. He stopped and took a series of photos. "We'll need to find the opening from above. These pictures will give us some landmarks."

Amanda studied the cave. "Even with a path, it'd be tough to drag a heavy object like a golden chest up there," she said.

"Agreed," Cam said. "And it must have been heavy, based on those thick poles. So I think it's likely Hurech had more than one friend with him. For expeditions like this, there'd usually be five or six Knights."

"And you think one of them made it back to Kinver and built the rock houses?" Willum asked.

"Seems possible. There's a theory called independent invention which states that identical inventions can bubble up independently of one another in different parts of the world. Sort of like the pyramids in Egypt and also in Central America—the theory holds it's just a coincidence that both cultures came up with the same idea to worship their gods. But I don't buy it. I think it is more likely that the ideas traveled across the oceans."

"Say, Cam, how do you feel about coincidence?" Amanda teased.

He mimicked her accent. "I think it's bloody poppycock."

She poked him with her walking stick. "Jerk."

Cam continued. "I suppose it's possible the idea of carving houses into the sandstone occurred independently. But it's also possible one of Hurech's mates went home to Staffordshire and brought the idea with him." The cliff houses in America predated Hurech, so the reverse was not possible. "The earliest recorded date for the Kinver houses is the early 1600s, but they could be much older."

They reached the saddle. Willum pointed to his left. "We have to climb that ridge line. Then descend from the top."

"And it's due east of the other cave?" Amanda asked.

"Almost exactly."

The morning sun glowed off to her left, in the southeast sky. In the summer, with the sun rising in the northeast, the angle would work. She poked Cam in the ass again with her stick. "Well, get moving then. History awaits."

Ellis found Astarte in a hotel conference room with Georgia. He had a lot to do today, but this was as important as anything. "Hello, Astarte," he said.

She looked up from the book she was reading. "Hello, Flying Fox," she smiled.

He handed her a couple of sheets of paper stapled together. "I though you might be interested in this. I found it on the internet." He didn't mention he had modified it before printing it out. "It talks about the Tucson artifacts—some researchers think the people in the Book of Mormon made them."

She reached out. "Really?"

Georgia turned away to focus on her phone call.

"Yeah," he said. "Both the Hebrew and the Latin writing could be first century AD. And I think the Book of Mormon talks about Jesus and his disciples coming to America during that time period, right? So maybe they made them?" The explanation wasn't perfect, but Ellis sensed the girl was looking for validation for her uncle's theory. Plus, after all, she was nine.

Astarte nodded. "Yes."

"And here's another thing. The Ark of the Covenant disappeared around 600 BC. When did the prophet Lehi come to America?"

She put her finger on her chin. "586 BC."

He tilted his head. "So maybe Lehi brought the Ark here. Maybe that's what that chest is."

Her eyes widened. "I don't think Cameron and Amanda thought of that."

He turned to go, then stopped. "You know, I'm not a Mormon. But it seems to me the Book of Mormon explains an awful lot of these unanswered questions." He paused and held Astarte's eyes. "I wonder if Cameron and Amanda aren't making this more complicated than it needs to be."

Ellis took a few more strides toward the door. "Sometimes it's hard to be the princess," he said. "Sometimes you have to make hard decisions."

Cam checked the harness, the carabiners, the knots on the climbing rope, the strap on Amanda's helmet. And then he checked them again. "Does your walkie-talkie work?"

"I'm fine," Amanda said, kissing him. "Willum bought top of the line equipment." She tapped the tip of his nose with her finger. "Just don't drop me."

Willum and Boonie had secured the climbing rope to a boulder using three spring-loaded camming devices, any one of which would have been sufficient to support Amanda's weight. The rope ran through a series of pulleys and attached to a carabiner on Cam's harness—through this system Amanda could lower herself as Cam let out slack but, in the event she fell, Cam would be able to catch her and arrest the fall. The use of pulleys reduced her weight so that Cam would not be pulled over with her. For redundancy, Cam himself was tied off and anchored to a second boulder.

"On belay," Amanda called.

"Belay on," Cam responded and let out a few feet of rope. They had done some indoor rock-climbing together so he knew a bit about the terminology. And she had done a bit of outdoor climbing. But never off a fifty foot rock cliff.

"Climbing."

"Climb on," he replied, peering over the side as she pushed off.

Using this system, in fits and starts Amanda backed down the cliff face, using her feet to bounce out away from the rock while she descended. "I'm here," she said. "Off belay." This gave her slack to walk about the cave.

"Okay, but I don't want to give you too much slack in case the ledge you are on gives way," he yelled.

She didn't respond.

"Amanda?" Nothing. He tugged on the rope but felt no tension. "Amanda!"

Using high-powered binoculars, Ellis watched as the men lowered Amanda down the cliff face. He cursed. Willum was wasting too much time looking for the chest and not enough time working on the fuel cell. And the fact they were sending her down there indicated they believed they had found the right cave.

He leaned back against a tree. He couldn't very well ask Georgia to order Thorne not to help Willum with his treasure hunt—that was what Willum had invited them to the compound for in the first place. And it was the thing that made Willum trust them. Ellis needed to add an external variable to the equation, something that would push Willum out of the mountains and back to his compound. The problem with adding external variables is that they often resulted in collateral damage. He shrugged. Such was the cost of doing business.

Amanda unclipped her carabiner as she examined the markings near the mouth of the cave. A few runic characters, and below them the distinctive splayed cross of the Knights Templar. "Bloody amazing," she breathed.

She leaned out and yelled up. "I found some markings. A Templar cross. This is the cave."

She didn't wait for a response. Flicking on her flashlight, she scanned the rest of the cave. It was smaller than the other, perhaps the size of a butler's pantry. But it dog-legged like a golf fairway to the left. Using her free hand to push aside the cobwebs she crept deeper in.

She jumped as her walkie-talkie buzzed. She put it on speaker and held it in her hand with the flashlight. "I'm walking toward the back of the cave," she reported. "There's a cavity or compartment in the back. It looks like an MRI tube." She froze and gasped. "There's some kind of crate or chest in there."

"Wait. Don't go near it," Cam said. "Remember the prospector got zapped by it."

She aimed her light deeper. "It's about the size of a blanket chest."

"What color?"

"I can't tell. It's covered in gray dust."

"I can't believe I'm asking this, but are there angels or anything on the top?"

"There's something decorative there, but I can't tell if it's angels or gargoyles or a partridge in a pear tree."

"Can you take a picture with your phone and text it to us?"

"Too dark." But she snapped a picture with her digital camera. The flash illuminated more of the cave, and she noticed a couple of poles standing at the dog leg. "I can touch the poles, right?"

Cam paused. "As long as you don't get too close to the chest."

She bent over and picked up a pole. Dusty but smooth, and heavier than it should have been even given its hefty diameter. She splashed some water on it and rubbed it with her shirt. "Gold," she breathed.

"What?" Cam said.

She held the light closer to the pole. "The pole is gold. Or at least gold-colored." The light played on the cave wall as her hand shook. She splashed some water on her face and took a deep breath. The poles used to carry the Ark of the Covenant were gold-plated.

"How close are you to the chest?"

"Perhaps ten feet."

"Hold on." He spoke to Willum in the background. "One of the things Willum put in your pack was a Geiger counter."

She slipped off her pack and pulled out an orange device that looked like a channel clicker. She flicked the power switch on and held it out toward the chest. It made a clicking noise for a few seconds, then displayed a number on the readout. "It's giving a reading of 7.4."

Cam spoke to Willum before returning to her. "Okay, that's counts per second. Normal levels are one or two. Dangerous levels are anything above ten. So you're not in danger, but whatever is in that cave is radioactive."

Amanda backed away. When she turned the dog leg, the readings fell to three. She still had the pole in her hand. "So now what?"

"Good question." He again consulted with Willum. "Are you sure you have a picture?"

She checked her camera. "It's as good a shot as I can get without cleaning it off." She also snapped a shot of the Templar cross and runic characters.

"Okay. Then let's get you out of there."

"Wait. I want to check the illumination." Again using the astronomy app on her phone, she projected the sun's path across the horizon on June 21. Just as the sun crested over the horizon to the east, its rays would squeeze past the front edge of the near wall of the cave and brighten a few inches of the far wall—in fact, she could see where a section of the near wall had been chiseled away to allow the sun to penetrate. Just enough sun to illuminate the carvings, and only on the summer solstice. Amanda smiled—these guys were good.

Cam grabbed Amanda's wrist and pulled her over the lip of the cliff. "You brought me a gift," he smiled, his jaw unclenching now that she was safe.

"Actually, I believe it belongs to Willum." She handed Willum the pole.

He, in turn, handed it to Boonie. "It's actually as much Boonie's as mine."

Boonie spoke. "It's heavy."

"I think it's gold-plated," she said. They all stared at it. She spoke the words on everyone's mind. "Would the Templars use gold-plated poles for any chest other than the Ark of the Covenant?"

A few seconds passed. "Wait, what's that clicking noise?" Amanda asked. She removed her pack and pulled out the Geiger counter. "I never turned this off. And now it's getting a radiation reading again." She moved it around herself in a circle—it increased in frequency when she held it toward Willum. "I'm getting a pretty high reading, Willum. Have you been around any radiation?"

His eyes widened. "So that's it. I've been losing hair and getting these rashes on my face, but I didn't know why. It must be from the experiments I've been doing in the lab."

"The white powder of gold stuff?" Cam asked.

"Yes. I was in the lab all night working with it."

"That's odd," Amanda said. She explained how their research showed that the Ark of the Covenant may itself have been radioactive. "It seems like quite a coincidence that both the powder and our chest also display radioactive qualities." She smiled. "And Cameron says we are not allowed to believe in coincidences."

Willum nodded. "Well, one of my theories is that the Ark might have been an ancient fuel cell, energized by the desert sand. If somehow this process produced radiation, it makes sense radiation would emanate from both the Ark and the powder that is the byproduct of the reaction."

Cam rubbed his face with both hands. "So wait. Are you guys saying that chest down there might be the *actual* Ark of the Covenant?"

Amanda exhaled. "Doubtful. But I suppose anything is possible."

"No, some things are *not* possible," Cam said. "The Ark of the Covenant is *not* in that cave below our feet."

Willum looked Cam in the eye. "You're the one who doesn't believe in coincidence, Cam. You explain it."

Amanda interjected. "Look, we'll know soon enough. We just need to examine and test the chest. But I agree with Willum—the golden poles and the radioactivity and the prospector getting zapped and the decorations on the top are all very ... curious."

"As am I," Cam said. "Whatever it is, we need to get down there again and check it out. Willum, I don't suppose you know where we can get some Hazmat suits?"

"That's some good work before lunch," Willum said as he led the way along the ridgeline. Cam nodded. It was good work. But they should have thought to bring some Hazmat suits with them.

He pulled a granola bar from his pack and devoured it in three bites, knowing he needed it to keep his blood sugar stable. They had traversed the ridgeline and were about five minutes into their descent when Cam turned to check on Amanda. As he did so, the loose dirt gave way beneath his lead foot and he began to skid off the trail. He looked up just in time to see a greenish-brown snake eyeing him from atop a low, flat rock. The snake flicked its tongue at Cam and rattled a warning as Cam clawed at the dirt to arrest his skid, but he came to rest with his foot covering the snake's rock, like a runner sliding into third base. *Shit.* A sharp sting punctured the back of his calf, followed immediately by the sound of another rattle, this one louder and angrier. "Damn it, I've been bit." The snake slithered away a few feet and hissed, warning Cam not to be so stupid again.

Amanda jumped to his side and nestled his head while Willum, cell phone in hand, approached the snake from below and snapped a shot as the snake slinked into the brush.

The original pain felt like a bee sting, but within seconds the pain magnified—it now felt like a hundred bees stuck sitting on his leg, stinging away furiously. Cam's heart pounded. "Shit that hurts."

Amanda's face blanched. "Was it poisonous?"

"It rattled," Cam said.

Willum scrambled over to Cam, knelt next to him and pulled up the pant leg of his jeans. "I got a picture of the snake. It was a Mojave Green. They're the most lethal of all the rattlers."

"Just my luck," Cam muttered. He felt the sweat break out on his forehead.

Willum probed the wound. "Looks like he got you pretty good." He opened his pack and removed a plastic case which contained a scalpel-like device, some rubbing alcohol, a tube of antiseptic and a couple of gauze pads. "This is going to hurt a bit," he said as he disinfected the scalpel. Cam bit on a leather glove as Willum made a clean cut into Cam's skin, connecting the two puncture wounds and going a bit beyond. "See that yellow stuff? That's the venom. I'm going to let that ooze out a bit. Some of it is already in your bloodstream, but the more we can get out the better."

Amanda held Cam's hand and dabbed his forehead as Willum worked. Cam alternately tried to focus on the mountains in the distance and the way the sunlight danced inside Amanda's emerald eyes, but mostly he chewed on the glove and fought back the tears. After a few minutes, Willum said, "I think we got out as much as we can." He squirted some antiseptic onto a gauze pad, pressed the pad against the wound and taped it securely in place. "We need to get you to a hospital. Soon." He removed his bandana and tied a tourniquet around Cam's leg just below the knee. "I don't want to totally restrict the blood flow, just slow it down. You need to tell me if your toes start to tingle."

Willum handed Boonie his pack. "Cam, I'm gonna carry you down."

"I can walk, I think," Cam said.

"No. No exertion. The harder your heart beats, the more quickly the venom spreads through your body. We've got a forty-five minute climb down, best case. And then it's a thirty mile drive to the hospital in Sierra Vista."

Amanda's eyes widened. "How long do we have?"

"With a Mojave Green bite, anything more than two hours is dicey."

"Then we should be fine," Amanda said.

He shook his head. "When we get there, they still need to prepare the antivenom." He handed Boonie the keys to the Land Cruiser. "Get to the bottom as quick as you can. Then bring the car as far up the trail as it'll go. If you have any cell coverage, call the hospital and tell them we're on our way. Make sure you tell them it's a Mojave Green."

Willum turned to Amanda. "Give me your harness." He loosened the straps and stepped into it. Quickly he looped a rope through the harness and handed the end to Amanda. "I want to move down hill as fast as I can without worrying about falling forward. If you walk behind me and keep some tension on this rope, that'll help." A memory flashed in Cam's mind from a few weeks earlier, Astarte angling down the slope as Cam snowplowed behind, leash in hand, keeping the girl's speed in check on her first day skiing. He'd like to be around to watch her grow into an expert.

Amanda slipped on her gloves. Willum crouched and Cam climbed onto him, piggy-back style. As Willum staggered forward, Cam began to feel dizzy. He tried to speak, but his tongue felt heavy and thick. And his throat was beginning to constrict.

"Best thing you can do is to close your eyes and relax. Slow that heart rate down." Willum turned and smiled. "You're going to owe me a beer for this."

Willum staggered under Cam's weight, his thighs burning as he picked a path down the trail. Cam's breathing, only inches from his ear, had become more and more labored. And he had begun to moan from the pain. From what Willum knew, a Mojave Green bite was about as painful a thing as existed in nature. Like fire ants crawling into an open wound.

Amanda did a great job supplying tension on the line and they were making decent time. But decent time might not do it. He thought about stopping to check on the tourniquet, but at this point Cam losing his foot was the least of his concerns. In retrospect, maybe he should have tightened it fully and sacrificed the foot from the beginning.

He called back to Amanda. "How long has it been?"

"Thirty-one minutes," she replied. He was afraid to look at her. The one time he had turned around it nearly broke his heart. Not just because of how concerned she was, but because it had been a long time since anyone had loved Willum like that. Probably not since his mother passed away almost twenty years ago. Gregory loved him, but how strong could that bond be when the boy only saw his father once a month? He sighed. It sucked being lonely.

Fifteen minutes later Willum spotted the long-legged Boonie loping up the trail toward them. "I'll take him, boss," Boonie said.

Willum transferred Cam to Boonie, dropped to his knees and gulped some water. His back was drenched and his breathing labored. And his legs felt like overcooked spaghetti. He was getting too old for this.

Boonie had driven the Land Cruiser a couple hundred feet up the trail and covered the final descent, Cam on his back, in less than five minutes. Willum, after a quick rest, plopped into the driver's seat just as Boonie and Amanda settled Cam in the back. "Amanda, don't let him lie down—make sure the wound stays well below his heart. We want to keep as much of that venom down in his leg as possible."

Willum bounced the SUV down the trail, anxious to rush but also aware that a flat tire or broken axel would likely be a death sentence for Cameron. Finally they hit the dirt road and Willum raced over the rutted path, bouncing and careening toward the highway.

He yelled over his shoulder. "Amanda, call 911 and tell them our situation. We are going to be on Highway 82, heading east, about fifteen miles west of Highway 90. If they can give us a police escort, that would be great." An ambulance would be even better, but they were few and far between in this secluded area of the state.

They hit the highway a few minutes later and Willum flicked on the hazards and pushed the accelerator to the floor. A mile later, as they cruised at ninety MPH, a sheriff's car, lights on, appeared in his rearview mirror and overtook him. Willum accelerated to near one hundred as they crested a rise and headed down out of the mountains. Twenty minutes later they screeched to a halt at the hospital entrance, a medical team lifted Cam onto a gurney, and Willum exhaled.

He looked at his watch. Elapsed time since the bite: eighty-seven minutes. He had done his job. Now it was up to the pros.

Amanda couldn't get the vision of the yellow, honey-like venom oozing from Cam's wound out of her mind. They didn't have rattlesnakes in England and she didn't realize how dangerous the situation was until she saw the grave look on Willum's face. That was reinforced by the emergency room doctor, a heavy-set Hispanic woman in her sixties whose apparent competence and confidence only served to undermine the seriousness of the situation.

"Someone said you had a picture of the snake?" the doctor asked with a slight accent, dispensing with any niceties.

Amanda pushed through the swinging doors and found Willum seated in the reception area. "I need the picture of the snake."

He handed her the phone and she rushed it to the doctor. "Yes, a Mojave Green," the doctor said. Her face was covered but a pair of concerned brown eyes met Amanda's gaze. "It's good you called this in. Different snakes require different antivenoms. We made up a batch of Mojave Green when you called."

They hung Cam's leg off the side of the gurney and hooked him up to a respirator and an IV. The doctor explained to Amanda, "We want to keep him hydrated. And we'll administer the antivenom intravenously."

"Will ... will he be okay?"

The doctor squeezed her shoulder. "I've been doing this almost forty years. Only seen a handful of fatal snake bites. But more than half have been Mojave Greens. It all depends on how much venom the snake sent into him."

Fatal. She steadied herself against the gurney. "It was a pretty big snake."

"That's actually a good thing. The older snakes know how to give either a dry bite or to limit how much venom they inject. They don't want to waste it on something like Cam that they know they can't eat. The younger snakes haven't learned that yet."

Amanda kissed Cam lightly on the lips, he smiled bravely up at her and they wheeled him away. Involuntarily, she followed the gurney, her hand out, until a nurse gently guided her back to the waiting room.

A half hour seemed to pass, but Amanda had no idea where it went. In some ways it felt like three days, and in some ways three minutes. It was almost like she had checked out of her body, the situation too difficult to bear. Someone must have given her a cup of water because an empty one sat on the end table next to her, and she had a vague memory of some kind of pill, but it was equally possible that the cup had been there all morning.

The appearance of the doctor striding toward her brought her back to reality. Willum also appeared, from somewhere; perhaps he had been in the waiting room with her all along.

The doctor sat next to her and looked her straight in the eye. "He's doing well."

Amanda slumped, a sob caught in her throat.

The doctor continued. "Whoever did the first aid on him did a great job. Probably saved his life. That and calling ahead with the species and getting him here so quickly. The antivenom is working and his vital signs are returning to normal. And it helps that he's in good shape."

Amanda reached out and took Willum's beefy hand. "Thanks," she whispered. "He might not have survived without you."

Willum grinned, a few bread crumbs still in his beard from lunch. "That's why they call me a Survivalist."

Amanda couldn't help but smile back. She turned to the doctor. "What next?"

"Well, usually we like to keep snake bite patients overnight. A lot of it depends on how much antivenom he needs. And he's going to be in a lot of pain for a few days—his lower leg has swollen to almost twice its size." The doctor smiled, one of those kind, caring smiles that told Amanda she had picked the right profession. "And it's already turning some funky shades of purple."

Now that she knew Cam was going to be okay, Amanda phoned Georgia, updated her on the situation, and offered a shorthand version of the events to Astarte.

Willum brought her a sandwich and a Diet Coke—only then did she realize how grubby she was and excused herself to wash up in the restroom. It was now mid-afternoon. The doctor wandered into the waiting room just as Amanda finished her sandwich.

She smiled again. "You can go see him now if you want."

"How's he doing?"

"Remarkably well. His blood is coagulating nicely, which means he doesn't need any more antivenom. Your insurance company will be happy—the stuff costs a fortune."

Amanda found Cam's room, grinned at him from the door and wrapped his head in her arms. "You had me a wee bit frightened."

"Yeah. Me too. That stuff coursing through my veins made my whole body feel like it had been shot up with Novocain. All numb and tingly."

"The doctor says Willum may have saved your life."

"Nice of him, given that we're here to spy on him."

"Yes, well, I think we owe him one going forward."

"Agreed." He sat up. "Other than the throbbing in my leg, I'm actually feeling pretty good. When can I get out of here?"

"Doctor said she'd like to keep you overnight."

Cam frowned. "I really hate hospitals. What if you promise to take really good care of me?"

She smiled. "What if I don't want to promise that?"

Willum actually welcomed the down time, just sitting in the hospital waiting room, his thoughts on the cave. He silently pumped his fist. They had found the golden chest. And it may actually be the goddamn Ark of the Covenant. Old Boone had been right.

In fact, in the past day or so, everything seemed to be coming together. First the fuel cell prototype, then the chest. He felt more alive than he had ever felt, more energized and motivated and focused. It was like the old Willum had died and been replaced by a new and improved version. Willum 2.0.

He thought about Cam and Amanda. These were good people. Really good people. The kind of people he wanted Gregory to meet and emulate. The kind of people that once made America great and would someday make it great again.

He had been right to trust them.

Cam and Amanda chatted quietly in the hospital room, Amanda in a chair by Cam's bed. "I feel bad that Willum and Boonie are stuck here waiting for us," Cam said.

"I asked Willum if he wanted to leave, but he said he'd wait another hour. If you get discharged, he can drive us back to the compound so we can pick up our car."

"I really want to get out of here." He still had the IV in. "My leg is going to throb no matter where I am."

"One more look from the doctor."

Cam nodded. "The hardest part of this whole thing is the feeling of helplessness. There I am on the mountain, a rattler bites me, and my first reaction is to fight for my life. But it turns out fighting, or doing anything, will just spread the venom through my body faster. So the best I can do is turn into a ragdoll." He sighed. "Talk about turning the survival instinct on its head."

"I suppose it's like playing dead when a bear attacks you."

"Good analogy. But I don't like it."

She smiled. "Can we talk about the chest now, or do we have to keep talking about your leg?"

"Since I practically gave my life for the thing, talk away."

"So I've been bothered by the Tucson artifacts being made of lead. Why not silver or gold? That's what most religious artifacts are made from."

"Maybe all they had was lead."

"Nonsense. There's almost as much silver and gold in these mountains as there are snakes."

He nodded. "Good point. So maybe lead has some religious significance."

"None that I've ever heard of."

Cam smiled. "So you have a theory?"

"Of course." She shifted in her chair. "Whoever these people were, they were far from home. We know they were Jews who had adopted many Christian practices as well. My guess is that over the generations, here with the natives, they probably adopted some Native American rituals as well."

"Fair enough."

"And it seems likely that whoever was here and whatever they were doing, radiation was a byproduct of their activities."

"Also fair."

"So put aside Hurech and his Templar mates for now—let's just assume they came looking for their lost ancestors from France. So these French Christianized Jews are here, and they're doing something that is creating dangerous levels of radiation. Now whatever they are doing must be pretty bloody important or otherwise they would just stop. But they can't stop, despite the risks. As the decades pass, at some point they stumble upon a phenomenon: Lead vestments and lead aprons and lead gloves and lead masks protect them from burns and hair loss."

"And hemorrhoids," Cam smiled.

"Yes, that especially. They don't understand why, but they do begin to value and even worship lead for its protective qualities—"

"I see," Cam interjected. "And since it is such a wonderful metal, they begin to make their religious and ceremonial objects from it."

"Precisely. It is heavy and unwieldy, but apparently God favors it."

"And that's why the Tucson artifacts are made of lead." Cam nodded. "Nice theory. I like it."

Willum was surprised to see it, but somehow Cam talked his way out of the hospital. He and Amanda sat in the back, Cam's leg wrapped and elevated, while Boonie rode shotgun as the late afternoon sun glowed low in the western sky.

"Quite a day," Willum said.

"Can't wait to see what we find tomorrow," Cam said.

Willum eyed him in the rearview mirror. "You think you're climbing tomorrow?"

Cam nodded. "Hoping to. It's all swollen, but the wound is stitched up. Doctor said it's just a question of pain management and making sure it doesn't get infected."

Willum shrugged. Everybody had a different tolerance for pain. "Okay."

His cell rang. "Hi, Clarisse."

"The sheriff is here again."

Damn. "At five o'clock on a Friday?"

"Probably figures it's too late to run to court to stop him."

"Smart play. He alone?"

"No. Looks like same crowd as last week."

"We'll be there in twenty minutes."

The gate swung open as Willum maneuvered between the police cars parked outside the compound security gate. As Clarisse reported, there were a dozen people milling around, half in police uniform and half in business suits. Willum expected the sheriff might deny him entrance, which would have forced him to sneak in via one of the hidden tunnels buried in the rear of the complex.

"Cam and Amanda, you can go back to the domes if you want. I'm going to have to handle this," he said as he guided the Land Cruiser back along the fence away from the gate. He drove slowly, making sure the gate closed before braking.

He took one step out of the vehicle. Suddenly the world exploded. The ground rocked, knocking him back into his seat. *What the--?* Ears ringing, he staggered to his feet, steadied himself against the car door and lurched toward the fence—the explosion had come from that direction. Flames rose from a maroon sedan parked on the shoulder of the highway just on the other side of the fence. Nobody moved for a few seconds, then shouts of panic, barely audible through the ringing, cut through the desert air. "Maria is in that car," someone yelled.

A woman screamed. As Willum staggered closer to the fence one of the armed deputies ran over and pulled a body from the burning car. He eased her mangled body, bloodied and charred, to the pavement and began applying first aid. Willum heard whimpering. A metallic, sulfurous smell assaulted his nostrils. He knew that smell from his time in the Marines: human flesh burning.

Sheriff Vaca caught Willum's eye from the other side of the fence. His face was red and the muscles in his upper jaw pulsated. "That was a bomb," he growled. "And it was set by a coward."

Willum's chest thumped. Who could have done this? He raised his hands. "Sheriff, I don't know anything about this."

Vaca glared. "Bombs just don't go off for no reason. If you didn't set it off, one of your people did." He moved closer to the gate. "Willum Smoot, I am placing you under arrest."

Willum backed away. "Arrest? For what?"

"You own this property. At a minimum, explosives are being stored here. Illegally." He looked at the lifeless body of the woman. "And we may be talking about murder." He put his hand on his gun. "Now open the gate and come out."

Clarisse, Boonie and a few other compound residents had gathered behind Willum. "Don't, Willum. You didn't do this," Clarisse said. Willum looked up; the guard on the roof of the guard house had readied his semiautomatic weapon.

He whispered to Clarisse. "If I go with the sheriff, I'll make bail or whatever and be back in time for a late dinner."

She pulled him away from Vaca. "Don't be crazy. Once they have you, they'll never let you go," she said. "We need you here."

"I'm not going to ask again," the sheriff said. He glanced up, no doubt counting Willum's soldiers on the rooftops.

Willum took a deep breath. Clarisse was right. Even if he got out on bail, the feds would make sure the bail conditions mandated that he stay away from the compound. "I'm sorry, sheriff." He pushed his people back. "And I'm sorry for whoever it is that got hurt. But I'm not leaving this compound."

Cam and Amanda watched from the picnic table area as the compound residents sprung into action. They had obviously trained for this kind of emergency—an alarm sounded, and within five minutes every resident was armed, the entire perimeter patrolled, the sniper nests manned, and the children huddled safely in a dome. Some kind of alert must have been sent out to residents outside the compound, because over the next hour a steady stream of cars raced along a dirt road leading to the rear of the property, got out of their cars and jogged through a hidden tunnel passing under the security fence.   "Update?" Willum said quietly to Clarisse as they took a seat at the table next to Cam and Amanda.

"All positions manned. Perimeter secured," she said. "Most residents have returned, but it won't be long before the police block off that tunnel." Apparently the sheriff didn't know about the rear entrance; that, or he didn't feel like he had the manpower yet to block it.

"Agreed."

She continued. "The children are being watched, and I've got a team to help me cook—I think group meals are in order until this blows over."

"Sounds good. How about the woman?"

"Ambulance came. But I don't think she's going to make it."

He sighed and stared into the distance. "Any idea who set that bomb?" Not that it really mattered—both the sheriff and the feds would assume it was Willum or one of his people.

Clarisse shook her head.

"What about the sheriff?" he asked.

"Still out there, with reinforcements streaming in. They're starting to surround the perimeter."

"Can you say Ruby Ridge?" Willum seemed to raise himself up, probably figuring the residents were watching. Willum's calm demeanor surprised Cam; he seemed in full control of the situation. And entirely rational, unlike the trigger-happy militant Georgia made him out to be. Cam was beginning to wonder where his allegiances should rest—he much preferred the burly Survivalist to the psychopathic Ellis Kincaid. "And what are our provisions?" he asked.

She consulted a clipboard. "We are above 98 percent for food, water, munitions and first aid supplies. The only thing we are low on is fuel—61 percent."

"Why so low?"

"Someone's been taking a lot of helicopter trips." She smiled. "We were expecting a delivery next week to refill the tank."

He nodded. "If this lasts for a while, I might need to perfect that fuel cell sooner than I thought. Is everyone back yet?"

"Yes."

He sighed. "Hopefully they all said their goodbyes. I think we're going to be here for a while." He turned to Cam. "Sorry you guys got caught in the middle of this."

Cam and Amanda exchanged glances. The compound was in complete lock-down mode. With them inside.

Cam and Amanda wandered off to a sheltered area behind one of the domes, Cam limping but able to put some weight on his leg. He phoned Georgia.

"You're at the compound?" She asked, surprised.

"Just arrived. How's the woman?" he asked.

"She died. Never really had a chance. The bomb was hidden under a rock right next to her car."

"Any idea who set it off?"

"Everyone's assuming it was Smoot or one of his people. Who else could it be?"

"Well, it wasn't Smoot. He was as shocked as anyone."

"Or he's just a good actor."

"Nobody's that good an actor." Cam rubbed his face with his hand. "Was it on a timer?"

"No. It was activated remotely, probably with a cell phone. This kind of thing is pretty easy to do—just type 'bomb-making' into the internet. There were hundreds of bombs like this in Iraq. The forensics people are examining the wreckage to try to get some leads, but these explosives can be made by anyone who has access to a computer and a Home Depot."

"The woman in the car, who was she?"

"She worked for the ATF."

"ATF? What are they doing here?"

"Once these guys arm themselves, the ATF jumps in."

"Any chance she was targeted because of Ruby Ridge?" The ATF agents were the primary aggressors in that standoff, so much so that the FBI agents called in late in the game were amazed at how confrontational the ATF agents had been.

"Could be," Georgia said. "If you were to ask the Survivalists who the bad guys were, ATF would be on the top of the list."

"I thought I saw Ellis there before the bomb went off," Cam said. If someone had to die, too bad it wasn't him.

"You did. He's here with me now. We need to contain this thing before it gets ugly. There's a lot of testosterone boiling over right now if you know what I mean."

"Well, you're going to need a small army to take this compound." He looked at Amanda. She should be back at the hotel with Astarte where it was safe. "What do you want us to do?" Assuming they even had a choice.

"Good question. Can you sit tight for a bit? It sure would be nice to have eyes and ears on the inside."

Cam and Amanda had discussed this—they weren't convinced Smoot had done anything wrong and weren't comfortable betraying him, especially after his heroism on the mountain today. On the other hand they might be able to help defuse things. And it's not like they could just saunter out the front gate. "You still able to watch Astarte?"

"Sure thing. She's a trouper."

"Okay. We'll sit tight. Oh, by the way, we found the gold chest. I'm not even going to tell you what we think it might be."

An hour later Willum found Cam and Amanda at the picnic area eating sandwiches. "Cam couldn't wait for the group meal," Amanda explained.

Willum nodded. "It's getting dark, so I don't think anything is going to happen tonight," Willum said. "If they're going to attack the compound they'll need to get clearance from Washington. That'll take time."

"That's comforting," Amanda said.

Willum smiled wryly. "Can't say I'm happy to be right, but we've sort of been expecting this."

"So what next?" Cam asked.

"We just wait. Not very exciting, to be honest. The only thing we can really do is try to get public opinion on our side—I actually have a PR firm in Phoenix on retainer." He shifted his weight. "I was really looking forward to going back up that mountain tomorrow to get a better look at the chest. I can't leave, obviously, but nothing is stopping you guys from going as long as Cam feels up for it."

"Really?" Amanda said. "You think they'll just let us walk out of here?"

"Sure. They might not let you back in, assuming you would want to return, but getting out should be easy enough."

Cam turned to Amanda. Georgia wanted them to stay put, but there was no way he was going to kill time inside the compound with that mysterious golden chest sitting out there. "I can make it if we take it slow. We could carry Hazmat suits in our packs and both of us could rappel down to the cave. Willum left the camming devices attached to the rock—all we would need to do is tie off to them again."

"And then what? It's not like we could carry the chest back up the cliff-face."

"True. But don't you want to get a better look?"

Willum interjected. "Look, not to be morbid, but I might be dead in a few days." He smiled. "If I die not knowing what that chest is, I swear my ghost will haunt you from the grave."

Amanda slept fitfully, partly because it had been years since she slept in a room with dozens of other people, partly because she didn't want to brush against Cam's wound, and partly because at any moment she expected gunfire to erupt. How did people live in war zones, or even in places like Tel Aviv, where at any moment their nighttime rest might be shattered by bombs or missiles? Finally, at the first hint of daylight penetrating the dome, she nudged Cam awake.

"Already? They just stopped singing a couple of hours ago."

Many of the residents had stayed up late, singing around the campfire. Things had finally broken up after they crooned "Go Down Moses" and Willum told them it was time for sleep.

"Sorry, I want to get going. These people are starting to creep me out. You were right—this place feels like a cult."

Cam sat up. "Okay. Let's wash up, get some breakfast and hit the road."

"Can we skip the breakfast and just get something on the highway?"

"Sure." He rolled to his side.

"How's your leg?"

He pushed himself up, tried to put some weight on it, almost fell, regained his balance and smiled. "Good to go."

"No way, Cam. You can't even walk." She bent over to examine his calf. It had swelled to almost the size of his thigh, and it looked like some over-sugared kindergartner had used his leg as a coloring book—greens and purples and yellows swirled over the surface of his skin. "How are you going to climb a mountain?"

"Once I put a compression sleeve on, it will feel better. And let's be serious. We just found an ancient golden chest, which may actually be the Ark of the Covenant. And we're going to just leave it there because I have a sore leg?"

"You don't have a sore leg. You have a rattlesnake bite that almost killed you."

"Like I said, we'll just take it slow." He slid a compression sleeve over his calf.

She felt his forehead. "No fever, at least."

"Look, we can at least try. If I can't make it, we just turn back."

Twenty minutes later they walked, Cam limping, toward the front gate. Willum met them in front of his saucer, his eyes red and his hair disheveled. "Morning." He held out a pencil-sized white plastic stick with a red bulb on the end to Cam.

Cam smiled. "Thanks for the lollipop, but my mother told me not to take candy from strangers."

"This is not just any candy. It's an Actiq stick. Made with fentanyl. One hundred times more potent than morphine." He smiled. "I'm only giving you one, so don't get used to it."

"What, do I just suck it?"

"No. Rub it onto the inside of your cheek so it absorbs into your bloodstream." Willum sealed the lollipop in a plastic bag and handed it to Cam. "It works quick. I'm guessing your leg is going to be barking pretty loud at you today."

"No grape?"

"Sorry, only cherry."

Cam shrugged. "Okay, thanks."

Willum shook their hands. "Good luck."

Cam and Amanda approached the front gate and nodded to the guard. "You leaving?" he asked.

Cam nodded. "Can you open the gate?"

Amanda retrieved the SUV; Cam sat in the back seat and kept his leg elevated and iced—Willum was right, the area around the bite was already throbbing. The guard opened the gate while two other armed guards positioned themselves to block entry from the outside. Amanda drove slowly between them.

As the gate closed behind them, a sheriff's deputy confronted them. "Names, please."

She gave them. Presumably Georgia had arranged for their exit.

The deputy's eyes registered recognition. But he wasn't stupid—if he let them pass too easily, that might arouse suspicion. "Please come this way. I'm going to need to question you."

Ten minutes and a few standard questions later Cam and Amanda were back in their SUV driving south on Route 10. "I've been thinking," Amanda said. "Why can't we make a harness out of the climbing rope and lower the chest down instead of heaving it back up the cliff face?"

Cam spoke from the back. "Good idea. And at that point we'd be almost halfway down."

"But after that we might need help from Georgia's men to get it to the road," Amanda said. "Especially with your injury."

"Well, I don't want that Ellis guy anywhere near it. And even though I'm not as paranoid as Willum, I'm not sure I want the federal government involved. The Smithsonian's been rumored to conveniently lose artifacts like this."

"Fair point."

"Besides, it really should be Willum's call. He found it."

They stopped in Tucson to grab breakfast and buy hazmat suits at an industrial supply warehouse. "Canary yellow," Amanda said. "Just my color."

"It's going to be awful hot in these things," Cam said, feeling the thick rubberized material. "Especially with the hoods on." The suit covered the entire body, including feet and head; a window allowed the wearer to see out.

"Hot is better than radiated."

"Well, for three hundred bucks each we're going to wear them out dancing when we get home."

They continued south.

"What do you think is going to happen back at the compound?" Amanda asked.

"It's one of those tough situations where both sides are in a box. The authorities have to investigate the murder, obviously. But Willum knows that once they take him in for questioning they're not going to let him go even if he's innocent."

"So is there a middle ground?"

Cam shook his head. "I don't see one. Maybe if whoever planted the bomb comes forward and confesses. But if not, at some point something has to give—either Willum surrenders or the feds storm the compound."

Clarisse pulled open the curtain in the corner of the communal dome they had converted to a kitchen area. "I'll make the pancake batter," she said to the two women already at work preparing breakfast for the residents. "Can you hang these posters?" Boonie had stayed up all night printing out color posters of a smiling, rifle-toting Willum with the caption, "Thanks for all you do for us!" Willum might not approve, but Clarisse would explain to him that the residents had insisted on the gesture.

She found an industrial-sized serving bowl and six boxes of pancake mix. This would make group meal number four. Almost universally, the residents seemed more focused, more aware, and best of all more committed to the welfare and future of the compound. There seemed to be a growing sense of pack mentality—the residents viewed the world less selfishly and more communally. It was as if everyone felt a mothering instinct for all the other compound residents. Included in this was the instinct to protect and nurture the pack's alpha male, Willum.

Which, the more Clarisse thought about it, made sense. Somewhere back in human history the need to act as a pack had been imprinted on human DNA as a survival necessity. Individuals perished, losing the battle for scarce resources to larger and stronger packs or tribes.

The looming danger was causing the compound residents to tap back into their core wiring.

They took it slow, with Cam keeping most of his weight divided between his uninjured right leg and his walking stick, but eventually they made it to the ridgeline.

"How you doing?" Amanda asked. She was actually glad for the slow pace—her back and shoulders ached from yesterday's descent, and today she had taken most of the supplies in her pack to unburden Cam.

He nodded. "Hurts like hell, but I'll live. Thank God for Willum's lollipop. Other than my leg throbbing, I feel sort of giddy. I can see how this fentanyl stuff could get addictive."

They reached the ledge over the cave, tested the equipment and had a quick snack.

"Ready?" she asked.

"Ladies first."

Amanda descended the cliff face first. While they were still in the car Willum had texted that his expert translated the runic writing from the cave entrance to read, not surprisingly, 'Hurech's secret.' Yet Amanda still had trouble accepting that the Ark of the Covenant, the world's most precious lost artifact, might sit in the cave just beneath her. How did she end up here? Two weeks ago she had been shuttling Astarte to ski lessons and volunteering with her Girl Scout troop. Today she was Indiana Jones, but without the monkey and two-day stubble.

The Geiger counter began to chirp periodically as she descended toward the cave opening. Her feet hit the ground. "Off belay," she called. She checked the counter—a steady three clicks per second, same as last visit.

She tied herself off to the cave wall, prepared in turn to belay Cam down the cliff face. "I'm ready."

"On belay."

"Belay on."

Cam dropped the last few feet to the ground, landing on his good leg. Amanda kissed him on the lips. "Welcome home, honey. How was your day?"

He smiled. "Same old same old."

"Well, can you help me move an old chest?"

They pulled the hazmat suits from their packs and helped each other seal all the openings. "You ready?" Cam asked, his voice echoing.

"Yup. Trick or treat."

"Treat, I hope." He carried a flashlight in one hand and a brush in the other; Amanda held the Geiger counter and a light of her own, along with a chamois cloth and some water.

They walked to the dog leg and stopped so Amanda could take a reading. "Same as yesterday. Three."

Cam edged closer, Amanda on his hip. "Four, now five," she said.

"These suits are good up to fifty."

"I'd rather not risk it."

"Agreed."

Click, click. "Reading seven now."

"You stay back a bit." He smiled. "We still need your ovaries." He handed her the brush and took the counter. Four short steps brought him to a body length from the chest. A couple of piles of powdered bones rested near the chest. "I bet those are animals that got zapped by the chest, just like that old prospector."

"Well don't get too close then."

Cam grabbed a handful of dirt from the cave floor and tossed it at the chest. Nothing. He opened his water bottle and flicked an ounce or two of water onto the chest, dancing back as he did so. Still nothing. "If it's some kind of battery, I think it's dead now."

"You think?"

"The water should have reacted if it's live. Plus I'm wearing rubber boots, so I'm not grounded." He exhaled loudly. "Theoretically."

"Ah yes, science geek."

He crept closer. Her eyes drifted to the piles of animal bones. She hoped he was right about the rubber boots.

"What's it reading?" she asked.

"Twelve."

Still safe. She approached, trying not to trudge up dust with her rubber boots. A tattered cloth, covered by a layer of fine gray ash, covered the chest. Cam handed her the counter, set his light down and reached slowly for the cloth. Extending a finger, he jabbed at the fabric and leapt away, staggering on his injured leg.

"Anything?" she asked.

"No. Like I said, it must be dead." He reached for the cloth with both hands.

"Gentle with it," she said. "We might want to carbon-date it. And it might be an important artifact."

He turned and smiled. "Like the Shroud of Turin?"

"Not exactly, but sort of."

Spreading his arms, he took hold of the cloth at either end and gently lifted it and folded it back on itself. Gray dust danced in the beams of their lights. He waited a few seconds and folded the cloth back a second time, exposing most of the chest.

Amanda grabbed Cam's shoulder. "Oh my God. Those are angels."

He nodded. "And I think they're gold-colored."

Holding the brush in a shaky hand and the chamois in the other, she brushed and wiped the chest clean of ash and bat dung and centuries of desert residue. Her mind wandered, back in time, perhaps 3500 years. Had this now-grimy chest carried the Ten Commandments, witnessed the Jews wandering in the desert, felled the enemies of Israel and eventually rested in the great Temple of Solomon? And later, had it become lost to history, spirited from Israel to Jordan to Africa to Europe, eventually finding a lonely home halfway around the world in this dusty, secluded mountain cave in the American southwest?

She took a deep breath, forced herself to work more slowly, more carefully. "Gentle," she whispered. Her work revealed an ornately-carved chest, the gold surface covered with flowing geometric patterns surrounding what looked like a holiday wreath. Inside the wreath, she brushed away the centuries to reveal a series of raised markings studded with emeralds and rubies. She applied water and rubbed more of the detritus away. *Odd.* It looked like writing. As she brushed and rubbed, her hood filled with warm air from her exertion; she forced herself to slow down. Two letters revealed themselves, then three more, then five, and finally six. Stunned, she dropped the brush. "Cam, look at this."

"What?"

She pointed. "Read that. It's Latin isn't it?" *But what would Latin be doing on an Old Testament artifact?*

It took Cam a second to get it. "Oh." His voice dropped, matching her mood. "Yup, Latin."

She sat back, deflated. They both stared at the object for a few seconds. "I don't suppose Moses and the ancient Israelites spoke Latin."

Cam shook his head and frowned. "No. And I don't suppose the Templars would deface the sacred Ark by adding Latin to it."

"Not bloody likely." She sighed. "So what does it say?"

He peered closer. *"In Hoc Signo Vinces."*

She nodded. They both knew the Latin was an old Christian battle cry, going back to the time of Constantine in the fourth century AD. The Templars often used it. It meant, 'Under this sign we are victorious.' But, again, it did not date back to the time of the ancient Israelites.

Cam pointed to another raised area above the wreath which Amanda had not uncovered yet. "I bet there's a cross carved up here. The cross is the sign they fought under—they carried a huge banner with a cross on it into battle."

So the chest dated back to the Templars or even earlier, but it clearly wasn't the original Ark the Jews carried through the desert. "This must be some kind of reproduction," Amanda said.

A thousand-year-old, gold-covered, jewel-encrusted, invaluable reproduction that would probably change American history. But a reproduction nonetheless.

Cam and Amanda retreated to the front of the cave. It was getting hot in the suits, and they needed to talk about this fake Ark. "Any theories?" Cam asked, leaning against the wall. He rubbed the last of Willum's lollipop along the inside of his cheek.

She shook her hair loose of the hood. "As a matter of fact, yes. There's no one to fool out here in the middle of the desert, so why make a fake Ark? The only reason to make a duplicate is because the original had some functional use. Otherwise why bother?"

"Fair point." He thought about it. "The original was used to carry the Ten Commandments. So you think the tablets are inside this chest?"

She smiled. "That would be fun. And I suppose it's a possibility. But I think it's more likely that Willum's theory is correct: They were using this fake Ark as some kind of capacitor."

"If so, we'd expect to find that white powder of gold inside, right?"

She nodded. "That may be what's setting off the Geiger counter."

Cam gulped some water and pulled his hood back on. "I guess there's only one way to find out."

She reached out and touched his arm. "Are you sure we should just go in and ... do this? Perhaps we ought to wait for the authorities?"

Cam removed his hood. In some ways this was not the time for this conversation, and in others it was the only time. He took a deep breath. "When I was a kid, I was told I'd be lucky to live to forty—and if I did I'd be blind. That's just the way it was with diabetes back then. So I used to spend a lot of time thinking about what would be written in my obituary."

"Heavy thoughts for a young lad."

Cam nodded. "Well, old habits are hard to break. I still think about that obituary." He smiled. "Other than having my law license suspended, I don't really have much so far."

"You could go for a full disbarment," she teased. "But I think it's safe to describe you as an expert on the Templars."

"Fair enough." He gestured toward the chest. "But this, if it's real, this is the headline, right? How many chances do people get to make a discovery like this?"

"I'll wait on the obituary if it's all the same to you, but I do see your point." She smiled and took his hand. "After you."

They trudged back into the cave, Cam's eyes drawn again to the small piles of bones. Sometime over the past century and a half the capacitor lost its juice. But it held its secrets.

He turned to Amanda; she nodded. He carefully pulled back the cloth shroud. Using his hand, he waved the dust away and peered at the gold-colored lid. Placing one hand under either end of the lid, he lifted the cover off the chest, steadied himself and wrestled the lid clear of the chest. The Geiger counter chirped louder. "Twenty-four," Amanda said as Cam leaned the cover against the cave wall.

Cam limped back and peered into the chest. "No Ten Commandments," Amanda said. "But fancy that." She pointed at a gold-colored bowl in the center of the chest, the only object within.

Cam leaned over, reached in with both hands and, holding the bowl at arm's length, removed an open-topped container that looked like something his grandmother put out to serve candies to guests. A whitish powder filled the bowl. "Just like you thought," Cam said.

Amanda held the gauge to the bowl. "Thirty-three," she said.

He set it back into the chest and they backed away. "Didn't you tell me the ancient Jewish texts talked about how the Ark used to levitate when they brought it out for holidays?"

"Yes. The Kabala describes it."

"Well, Smoot told me the white powder also levitates—"

"So if enough powder were in the Ark," she interrupted, "the entire Ark would levitate."

"Exactly." He exhaled. "So this is the secret Hurech and his Templar mates were hiding. A fake Ark, filled with white powder of gold."

"But why? Why come all the way here just to do that?"

"Good question," he said. "I bet the answer has something to do with the Tucson lead artifacts."

In the end they decided to leave the fake Ark in the cave. Cam had gone back to retrieve a sample of the white powder and take some pictures, but for now the artifact would remain hidden. "This needs to be Willum's call," Cam said. "Plus I don't think we could wrestle it down ourselves."

"Agreed."

Amanda wasn't sure whether to feel elated or disappointed. She had never really believed they would find the Ark of the Covenant, but as every step continued to bring them closer and closer, and as she brushed away the detritus from the golden chest, she had pretty much convinced herself that the impossible had happened. And even though she had been wrong about the impossible happening, what had happened was pretty damn improbable in its own right. The fake Ark would need to be carbon-dated and tested, but she had no doubt that it would conclusively prove that Templar Knights had been exploring the Arizona desert long before Columbus was born. And once that Rubicon had been crossed, the dozens of other artifacts and sites that evidenced early exploration of America would need to be reanalyzed. It was like Cam always said—the only thing the archeologists were consistently right about was being wrong. The history books would need to be rewritten.

Ellis trained his binoculars on the rented SUV as Cam and Amanda bounced down the dirt road toward the highway. Based on the conversation being transmitted to him through the listening device he had imbedded in their car, they had found some kind of ancient chest. Not the actual Ark of the Covenant, but a duplicate made a thousand or more years ago. Ellis didn't know enough about this stuff to understand the ramifications of the find. And though there was talk of radiation, the fake Ark didn't seem to have much to do with the fuel cell Willum was working on. But Ellis knew you didn't pass on the chance to take out an unprotected piece on the chess board.

Traffic slowed to a stop about a quarter-mile south of the compound. "This can't be good," Cam said from the back seat, a bag of ice on his lower leg.

Amanda nodded. "You want to call Georgia?"

"Wait. Someone's coming over now."

A policewoman approached and smiled. "Good afternoon. I'm sorry, but the road is closed. You'll need to turn around in that parking lot."

"We're trying to get to the domes up on the right."

She nodded. "That's why the road is closed. Nobody's allowed near it."

No reason to argue. "Okay, thanks."

As Amanda turned into the parking lot, a dull explosion rumbled across the desert from the direction of the compound. "That can't be good either," Amanda said.

"No. I'll get Georgia on the phone."

Willum had watched all day as law enforcement personnel rolled in. Federal, state, local—but it would be feds who called the shots. Literally.

Though he had planned for this day for years, he was disappointed it had come. The more he thought about it the more convinced he was that the roadside bombing was a hoax. It probably wasn't even a real body—the special effects guys in Hollywood could make anything look real. And none of his people had actually seen the woman in the car. But the feds now had justification for an armed assault on his compound.

He sat at one of the picnic tables sheltered by the domes and sipped a lemonade. No sense giving them a clear shot at him—some Nazi FBI sniper took out Randy Weaver's wife at Ruby Ridge while she stood in the kitchen with a ten-month-old baby in her arms.

As if on cue, a whistling noise pierced the air. Willum knew that sound. "Duck!" he yelled. Seconds later the ground shook and a thunderclap emanated from the rear of the compound. He whipped his head around—black smoke rose up from where the generator was. Or used to be. "Assholes," he cursed. His chest pounded. He hoped none of his people were back there.

Even before the air raid siren sang out, compound residents rushed from the pods. As trained, some manned security posts while others rushed to the impact site. Willum punched in Boonie's number on his cell phone—Boonie was in that area checking on the rear tunnel. Nothing. No service. Clarisse arrived at his side. "Do you have cell service?" he asked.

She punched at her phone. "Nothing."

"Fuck them. They're trying to take out our infrastructure. First power, then communications."

"I'll get the radios and distribute them."

"Good. And also get on the ham radio and let the other Survivalist groups know what's happening. I'm going to check on the generator."

"Get some good video." She paused. "Especially if there are casualties. Our Internet is probably down also, but we can smuggle it out somehow and get it posted. It'll go viral, just like in Egypt. What kind of government drops missiles on its citizens?"

He turned and looked back at her. "An illegitimate one."

CHAPTER 7

Georgia had secured a conference room at the hotel, and she, Cam, Amanda and a couple of agents sat around a table picking at pizza and salad. Cam appreciated that she hadn't invited Ellis. The agents excused themselves to take a call, which gave Georgia a chance to get Cam and Amanda up to speed.

"Obviously, things are getting out of hand at the compound," she said. "FBI is in charge now. But ODNI still has a seat at the table, at least for now."

"So who decided to take out the generator?" Cam asked. The solar panels were also destroyed.

"Honestly, it feels more like a political decision than a tactical one. Someone convinced the President to authorize a drone strike. Thank God nobody was seriously hurt. Plus the cell phone carriers agreed to de-power their towers. So Smoot is without power and cell phones."

Cam spoke. "Smoot still has power— I'm sure they have plenty of smaller generators, and they have thousands of gallons of gasoline buried. Plus they have radios to communicate. All you really did is feed his paranoia."

"I didn't do it, Cameron," Georgia said, straightening herself in her chair.

"Sorry," he smiled. "I mean you in the plural sense, as in the government."

She nodded and relaxed her shoulders. "We're all getting a little edgy."

Amanda spoke. "Why be so aggressive? Why not just wait it out?"

"That's what I would do," Georgia said. "But this thing is starting to feed on itself. All the Survivalists and militia folk and right-wing whackos are starting to mobilize. The President doesn't want this to mushroom. There's already talk in places like Idaho and Wyoming and New Mexico about states seceding. And the people in Arizona aren't too happy about the feds dropping missiles on their neighbors."

"All the more reason to just back off," Amanda persisted.

"Again, I agree with you. But I think the President is tired of taking shit from what he considers the radical right—they've been beating him up for years. I think he wants to show them who's boss. You can't detonate a bomb and kill an ATF agent and then barricade yourself in a fortress compound." She shrugged. "I mean, you just can't."

"I don't think Smoot knows anything about it," Cam said.

"Based   on?"

"Based on I saw his reaction when it happened. Like I told you, he was as shocked as anyone."

"Well," Georgia said, "if that's true he probably has nothing to be afraid of."

Cam caught Amanda's eye just as she was about to argue the point. People went to jail all the time for crimes they didn't commit. Cam knew it, Amanda knew it, Georgia especially knew it.

The two agents returned to the room. Georgia addressed them. "Cam and Amanda have spent a lot of time in the compound. In addition to the description of its layout, which has been very valuable to us, they have gotten to know Smoot a bit." She sat back. "They don't think he set off the bomb; in fact, they don't think he knows anything about it."

The older agent, a heavy-set guy with nicotine-stained fingers and a lazy eye, drummed his fingers on the table. According to Georgia, he was an expert on the Survivalist movement and in particular the residents of Smoot's compound. "It's possible," he grumbled. "Almost a hundred people in the compound. A bunch of them not only expect the world to end, they're hoping for it. I can give you a dozen names of people who could have set the bomb."

The other agent was about Cam's age, hard and good-looking—if this were a movie, he'd be the leading man. "We've got nothing yet on the bomb. Pretty basic. Anyone with a little training could have built it from supplies at the local hardware store and then set it off."

Georgia took a deep breath. "Okay. So the question is, what do we do next? Is there any way we can get Smoot to come out peacefully?"

Lazy eye spoke. "Maybe use his kid?"

"What," Georgia asked, "start cutting off his fingers?"

The agent shrugged. "You asked for ideas."

"I have an idea." Ellis Kincaid strolled in, his auburn-tinted hair thick on his forehead. He flopped into an empty chair. "I can end this all now. You might not like it, but I can get it done."

Georgia narrowed her eyes as Cam rolled his. "Don't play games, Ellis. If you can end this, tell us how."

He smirked. "I can't tell you how. At least not yet. But if you give me fifteen minutes with him, I can do it."

"You're not James Bond, Mr. Kincaid, and this is not the movies. That's not how things work here. If you have a plan, I want to hear it." Georgia was not Ellis's superior, and she had told Cam she had the sense Ellis and his bosses were pursuing some hidden agenda. But Cam admired her for her attempt at a little bluster.

Ellis shrugged. "I don't have an actual plan. I just think if I talk to Smoot I can convince him to come in for questioning."

Cam looked at Amanda. It was not his place to say anything, but clearly Ellis was hiding something.

Georgia sighed. "You must have some sort of plan, or how would you know we won't like it? What won't we like?"

Ellis ignored the question. "Actually, I can't do it alone." He paused and smirked again, this time at Cam. "I'll need Cameron's help."

"Desperate times require desperate measures," Georgia said as they drove out to Smoot's compound. She was up front with the lazy-eyed agent, who was driving. "Are you sure you're comfortable with this, Cam?"

"Why not? We're just going to talk to Smoot. What's not to be comfortable with?"

Amanda sat next to Cam in the back seat; she turned to him. "Well, it's likely a small army of Smoot's men will have automatic rifles trained on you, for one thing."

"Good point. I'll be sure to stand behind Ellis."

Ellis Kincaid's car had already arrived at the compound. Like Cam, he wore a pair of jeans and a tennis shirt. Ellis also carried a thin leather portfolio. He said, "I figured Cameron can set up our meeting. Smoot will trust him." When he pronounced Cam's name, he did so in an affected way, with perfect diction— as if it were being spoken at a country club or prep school.

Cam nodded and limped to the guard house. "Any chance Willum can come out and have a chat?" he asked.

The guard spoke into his radio for a few seconds. "He says you are welcome to come in."

"Can I bring someone with me? He's a federal agent. He'll be unarmed." But he is a prick.

After another quick conversation through his radio the guard replied. "I'll need to search him. And you."

Cam nodded.

"Oh, and one more thing," Ellis said as he sauntered over. "Tell Smoot to bring that woman Clarisse with him."

The guard looked at Cam, who in turn looked at Ellis. "Work with me here, Cameron," Ellis said. Cam wanted to rub his face in the desert sand, but instead he sighed and nodded again.

A few minutes later one of the guards opened the gate, searched them and escorted them to the picnic table area in the center of the compound. Willum and Clarisse stood framed by the late afternoon sun, their shadows elongated across a rectangular table. Unlike the last time Cam was inside the compound, both Willum and Clarisse wore holstered handguns over their cargo shorts. Cam made the introductions. "I'm going to be perfectly honest with you guys. I have no idea what Agent Kincaid is up to, and I don't really trust him."

"Speaking of trust, why are you involved with this in any way, Cam?" Willum asked, jaw clenched and hand on gun.

"Fair question." Especially from a guy who just saved his life. "I think you know about our encounter last fall with the Mormon extremists and the rogue federal agents?"

Smoot nodded.

"Well, we became friendly with one of the agents, one of the honest ones. She asked me to intervene to see if this can be resolved."

"So you were lying to me."

Cam shifted his weight. "You contacted me. Then the feds contacted me. I agreed to help try to keep this compound from being blown up."

"And now I'm supposed to trust you."

Cam shook his head. At least Willum hadn't thrown them out yet. "Look, I don't care if you trust me. But you should at least listen to what Kincaid has to say."

Ellis interjected. "Maybe you two can go on Dr. Phil when this is all over." He sniffed. "Talk out all your differences, maybe share a big hug afterward."

Willum glared at him.

Ellis turned and addressed Clarisse. "You and I both know who set that bomb."

Clarisse stared at him for a couple of seconds before nodding slowly. "Yes," she breathed.

Willum straightened. "Who?"

Ellis responded. "Your man Boonie. Last week he bought the bomb-making supplies at Home Depot. We have him on a surveillance camera. Clarisse knows because he submitted his receipt for reimbursement. And, always the efficient little worker bee, she issued the check that day." He tapped the cover of his portfolio. "We have a copy of the check."

Clarisse turned to Willum. "It's true. I sent him for supplies. But he came back with a bunch of extra stuff."

"I can't believe Boonie is sophisticated enough to make a roadside bomb," Willum said.

"From what I've read in his file, I tend to agree," Ellis said. "In fact, he doesn't sound smart enough to wipe his own ass."

Willum lowered his voice. "Fuck off."

Ellis waved the comment away, his auburn bangs swinging as he did so. "Someday, perhaps—but for now you're stuck with me. Anyway, Boonie being an idiot is why we suspect he had help. We just don't know who."

Willum's face turned red and he worked his jaw. "I'm not giving Boonie up."

"Listen. We all know he's mentally challenged, or whatever they call it today. No way will he do any time on this. All he has to do is tell us who helped him make the bomb."

Willum shook his head. "No."

Ellis nodded. "I figured you'd say that. I know you did time with his grandfather. Which is why I'm willing to sweeten the pot a bit."

"What do you mean?" Willum said.

Ellis slid a photo across the table. Cam leaned over it as Smoot and Clarisse did the same. The fake Ark. "You asshole," Cam said. "Where did you get that?"

"In the mountains, where you left it." He turned to Smoot. "And thanks for leaving the climbing lines—it made it easy to lower the chest to the ground."

"Wait," Cam said. "You know it's radioactive, right? I hope your men were protected."

Ellis nodded. "Your concern is touching. But we're not idiots."

Cam pursed his lips. So Ellis had been spying on them. Not really a surprise. "Well, anyway, the fake Ark has nothing to do with the bomb," Cam said. "You have no right to steal our artifact."

Ellis smirked. *"Our artifact?* Did you by chance get permission from the landowner to keep it?" He waited a few seconds. "I thought not. In any event, there are no rules here, Cameron. One of our agents is dead. It's my job to find out who did it."

"So what's your offer?" Smoot asked.

"Like I said, we just want to question Boonie. You can lawyer him up all you want—but we need to bring someone in to show we are making progress on this case."

"And then what?"

"Well, then he tells us who helped him make the bomb and we arrest him." Ellis smiled at Clarisse. "Or her."

"And if we won't let you back in?"

Ellis shrugged "Then we're back to square one, I suppose. In this area of the country I believe they call it a Mexican stand-off."

"What about the golden chest?" Smoot asked.

"It's in a van a few miles away. As soon as we have Boonie, you get the chest."

Smoot turned from the table. "I need to talk to Boonie and call my lawyer."

Cam waited at the picnic table with Ellis Kincaid for Smoot's response. His leg throbbing, Cam had sat when Smoot left. He hated the idea of making small talk with the agent, but his curiosity won out. "Do you think he'll accept the deal?"

Ellis rolled his eyes. "Of course not."

Jerk that he was, Ellis didn't give a reason for his answer, instead forcing Cam to grovel. "Why not?"

"No way will he give up Boonie. What kind of message would that send to his followers?"

So what game was Ellis playing? "Then why are we here?"

"Because once he rejects our first deal he'll want to show his good faith by accepting my second offer."

"Which is?"

Ellis smiled but did not respond.

Forty-five minutes passed and the sun was now low on the horizon. Willum trudged back to the picnic area, Clarisse close behind. Cam stood. "Sorry," Willum said, "no deal."

"You know that means you'll be harboring a fugitive, right?" Ellis said.

Willum nodded.

Ellis sighed. "Look, Willum, you have to give me something here. Something I can take back to the trigger-happy yahoos just looking for an excuse to go all Rambo on you. I need you to make some show of good faith."

"I understand. But I'm not giving up Boonie."

Clarisse didn't know what game this oddball federal agent was playing, but whatever it was he was pretty good at it. He had sent her a text message a couple of hours earlier reading, simply, "Play along. You'll understand." She didn't understand, and didn't trust him, but she also knew enough to keep an open mind.

So when Agent Kincaid accused Boonie of making the bomb, Clarisse went along with it as a tidy solution to this mess: Willum would avoid arrest and the feds would have their man. More importantly, nobody would blow their compound into a million pieces.

Now the game had reached stage two. Still Clarisse had no idea of the rules. But somehow Kincaid must have known Willum would never give up Boonie. She took a deep breath and eyed the three men standing around the picnic table. "How about the fuel cell, Willum?" she said.

"The fuel cell?"

"Yes. The prototype." She leaned in closer. Now that it turned out even Thorne was not totally trustworthy, her counsel would be even more valued. "You said the Defense Department has been trying for years to get you to help them build the next generation fuel cell. Well, you've done it. You have it, they want it. Why not play the card?"

Kincaid caught her eye and nodded almost imperceptibly. "What does that have to do with anything?" Kincaid asked.

Willum sighed and rubbed his hand through his hair. "You know, Clarisse, that's not a bad idea." He turned to the agent. "I wouldn't expect you to know anything about this, but tell your boss to tell his boss that I've invented the next-generation fuel cell. And I'm willing to trade it for Boonie's freedom."

"Why would that be enough to back off a murder investigation?" Kincaid asked, though Clarisse sensed he was just playing dumb.

"Well, there are people in your government who would wipe out a whole neighborhood to get this technology. They would probably think one corpse is a damn good deal."

Cam interjected. "And you need to return the ark also."

Kincaid nodded. "So the deal is we get this fuel cell and you get the ark."

"And you need to stand down," Willum said. "And Boonie walks."

Kincaid nodded again. "Basically we'll need to make believe this whole bomb thing never happened." He stared into the distance. "I'll need your help on this. We'll send a doctor in to question Boonie. The doctor will conclude he's not capable of understanding right versus wrong and recommend no charges be brought. We'll write a big check to the deceased's family and this whole thing will go away."

Willum looked to Cam. He seemed to be weighing whether to trust him or not. "You're a lawyer, what do you think?"

"Assuming we can trust him to do what he says?" Cam asked.

"Yes, assuming that," Willum responded. "I'm not giving them the fuel cell until the end."

"Well, then, it should work. There are plenty of cases of defendants let go because of low intelligence."

Kincaid looked back and forth from Cam to Willum to make sure they were finished talking. "Okay," he said. "But first I need to sell my bosses on this magic fuel cell of yours." He looked at Willum. "I sure hope you're right about this."

The sun had not yet begun to brighten the eastern sky. But Clarisse was playing a dangerous game here with the federal agent, and she needed to know if she was still winning.

She dabbed some perfume on her neck and wrists, grabbed a couple of cold Coronas from the fridge and radioed to Willum. "Where are you?"

"Parking lot, near the guard house."

"Everything okay?"

"Yes, quiet."

"Thirsty?"

"You buying?"

She found him leaning against the Land Cruiser. Did he suspect her of anything duplicitous? She approached, came perhaps a half-step closer than was necessary. "Howdy Cowboy."

He smiled. His eyes shone bright in the moonlight, even with the dark circles underneath. He mimicked doffing his hat. "Ma'am." Willum had risen to the occasion, as she knew he would; command suited him. He just needed a kick in the ass sometimes. And maybe also a reward.

Had Moses similarly risen to the occasion to exercise his authority over the ancient Israelites? If they could somehow end this current standoff, and just wait for the inevitable collapse, there was nothing to prevent Willum from eventually becoming a Moses of his own. Willum might be a reluctant savior, but then again so too was Moses at the beginning. Willum would lead if necessary. Especially if his people insisted on it.

"Here's your beer." She leaned closer and nibbled his ear. "And is this car unlocked?"

Twenty minutes later she kissed him a final time and let herself out. Adjusting her shorts, she peered in and smiled. "Not a bad way to start the day."

He grinned back at her as she closed the door. Men were easy. Even those destined for greatness. Give them beer and sex, and they were happy.

Cam, Amanda and Astarte were supposed to fly back to Boston today, but Amanda knew there was little chance of getting Cam on a plane with so much still unresolved. Instead they were meeting Georgia for Sunday brunch in the hotel restaurant.

"Your man Ellis nicked our chest," Amanda said as Georgia approached the table with a cup of coffee.

She flopped into a chair. "And a good morning to you also."

Amanda clenched her jaw, glanced to make sure Astarte was out of earshot getting some fruit. "You promised you could control him. Cameron almost died finding that chest."

Georgia smacked the table, the silverware clattering against the plates. "Don't you think I know that? Do you think I like feeling powerless?"

"But you said you could control him," Amanda repeated. Cam rested his hand on her arm.

Georgia blew over the lip of her cup, her hand shaking. "Obviously I was wrong. Ellis seems to be answering to someone over my head." She sighed. "I've been trying to figure out his game but I'm not getting anywhere." She paused. "I'm sorry to have dragged you all into this."

Astarte joined them, ending the conversation. They ate in silence for a few seconds. The television above the bar was tuned into *Meet the Press*. A picture of the bearded Willum, steely-eyed and carrying a rifle, flashed on the screen while the director of the FBI answered questions about the standoff.

Georgia glanced at the screen and straightened herself. "Well. Looks like we're the story of the week." She turned away from the television. "You know, I'm surprised the White House is even considering the deal Ellis brokered."

"The White House?" Cam asked. It was hard to stay mad at the woman—it wasn't her fault control of this mission had been taken away from her.

She nodded. "Yes. Apparently they are calling the shots on this now."

"Why are you surprised?" Amanda asked, a bit calmer.

"A federal agent is dead. Usually that doesn't leave much room for negotiation." Georgia sipped her coffee. "That fuel cell must be pretty important."

"When do you think we'll hear something?" Cam asked.

"The way this works is that these Sunday morning shows are a way to take the nation's pulse. The President and his advisors will sit around this afternoon and the spin-masters will help him decide what the next step is." Cam knew that for decades Georgia had been a political operative—a perfect cover for a CIA agent. When she earned a promotion to deputy director and left the field, she no longer needed the cover. But she still possessed keen political instincts. "Based on the tone of these questions, and some of the demonstrations around the country, my guess is the White House is going to want to end this quickly—one way or another. The last thing they'll want is for this to drag out and turn into a daily watch like the Iran hostage crisis. That was death from a thousand small cuts for Carter. So I would expect a call this afternoon."

They ate in silence for a few seconds until Georgia spoke again. "I want to hear more about this ark you found. Tell me why you think it's a replica and not the original?"

Amanda deferred to Cam. "There's an old Christian battle cry, *In Hoc Signo Vinces*, carved on the side of the ark. The ancient Israelites didn't speak Latin, so there are only two choices: Either some Christians added the inscription to the original Ark, or this ark is a replica of the original."

Georgia nodded. "And you think it is unlikely any Christians would have defaced the original Ark."

"It would have been unthinkable," Amanda said. "It was the most holy object in the Old Testament."

"Well, could it have been defaced by some other group, someone not Jewish or Christian, someone who wouldn't have viewed the Ark as holy?"

"No," Amanda said. "The *In Hoc* slogan is a Christian one."

Cam turned his laptop screen toward Georgia. "You've seen the Newport Tower, right?"

THE NEWPORT TOWER, NEWPORT, RI

Georgia nodded.

"And you know we think the Templars probably built it?" There were a number of architectural, astronomical, historical and allegorical connections between the round, arched Rhode Island tower and the medieval Templars. Cam and Amanda had spent the past couple of years documenting these connections. "Well, about a mile away, along the shore, someone found this boulder after a massive storm."

THE *IN HOC SIGNO VINCES* STONE, NEWPORT, RI

Georgia leaned closer to the screen. "Does it say *In Hoc Signo Vinces?*"

Cam nodded. "Yes. It's only uncovered for about twenty minutes per day at low tide; it had probably been buried for decades if not longer. We think when it was carved, maybe six or seven hundred years ago, the water levels were lower and it would have been more visible."

"This is on the shore where ancient travelers would have landed when visiting Newport," Amanda said.

Georgia nodded. "Okay, I'm convinced. So your ark is a replica, with this *In Hoc* slogan carved onto it by some Christian group. I'm not surprised—I know some historians believe there are a bunch of copies of the Ark spread around Europe. But I still don't understand why it's here in Arizona."

Amanda responded. "I've been thinking about it and here's what I've come up with. Like you said, there are probably quite a few replicas of the original Ark. Maybe the original was taken to Ethiopia, or maybe it was destroyed, or maybe it simply stopped functioning. But the high priests who were trained to guard and watch over the Ark—these were the descendants of Aaron, called the Levites—must also have known its secrets and how to build a new one. So when some of these high priests ended up in France after the fall of Jerusalem, they probably built themselves a new ark."

Cam interjected. "And they would have incorporated the same technology as the original and used it the same way—as a way to produce the white powder of gold. The Jews of Europe were always rumored to have secret knowledge of alchemy."

Amanda put her finger to her mouth. "I'm confused. Does the white powder fuel the Ark, or does the Ark produce the white powder?"

"Good question. I think it's both, sort of like the chicken and the egg. The original process of turning the gold or heavy metals into white powder was done at the smelting workshop at *Serabit el Khadim.* Then, once they had the powder, it powered the Ark, turned it into a fuel cell. The fuel cell could in turn be used to produce more of the white powder without having to go all the way back to *Serabit el Khadim."*

Amanda nodded. "So when the French Jews decided to come to America, they brought the duplicate ark with them. That must have been sometime after the fourth century, because that's when the *In Hoc Signo Vinces* battle cry was first used by Constantine."

"But why come to Arizona?" Georgia asked.

Cam responded. "Probably for the same reason pioneers came here and to California in the 1800s—there's gold in them there hills. And silver too."

"And perhaps also because of the soil," Amanda added. "I don't think just any soil can be used to make the *mfkzt.* I think they needed a specific desert soil. One rich with heavy metals."

"So how did our man rough Hurech end up with the replica ark?"

Amanda continued. "I'm guessing the Templars came looking for their long-lost ancestors. Remember, the Templars and the Calalus settlers—the people who made the Tucson lead artifacts—were all part of the same lineage, the French Merovingians. But by the time Hurech and his mates got here their ancestors had been wiped out by the native Toltecs. That was around AD 900, right Cam?"

"Yes, 895. So it was probably three hundred years later that Hurech came looking for them. And somehow he found the ark."

"Perhaps one of the reasons they came was because the knowledge of how to build the Ark had been lost," Amanda said. "During the Dark Ages much of the accumulated knowledge of Western society was wiped away. Perhaps the ark we found was the last prototype."

Cam interjected again. "Ralph de Sudeley."

"What about him?" Amanda said.

"We were wondering why he was in the Catskills. What if the ark that he found in Jordan didn't work? It was too old, or it got damaged somehow—he's just found an amazing weapon or tool or power source but he can't even turn the damn thing on. But he heard rumors that the Calalus folks had crossed the ocean with a duplicate ark a few hundred years earlier. So maybe he and his buddies come across the pond themselves trying to track them. They scout around the east coast, but of course they're thousands of miles away."

Amanda nodded. "I like it. It makes sense." And there was even more to it than that. "And it helps explain rough Hurech returning a generation later—de Sudeley and Hurech lived close by to one another in the English Midlands, so Hurech would have been a natural ally. The Templars sent a second group over to try to find the Calalus settlers. This time they sent them into the Gulf of Mexico rather than to the New England coast. Bingo. But Hurech never made it home."

Georgia nodded. "It sounds like a lot of people have been looking for this ark before you." She lowered her voice so Astarte couldn't hear. "I'm sorry Ellis stole it from you. I've tried a couple of times to have him removed from this case, but for some reason somebody high up wants him involved."

Georgia's phone rang, interrupting their conversation. A half-minute later she hung up. "Well, maybe I was too quick to judge Ellis. Your ark is on its way here. Ellis says it's a show of good faith." She glanced around the dining room and smiled. "I'm assuming you don't want it delivered to your room."

Later that afternoon a couple of guys wheeled a dolly out of the back of a moving van and delivered a thousand-year-old, gold-covered, two-hundred-pound, radioactive artifact. Somehow Ellis had found a large lead box to encase the ark, which more than doubled the relic's weight. It also sealed the radiation in, as Amanda's Geiger counter confirmed. After a long conversation between Georgia and the hotel manager, it was finally agreed that the ark would be stored in a locked storage shed located in the rear of the hotel parking lot.

"So what next?" Amanda asked.

"At some point we need to get this out to Willum's compound. After all, it's his. But for now I'd like to finish examining it. Who knows what other markings we'll find." Cam had hosed down their Hazmat suits and tested them with the Geiger counter to make sure they were free of radiation. "Any interest in getting back into your bunny suit?"

She rolled her eyes. "You sure know how to show a girl a good time."

Georgia agreed to take Astarte to see a movie, and a half-hour later Cam and Amanda drove the rental SUV to the rear of the lot, crouched behind the vehicle and stepped into their Hazmat suits a second time.

Closing the storage shed door behind them, Cam studied the lead box while Amanda found the switch for the overhead light. "I don't think we're going to be able to lift the ark out of the case by ourselves," he said. He fingered a couple of latches. "But it looks like the top and side panels come right off." Cam wrestled the lead panels aside, leaving the ark sitting on the lead base. "And I think Ellis cleaned it."

"Yes. I only cleaned the front face." She pointed to the *In Hoc Signo Vinces* inscription inside the ornate gold wreath. "But it looks like all the faces have been scrubbed. I hope he was careful with it."

Cam circled the artifact, still favoring one leg. They had so far only examined the front face. The two end faces were merely decorative, but the back of the ark had additional writing on it. He called Amanda over.

"Can you read it?" she asked.

As on the front face, the writing filled the space inside an oval-shaped decorative wreath. He crouched and angled his flashlight. "It's Hebrew." He peered closer. There were two words, written right to left in the Hebrew fashion. "The first word says *Beit*, which means 'house.' The second I think says *Levi*, but I'm not quite sure of the 'v' letter—it might be an 'h,' which would make it *Lehi*." Cam pronounced both *Levi* and *Lehi* as if the final 'i' made the sound of a final 'y,' as was indicated by the Hebrew—so *Levi* rhymed with 'heavy.'

Amanda responded. "So it says 'House of Levi' or 'House of Lehi'?"

He stood up. "I think so."

"Well, 'House of Levi' makes perfect sense," Amanda said. They both knew that the descendants of Aaron were called Levites, or the House of Levi. It was the Levites' job as the high priests to take care of the Ark—nobody else was allowed to touch it or even come near it. And if anyone knew the secrets of the Ark and how to build a replica, it would be the Levites. "If this was their ark, no surprise they'd put their name on it."

Cam stood. They had not yet examined the ark's lid, which Ellis and his men had also cleaned. An ornately-carved gold angel sat at either end of the lid, each angel leaning forward so that their outstretched wings almost touched in the middle.

Amanda motioned to the space between the wings. "There's your spark gap."

He nodded. "And look. There's a face carved on the lid." He leaned in. "And I think a name carved beneath it."

"Can you read it?"

"It's more faded than the others, but I think it says *Bezaleel.*"

"That name sounds familiar. I think it's from the Bible."

Cam shrugged. "Not to me. But it's weird to have a face on a relic like this."

"How so?"

"Jews aren't allowed to glorify anyone except God. To carve his face on the ark doesn't seem right. Almost like a false idol."

"Well, don't forget these were Christianized Jews. So maybe the old taboos don't apply."

"Maybe." He backed away. It was getting hot in his suit. "Let's snap some pictures and get out of these things."

"Right. And I'd like to do some research on this Bezaleel chap."

Using the printer in the hotel's business suite, Cam printed out images of the carvings they had found on the ark. He was examining the shot while Amanda researched Bezaleel on the internet when Georgia and Astarte strolled into the hotel lobby.

"How was the theatre?" Amanda asked, hugging the girl. It was difficult to remember what life had been like before Astarte arrived.

"Good. We saw *Little Mermaid*."

"Another princess movie." Amanda smiled. "What a surprise."

Astarte put her hands on her hips. "If I'm going to be princess someday, I need to learn all I can about it."

"Fair enough," Amanda said. "But do you know what these movies are *really* about?"

"What do you mean?"

"Well, these princess movies are all made by a company called Disney, founded by a man named Walt Disney. Mr. Disney was a member of the Freemasons, a very high-ranking member at that. Do you remember what we told you about the Freemasons?"

"Yes," Astarte said. "And Uncle Jefferson told me about them also. They are the keepers of the ancient knowledge."

Amanda nodded. "Yes, well said—the keepers of the ancient knowledge. If you study the Disney princess movies, you'll find that what they are really telling us is that society can not function well if the king and queen don't sit on the throne together. Nature requires this kind of balance in all things—light and dark, hot and cold, heaven and earth, and also male and female."

She waited as the girl processed this. "Okay," Astarte said.

"So in these stories—whether it is *Snow White* or *Cinderella* or *Sleeping Beauty*, the prince is looking for his princess so they can rule together. In the meantime, the kingdoms are dysfunctional—they don't work. The people are poor and unhappy."

"Okay," she said again.

"Now, this is the part Mr. Disney understood that others didn't. We have been taught that God is a bearded, male figure. But the truth is that God is part man and part woman. Nature requires it."

Cam interjected. "We talked about this the other day in the car, Astarte."

"But God is a man. And so is Jesus. I've seen pictures."

Amanda met Astarte's gaze. "Yes, Jesus is a man. But he was married to Mary Magdalene. She was supposed to sit on the throne in heaven with him, as his queen. But the male leaders in the ancient Church wanted to keep power for themselves. So they changed the story to make Mary Magdalene be a ... bad person."

"You mean a prostitute."

Amanda smiled and took a deep breath. "Yes." This was going on longer than she intended. "So in these princess movies, the prince is meant to represent Jesus and the princess meant to represent Mary Magdalene. When they finally marry, the kingdom is saved."

Cam interjected again. "And until they do, the people are ruled by the evil stepmother. She's not really a mother, she just tries to act like one. Just like the Church calls itself the bride of God and the Mother Church when it really is controlled by men, not women."

Amanda continued. "And *Little Mermaid* is the same message. Eric, the prince, can't rule his kingdom without Ariel, his princess."

Georgia, who had been sitting back on the couch with her arms crossed, leaned forward. "So you're saying Ariel is supposed to represent Mary Magdalene?"

Amanda smiled. "Yes. Long red hair and all."

"It seems like a bit of a stretch to me."

"Actually, Ariel is more on point even than the other princesses. You've heard of the dawning of the Age of Aquarius?"

"You mean like the song?"

"Yes. It refers to the zodiacal procession of the equinox. The Age of Pisces ushered in Jesus Christ, which is why his symbol is the fish. Before that was the Age or Aries, and before that Taurus. Today, we are transitioning to Aquarius. Water. That's why Eric needs to look to the sea to find his princess in *Little Mermaid.*"

Georgia shook her head. "I know this is your area of expertise, Amanda. But I think you're taking this too far. What's the saying, sometimes a cigar is just a cigar? For you to associate Ariel with Mary Magdalene is just … a stretch to me."

Amanda leaned over her laptop. "I bet I can change your mind." She poked at the keys. "Remember when Ariel is singing 'Part of Your World'? During the song she's looking through her treasure chest. In addition to jewels and heirlooms, she pulls out this painting." Amanda held up her screen. "Have a look."

"MAGDALENE WITH THE SMOKING FLAME"
BY GEORGES DE LA TOUR
AS SEEN IN *THE LITTLE MERMAID*

"Well I'll be," Georgia exhaled. "It's Mary Magdalene all right. I missed that in the movie."

"It passed quickly," Amanda said. "I don't think we need to ask Cameron if he thinks a young mermaid treasuring a portrait of Mary Magdalene is a random coincidence."

Cam shrugged and patted Georgia on the shoulder. "It's usually not worth arguing with Amanda about this stuff."

Georgia cleared her throat. "Well, you'll probably argue this with me. You should know that after the movie Astarte and I spent a half-hour inside a Mormon church."

Amanda's head whipped around. "You what?"

Georgia stood and held up her hand. "We drove by it on the way to the movie, and on the way back Astarte asked if we could stop. She said she wanted to pray for the woman who got killed at the compound." Her shoulders sank. "I didn't know what to do."

"Well, what did she do there?" Amanda directed the question to Georgia.

"We went in, a little girl came over to say hi, and the girl took Astarte into the temple area to pray. I watched from the back."

"Please don't be mad at Georgia," Astarte said. "It was my idea. I wanted to ask God to take care of the woman who died. She wasn't married, so she can't go to heaven like the other wives."

Amanda unclenched her job, took a deep breath and spoke. "Okay. We can discuss this later."

Fighting to contain her aggravation, Amanda pointed to the images on the coffee table as Astarte sat on the couch next to her. Georgia remained standing. "We found some new carvings on the ark. Astarte, you know a lot about the Bible. Who is Bezaleel?"

"He's the man who built the Ark of the Covenant."

Amanda nodded. "Yes. We found his name and portrait carved on the lid of our ark. And we found 'House of Levi' carved on the back panel."

"Can I see the pictures?" Astarte asked.

"Sure ... honey," Amanda said, her voice still strained. She made a point not to angle the pictures so Georgia could see them.

Cam explained to Georgia who the Levites were as Astarte studied the pictures. "Astarte, can you read Hebrew?" Cam asked.

She nodded. "Uncle Jefferson taught me."

"So do you see where it says *Beit Levi*, or 'House of Levi,' on it?"

"It looks like *Beit Lehi* to me," she said.

Cam shrugged. "Could be. But 'House of Levi' makes more sense."

The girl's eyes narrowed. "No it doesn't."

Cam started to respond but Amanda grabbed his arm. "Hey, shush for a second, Georgia's on the phone with the White House. I think they've approved the deal."

Willum hadn't slept in, well, he was no longer sure. On Thursday night he stayed up all night working on the fuel cell. On Friday the car bomb went off and the compound went into lockdown, so he didn't sleep that night either. And yesterday the feds declared open war by dropping a bomb on the generator—Willum spent all night on patrol with the other residents. Other than, that is, twenty minutes in the backseat of the Land Cruiser.

Somehow, amazingly, he didn't feel tired. It was as if his body no longer needed sleep, as if it had itself become the perfect fuel cell. The other residents seemed to have the same super-human stamina also. Clarisse and her kitchen team kept them well-fed, and they all pounded coffee, and of course adrenaline coursed through their veins. But sleep? Apparently no longer necessary.

This morning he and Clarisse had rigged up a television with a pair of old rabbit ears and watched the Sunday morning roundtable discussion programs. A few other residents joined them, and everyone leaned forward when an image of the compound, with the highway turned into a staging area for an armed invasion, appeared halfway through the segment. Well, so much for moving to the desert and laying low.

A surprising sense of harmony had settled over the compound. There were a few minor squabbles, but for the most part everyone did their jobs without complaint. It was as if they were a team of professional soldiers rather than a ragtag group of societal outcasts. Strangest of all, everyone obeyed his orders as if he were Patton or Truman or Alexander the Great rather than some overweight chemist in a Grateful Dead t-shirt.

Most dutiful of all, as always, was Boonie. He had followed Willum around for the past few days like a kid chasing the ice cream truck. Was it because he felt guilty about setting the bomb? Or did he sense he might be bartered to the feds? Only now, as they ate sandwiches made with fresh-baked bread, did Willum finally have a few minutes alone with Boonie.

"I still remember the day you stood outside the compound fence waiting for me to see you." It had been a couple of years ago, not long after Willum bought the place and moved in. "I didn't even know old Boone had a grandson." He laughed. "Well, that's not accurate. I knew he had dozens of grandkids; I just didn't know who they were. He kept busy when he wasn't in jail."

Boonie didn't respond, nor did Willum expect him to. "You know, the feds think they know who set off that bomb."

Boonie nodded as he chewed. "Okay."

"Do you want to know who they think did it?"

He shrugged. But he had also stopped chewing, the mouthful of bread and turkey and lettuce balled into the side of his mouth like a December chipmunk.

Willum sighed. Poor Boonie. This was probably the first time in his life he fit in, felt important. He had jobs to do, was part of a community, even had a little bit of status as Willum's ward. Had he set the bomb out of a sense of loyalty? And had he done it for Willum?

Willum slapped the table. "You know what? Who gives a shit what the feds think. They can go fuck themselves." He patted Boonie on the back. "You want me to get you another sandwich?"

Ellis watched from the far side of the lobby as Thorne, his fiancée, the girl and Georgia studied the images of the ark. He strolled over.

"I see the ark was delivered."

Thorne glanced up. "Yup."

"You guys are the experts on this stuff. I didn't understand the 'House of Lehi' inscription."

Neither Thorne nor his fiancée responded so, after a few seconds, Georgia did. "We think it says 'House of Levi,' not 'Lehi.'"

Astarte was following the exchange, and Ellis caught her eye. He raised an eyebrow. "Really? I could have sworn it said 'Lehi.' And the guy who helped me clean it thought so too," he lied. "But, like I said, you guys are the experts. If you think it says 'House of Levi,' you must be right."

Astarte spoke. "I think it says 'Lehi' also--"

The British woman cut her off. "Thank you, Astarte."

Ellis shifted his weight. "Anyway, we should head over to the compound and tell Smoot he has a deal."

Georgia nodded. "Cameron, Amanda—are you two joining us?"

Ellis studied the older woman's body language. She was upset, her face flushed and her breathing rapid. And Amanda had turned away, specifically not responding to the question. Ellis smiled. Perhaps he could exploit the growing tension.

Astarte finally answered. "I'd like to come. I've never seen the compound."

Thorne and his fiancée shared a glance. "She can't very well stay here alone," Thorne said.

Ellis thought about offering to let the girl ride with him, but instead smiled and jogged out to his car.

One of the things Cam liked best about Amanda was that she didn't let things simmer. No doubt she would discuss the trip to the Mormon church with Georgia at some point, but for now at least she had let it go.

"So, this is what I found out about Bezaleel," Amanda said as Cam navigated out of the hotel parking lot. "As Astarte said, he was the man who built the Ark of the Covenant. In fact, he was so smart and so pious that God himself requested he do the work."

"Wow. Tough to turn down that assignment," Cam said. "Sorry, God, I'm doing an addition over the garage now. Can this Ark project wait a few weeks?"

Amanda laughed. "But there's more: Remember the story of Moses melting down the golden calf?"

Cam nodded. Astarte said, "He was angry that the Israelites were worshiping false idols."

"Precisely. Well, what Moses actually did was order that the calf be melted and the gold be ground into powder and put into the water. Then the people were forced to drink it."

"Drink the gold?" Cam asked. "Odd."

"And here's the other odd thing. Moses also ordered that the gold be baked into loaves of bread he called the 'Bread of God' or 'Bread of Heaven.' He put the bread into the Ark and they carried it around the desert with them for forty years. And guess who he ordered to do the baking?"

"His mother-in-law?"

She cuffed him lightly on the shoulder. "Bezaleel."

"But I thought he was a goldsmith," Astarte said from the back.

"Yes," Cam said. "With God as a client."

Amanda nodded. "He was. That's why it seems strange Moses was treating him like the kitchen help, ordering him to bake the bread."

Cam stared at the highway ahead. Unless there was something special about that bread....

Astarte liked living with Amanda and Cameron. But she didn't like them not letting her go to the Mormon church. And she didn't like them always trying to prove the Bible was wrong.

Astarte was happy to change the subject. "How many people live at the compound?" she asked as they drove towards it.

"About seventy or eighty," Amanda said.

"Are any of them children?"

"Yes. I think I counted twelve or thirteen."

"So anyone can move in there?"

"I believe so."

Cameron spoke. "The only requirement is that you have to agree to the rules of the compound and do your chores. So it's sort of like joining the army."

Astarte nodded. "So what are the jobs for the kids?"

Amanda said, "I saw some of the older ones helping with the food. And the younger ones worked in the garden and helped clean up after the meals."

"Is there a church inside the compound?"

"Not that I saw," Amanda said. "But I think many of the residents leave on Sundays to go to their churches."

"So it's not against the rules?"

"Of course not," Amanda said. When Astarte didn't ask any more questions Amanda turned to Cameron. "Say, Cam, if we're right about Bezaleel being a key to all this, then it stands to reason that the Templars would have made a big deal of him, right?"

Astarte sighed. Here they go again. She stared out the window and thought about Uncle Jefferson.

"I agree," Cam said. "Can you find anything tying the Templars to Bezaleel?"

"Give me a few minutes." She punched at her smartphone. Twenty years ago the research she and Cam were doing in an hour-long car ride would have necessitated a team of researchers visiting libraries scattered around the world. In many ways it was this explosion in technology that had allowed for so many breakthroughs in historical research.

"Okay," Amanda said, "I have something. I'll read it to you: 'Bezaleel bears a remarkable similarity to Azazel, one of the fallen angels who rebelled against God in the Book of Enoch.'"

"The Book of Enoch," Cam said. "Hmm." She and Cam had often come across the Book of Enoch in their research as it was an important part of Freemasonry.

She continued reading. "'Azazel released to humankind the secrets of metallurgy and the manufacture of jewelry—'"

"Sounds like Bezaleel, a goldsmith," Cam interrupted.

"'—and also taught women to be promiscuous and enjoy sex,'" Amanda whispered, glancing at Astarte in the back seat.

"Aha. Now you're talking."

"'For these transgressions God condemned Azazel to remain forever bound, hung upside down.'"

"Can't be having women enjoying sex," Cam said.

"At least not in a patriarchal church," Amanda responded. "So there's more: 'The only known statue of Azazel is in the choir area of Rosslyn Chapel, in Scotland.'"

Cam grinned. "You're kidding."

"Nope." Again, through their prior research Amanda and Cam knew all about Rosslyn Chapel. Purportedly a Christian house of prayer, it was in reality a monument to Freemasonry, paganism and worship of the Sacred Feminine. Not surprisingly, it was built by a family—the Sinclairs—with prominent historical ties to both the Templars and the Freemasons.

"That's perfect."

"Some people say he also taught women the art of witchcraft. Here's a picture of the statue; the official literature says the statue depicts Lucifer, but this website I'm on insists it's really Azazel." She angled her screen toward him.

CARVING OF AZAZEL, ROSSLYN CHAPEL

"Yup. Bound and hung upside down," Cam said. "So is it too big a stretch to say the Templars would have venerated this Azazel guy—or angel—not only because he built the Ark of the Covenant but because he was, well, a feminist? You know, teaching women to enjoy sex and wear makeup and all."

"I think that's fair. That was the big fight the Templars were having with the Church. They recognized the need for balance between the masculine and the feminine, both in the Church and in society as a whole." She paused. "And for our purposes I think we've figured out why Bezaleel is decorating our ark. It's another strong connection to the Templars."

Cam glanced again at the image of the statue from Rosslyn Chapel. "I just love that they put a statute of this angel in there. Talk about standing tall and giving the finger to the Church."

Willum met them at the front gate of the compound. Astarte waited in the car with Amanda while Cam and Ellis approached Willum.

"They accepted the deal," Ellis said. "Congratulations." He smiled. "Now the government won't blow up your compound."

Willum took a deep breath. "I'm afraid I've changed my mind. Deal's off. I'm not giving up the fuel cell."

"What?" Cam sputtered. "Why?"

Willum shrugged. "I thought about making some speech about not wanting to make the world a more dangerous place, about not wanting to be looked at like the guys who invented the nuclear bomb. But in the end it's simpler than that. I don't like the pricks at the Defense Department getting their way. Fuck them."

Ellis nodded, trying to act like he saw it coming all along. "So maybe they will blow up your compound after all."

Willum shrugged again and pointed his jaw toward the armed troops mulling around outside the gate. "I don't think there are many guys out there willing to murder their fellow Americans."

"Well," Ellis said, "for your sake I hope you're right."

Willum turned to Cam. "According to your friend here, I may be dead by morning. You owe me an explanation about the ark."

Cam nodded. He did owe him at least that.

Ellis hadn't expected Smoot to renege on their deal. It simply didn't fit his personality profile. From everything Ellis had read Smoot was risk-averse, apprehensive, even a bit meek. That was why he built this compound and retreated to it—he wanted to insulate himself from conflict. But now he was almost inviting it. It was almost as if he had undergone a personality transplant. Odd.

In any event, even though Ellis hadn't expected it didn't mean he wasn't
prepared for it.

He hopped into his car and pulled out a satellite phone. "Elder Bigelow," he said. "I'm calling about the matter we discussed earlier today. If you're free in, say, one hour, I can meet you at the hotel and show you the relic."

"And what about the girl?"

"I don't think she'll be available tonight. But we can discuss that matter as well."

Amanda wasn't comfortable bringing Astarte into the compound so she took the SUV and drove back into town for some dinner. Willum opened the gate for Cam to enter and the two of them walked the perimeter fence in the fading daylight, the pace slow to accommodate Cam's wound.

"Hey, I'm sorry if you think I lied to you," Cam said.

Willum shrugged. "Truth is the first casualty of war."

"But I'm not a soldier. And I'm trying to stop a war before it starts." He put his hand on Willum's shoulder. "Honestly, Amanda and I are just trying to help."

"Okay. Whatever."

They walked in silence. Every fifty feet or so a pair of armed National Guardsmen crouched, hunkered behind Plexiglas barricades on the other side of the electrified fence.

Willum gestured toward them. "What, they think we're going to start shooting at them?" He shook his head. "What a waste this all is."

Cam lowered his voice. "You really can't just give them the fuel cell and get this all over with?"

He sighed. "You know, if I thought it would, as you say, get this all over with, I'd do it. But our government is out of control. If they don't attack here, they'll attack somewhere else; if not me, some other imagined enemy. This country has to wake up and understand the government serves the people, not the other way around."

Cam nodded. He didn't agree, but then again nobody had thrown him into jail and took his son away and dropped a missile into his compound. So he understood where Willum was coming from.

"So," Willum said, "tell me what you've learned about our ark."

"Your ark."

Willum smiled. "For now, I think it'd be best if you kept it. If we put it into the compound it might end up as scrap metal."

Cam explained how they believed the arks—both the original and the replicas—were capacitors used to convert heavy metals, often contained in desert sand, to the white powder of gold. The powder in turn was then used as some kind of energy source to power the ark.

"Hmm." Willum stared out into the desert dusk for a few seconds. "Interesting."

"This goes back to the time of the Pharaohs. The Egyptian priests fed the white powder—they call it *mfkzt*—to the Pharaohs supposedly so they could communicate with their gods. Apparently the ancient Jews did the same thing."

"Fascinating. And you think the ark we found was made for the same purpose?"

"Yes. Again, the Jews are wandering the desert. Again, their leaders want to communicate with God. The Calalus leaders are part of the Levi tribe—the priests—so they know all the secrets of the ark and the white powder and how to handle the ark without getting electrocuted."

"You know, if the priests ate the white powder of gold, it might put them in some kind of resonance with the ark itself. That would allow them to approach and even touch it. I can explain the science to you if you'd like...."

Cam held up his hand. "No, no, I trust you. But it does explain how the priests could approach when others couldn't. Anyway, we found 'House of Levi' inscribed on one of the faces of the ark. Also a portrait of a guy named Bezaleel, the goldsmith who built the original Ark. I won't bore you with the details, but all this ties everything back to the Templars and the French noble families. It all fits."

Willum shook his head. "So the Templars really were here."

"Yes, they came looking for their Calalus ancestors. And they found the replica ark."

"And they probably died here. At least rough Hurech did. And the others left the ark for some lucky bastards like us to stumble upon." He clasped Cam's shoulder. "I might not live through the week, but I'm sure glad you solved this mystery for me." He smiled. "Now I won't have to haunt you from the grave."

Cam slowed as they approached another pair of soldiers. "Speaking of graves, are you sure it's okay to walk around in the open? What if they decide to take you down?" Cam had grown to like the paranoid Willum. And it wasn't even clear how paranoid he really was—maybe they really were out to get him.

Willum shrugged. "Not going to happen. At least not yet. I turned down their deal, so it's going to take a day or two of meetings in Washington to figure out what they want to do next."

"So what are *you* going to do?"

"Well, tonight I'm going to talk to my people. Clarisse is writing the speech now—I'm not very good at this kind of stuff."

"Mind if I stick around?"

"For good? Or just for the speech?"

Cam chuckled "Just the speech. Then I'll go back to the hotel." They walked in silence for a few seconds. "So you think this will go on for awhile?"

"Yes. Remember the story of Masada, where the Israelites held out in a mountain fortification against the Roman army for, like, six months? Well, that could be us."

"Eventually the Romans won, right?"

"Well, the Jews all committed suicide. So I guess you could call it a win."

"But they stayed true to their beliefs."

"Yes." Willum smiled. "Not just that—before they died they emptied the sewerage cisterns onto the Roman troops below."

"Ugly."

"Just one final 'fuck you' to the authorities before meeting their maker."

"You have something like that in mind?"

Willum bit his lip. "It's not nearly as ... aromatic. But not giving them the fuel cell makes me feel pretty good about myself."

With Smoot having rejected their deal, there was nothing for Georgia to do at the compound so she returned to the hotel.

The day had pretty much been a disaster. Amanda was angry at her over the visit to the Mormon church. And understandably so. But how do you say no to a scared little girl who begs you to let her go pray?

And with Smoot reneging on the deal the chances for a peaceful resolution at the compound had dimmed. Georgia had been amazed when Ellis had orchestrated the original deal—it had seemed too good to be true, and now it turned out that it was. The longer this went the more likely it would be that some trigger-happy redneck would give the order to fire. It only took one idiot to start a war.

She flicked on the television set in her room, ordered a burger from room service and found a bottle of wine in the mini bar. Unable to find a good movie, she settled on a cable news channel. A Survivalist from Idaho, a heavy-set woman with her hair pulled into a ponytail and her fleshy chin jutting out challengingly toward the camera, discussed the Casa Grande compound standoff. "This just shows how messed up our country is right now. If the people in that compound were illegal immigrants, the government wouldn't have bothered them. But instead they harass and intimidate and basically goad them into fighting back. Now an innocent woman is dead and who knows how many others will die also?"

The interviewer, a Ken-doll whose dark, tailored suit contrasted with his guest's threadbare floral blouse, asked, "So what are others in the Survivalist community doing?"

"You know, this has really mobilized us. One of the things that has really caught on is that thousands of people—many of them Survivalists, but also many other Americans who are just fed up—are taking steps to quit their jobs."

"Quit their jobs?"

Georgia leaned forward. How would that help?

"Well, it's like this. Our government is a hungry beast. Insatiable, in fact. And we feed it with tax revenue, right? Well, how are taxes in this country collected?"

"Income taxes and sales taxes, mostly," Ken-doll said.

"Exactly. So, for example, in our compound in Idaho we have thirty families living there—let's say fifty adults. We grow our own food, make our own clothes, etcetera. We are not totally self-sufficient, but nearly so. And when we need to buy anything, we go into town and barter. So cash almost never changes hand. None of us have an income, and we don't really buy anything."

"So you don't pay income tax or sales tax."

She showed a mouth of clean, crooked teeth. "Right. We call it going off the grid. Like I said, we have thirty adults. When we lived back in society, we each would have paid, maybe, ten thousand dollars a year in taxes. Now, we pay almost nothing. So just from our little compound we are denying the beast $300,000 per year. When you start to get tens of thousands of people doing the same thing, you're talking hundreds of millions of dollars in lost tax revenue."

"Do you really have that many people?"

"We didn't last week." She smiled again. "But we do now."

Clarisse gathered the residents in the picnic area and fed them burgers and mashed potatoes. She sent runners out to feed the sentries the same meal—no sense making people fend for themselves.

The plan was for Willum to address the residents at seven o'clock. The speech would be broadcast through the entire compound—not only could the sentries hear it but also the Guardsmen outside the fence. In many ways, the words Clarisse had written were intended for them.

Willum slowly eased himself off the picnic bench and, standing on a wooden platform, took the microphone and cleared his throat. "Good evening, good evening to my friends."

It was not a word used often within the compound or generally in the Survivalist community. Sure, friendships were made. But people generally thought of themselves as business associates or teammates.

"I believe we are at a crossroads. I believe America is at a crossroads. What happens here over the next few days and weeks will determine the course of history for our country." He paused and took a deep breath. Clarisse looked around—not a single eye was not on him. Willum was not normally a dynamic speaker, but the enormity of the situation seemed to have lifted him.

He continued. "Will our leaders call for an attack on American citizens? Will this country pursue a path that elevates the rights of the governing over the rights of the governed? Will this turn into Kent State or Waco or Ruby Ridge all over again?

"Over the past decade or so we have witnessed a fundamental change in the way our government sees itself. We have become a mirror-image of the old Soviet Union and China models, where the people exist to serve the state. Today, in America, our leaders do not believe they work for us—rather, they see themselves as queen bees, ensconced in Washington, while we workers devote our lives to paying taxes. We are nothing more than pollen collectors to them. And, if need be, we are disposable."

Willum spread his hands. "Well, I for one do not appreciate being a slave to my government. Or of being disposable. And I don't believe millions of other Americans like it either. As many of you know, they offered me a deal to end this standoff. But it required me giving them technology that would only strengthen their power over us." He shook his head. "I couldn't in good conscience do that. Just as I couldn't in good conscience give up Boonie to them."

Clarisse had been blind-sided by this decision. But she shouldn't have been—the looming danger had altered Willum's personality just as it had the others. He had become more idealistic, more spiritual, more messianic. The world in his eyes had become a palate of black and white, with little gray area in between. She shook her head—he had become the Moses-like figure she had pushed him to be.

He continued. "So now, tonight, I am making a choice. The leaders of this great country can push a button and wipe this compound off the face of the earth. We all know that. But if they do so, they are going to have to do so while millions of Americans bear witness." Willum smiled. "And I don't think they have the guts to do it!"

After the applause died down, Willum gave the compound residents a final chance to leave. The children had been evacuated earlier in the day, with some of their parents accompanying them. But none of the remaining adults chose to follow. Clarisse knew they wouldn't. Now she just had to hope Willum was right about the White House not having the guts to take them out.

Well, so much for getting that fuel cell peacefully. Ellis clicked the stop button on the video link, ending the clip of Smoot's speech at the compound. Smoot and his gang weren't coming out without a fight. And the problem with a fight is that it might destroy the fuel cell prototype. Smoot likely hadn't figured it out yet, but keeping that fuel cell was probably the only thing keeping him alive. But at some point the White House would value the President's falling opinion poll numbers more than the fuel cell—they couldn't let him continue to look weak indefinitely.

Ellis checked his watch. Almost seven o'clock. The Mormon Elder, Bigelow, was due to arrive any minute. They had probably an hour before Cam and Amanda returned to the hotel.

Flashing his badge, he got a key to the storage shed from the front desk. He hadn't quite figured out why the ark was radioactive, and in fact really didn't care. But that didn't mean he wanted his testicles to shrivel up. So when Elder Bigelow arrived, they took the elevator up to Ellis's room to step into Hazmat suits. Ellis wondered whether Bigelow wore the 'magic underwear,' the one-piece undergarments worn by observant Mormons.

Elder Bigelow really wasn't elderly—maybe early thirties. Tall, gangly and bespectacled, he parted his hair on the side like a school-kid from the 1950s and wore a light blue button-down shirt and a pair of khakis. No doubt he ate vanilla ice cream and maintained a meticulous lawn as well.

"I'm curious to see this artifact," he said, "but I'm also concerned about the girl. My daughter Naomi befriended her, and she tells me the girl is being kept away from our church."

A couple of people gave them funny looks as they walked through the rear parking lot in bright yellow suits. Ellis nodded. "It's really a sad story. She was raised Mormon by her uncle, who died. A young couple have temporary custody of her, but they have a … I guess you would call it disdain … for Mormonism. They won't let her attend or pray or contact her old teachers.

And from what I can tell the poor girl is really torn up by it. She feels like she's being forced into being a sinner."

"My daughter is about the same age. And I also have two older boys. Their lives revolve around our church. I can't imagine what this girl must be going through." He sighed. "God help her."

Because Bigelow was sweating in his suit, his glasses had slid down his nose so that he had to arch his neck back to look through the lenses. Dressed in yellow, knees bowlegged and chin pointed upwards, he looked like Chicken Little watching for a falling sky. Or perhaps a nervous Mormon awaiting the wrath of his angry God.

They put on their hoods and Ellis opened the shed. He allowed Bigelow to examine the ark for a few seconds before speaking. "Obviously, this is not the original Ark of the Covenant—the Latin inscription tells us that. But we think it may date back to the early centuries after Christ." He shined a flashlight on the Hebrew. "What do you think that says?"

Bigelow crouched. *"Beit ... Lehi."* His voice dropped and echoed inside the hood. "House of Lehi."

Ellis waited a few seconds before prompting. "Is that important?"

Bigelow dropped to his knees, his eyes glued to the inscription. Ellis leaned closer to hear. "Lehi is a Mormon prophet who came to America before the time of Christ. But his descendants would have been called the House of Lehi. If this is authentic, it might actually prove the Book of Mormon."

"Really," Ellis feigned.

"As God is my witness."

CHAPTER 8

Cam woke at six, rode the exercise bike in the hotel gym for a half-hour using only one leg, and returned in time to shower and join Amanda and Astarte for breakfast at the hotel buffet. Georgia would have contacted him had the situation flared at the compound overnight.

"I could get used to this fresh fruit every day," Amanda said.

"Me too," Cam responded. He turned to Astarte, expecting her to chime in as well, but she had been unusually quiet the past couple of days and it continued today.

Amanda filled the void. "We've been here for the better part of two weeks now. I think it's time to go home."

"What about the ark?" Cam asked.

She shrugged. "It belongs to Willum. I imagine he'll bring in some experts to test it—metallurgists, what have you."

"You're assuming he lives out the week."

Astarte interjected. "I don't want to go home yet. I made a friend at the Mormon church. Her name is Naomi. She invited me to come to her house tonight for Family Home Evening."

Amanda looked to Cam questioningly. "It's basically family night," he said. "They pray and play games together." He tried a smile. "No speaking in tongues, as far as I know."

Amanda didn't see the humor. She glared at Cam before turning back to Astarte. Pulling at her own fingers, she took a deep breath. "Cameron and I will discuss this. I understand you want to go, but we have some concerns."

"But I want to go." She folded her arms across her chest. "It's not fair you won't let me pray."

"I said we would talk about it. Now please finish your breakfast."

Astarte sat on a barstool in the hotel lobby, painting with water colors on an easel Georgia had bought her. Painting always seemed to calm her down—but today she found herself drawn to the grays and dark blues and blacks in the color palette.

"What are you painting?"

She looked up to see Flying Fox smiling down at her. She hadn't heard him approach. "A boat. In a storm."

"I see." He cocked his head. "I like the way you've made the sea so angry."

"I feel angry." She hadn't meant to say it.

He looked at her painting again. "Who's the man in the boat?"

She knew she wasn't supposed to talk to strangers, but Flying Fox worked with Georgia. And he was sort of like a policeman. "The prophet Lehi."

"Really?" He paused. "Say, did I hear you made friends with a girl named Naomi Bigelow?"

"Yes." How did Flying Fox know that?

"Her father was here last night looking at the ark. You mentioned the prophet Lehi—Elder Bigelow thinks that's one of the names carved on the side of the ark."

She knew it!

"He thinks it might help prove the Book of Mormon," he said.

Her teeth ground together and she steadied her hand as she painted the clouds. She was glad Mr. Bigelow agreed with her. But why didn't Cameron and Amanda listen to her in the first place?

Flying Fox seemed to sense her frustration. "It's tough being a kid sometimes. Adults always think they know what's right." He smiled again. "You know, usually they do."

"But not always."

He leaned against the back of an easy chair. "You're right, not always." He turned his palms up. "Just look at the situation at the compound—all the adults can't *all* be right, otherwise what would we be fighting about?" He watched her paint for a few seconds. "You've been to the compound, right?"

Astarte put her brush down. Her eyes began to water. "I've been there. But Amanda and Cameron won't let me go inside." Just like they wouldn't let her go to the Mormon church. Or to Naomi's house. Or listen to her opinion about the writing on the ark.

"Really, they wouldn't let you? They told me you were too afraid to go in."

She spun on the stool. "I am not afraid."

He shrugged. "Whatever. I'm heading out there now. I'm going to show Elder Bigelow and his daughter around. It's really neat inside those domes. There really is nothing to be scared of."

Wasn't he listening? "I ... am ... not ... afraid."

"Well, today is probably the last chance to see it. I think tomorrow the soldiers might take some action." He stood. "You know, there's nothing wrong with being scared."

She hopped off the stool. Why were grown-ups such bad listeners? "I would like to come with you." Suddenly her face felt very hot. But if Naomi was going, she should be able to go too.

He nodded and glanced at his watch. "Sure thing. But I'm running late." He motioned to her palette. "Leave your paints here; we won't be gone long. You can call Amanda from the car."

Astarte nodded. Good idea. If she asked permission, Amanda would just say no anyway.

Today she was making potato salad for lunch. As she was stirring in the mayo, a text arrived on her cell phone.

From Ellis Kincaid: "I am bringing a human shield. Be there in forty-five minutes. Put on your Mormon hat." What was this? And how did Kincaid even know she was Mormon? He seemed to enjoy keeping her off balance while at the same time trusting her instincts and intelligence to do the right thing. Or the thing he wanted her to do.

She left instructions for her kitchen staff to finish preparing the meal. Kincaid was not an ally, but for whatever reason his interests and objectives seemed to jibe with hers. She made sure

Willum was occupied in the rear of the complex, then strolled to the front gate to wait for Kincaid and whatever scheme he had cooked up this time.

"Oh my God, Cam," Amanda said, reading a text on her phone.

"What?"

"It's Astarte." She dropped into a chair. "She's with Ellis Kincaid. They're heading to the compound."

Stomach tightening, Cam swung open the door of the conference room. "She's supposed to be out in the lobby painting." He jogged down the hallway, ignoring the pain. Easel yes, Astarte no. *Son-of-a-bitch.*

Amanda pulled up behind him, her eyes wide with fear. "I can't believe she left without telling us."

"I think she's pissed at us."

"But still."

"I know." He flashed-back to his fall through the ice. "I'm going to kill that piece of shit if anything happens to her."

"What do you think he's up to?"

"I don't know. Can you call her cell?"

"I just tried. No service."

"Or he turned it off. And we can't reach anyone at the compound either." He stared out the front window of the lobby. "I'm going up to get our keys." He sprinted to the elevator and called over his shoulder. "We need to get out there."

As soon as Astarte sent her text to Amanda, Ellis flicked a switch on a box at his feet to jam further cell communication. He thought about blocking the initial text as well, but figured Thorne and Amanda would be less panicked if it looked like Astarte had accompanied him voluntarily. Once he got her inside the compound, it wouldn't really matter anymore.

Ellis knew he needed to keep the girl calm, so he asked her about her favorite desserts and toys and hobbies. He told her funny stories from his childhood—about the ice cream truck driver letting him hide in the freezer and then jumping out to scare the little kids; about persuading his friends to go swimming on a cold May day and then stealing their towels; about putting cracker crumbs in all the sleeping bags at his sister's sleep-over party.

"Why are all your stories about doing mean things to other people?" Astarte asked.

Ellis blinked. *Why indeed?* He changed the subject. "So did you ever have any pets?"

He half-listened as he drove, the compound now looming on the desert horizon. "Did you know that the woman who helps Willum Smoot run the compound is a Mormon?" he asked.

She shook her head.

"She is going to show us around. And I thought maybe also you could talk to her about the words carved on the ark. I know Cameron and Amanda are telling Mr. Smoot it says 'House of Levi.' But I think they should know that Elder Bigelow thinks it says 'House of Lehi' instead."

The girl nodded. "It does."

Clarisse met them outside the front gate. She wanted to get a better sense of things before opening their doors to a federal agent.

"So you must be Astarte," she said, smiling.

"Yes. Hello."

"You can call me Clarisse."

"That's a pretty name."

The girl looked like any other nine-year-old—pink leggings, sneakers, a floral short-sleeve shirt. But her cobalt eyes, framed by almond skin, were striking—she would be a beauty someday. "So I heard you want to see our compound."

"Yes. Is it true it looks like a flying saucer?"

"One of the buildings does, yes. The others are giant domes—it feels like we're living inside a basketball."

"Does it echo?"

Smart kid. "As a matter of fact, it does. And sometimes when you whisper in one corner of the dome you can hear it way on the other side."

Ellis stood off to the side, his auburn hair pushed down over his eyebrows, wearing his self-satisfied smirk. But he didn't seem to be a threat. At least no more than usual. "Okay, you want to come in?"

Astarte nodded.

"Follow me." The guard closed the gate behind them, the echo of metal-on-metal reminding her of some old 1950s prison movie. Clarisse motioned with her chin and a guard they called Rattler, a tightly-wound guy who had a fascination with snakes, followed a few feet behind, just to make sure Ellis behaved himself.

As they walked, Ellis spoke. "I was wondering, do any Mormons live here?" He gave Clarisse a quick look.

"Sure. In fact, I'm a Mormon."

Astarte looked up. "Do you hold worship services inside?"

"No. Members go to a meetinghouse in Casa Grande to pray. It's not far."

Ellis pulled out his phone and feigned reading a text—the girl didn't know there was no coverage. "Looks like Elder Bigelow and his daughter are running late." But the girl was too curious to really care.

They approached a dome. Clarisse pushed open a screen door. "You can go in. This is the women's pod, where the single women live. Just please don't touch anything."

Astarte tip-toed around the cots and hammocks, occasionally peering into one the tents. "So," Clarisse whispered, "what are you up to?"

"Like my email said, human shield."

She glanced at the girl. "You want me to keep her here against her will? Like a hostage?"

"If necessary, yes. Our story is that she asked to stay. Which she may actually do—she's upset they won't let her attend Mormon prayer services."

"I don't know. She's just an innocent kid."

"Look, this is getting serious. And she's not in any danger—no way will they attack with her in here. And she can leave tomorrow."

"What if she wants to leave tonight?"

Kincaid shrugged. "Once the gate is locked, she's not getting out unless you let her."

"Why her? What makes her a better shield than the other dozen kids who were living here?"

He looked around. "Well, for one thing, the other kids are gone. Plus it's personal with her and one of the lead agents."

"So maybe she buys us some time. But what for?"

"For you to steal the fuel cell."

"Why would I do that?" It actually wasn't a bad idea.

"Because if you can deliver that prototype, the government will back down." He tossed his head so his bangs didn't cover his eyes. "Think what a hero Willum will become in the Survivalist community. Standing up to the feds, forcing them to skulk away."

He was right. With a victory like that, Willum would become a legend. And when the collapse finally did come, he would be the natural choice to lead the people. The next Moses. But it wasn't that easy. "He'll know I took it," she sighed.

"So what. He almost gave it to us voluntarily. I bet in some ways he expects you to steal it—he needs to save face, but he also realizes it's the best resolution to all this. You'd just be doing what he expects his lieutenant to do."

"And if I don't agree?"

"I take the girl with me. And the troops move in tomorrow."

She nodded. "Well, then, I guess we have a deal."

Ellis slipped away while Clarisse was showing the girl around the compound and drove until he had cell coverage. He sent a text to Duck Boots requesting a call, as was their protocol. Ten minutes later his phone rang.

"You wanted to speak to me."

"Yes, sir. I need you to issue a new order," Ellis said. "Nobody gets in or out of the compound, effective immediately. Including children."

The man grunted. "What are you up to?"

"Horse-trading. We should have that fuel cell by tomorrow."

Another grunt. "About time."

Ellis pursed his lips. A couple of grunts was nothing compared to what he would have to face from Cameron Thorne and his fiancée.

Cam skidded to a stop on the shoulder of the road outside the compound gate. Somewhere inside was Astarte. He jumped from the car and strode toward the guard house. A soldier in a camouflage uniform carrying an M16 sprang from his post and intercepted Cam.

"I'm sorry, sir, this compound is locked down."

Amanda pushed up next to him, her face as pale as he had ever seen it. "We have clearance. You can check with your commanding officer." Cam gave their names.

The soldier motioned for a cohort to take his position while he radioed in the request. He returned in less than a minute. "I'm sorry. New orders. Nobody in or out. Straight from the White House."

"But our daughter is in there," Amanda pleaded.

The soldier's face softened. "I'm sorry, Ma'am. Those are my orders." Cam didn't know how the guard resisted her—Cam would have done anything to lessen the pain in her eyes.

Cam eyed the guard. "You said the orders were new. How new?"

He probably shouldn't answer. But he was human. "Ten minutes ago." He bit his lip. "I'm sorry. I saw the girl go in. She seemed okay."

Ten minutes. So somehow Ellis had gotten the White House to issue new orders instantly.

Cam peered past the guard, looking for a pair of black pigtails. Would they shoot him if he made a run for it? But even if he made the gate, it was locked. And Smoot wasn't there to open it for him. He sighed. "Come on, Amanda. I think we need to have a talk with Ellis Kincaid."

Alone in his hotel room, Ellis removed his golf shirt, slipped on a black Kevlar flak jacket and threw on a loose-fitting grey hoodie to hide the bulk underneath. He then pulled an unmarked pill bottle from a side pocket of his Dopp kit, opened the lid and popped four Percocets. He rarely took pain medication, especially something as strong as Percocet, but he knew he'd set himself up to take a beating when Thorne returned—flak jacket or not—and he wanted a head start on managing the pain. From his Dopp kit he also removed a dental retainer, rinsed it off and snapped it into place against his upper teeth—it might prevent a tooth or two from getting knocked out. Finally, he emptied his bladder and his bowels in the toilet; getting knocked cold is no fun, but it's even less pleasant when you wake up soaked in your own urine and feces.

Ellis didn't look forward to the next couple of hours, but understood it was part of the job—sort of the way a boxer knew that, win or lose, champion or bum, he'd be in agony for days just from entering the ring. Ellis was well-trained, in decent shape and about the same size as Thorne, but in order for this to work he needed to let his adversary vent a little anger and exact a little revenge.

Not that he blamed Thorne—he had it coming to him.

Cam raced toward the hotel. Almost as bad as the thought of Astarte held hostage in the compound was the wretchedness that oozed from Amanda's pores.

"Cam," she whispered. "Please pull over."

Before he fully skidded to a stop on the shoulder of the highway, she had opened her door and dropped to her knees. Her body heaved, chunks of breakfast and bile pooling beneath her. Cam jogged around the Explorer and held her hair away from her face.

"You okay?"

She shook her head. She heaved again, this time only a few drops of stomach juice dribbling down her chin. Cam had never seen her like this.

After another dry heave, she sniffled, wiped her chin on the shoulder of her blouse and allowed Cam to pull her to her feet. He tried to embrace her, but she stiffened and pushed him away. "I will never forgive myself if anything happens to her, Cam."

"Nothing's going to happen," he responded, both of them knowing he had no way of knowing for sure.

Ten minutes later he skidded to a stop at the Tucson hotel. He jumped from the vehicle, surprised to see Ellis Kincaid leaning against a planter near the hotel entrance.

Their eyes met and Kincaid walked toward them, his hands raised in front of him in a sign of surrender. "Just hear me out. I know you're pissed, and I don't blame you. But the girl wanted to stay at the compound." Ellis stopped ten feet away. Close enough to be heard but out of Cam's immediate range. "She wouldn't leave with me. When Clarisse saw Astarte wanted to stay, she had the guards throw me out."

What? "You're lying," Cam said. Amanda sagged and gasped, steadying herself against the door.

"No," the agent responded. "She said you hated Mormons. Said you won't let her go to Mormon prayer services. Said you're forcing her to live a life of sin."

Cam's eyes blurred. "So you left a nine-year-old-girl in a goddamn war zone?" He rushed at Ellis and sunk his fist into the agent's midsection. As Kincaid doubled over, Cam lifted him and threw him against the back of the SUV, the agent's head smacking back against the vehicle's roof. Cam was about to punch him again when Amanda called out.

"Stop, Cam!" She rushed over and wedged her body between the men. "He's right. This is our fault. My fault. I drove her away." She sobbed and turned toward Kincaid. "This … maggot … just happened to be in the right place at the right time."

Cam pushed past Amanda and wrenched Kincaid's arm behind his back, holding him firm. "I don't think it's that simple. I don't think it's a coincidence he just happened to be going to the compound."

The agent nodded. "You're right," he gasped. "I wanted Astarte's help trying to understand what was so important about that ark of yours. When she said she wanted to see the compound, I figured the car ride would be a good chance to pick her brain."

"Pick the brain of a nine-year-old?" Cam hissed.

"She knows a hell of a lot more about the Book of Mormon than I do. She explained the House of Lehi carving to me."

Cam clenched his teeth. "It's House of *Levi*, asshole!" He shoved Kincaid against the SUV again, his face squishing against the rear window.

"If you say so." Kincaid grimaced, his teeth reddened by a split lip. "But that's not what Astarte thinks."

Cam burst into the hotel conference room, interrupting a meeting between Georgia and a handful of white shirts. "Your piece of shit agent kidnapped Astarte and left her at the compound."

"What?"

"You heard me."

Her face blanching, she nodded to the group. "Please give me a minute."

She reached for Cam's arm to guide him out of the room but he shrugged her off.

"You said you could control him," Amanda said.

She stared back at Amanda, then at Cam, her eyes wide and sad. "I'm sorry." She sighed. "What can I do?"

"Use your satellite phone," Cam said. "Get Willum on the line."

She nodded. "Come to my room."

Twenty minutes passed, presumably while someone at the compound persuaded Willum to take the call. "Cam, what the fuck is Astarte doing here?"

"Is she okay?" Amanda leaned in close to Cam to listen.

"She's fine, she's with Clarisse. But I have no idea why she's here."

"Me neither," Cam said.

"Clarisse says she refused to leave. Started crying and howling and whatnot. Something about you guys making her live a life of sin."

So Ellis was telling the truth. Amanda's eyes pooled and Cam bit his lip. "Yeah, well, it's not quite as simple as that," Cam said.

"Listen, Cam, I hear you; I'm a parent also. And I don't want her here either. Maybe Clarisse shouldn't have let her stay in the first place, but I'm not sure how we get her out. You need to convince the feds to give her passage."

Cam relayed Willum's request to Georgia. "Can you do that, at least?"

She shook her head slowly. "While you were waiting for Willum I called my boss. He just texted back. They won't reverse the lockdown order."

Amanda slapped the desk. "Damn it, Georgia! Do you have any power at all?"

The older woman sighed. "Apparently not. I don't know what's going on here. Honestly. But whatever it is, I'm not a part of it. None of this makes sense." She jabbed at the speaker button on the phone before slumping onto the bed.

Cam spoke into the speaker. "What about the tunnel? Can I sneak in there and bring her out that way?"

"No. That worked the first day, but they figured it out pretty quick. They blocked it."

"So there's no way to get her out?"

"I suppose we could just open the gate and push her out."

Georgia interjected. "I wouldn't try that. The orders are that anyone who opens that gate is to be shot."

"Would they really do that?" Amanda asked.

Georgia shrugged. "Who knows these days? It just takes one yahoo with an itchy finger. And my guess is that Willum's men will return fire."

Willum grunted. "Ten-four on that. My guys aren't getting much sleep. Fingers are getting twitchy, not just itchy."

"And then Astarte will be in the middle of it," Cam said.

"Listen, Cam, I sent the kids away for a reason." Willum lowered his voice. "I can't protect her if the shit hits the fan."

Amanda asked, "Can you put her on the line?"

"Sorry. She's on the other side of the compound with Clarisse. I think they're getting eggs from the chickens—they're making cupcakes for dessert. You know, just trying to do normal stuff."

Amanda sagged against Cam's chest. "Okay," Cam said. "I guess the last thing we want to do is panic her. Tell her we called and we'll call again in the morning."

"What's that stuff you put into the frosting?" Astarte asked.

Clarisse avoided her gaze. "Just some cinnamon powder to add a little extra flavor." She forced a smile. "It's an old Mormon recipe my grandmother taught me."

"It doesn't look like cinnamon," Astarte said innocently.

"It's organic; we grew it here," Clarisse answered. A few other women were outside grilling burgers and dogs for tonight's dinner.

"When are Amanda and Cameron coming to pick me up?"

"I think after dinner. Mr. Smoot just talked to them. But he said there's a chance they might not be able to come back for you tonight. So would you mind sleeping here? You can stay in my tent with me."

The girl frowned. "I suppose that would be okay." She stirred the cupcake batter. "But I was supposed to go to Naomi's house for Family Home Evening."

Clarisse smiled. "I remember those nights." It was one of her few happy childhood memories. She was probably five or six, even younger than Astarte, and she would sit around the kitchen table with her mom, dad and older brother and play board games. Candy Land, Chutes and Ladders, Mousetrap. A year or two later her father ran off with the Avon Lady and that was the end of their family as well as Family Home Evening. "We could play some games if you want. I have cards. Do you like Crazy Eights?"

Astarte nodded. "I should warn you, I don't often lose."

"Perhaps we should play for money," Clarisse said.

"I don't have any money," the girl said, her face serious. "But we could play that the winner gets to have her toe nails painted by the loser."

Clarisse put out her hand. "It's a bet."

It had been many days since anyone at the compound paid much attention to personal grooming. Which reminded Clarisse, she needed to shower at some point if she was going to implement her plan—join Willum in his bed, wear him out with a few beers followed by sex, then sneak into his lab to steal the fuel cell. Not very sophisticated, but why make things more complicated than they needed to be? But now it looked like, in addition to a shower, she also needed an overnight body-double. She couldn't really leave Astarte alone in her tent—the last thing she needed was for the girl to wake up and wander around the compound in the middle of the night. And she obviously couldn't bring the girl to Willum's tent. She shook her head. Even for the Mormons, nine was too young.

Willum had the haunting feeling that he was being manipulated, pulled by puppet strings by some unseen set of hands. The girl showing up at the compound was just the latest example—how had this come about, how did his armed, besieged fortress end up hosting a sleep-over for a nine-year-old girl? It just didn't seem to be the way the world usually worked.

As he had for the past four nights, he sat at the picnic tables and shared a communal meal with his fellow compound residents. Not much had changed. Once again the warm, clear desert day had turned into a cool, clear desert night; weary compound residents eyed the perimeter fences as they ate; Boonie stuck by him like a flea on a dog—it was like that *Groundhog Day* movie with Bill Murray.

The only real difference was the girl. She sat with Clarisse, playing cards. Willum had never seen Clarisse interact with children—he was surprised to see her joyful and even a bit carefree. Clarisse had always struck him as one of those people who had been born with the soul of an adult. For a few seconds he indulged in a fantasy of marrying and having children with his lieutenant, but the thought evaporated in the echo of a military truck repositioning itself outside the compound fence. Hard to think about the future when the odds were long that you would survive the week.

Clarisse poured the milk into a coffee mug, ground the Ambien into powder using the butt end of a knife and added half of it to the beverage. "My mother always gave me warm milk before bed." She stuck the mug into the microwave.

Astarte sat atop a sleeping bad inside Clarisse's tent. She wore one of Clarisse's tee shirts as a nightgown. "I've never had warm milk."

"Really? It's a Mormon tradition."

"Like the cinnamon in the cupcakes?"

Sure, why not. "Exactly." She remembered hearing something about the girl being raised by her uncle, but Clarisse didn't have time for that now. She handed the girl the milk. "Drink up. Then you can read for a bit before going to bed."

"Can we talk instead? I want you to tell me more about the Mormon traditions." She paused. "Especially the things your mother did."

Clarisse sighed. This was not part of the plan. And reliving her childhood was making her a bit melancholy herself. But the girl would be out cold within minutes if the warning on the Ambien label was correct; it was not meant for children, and crushing the pill caused it to enter the bloodstream faster. So even half a pill should knock her out. "Well, I remember on Sundays we always sang on the car rides home from church. It was the only time I remember Dad singing." She wouldn't have spoken the next words to an adult. "There was love in the car. It was nice."

Astarte yawned. "It sounds fun. Do you like to sing?"

Smiling, Clarisse shook her head. "I have a bad voice. But I'm great in the shower."

"What kind of songs?" She lay back on her pillow.

"Well, my dad's favorite was *Camptown Races*. After we'd sing it the regular way, there were special Mormon words he had for it, something about Brigham Young making a stand and sweeping his enemies from the land." She hadn't thought about this in decades.

Astarte yawned again. "My uncle sings that song also."

"Do you want to sing it now?" Clarisse sat at the foot of Astarte's sleeping bag. "Astarte? Are you awake?"

She moved closer. Nothing except the steady breathing of a sleeping child. Clarisse was surprised she felt so disappointed. She was actually looking forward to singing a few songs with the girl.

"All right, that's enough." Clarisse had found Willum up in a sniper's nest atop one of the domes. "You've been awake for, like, a week. Time for bed."

He smiled at her, the bags under his eyes reminding her of the eye black her brother used to wear when he played high school football. "I'm good. Really."

She leaned closer so the guard on duty couldn't hear. "I have a six-pack of Corona on ice. And I was thinking, if the feds attack tomorrow I'd really like to get laid tonight." She flicked her tongue against his earlobe. "I can ask around if you're too busy...."

Willum grinned. "Randy," he said to the guard. "You're on your own for a while."

He stood and took her hand. As they descended the ladder down the side of the pod, he called up to her. "What I wanted to say was, 'Randy, I'm feeling randy.' But I resisted."

"What, did you think you'd offend me?"

"No. But it didn't seem fair to leave him up there alone with thoughts of me getting lucky while he was stuck on guard duty."

She knew he was peering up the leg of her cargo shorts as she descended. "Maybe if you don't do the job I'll come back up and give him a go also."

Amanda tried to keep busy reading more about the Ark of the Covenant—but her mind kept wandering to thoughts of Astarte so she gave in and rented *Raiders of the Lost Ark* from the hotel on-demand system. Cam didn't even made a pretense of trying to be productive—he went to the hotel gym an hour ago with a large bottle of water and some headphones.

She was glad for the alone time. Cam hadn't come right out and said it, but they both heard his words nonetheless: It was Amanda that sparked this crisis. Her refusal to allow Astarte to be part of the Mormon community had pushed the girl into Ellis's car. Had it been up to Cam, he would have been more accommodating. Recently, not far from their house, a distracted father with a toddler in the car had run a stop sign. A box truck rammed them, tragically killing the child. Obviously the father hadn't intended his child to die, but how would the mother react? Could their marriage survive? Would the combination of his guilt and her resentment be fatal to their relationship as well? It had been something Amanda thought about often when the accident occurred. Now, with Astarte in danger, she couldn't help but wonder whether she and Cam could survive if anything happened to Astarte.

At least, according to Willum, Astarte was safe. The worst had been the thought of her alone in the car with the creepy Ellis. It was incredibly frustrating that the feds insisted on keeping the gates locked—how hard would it have been to make an exception for a young girl? But Amanda took some solace: Those same gates kept Ellis safely away from Astarte.

She glanced at the clock radio on the night table. Just past ten o'clock. By now Astarte would be asleep, probably enjoying the adventure of spending the night in a tent inside one of the domes.

Just as the Nazis were getting zapped by the Ark, Cam's key card interrupted her musings. "Heard anything yet?" he asked.

"Nothing. How was your workout?"

"Rode the bike for an hour. Didn't get anywhere."

"Been one of those days."

He looked at his watch. "You thinking what I'm thinking?"

She smiled. "As soon as you're out of the shower, I'm ready."

"We probably won't be able to even get to the gate."

"Well, it's better than sitting here all night worrying about her."

He shook his head and sighed. "And I thought the worst would be when she's a teenager out on a date."

Cam and Amanda sat in the SUV, parked a hundred yards down the highway from the compound gate. They had tried to edge closer but a soldier turned them away.

They sat in the dark, staring at the high concrete wall surrounding the compound. Cam felt helpless—Astarte was on the other side of the wall, perhaps frightened and lonely, and he couldn't do a damn thing about it.

"I know this is my fault," Amanda said.

"No it's not. It's Ellis's."

She shook her head. "Astarte wouldn't have gone with him if she wasn't so ... desperate ... to reconnect with her religion."

Cam took her hand. "You were just trying to do the right thing."

"But I took it too far."

He shrugged. "Maybe. Maybe not. If I really disagreed with you, I would have fought you harder on it."

"It's just, I can't bring myself to see Astarte be fed all that ... rubbish ... about women being inferior to men."

"You know, all religions have archaic beliefs. The Jews call themselves the 'Chosen People'—well, does that mean they think they're superior to everyone else? Looking at it from the outside, you could see why people would be concerned it does. But the Jews I know don't feel that way." He smiled. "At least no more so than any other group of people."

"That's not the same thing at all. I would have no problem with the Mormons teaching Astarte that women were *superior*."

"Fair point. Maybe a better analogy is the whole original sin idea taught in the Catholic Church. Or better yet, the story of Lilith—God makes her a demon because she won't let Adam always be on top during sex. Then he makes Eve, who is supposed to be all obedient. That's a pretty misogynistic message. But there are plenty of Christian women who are strong and assertive."

"Sure, it happens. People can rise above their teachings. But what about all the little girls out there who hear those stories and buy into all that sexist poppycock?" She slapped her thighs with her fists. "They end up cowering in some corner, afraid their drunk husband is going to beat them." She sniffled. "I know," she whispered, "my Mum was one of them."

Cam reached over and squeezed her shoulder. "I know. I understand." He kissed her head. "And I'm not saying you're not right to be concerned about this. But by shielding Astarte from all this chauvinism, we've also taken away some stuff that's pretty important to her. She's lost her family already. I think it's hard for us to ask her to walk away from her faith also."

Amanda nodded. "I get that now. I do." She swallowed a sob. "I just hope it's not too late."

They sat in silence for half a minute, Cam stroking her hair. She sighed, blew her nose and smiled through reddened eyes. "Enough of that. I have some movies we could watch. Or at least try. Maybe distract ourselves a bit."

Cam smiled. "Sort of like the drive-in. Did you bring any popcorn?"

"Sorry, only a couple of granola bars."

"A movie sounds good. I'm not sure what else we can do." He opened his door. "Might as well get comfortable." He slid into the backseat and waited for her to join him.

She opened her door, slid up against him and smiled sadly. "We're in the back seat, out in the desert, in the middle of the night. And neither one of us has an amorous thought in our body. This raising kids thing is tough."

Maybe it was the sense of looming danger outside the compound fence, or maybe the need to wear Willum out so she could steal the fuel cell, or maybe the kick of adrenaline as her body prepared for the heist. Whatever the cause, the sex with Willum was the best it had ever been. Round one ended fairly quickly in a desperate, almost-violent coupling, but round two was more ballet than boxing match. Though he moved one way and she another, their bodies in rhythmic concert, they remained permanently joined at the pelvis like a pinwheel spinning on a

244 *David S. Brody*

stick. Finally they climaxed a second time and the sounds and smells of the night slowly refilled his tent.

"That was amazing," Willum breathed. "I'm ready to die now."

Clarisse propped herself up on one elbow. "Not bad." She kissed him lightly. "I guess old Randy is on his own up there."

He sighed and closed his eyes. "I'm really beat."

"You sleep, darling." She never called him that. "I'll take care of the compound." She shifted her weight, the movement confirming to him what she said. "Sleep. You need it." She kissed him again on the forehead. "I'll let myself out."

She waited a few minutes, rolled out of the tent and puttered around for another ten until she heard him begin to snore. Snoring usually occurred during a deep sleep cycle, so now was her chance.

She pulled an insulated lunch bag from her backpack. Inside was a dead but still-warm tabby cat she had poisoned earlier in the day. Illuminating her way with a small flashlight, she found the hatch, climbed down the ladder and tossed the cat against one wall of the passageway. If Willum happened to awake, her story would be that she heard a cat screaming, came down to investigate, discovered a rattlesnake slithering away from the cat into the laboratory, and followed the snake to try to kill it. Not a great story, but Willum would have no reason to doubt it.

She flicked on the light to the lab. Where would he keep the prototype? Paranoid as he was, he probably hid it away. She looked for a safe or even a locked file cabinet but found nothing. As she wandered to the back corner of the lab, she spotted a six-sided glass box the size of a small fish tank—inside the glass walls sat a shiny cube of metal with tubes and wires running from it. There it was, just sitting on a workbench.

She reached down and began to lift it, thinking to herself how odd it was that he hadn't hidden it. Something caught as she pulled up, as if the fuel cell had been connected to the table with putty.

A flash of light blinded her as a burst of furnace air threw her across the room. She flew through the air for what seemed like many seconds, surprised that her thoughts had turned to

Astarte. Would the girl be frightened when she awoke, alone? Clarisse waited, suspended above the ground, floating and dreamlike, expecting any moment to crash to the floor. And then she realized she never would.

Willum stumbled to his feet, disoriented. Had the earthquake occurred in his sleep or for real? Voices yelled outside, alarmed. So it had been real. He replayed his dream—he had been walking in the desert and the ground began to shake beneath him. Beneath him. *The laboratory.*

Fumbling for his glasses, he stepped into his slippers, flicked on a light and found the hatch. As he lifted it, a wave of acrid smoke blew over him. He lifted his t-shirt shirt over his mouth and nose and, waving the smoke away, descended the ladder and pushed his way into the lab. He flicked at a light switch but nothing happened—the explosion must have knocked out the lights. Stumbling in the dark, his foot stubbed against a body. An icy fist squeezed his heart. He dropped to a knee and probed the body, his hand dipping into warm, sticky blood. The smell of charred flesh penetrated his shirt and filled his nostrils; he swallowed back a sour gag. He found a head, covered by thick hair. Using his watch, he illuminated the face. *Clarisse.* Hand shaking, he felt for a pulse. Nothing. Gasping and coughing, he retreated from the lab to find some fresh air. He hoisted himself up the ladder, closed the hatch, pounded the wall and vomited. Dropping to the floor, he began to sob. She had just shared his bed, called him darling. Was it all a ruse? Or was it possible she had a legit reason for being in the lab?

A few seconds later his body froze, his sadness turning to dread. There wasn't any white powder of gold inside the fuel cell prototype—it was a fake, just in case the feds stormed the compound. The real one was locked away in a safe; Willum planned to take it with him if he needed to flee. But there was a half-gallon jug of the powder he had produced for future experimentation stored in a lead chest nearby. If the explosion blew open the chest....

A fist pounded on the door, jarring him out of his stupor. He opened it to Boonie. "What's going on, boss?"

"It was Clarisse. I think she was trying to take the fuel cell."

Boonie looked at him blankly.

"I booby-trapped it so the feds wouldn't get it if they stormed the compound." It had never occurred to him that one of the residents would try to take it. Especially Clarisse. "She's dead."

Something almost like anger passed across Boonie's face, but Willum didn't pay much attention to it. "We need to get everyone away from here. That explosion may be releasing radioactive particles into the air."

Sprinting through the compound, Willum banged on the pod doors, rousing the residents. The night wind blew steadily across the desert. His Geiger counter read increasing, but still safe, levels of radiation. The explosion was likely the equivalent of a dirty bomb—anyone in close proximity could be exposed to potentially-lethal levels of radiation. A dirty bomb's reach was limited, but that was small comfort to those in its direct path. Including himself.

"Everyone, move to the back side of the complex," he yelled. Unlike in the mountains, the wind here often blew east to west, pushing the radiation toward the front gates. He opened the supply pod and pointed at a dozen hazmat suits hanging along one wall. "Rattler, get some help and distribute these suits to the guards."

He barged into the bath house, tore off his clothes and slippers and stuffed them into a plastic garbage bag. He turned the water as hot as he could stand it and stepped into the shower, scrubbing his skin, hair and beard with his fingernails and an abrasive loofa brush. He felt incredibly selfish doing so, but on the other hand his clothes and skin were covered with radioactive particles—he had become a lethal weapon himself.

After scrubbing his skin raw, he jogged toward the front gate, wearing only a towel and waving his arms. "Listen to me," he called to the soldiers. "We've had a radiation leak."

A young sergeant stepped forward, smirking, his eyes on Willum's ample white belly. "What, do you think we're nine years old?"

Astarte. Was she still in Clarisse's pod? Willum turned. "Do what you want. But don't blame me when your dick shrivels up and falls off." He ran toward Clarisse's dome, the towel barely covering his own dick. "Has anyone seen the girl?" he yelled. Why hadn't she woken up?

Cam sprinted from the SUV, the echo of the explosion rolling across the desert still fresh in his ears. Yelling from inside the compound mirrored the chaos of the soldiers near the front gate. He angled toward the friendly soldier he and Amanda had spoken with earlier. "What's going on?"

"Explosion inside. Maybe also a radiation leak. We're all pulling back—wind is blowing this way."

Amanda had matched his stride. "Our daughter is in there."

"I know."

"I'm going in," Cam said.

The soldier shrugged. "Do what you have to do. I'm not going to stop you."

"I'm going too," Amanda said.

Cam put a hand on her shoulder. "Please, please don't come. We need your ovaries. Go back to the car. I'll find her." He kissed her quickly and handed her the keys. "Seriously, get back."

He turned and ran to the gate, shouting. "I need to get in. Open the gate!"

A guard recognized Cam and the gate latch clicked open. Cam pushed through. "Are those Hazmat suits?"

The guard nodded.

Cam didn't ask permission. He grabbed the top one, kicked off his shoes and began to pull the yellow rubberized suit on. "Which dome is Clarisse's?" he asked.

"Middle one."

"Thanks." Cam slipped on the hood, snapped it in place and ran toward the cluster of domes as fast as the bulky outfit and his injured leg allowed.   Most of the compound residents were fleeing toward the back of the compound but Cam noticed Willum's hulking form moving through the mass, giving orders. He saw Cam running toward him and raised his rifle. "Identify yourself," he commanded.

Cam stopped. "It's Cam Thorne." His voice echoed inside the hood. "I'm here to get Astarte."

Dressed only in a pair of ill-fitting shorts, Willum nodded and lowered his gun. "Nobody's seen her. I was just going to check Clarisse's tent. Follow me."

Cam spoke as they jogged, Willum's belly bouncing. "Did the explosion release the radiation?"

Willum nodded.

"Where was it?"

"In my lab." He jerked his chin over his shoulder. "Under the saucer."

"Shouldn't you be wearing a Hazmat suit?"

"I got a heavy dose already when I went into the lab."

Cam stopped. "Shouldn't you get some treatment?"

Willum shrugged. "Not much they can do for it. Come on."

At least they were upwind of it now. Willum pushed open the pod door and flicked on a floor lamp near the entrance. A couple of dozen tents along with a few hammocks were scattered around the perimeter of the dome; a few couches, a television set and a couple of picnic tables helped fill the vast space in the center of the room. "Clarisse's tent was over here." Willum cut across to the far corner. "This one."

Cam pushed open the flap and dropped to one knee. "Astarte? Astarte?"

No response. Where else could she be? Struggling inside his suit, and now sweating profusely, he crawled through the opening. A clump of blankets piled in the back corner of the tent caught his eye. Could she be sleeping through the commotion? He pulled the top blanket aside. His shoulders slumped. Nothing.

Cam and Willum spent the next hour searching the compound but could not find Astarte. Nobody had seen her since she said goodnight and joined Clarisse in her tent.

Gathered in the back of the compound with the other residents, Cam removed his hood. He gulped some water and toweled the sweat off his face. "The one place we haven't looked is your laboratory," he said to Willum. "Is it possible she was in there with Clarisse?" The possibility hit him like a fist to the gut; he reached for a tree to steady himself.

Willum bit his lip. "I suppose it's possible. It was pretty smoky in there and I couldn't see much."

"I'm going in."

"Give me a minute to put on a Hazmat suit. I'll come with you."

Ten minutes later, flashlights in hand, Willum led Cam into his saucer.

Cam said, "It's really smoky in here."

"Good. The saucer is containing the radiation."

The suits they wore contained respirators, but they wouldn't protect against high levels of radiation. Willum held the Geiger counter out in front of him as he walked to the hatch. Cam crouched to lift it. "Careful when you open the hatch," he said to Cam, his voice echoing. "If there's anything smoldering down there, the oxygen will ignite it."

Cam nodded. He opened the hatch an inch and waited a few seconds. Nothing. He opened it further and waited for Willum to get a reading from the Geiger counter. Willum nodded and Cam, using his flashlight to guide the way, descended the ladder. Thin gray smoke filled the passageway; despite the respirator, Cam could taste ash as he breathed. Willum joined him at the bottom of the ladder and again read from the clicking Geiger counter.

"It's getting higher. We don't want to stay down here any longer than we have to."

At the entrance to the lab Willum took a final reading. "Steady. But no more than five minutes."

One walking clockwise and the other counter-clockwise, they circled the lab, their flashlights arcing back and forth. Cam was looking for Astarte, in fact desperate to find her. But the last thing he wanted to do was actually find her. Not here, not like this. They met in the middle of the room. "Anything?" Cam asked.

Willum shook his head. "No. And all the closets are locked. She's not here."

Cam surveyed the room once more with his flashlight, looking for any clue. Nothing. "Okay."

Willum bent over Clarisse's mangled body. "Can you give me a hand?"

Cam nodded. They couldn't leave Clarisse here. He moved around to grab her under the armpits.

A sob erupted from Willum's hood. "I killed her. I booby-trapped the fuel cell."

Cam clasped his shoulder. "That sounds like blaming the victim. She was stealing from you."

Willum shook his head. "And it wasn't even the real prototype. That one's locked away."

Cam bent down to help with the body.

"Wait," Willum said as they began to lift. A Ziploc bag partly protruded from one of the pockets in her cargo shorts. He pulled it out.

"What is it?"

"It's the white powder of gold."

"Was she stealing it, along with the fuel cell?"

Willum shook his head. "No. This bag went missing about a week ago. I thought I just misplaced it."

"Well, what was she doing with it?"

Willum stared at Clarisse's body. "I have no idea."

Cam and Willum wrapped Clarisse's body in a sheet and carried it to a locked storage room in a remote corner of compound. They spent another hour searching the compound for Astarte. Finally, exhausted from the exertion and heat created inside the Hazmat suits, they retreated to the rear of the compound with the other residents, who had made a fire and set up some tents.

As Willum addressed the residents, Cam gulped some water and poured the rest over his head. "Any updates?" Willum asked.

A few men looked at each other, apparently unsure of how the chain of command fell now that Clarisse was dead. Finally Rattler stepped forward. "The army pulled back for awhile, but now they are redeploying, using soldiers in Hazmat suites. But they've allowed us to open the gates. Anyone who wants to leave can."

"Okay. Spread the word. People can leave if they want. But tell the guards to be alert. This kind of chaos is a great chance for them to attack."

Rattler nodded. "They say they have a Hazmat team ready to come in. I refused to open the gate."

"Good. How are the radiation levels?"

"Beginning to fall."

Willum exhaled. "Anyone seen the girl?"

"No."

"Why aren't we using the bunker?"

"According to Boonie, it collapsed from the explosion. I think it was built to withstand a hit from above, but not from the side."

Willum nodded. "We'll need to shore that up." He glanced at Cam. "Fully-stocked bunker, with food and cots and running water and a generator, and we're out here getting zapped by radiation. So much for great planning."

Willum turned back to Rattler. "Speaking of Boonie, where is he?"

Rattler shrugged. "Last I saw he was helping hand out the bunny suits to the guards."

"Okay." Willum checked his watch. "It's almost three now. We'll camp out here for the night. Rotate the guards every hour—it's hot as hell in those suits. In the morning we'll look for the girl again."

Cam couldn't really argue—Willum had other things to think about besides Astarte. "I'm going to keep looking if you're okay with that."

Willum nodded again. "Of course."

"But first I better give Amanda an update. Can you let the guards know I want to talk to her through the gate?"

Astarte woke up in a dark room. She still felt very tired, like her body had sunk deep into her mattress. But she wasn't on a mattress.

She fought to remember where she was—not home in Westford, and not in a hotel. It came to her—in the dome with Miss Clarisse. She reached up, her arm heavy, expecting to feel the tent above her. But there was only air. She couldn't see much, but it didn't feel big and airy like the dome she fell asleep in. And it smelled like a basement.

"Miss Clarisse?" she whispered. "Are you there?"

A flashlight flicked on, its beam shining right in her eyes. A man's voice: "Don't be frightened."

Astarte gasped. She held her hand up to shield her eyes. "Who are you?"

"My name does not matter. I won't hurt you as long as you do as I say."

"Where is Miss Clarisse?" She knew she had to be brave. Like the princesses in the movies.

"I'm going to leave now. When I do, I'll turn a light on for you. There's some food and juice here for you." She didn't recognize the voice. "I'll be back in a few hours. Don't try to yell—nobody can hear you."

Astarte heard a door open, then close. A light came on as the man promised. She looked around—she was in a bathroom.

The cot she was on had been wedged into the bathtub; a tray with her breakfast rested on the sink near the door.

Climbing out of the tub, she walked to the door. She knew it would be locked, but she tried anyway. And there were no windows in the room either. She collapsed onto the toilet and eyed the food, her eyes pooling with tears. She should be hungry. But she was too scared to even try to eat.

Cam staggered through the front gate just before dawn. He had searched the entire compound but couldn't find any sign of Astarte.

The explosion and radiation leak had, apparently, resulted in a change of orders. The lockdown had ended and compound residents who wished to leave were being ushered directly into a decontamination tent. Cam allowed himself to be hosed down and examined by a young medic.

"Looks like that bunny suit worked well. I'm detecting only low levels of radiation on you."

"Should I take iodide pills?"

"They only work if you take them before exposure. But you should be fine."

Cam jogged along the highway shoulder toward the SUV, barely visible in the dim light. At least he had been active—Amanda was stuck out in the desert, pacing, waiting for word. She ran out to meet him as he approached.

He shook his head. "Sorry. I couldn't find her."

Amanda buried her face in her hands and let out a single wail, the cry cutting through the night like a feral cat.

He wrapped her in his arms. "Listen," he said. "If we didn't find her that means she went someplace. Maybe she just took off during the commotion."

"I've been in touch with Georgia," she sobbed. "She's been on the phone with the military people. Nobody's seen her."

"All right. Then she must be inside the compound still. We'll just keep looking...."

254 David S. Brody

Cam's cell interrupted. He pulled it from his pocket. "Unknown. Should I take it?"

"It's five in the morning and Astarte is missing," she sniffled. "Of course take it."

He nodded. "This is Cam."

"I have the girl." Cam's breath caught in his throat. A deep voice, unfamiliar. Maybe a New York accent. Cam pressed the speaker button.

"Is she okay?"

"For now, yes."

For now? "Who is this?"

"Charlie Boone." He paused. "You know me as Boonie."

Amanda's eyes widened. She leaned into the phone. "What kind of game are you playing?"

"Believe me, this is not a game." He sounded different, more authoritative. A chill passed through Cam—had Boonie's dim-wittedness been an act?

"What do you want with her?" Amanda asked.

"It's not what I want from her. It's what I want from you."

CHAPTER 9

"Cam," Amanda said, "we have to do it."

They were in the SUV, still parked on the side of the highway outside the desert compound. Boonie had made a simple demand: Persuade Willum to make another fuel cell and deliver it to him. It was no easy task, but at least Astarte was alive and safe. And there was no sense debating the morality of the action—they both knew they would do almost anything to ensure Astarte's well-being. "It's going to be tough. Willum is going to be more paranoid than ever. And more pissed at the feds—he probably thinks Clarisse was working for the them"

"Maybe she was."

"Now Boonie says he's working for the feds also," Cam said. "But I'm not sure I believe him."

"I do. It's a perfect cover. It reminds me of an old Cold War thriller I read once, where an American spy lives as a homeless person in Eastern Europe for, like, thirty years, just waiting to make one drop."

"So if they already have someone imbedded in the compound, why did they need to recruit me?"

"Good question. If you think about it, it's a pretty good feint—recruiting someone to go undercover to distract from the bloke you've already snuck in. Or maybe the answer is that Boonie's so imbedded that even Georgia and her team don't know about it."

"Well, if he really is working for the feds, I'd like to know when they got in the business of kidnapping little girls. First Ellis, now him."

"Perhaps Willum is right to fear them. Perhaps they are out of control."

"So how are we going to convince Willum to give them the fuel cell?"

Amanda shook her head. "We're going to have to fool him, or trick him somehow. And we agree, right? We can't tell Willum or Georgia that Boonie has her."

"For now," Cam said. Boonie had been clear: The deal was off if they blew Boonie's cover. It was his only condition. "But it was weird he said we could tell Ellis and ask for his help."

"Great. Just who we want to trust." Amanda had rallied, as Cam knew she would. Now that she knew what they needed to do to free Astarte, she would devote her full energies to it. It was the not knowing that debilitated her.

"We might need his help. We might need him to get the government to back off."

Amanda said, "This is the same deal Willum rejected a couple of days ago." Ironically, because he had been loyal to the disloyal Boonie.

"Well, it's our job to get him to accept it now."

They sat in silence for a few minutes, watching the sun rise over the foothills. "So, it turns out there was a lot going on inside that compound that we didn't know about," Cam said. "Boonie not being who he said he was, Clarisse trying to steal the fuel cell, who knows what else...."

"And we mocked Willum for being paranoid." Amanda said. "So was Clarisse working with Boonie; is that why she was trying to steal the fuel cell?"

"I don't think so. Willum mentioned that Boonie was the only one who knew the fuel cell had been booby-trapped. If Clarisse and Boonie were working together, he would have warned her."

"So why was Clarisse trying to steal it?"

Cam shrugged. "I don't think we'll ever know. Money, maybe? But it does make me wonder about her. When we found her body, she had a bag of the white powder in her pocket. Willum said it had gone missing."

"So she stole that also?"

"Yup." Cam reached into his pocket and pulled out a folded sheet of paper. "And check this out; I almost forgot about it. When I went back to search Clarisse's tent, I found a Bible. This page was marked. Read the highlighted text. It's Exodus 32, Verse 20."

"You ripped a page out of a Bible?"

Cam sniffed. "Damn straight. It might be a clue to help find Astarte."

Amanda unfolded the paper and read aloud:

"Moses took the golden calf which they had made, melted it, ground it into fine powder, and mixed it with water. Then he made the people of Israel drink it."

"We talked about this already. Making the people ingest the gold was an odd thing for Moses to do, but why did Clarisse focus on it?"

Cam felt like a guy in the eye doctor's office as the ophthalmologist clicked through varying lens magnifications. "Which is clearer, lens one … or lens two? One … or two?" Nothing was clear; everything was blurry. But every click of the lens brought the picture more into focus.

He turned to Amanda. "Hold on. If you melt down gold, you get molten gold, not powder. So someone who knew the secrets of alchemy—one of the priests—must have transformed it to powder first. Powdered gold. Amanda, this passage is talking about making *mfkzt*."

"Oh my God, you're right. How did we not figure this out?" She stared at the Bible page. "But why would Moses feed the *mfkzt* to the people? Wasn't this stuff supposed to just be for the pharaohs so they could speak to the gods?"

"Think about it. The Egyptians used the *mfkzt* to enhance spirituality. It was some kind of aphrodisiac, or mind-expander— that's why the pharaohs were supposedly able to converse with their gods after ingesting it. So look at the timing of this passage. Moses comes down from the mountain with the Ten Commandments and finds that the people are worshiping the old gods, the golden calf. He's pissed, but he also needs to convince them to abide by these new laws. Think about the story he's trying to sell: *'Listen up. I spoke to God. He told me to be your leader. He wrote down all these new rules you need to follow, including getting rid of your other gods. And one other thing: Only I can see him and talk to him. So you have to do everything I say.'"* Cam shook his head. "It's a pretty tough sell."

Amanda brushed her hair out of her eyes with her hand. "So Moses melts down the gold, transforms it to *mfkzt,* and makes all the people drink it."

"He knew how to make *mfkzt* from his days in exile, when he was in *Serabit el Khadim,* where they made the stuff."

Amanda nodded. "Soon they start to feel all spiritual." She paused for a second. Cam knew she had reached the same conclusion he had. But it was a tough thing to wrap your brain around.

Finally she took a deep breath. "Are we saying Moses got the Israelites to accept the bloody Ten Commandments by drugging them?"

Willum sat atop one of the domes, alone in a sniper's nest, watching the sun rise. He tried to fight back the nausea, but finally gave into it and puked over the railing onto the curved dome roof. But the queasiness didn't dissipate. *Radiation sickness.* He swigged some water and rinsed his mouth. At some point he'd need to get to the hospital. But he knew once he left the compound the feds would never let him back in.

Worse than the nausea was the depression. The realization that Clarisse had betrayed him had wormed its way into his gut and wouldn't stop twisting. It had been bad enough that she tried to steal the fuel cell. From what he had figured out, she was trying to consummate the deal he had reneged on earlier in the week: Trade the fuel cell for an agreement the feds wouldn't storm the compound. If so, and if that's all it was, maybe she had the compound's best interest at heart.

But the bag of white powder in Clarisse's pocket was like a key unlocking a door that revealed a whole other layer of plotting and subterfuge. There was no denying the obvious: Clarisse had been drugging the compound residents, experimenting first on Boonie, using her position as self-appointed kitchen chief to feed white powder, the stuff the ancient Egyptians used to call *mfkzt,* to them all. Including Willum.

It hadn't taken Willum long on the internet to retrace Clarisse's steps. A quick Google search for white powder of gold revealed numerous testimonials regarding the spiritual benefits of the substance. The powder didn't appear to be mind-altering like a drug or alcohol; rather, the substance seemed to make people more communal and self-sacrificing. As Willum read the testimonials, he pictured sit-in rather than rock concert. Not that Google was always the most reliable source, but most of the recipes called for one-quarter of a teaspoon of the powder to be diluted in a gallon of water, with a daily dosage of three ounces. So the bag Clarisse stole could easily feed the compound for weeks. Apparently the powder didn't fully dilute, instead remaining suspended in a semi-gelatinous state in the distilled water. That's probably why Clarisse had made things like clam chowder and pancake mix—thick, creamy meals that would hide the powder.

Now that he had solved the mystery, so many unexplained things suddenly made sense. The two-day fast Clarisse suggested was obviously a ruse to cleanse their systems in preparation for the *mfkzt.* Clarisse's willingness to serve as head chef put her in perfect position to carry out her plan. The residents' boundless energy, their enhanced spirituality, their new-found pack mentality, and even their willingness to die for their cause—all attributable to the ingestion of the white powder of gold. He shook his head. Clarisse had brought them to the edge of a Jim Jones-like catastrophe, the Kool-Aid taking the form of white powder of gold. And the terrifying, mind-numbing truth was that he, Willum Smoot, was the messianic figurehead they were willing to follow to the grave.

And he hadn't even known it. Hadn't a clue as to what she was orchestrating. Shit, he didn't even get suspicious when she put up those goddamn posters of him.

He smacked himself on the side of the head. What, did he think he was so charismatic, so dynamic, such a natural leader that the residents would blindly follow him? Did he think he was some modern-day Moses? How could he have not realized how stupid that was, how utterly unfathomable it was?

He was Willum Smoot. A science geek. A fat loser. A paranoid ex-con. About as far from Moses as you could get.

Ellis Kincaid had been monitoring the situation at the compound. Frankly, he had no idea what was going on. Apparently Clarisse had done as instructed and tried to steal the fuel cell. But Smoot had booby-trapped it, killing her. Not a great situation—she had been a useful ally—but not a fatal blow to Ellis's plans either.

But Ellis hadn't foreseen the radiation fallout. And he hadn't foreseen the abduction of Astarte. The first was simply bad luck—but eventually the radiation would dissipate and the compound would probably go back into lockdown. So no real change. But the second meant there were forces at play here that he knew nothing about. Ellis was not the only puppet master on the stage.

And the other guy seemed to have the bigger puppets.

Cam and Amanda spent the night searching the compound. They hung as the residents began to stir, hoping perhaps someone would have found Astarte. But after a couple of hours it had become obvious they were wasting their time. Boonie had her well-hidden.

"I'm not sure we're doing much good hanging out here," Amanda said. "We need to come up with a plan to get Willum to hand over the fuel cell." Boonie had said he would phone them again at noon.

Cam started the engine of the SUV. "I've been trying to come up with something, but no luck," Cam said.

"Maybe we should talk to Kincaid. He might have some answers. And if not, much as I despise him, he's got the kind of devious mind that might concoct something."

"We need to be careful with him. I think we have to assume he's working with Boonie. Why else would Boonie suggest we contact him?"

Amanda mulled it over. "Which makes sense, if Boonie really is a federal agent."

"It also makes sense if Boonie is a crook, and Kincaid is in cahoots with him," Cam said. "That fuel cell would be worth millions, maybe even billions. I could see Kincaid selling out for that kind of cash."

Amanda nodded. "Fair point. Either way, we should assume Kincaid will be reporting back to Boonie."

They drove for a few more minutes. Amanda sighed. "This still doesn't add up. If Boonie and Kincaid are working together, why did Kincaid accuse Boonie of setting the roadside bomb?"

"You're right. There's something we're missing." Cam turned and smirked. "Mind if I try to beat some answers out of Kincaid?"

"Only if you get to him first."

Ellis was only half-dressed, his hair still wet from the shower, when someone banged on his door. He zipped up his jeans. "Who is it?"

"Cam. And Amanda. Open the door."

Shouldn't they be at the compound, looking for the girl? He flicked the deadbolt and pulled the door open. Before he could brace himself Thorne bull-rushed him, driving his shoulder in Ellis's bare chest and driving him to the carpeted floor. Straddling him, Thorne grabbed Ellis's hair with his left hand, lifted his head a few inches and drove his right fist straight into Ellis's nose. Ellis saw the rage in Thorne's eyes, saw the determination in his clenched jaw, even saw the desperation in the way he threw the punch—as if the harder he hit Ellis, the more likely he would be to rescue Astarte. And there was nothing Ellis could do about any of it other than wait for the blow to land....

He must have passed out for a few seconds because when he awoke, still on the floor, Thorne was standing above him and Amanda was holding a bloodied white towel over his nose. He pushed her hand away, took the towel himself, and worked himself into a sitting position against the bed. Even the slight movement made his nose throb. Blinking back the tears, he forced his eyes to focus, then took an extra few seconds to calm himself before speaking. *Ignore the pain; swallow the anger.* At some point he would bloody Thorne a bit also, but for now he needed information.

"If you think I had anything to do with Astarte's disappearance, you're wrong." He spat out some blood that had dripped into the back of his throat.

"You mean other than kidnapping her and driving her out there," Thorne said.

Implicit in the statement was that Thorne didn't think Ellis had anything to do with the disappearance, *other than driving her out there.* And if he knew Ellis didn't, he must know who did. Simple deductive reasoning. "You already know who took her. So what do you want from me?"

Doubt flickered in Thorne's eyes. In some ways it was better than knocking him to the ground. "How do you know that?" Thorne asked.

Ellis pulled the towel away from his nose. But he still sounded nasally. "Because I'm smarter than you."

"Well, if you're so smart, tell us what Boonie is up to."

Ellis tried to hide his surprise by pushing the towel back over his face. Boonie? "How would I know?"

Amanda responded. She really was a nice piece. And her accent was hot also. Maybe instead of pummeling Thorne he'd steal the girl from him. "He claims to be a bloody federal agent."

What? "That's ridiculous. The guy's a retard."

Thorne sneered. "It's a cover, smart boy."

This made no sense. Georgia was in charge, and Ellis the one assigned to work behind the scenes. "He's lying to you."

"Well, explain this," Thorne said. "He swore us to secrecy. But he said the one person we could confide in was you." He paused. "He told us we could trust you because we were all Patriots fans."

Ellis pulled himself to his feet. "I need to use the bathroom." He staggered away from Thorne and Amanda, the towel pushed against his nose.

Thorne pushed past him and entered the bathroom first, removing anything Ellis might use as a weapon. Satisfied, he left Ellis alone.

Ellis turned on the shower to hide the noise and, as silently as possible, puked into the toilet.

Patriots fans. Just like in the bathroom stall at the highway rest area. So Boonie was the guy in the duck boots. The meeting in New Hampshire was a goddamn set-up, about as far away from Arizona as you could get.

Throwing the bloodied towel into the bathtub, Ellis washed his hands and face, rinsed his mouth and stared at the bloodshot eyes reflected in the mirror in front of him. "Holy shit," he breathed. This was close to checkmate. Really close. Not only was his career in jeopardy, but he could easily spend the rest of his life in jail. "Fuck."

And he never saw it coming. Which made sense, of course. If he had seen it coming, he would have taken countermeasures. But he had swallowed the ruse like a baby suckling on his mother's tit.

He splashed more water on his face and replayed the past week in his head. He had framed Boonie for the roadside bomb. Nobody had questioned him on it—the only one who might have, Clarisse, was now dead. But Boonie knew the truth, knew he hadn't planted the bomb. And so Boonie must also have deduced that Ellis planted it—the one person who had motive to frame Boonie was the real bomber. That is why Boonie told Thorne to contact Ellis—Boonie wanted Ellis to know that

Boonie knew the truth. Implicit in that message was a clear threat—*if this mission goes bad, young Ellis, you are taking the fall for the car-bomb that killed the ATF agent.*

This mission had just become personal. Very personal. If Thorne and Amanda couldn't persuade Smoot to deliver the fuel cell to Boonie, Ellis would be spending the rest of his life in jail.

"What do you think he's doing in there?" Amanda asked. Ellis had stumbled into the bathroom almost ten minutes ago.

"Maybe combing his hair," Cam sniffed.

Whatever it was, it wasn't helping rescue Astarte. Amanda slapped the door with an open hand. "Get your ass out here!"

The water stopped running. "Coming."

A minute later Ellis stepped out of the bathroom, a wadded-up tissue in one nostril. "Okay, I'll help you," Ellis said. He seemed different, less haughty. He pulled a navy blue golf shirt over his head and flopped into a desk chair. "We need to think of a way to convince Smoot to give up the fuel cell."

Amanda sat on the edge of the bed. "Thanks for stating the obvious."

They sat in silence for a few seconds. "The problem," Cam said as he stood next to Amanda, a wary eye on Ellis, "is that Willum's not going to trust anyone. First it turned out we lied to him and we really were helping the feds. Then it turned out Clarisse was trying to steal the fuel cell. How do you think he'll react when he finds out Boonie isn't what he says? It's not paranoia if everyone really is out to get you."

"What about just telling him the truth?" Amanda said. "Ask him to help us save Astarte."

Ellis shook his head. "I hate to agree with Cameron," which, for once, he did not pronounce in his affected way, "but Smoot isn't going to trust you. He'll think the whole thing is just a ploy to get the fuel cell from him."

"And if we tell him," Cam said, "and Boonie finds out, who knows what he'll do to Astarte?"

Poor Astarte must be petrified, held hostage in some dark room by a strange man. Amanda wrapped her arms around herself to suppress her shudder and tried to focus on coming up with a plan. But her mind was mush. "It's not much of a plan," she said, "but what about just appealing to Willum's sense of right and wrong? He can end the siege and save the compound just by giving up the fuel cell."

Cam bit his lip. "That hasn't worked so far. He really doesn't want the feds to get this technology. And I don't think he'll trust that the feds will keep their word. Again, he's not going to be in a trusting mood." Cam paused. "I wonder if there's a way to convince him the ark needs the fuel cell to operate. By showing that the ark works we can prove it's ancient."

"I like your approach," Amanda said. "But we wouldn't have to give the fuel cell to the feds to test the ark. We could just test it ourselves."

Cam nodded. "Good point." He paused. "What about if Willum gave them a fake prototype, one that didn't work?"

Ellis rolled his eyes. "Please. Boonie's not going to fall for that. You're not going to see Astarte until they're sure the prototype works."

Ten seconds passed, with no further discussion. "So it seems like we have bad ideas and very bad ideas," Amanda said. "So I vote we try out one of the bad ideas and see if it works." She stood. "Because doing nothing is not an option."

Cam and Amanda agreed that, of the bad ideas, the plan to approach Willum to see if he would give up the fuel cell to end the standoff was the one with the least risk. And, as Amanda said, at least they'd be doing something.

Cam drove, for what seemed like their hundredth trip to the compound. "I really want to get back to Westford," Amanda said.

"Yeah, I'm getting sick of the desert and the never-changing weather and living in a hotel and dealing with all these fruitcakes."

"We need to call Georgia. I've been dodging her calls all morning."

Cam nodded. "I got this one." He punched at his phone, one eye on the road. "It's Cam," he said. "Listen, you promised us you would control your boy Ellis, and you didn't. And Astarte is missing because of that. So Amanda and I are going to try to handle this ourselves, without help from you or your people. Just make sure we can get into the compound, okay? And make sure they don't storm the compound until we get her out."

Georgia stammered a reply. "I'll do whatever I can to help, you know that. But I can't make any promises...."

"Frankly, Georgia, we're not interested in any more of your promises. We need some results. Threaten to go public, call the President yourself, I don't care. Just do what needs to be done."

"That was harsh," Amanda said.

"Sorry. But I'm pissed."

"Don't be sorry. She deserves it."

Cam exhaled. "Besides, Boonie said we couldn't tell her anything. So this was the best way to handle her. If he saw her with us, or saw her snooping around the compound, he might get the wrong idea."

She nodded. "Okay, so assuming we get into the compound, what are we going to say to Willum?"

Cam sighed. "I don't know. But we've got a half hour to come up with something. Something brilliant."

Amanda put her palm over her forehead. "Bloody hell."

Ellis hadn't mentioned this to Thorne and Amanda, of course, but there was another way for Ellis to save his skin besides orchestrating a trade of Astarte for the fuel cell: A raid on the compound which killed Boonie.

With Boonie dead, there would be nobody left to tie Ellis to the roadside bomb.

Would Ellis be willing to allow the compound to come under siege, allow innocent people to be killed? What about honor and loyalty and the self-sacrifice required of a federal agent? He spit more blood into the bathroom sink. These were silly sentiments, empty words. If he didn't look out for himself, nobody else would. Even the people he worked for were playing him.

And those chuckleheads knew what they were getting themselves into when they moved into the compound. Heck, half of them probably have a martyr complex and want to die anyway. Ellis ran a brush through his hair, fluffed his bangs. He expected Thorne and the Brit to succeed. But if not, Ellis had a back-up plan.

He picked up the phone and dialed a number in suburban Virginia. After being shuttled and put on hold and asked repeatedly for his security clearance, he finally was connected. "Hayek here."

"This is agent Ellis Kincaid, sir. I'm stationed out in Tucson, at the Smoot compound."

"Why are you calling me directly?"

"Because, frankly, I'm not sure who else to trust with this, sir. I just received a tip that someone inside the compound has been seen meeting with the Chinese. Apparently he is trying to sell them a state-of-the art fuel cell."

A sharp intake of breath. "Do you know who it is?"

Ellis smiled. Now was not the time to overplay his hand. "Not yet. But I think the information is solid."

Georgia's call must have done the trick, because the military guard waved their SUV past the checkpoint outside the compound. They rolled to a stop near the front gate, where a camouflaged soldier greeted them.

"No Hazmat suit?" Cam asked. At this point most of the soldiers knew Cam and Amanda by sight.

"Wind shifted; readings are down," the soldier answered. "I've been instructed to allow you to approach the gate. But I can't promise they'll let you in."

Cam nodded and turned to Amanda. "I still think you should stay out here. Obviously, radiation levels will be higher inside."

She shook her head. "Absolutely not. I'll put on a suit if I have to. But I'm coming with you."

They walked slowly to the main gate. Inside the compound the guards had removed their Hazmat suits as well. Cam spoke into an intercom and they waited for a few minutes, presumably while the guards checked with Willum. An electronic deadbolt clicked and the gate swung open.

They found Willum in the picnic table area, sheltered from possible snipers. Dark crests of skin sagged beneath his eyes, and his brown eyes themselves seemed less alive and vibrant than they had only a few days earlier. He didn't smile or offer a hand. Obviously his paranoia had been hard at work—was he now wondering if the Astarte abduction was some kind of a ruse? "What can I do for you?" he asked.

Amanda answered, taking his hand in hers. "We need your help, Willum." She waited until he made eye contact. "I know nothing has been as it seems. I know the people you trusted have turned on you. But this is real. Astarte is in danger. We need your help."

He nodded slowly. "Tell me what you know. Have you heard from the kidnapper?"

Cam nodded. "Yes, we have. He says he'll trade her for the fuel cell."

"He will, huh? And you believe him?"

"Yes," Amanda said.

"And who is this honest man, this trustworthy kidnapper?"

Cam and Amanda glanced at each other. Cam took a deep breath. "We can't tell you."

Willum crossed his arms in front of his chest and exhaled. He leaned back against the wall of one of the domes. "You can't tell me."

"He said he would harm Astarte if we did," Amanda said.

He exhaled again. "So let me get this straight. You guys lied to me when we met, not telling me you were working with the feds. Then you lied to me again, not telling me Clarisse was trying to steal the fuel cell."

"We didn't know about Clarisse," Cam said.

"Okay, so you only lied to me once." Willum smiled sadly. "That actually makes you among my most reliable friends."

"So will you help us?" Amanda asked.

He didn't answer directly. "So whoever has her wants to end this standoff and figures giving the feds the fuel cell will do the trick. Same idea Clarisse had. And they probably are thinking the girl is some kind of human shield, protecting us from the army bombing the shit out of this place. I assume she's in one of the underground tunnels. To be honest, I haven't looked for her because I like the idea of a human shield. We can use any shield we can get at this point." He lifted his chin. "I'm inclined to leave her where she is."

Amanda took his hand again. "You're a father, Willum. You know how we feel." Tears welled in her eyes. "Astarte must be petrified. She's just a young girl. I know you don't trust us. But trust your heart. If you do nothing else, if you can hold nothing else dear, at least do what you know is the right thing for Astarte."

"The innocence of children," he whispered. He stared past Cam and Amanda, at the compound he had built and which now entrapped him. Thirty seconds passed, which for Cam seemed like an hour. Finally Willum spoke. "I'm sorry. I'd like to help. But I can't give the government that fuel cell."

Amanda gasped. She dropped to her knees as the gasp turned into quiet sobs.

"Wait, can you repeat that?" Georgia pushed back her conference room chair and stood, as if standing would help her hear better.

"I said that the troops are going in tonight," said Hayek, her boss at ODNI. "Pre-dawn. The White House just signed off."

"Are you crazy? Do you know how many people are likely to die?"

"I can't give you an exact number, no. But you know how this works: When we get to the point where we know someone is going to die, we always make the choice that it be the other guys."

"And how can you be sure someone has to die?"

"Really, Georgia? Do I need to remind you that someone already did? We know now they are manufacturing dirty bombs inside that compound. Are we just supposed to wait for Smoot to drop one on our troops?"

"You don't know they're making dirty bombs. I told you, that radiation came from an explosion involving the white powder of gold."

"Listen, I know you are emotionally invested in this. And our scientists are looking into this white powder stuff. But I gotta tell you, it sounds like hocus-pocus to me. When a crazy man in a fortified bunker who already killed one of our people sets off a dirty bomb, I have to think it's a real threat."

She wanted to scream. Obviously Hayek had been behind a desk too long. She was here, eyes and ears on the ground—why bother having agents in the field if you weren't going to trust their judgment? "What about the girl?"

He sighed. "You've got all day to find her."

"I just don't see what the big rush is."

"Look, they are at the most vulnerable right now. We know they're expending a ton of resources dealing with the blast and the radiation. Attack while they're weak."

She replayed the statement in her mind. "Wait, how do you know they're expending a ton of resources?"

He cleared his throat. "It's a reasonable conclusion to draw."

"But that's not how you worded it." She started at the conference room wall. "You have a man inside the compound, don't you?" Lies hidden inside lies.

Another pause. "We do. He's been imbedded there for a couple of years. But that fuel cell is worth billions. We're worried he may have gone rogue on us. If we don't attack now, that fuel cell may slip through our hands forever. We go in tonight."

Cam took Amanda by the arm, lifted her gently to her feet and turned to Smoot still seated on the picnic table bench. He played his last card. "Is that all it is, just that you don't want the feds to have the cell?"

"Yup. I don't trust them to use it for the right reasons. Not this government. They have too much power already." He shook his head. "I got a bad dose of radiation last night. I might be dead in a few months. I don't want my legacy to be that I'm the guy who sold out to the feds."

Cam nodded. "Then I think I have a plan that might work."

"Well then let's hear it."

As promised, just after noon Cam's cell phone rang. He and Amanda had driven down the highway a few miles to ensure cell coverage; Boonie must be using some kind of satellite phone.

"Before you ask, the girl is fine," Boonie said. "For now."

"Can we talk to her?" Amanda said.

"No. Tell me you have the fuel cell."

Cam spoke. "We don't have it, but Willum has agreed to give it up in exchange for Astarte's release."

"Did you tell him I was involved?"

"No."

"I'll know if you're lying."

"Which is why we wouldn't risk it."

"So when can I expect the cell?"

"In an hour, if you want."

He guffawed. "Now I know you're lying. You must not care too much for the girl."

"We're not lying," Amanda said.

"I know the fuel cell got destroyed in the explosion. It'll take Smoot at least a day to make a new one."

"The one that got destroyed was a fake," Cam said. "The real one is locked away in a safe." This time Willum's paranoia played to their advantage.

"I hope you know what you're doing here. I'm not giving up the girl until I test that fuel cell. If it's a fake, I'll know it. And the girl will suffer."

Cam swallowed. The fuel cell better work. "We understand."

Boonie chewed on a piece of grass as he made a sandwich. Most kids were plain eaters, so he kept it simple—turkey and lettuce on white bread. And a couple of cookies. He shook his head. He should be making lunch for his grandkids, not some innocent girl he had just kidnapped.

At least this mission would soon be over. When he had taken it on, a few years away from retirement, he had figured it would be a six-month gig, maybe a year at most—one last adrenaline rush out in the field, a perfect way to end a thirty-five-year career. Befriend Smoot, win his confidence, learn what he could about the fuel cell technology. Show the young agents that even the senior members of the intelligence community were willing to make sacrifices, to take the hard missions. That was twenty-six months ago. Twenty-six months of playing the fool, of pulling his hat low over his face, of listening to Smoot rail against the country he loved.

He nodded at Smoot. "Hi boss," he said.

Willum clapped him on the back. "Haven't seen you much today, Boonie." He said it without any edge; Thorne had been honest—he had not said anything to Smoot.

"Been looking for the girl. Lots of tunnels down there."

"I appreciate that." Smoot looked out over the desert. "At one point it was just you and me, Boonie." He sighed. "I wonder if we wouldn't have been better off if we had just left it at that."

Boonie nodded. After twenty-six months together, Boonie had come to like Willum. Not his politics, or his paranoia, or his lack of patriotism. But he was a good man. Whatever happened, Boonie hoped Willum would find some happiness. And, once this mission ended, Boonie would insist the man be reunited with his son.

But first things first. He needed to recover that fuel cell. Otherwise nobody would be spending time with their families.

Willum finished his lunch, patted Boonie on the back and went to the supply pod to don a Hazmat suit. He pulled it on and trudged back to his saucer, the first time he had returned since the explosion. Geiger counter in hand, he opened the door and allowed his eyes to adjust to the dark.

Being back in the pod made him think of Clarisse. He would need to decide what to do with her body soon—it would need to be decontaminated before anything else. Then what? Bury it, return it to next of kin, turn it over to the coroner's office? She deserved a decent burial, preferably someplace where he could visit once in a while. She had betrayed him, but in the end he had to admit her intentions were probably noble. She wanted to protect him, protect the compound. But first things first.

Moving methodically, he opened the hatch and navigated the steep ladder. Some of the smoke had dissipated but his flashlight illuminated thousands of tiny particles of dust and debris in the air.

The Geiger counter chirped, increasing in regularity as he moved toward the explosion site. Thankfully the levels had dissipated in the past twelve hours.

Keeping to the perimeter of the room, he made his way to the back wall and opened the door of a badly-dented steel storage cabinet. He removed the lid from a green plastic trash barrel within, revealing a white plastic bag filled with coffee grounds, banana peels and other decaying refuse. He removed the bag to reveal a two-foot-square cast-iron safe hidden inside the barrel. Having previously cut away the bottom of the barrel, he easily lifted the empty barrel up and over the safe. He dropped to a knee, spun the dial a few times back and forth, opened the safe and shined his light on the fuel cell prototype, examining it carefully.

"Snug as a bug in a rug," he said as he removed the object.

Cam stood near the picnic tables, kicked at the dirt and glanced at his watch. Two minutes past one o'clock. Willum was late. And every minute he was late was another minute Astarte remained locked in some closet or something.

Had something happened? Had the fuel cell been damaged in the explosion? Had Willum changed his mind?

He kicked at the dirt again. Somewhere beneath the ground, perhaps directly beneath where Cam was standing, Astarte was being kept captive. Was she cold, hungry, frightened? Cam took a deep breath. Boonie was just interested in the fuel cell—he had nothing personal against Astarte so presumably he was not mistreating her. Presumably.

Willum turned a corner and ambled toward Cam. Cam exhaled. *Thank God.* Willum dragged a red and white rectangular cooler behind him like a man heading to the beach.

"Does it need to be kept cold?" Cam asked.

"No. But I couldn't find a box."

Cam lifted the lid. The cooler was filled with packing worms; he pushed a few aside to see a six-sided glass case with tubes and wires inside it. "Is it … unstable?"

"Do you mean will it explode?" He chuckled. "No."

Cam exhaled. "Willum, I really appreciate this." He didn't want to insult the man, but he had to ask. "Are you sure it will work." If not, they would suspect a trick. And Astarte would pay.

Willum smiled sadly. "Cam, that's what all this is about." He waved his hand at the compound, then at the soldiers outside the gate. "If the feds weren't so sure I could build this, none of us would be here right now. They put me in jail, took my son away, forced me to become a Survivalist and build this compound, sent you to spy on me, and eventually put us under siege." He chuckled again. "It'd be pretty damn ironic if after all that it turned out I didn't know my ass from my elbow when it came to building a fuel cell."

Cam smiled. "So it'll work."

"It'll work."

Cam offered his hand, which Willum took. "And the rest of the plan is in place?"

Willum nodded.

Cam passed through the gate, wheeling the cooler. A soldier in an army jeep motioned to him and Cam climbed aboard. In the distance a helicopter waited, alone in the desert like a dragonfly on a beach.

The plan was for Cam to fly to a nearby military base, where government scientists would examine the fuel cell. If it checked out, they would notify Boonie and he would free Astarte. Cam and Amanda had originally balked at the plan, wanting some security Boonie would do as he promised, but Boonie asked a valid question: "Why would I want to keep the girl once I have the fuel cell?"

Five minutes later Cam was airborne, heading southeast, tracking Route 10 on a path similar to the one he and Willum had taken to visit Mustang Mountain. The army copter flew much faster than Willum's civilian chopper, and they covered the sixty-mile distance to Tucson's Davis-Monthan Air Force Base in just over twenty minutes. The copter set down and a soldier wearing the standard Air Force blues escorted Cam to a small waiting room while another wheeled the cooler away.

Cam dialed Amanda. "Eagle has landed."

"Are they examining the fuel cell?"

"I assume so. I'm guessing they flew in some top people from around the country."

"How long will it take?"

"According to Willum, not long. It either works or it doesn't."

Two-and-a-half hours later the same soldier in his Air Force blues opened the waiting room door. "Mr. Thorne, you're all set for your return trip."

Cam stood. "Did the fuel cell work?"

"I'm not at liberty to say, sir." The soldier offered a wry smile. "But I did hear some hooting and hollering from inside the lab."

Boonie took the call on his satellite phone. "Bingo," said the voice on the other end of the line. "It's the real deal."

He exhaled. "You're sure?"

"We've got three of the best guys in the country. They all agree."

"Okay, thanks."

Slipping into one of the abandoned domes, Boonie lifted a hatch hidden under a steamer trunk pushed up against one wall. He dropped through the hatch and into one of the many tunnels snaking underneath the complex—the idea, apparently, was that workers would never have to go out into the desert heat during the summer months. Over the past couple of years Boonie had modified the system, blocking off some tunnels and hiding access points to others.

He followed the tunnel a couple hundred feet to the room Smoot called the bunker, the one Boonie reported had been damaged by the explosion. As he walked, he dropped M&M's on the floor every few feet. When he arrived at the bathroom door, he turned on his flashlight and knocked gently. "Astarte, you in there?" Where else would she be?

"Yes," came the whimpered reply.

"Listen carefully. I'm going to let you go now. Here's what you need to do. First, I'm going to turn off the light for a few seconds. Then I'm going to open this door and shine my flashlight in your face again."

"So I can't see you?"

"That's right. But this time I want you to follow me out of the bathroom. I'm going to leave another flashlight for you here on the ground. Turn it on and use it to follow the trail of M&M's I left for you." He paused.

"Okay."

"When you get to the red M&M, stop, like a stop sign. You'll see a ladder along the wall of the tunnel. When you climb the ladder, you'll be outside near the picnic tables. I'll make sure Amanda is there waiting for you."

Amanda sat at a picnic table, as instructed, her eyes sweeping the compound for Astarte.

Out of nowhere the girl appeared, like an apparition. "Astarte," Amanda called, running toward her.

Astarte stood motionless, tears running down her cheeks, their tracks visible on her dust-caked face.

Amanda scooped her up, hugged her to her chest. "Are you all right?"

The girl sniffled, her hands balled into fists as she squeezed Amanda's neck. She did not speak, but merely nodded her head. Sobbing now, she burrowed her head into Amanda's shoulder.

"It's okay now ... you're safe ... I've got you ... it's okay ... I'm here," Amanda whispered. "It's okay."

Amanda held her for another thirty seconds until the sobs gradually subsided. She pulled her face back so she could see Astarte's face. She brushed the girl's hair out of her eyes and kissed her on the nose. "I was so very frightened we had lost you, Astarte." Her own eyes filled with tears. "I don't know what I would have done without you."

"So you're not angry with me?" Another sniffle.

"No, this was all my fault."

Astarte's lower lip trembled. "Do you still want to be my parents?" Her words were barely audible.

Amanda melted into her. "More than ever, darling. More than ever."

Ellis had watched the copter take off, the crushing weight of trepidation lifting off his shoulders in concert with the bird's ascent. Now, three hours later, he scanned the horizon for the sign of a return flight.

Assuming Thorne delivered the fuel cell and it worked, Ellis's mission will have ended in success. He had been assigned to somehow orchestrate the delivery of the fuel cell—mission accomplished. That he may have cut some corners along the way would be overlooked. The ends justified the means, at least as long as the mission succeeded. If the mission failed, every decision you made would be questioned. That's the way it worked.

In the distance a chopper appeared, mosquito-like on the horizon. As it did so, he heard the compound gate open. Amanda and the girl walked out, hand-in-hand. Ellis smiled. "So the fuel cell must have worked."

Amanda nodded, her eyes cold. She put her body between Astarte and him. "If you ever come near my daughter again," she hissed, "I'll hunt you down and rip your heart out."

He tossed his head. "I'd look forward to that."

She began to walk away, then stopped. "Actually, that would be impossible. My bet is you'll soon be locked away in some jail cell, rotting."

Now why would she say something like that? Didn't she realize his mission was a success?

Cam jumped from the copter and he and Astarte shared a long, tearful embrace. Amanda cut it short. "I'm sorry, but I really want to get as far away from this place as we can."

Cam nodded. "Agreed. The shit is going to hit the fan soon. And it's going to be ugly."

They jogged to the SUV, Cam holding Astarte's hand. Cam pointed the car in the opposite direction from the hotel and floored it. "Where to?"

Amanda had loaded all their gear into the SUV earlier in the day. "Let's drive for half an hour, then find a hotel with an internet connection."

Twenty-five minutes later, just outside Phoenix, they pulled into the parking lot of a Hampton Inn. They rented a suite, ordered a pizza from room service and threw their bags in the corner. While Cam helped Astarte wash up and put on clean clothes, Amanda popped open her lap top and connected to the Wi-Fi signal. She smiled and turned to Cam as he stepped out of the bathroom. "You ready?"

He sat next to her, pulled Astarte onto his lap and nodded. "Ready."

She typed the words "prototype fuel cell" into the search engine, restricting the search to web entries created within the past twenty-four hours. They stared at the screen, waiting for the engine to load. "There," she said. "That's it."

She clicked on the YouTube link, turned up the volume and sat back. Willum's voice filled the hotel room. "My name is Willum Smoot. And I'm here today to share with the world the new fuel cell technology I've invented...."

Cam clapped. "Beautiful. He also downloaded the specs and all the technical info on a bunch of different science chat rooms. Within hours the whole world will be able to build a version of his fuel cell."

Amanda smiled. "It worked perfectly, Cam." She kissed him on the mouth. "Well done."

He grinned. "I just wish we could see the looks on Boonie's and Kincaid's faces. They are going to be pissed."

"I just hope they don't take it out on poor Willum."

"Take it out on him? They've already mobilized armed forces to attack his compound. What else could they do to the guy?"

"Bloody true." She smiled. "And you know what? No matter what happens later, I think Willum is sitting there with a cold pint right now, laughing his ass off."

CHAPTER 10

Willum climbed to the top of the sniper's nest nearest the front gate, plopped into a lawn chair, opened a Corona and lifted his binoculars. The soldiers had already begun to pull back even before the chopper carrying Cam had returned and now, three hours later, only a few stragglers remained. Would they spin around and return once word of the YouTube video reached central command?

He kept the binoculars trained on one man in particular, Agent Kincaid. Cam had said Kincaid would probably get the first call regarding the YouTube video since he was the agent at the scene.

A beer and a half later, Kincaid reached for his satellite phone. Willum focused in, watched the color drain from the man's face, read the "Are you sure?" on the man's lips.

What happened next surprised even Willum. Kincaid ran to the nearest soldier and grabbed for her rifle. Holding tight, the soldier fended Kincaid off with a knee to the groin. Doubled-over, Kincaid bellowed, his angry voice carrying across the desert air. "They tricked us! Storm the compound! Attack, attack!"

The soldier stared at him for a few seconds, shrugged and walked away.

Cam, Amanda and Astarte spent the night at the hotel—swimming, playing board games, watching a movie. In the morning Cam checked his phone for messages. "Georgia, six calls."

"Four for me," Amanda said.

"Should I call her?"

"Sure. Maybe she can meet us out at the compound." Amanda had made reservations for a flight back to Boston late that afternoon. But they wanted to say goodbye to Willum first. "Ask her to bring the ark. It belongs to Willum, after all."

Two hours later, after breakfast and another swim, they pulled up to the front gate of the compound.

"Sure looks different with no army surrounding it," Amanda said. A few tumbleweeds raced across the desert.

"Almost abandoned. Imagine what it must have looked like when Willum first found it."

"And my cell phone works now. Guess the troops really are not coming back."

A lone guard sat in the guard house. Cam waved, he buzzed them in and Willum ambled out to greet them. "I'm a YouTube star," he said. "Over three thousand views so far, and a couple dozen emails with questions."

"Won't be enough sand in the desert to run all those fuel cells," Cam said, laughing.

Georgia pulled to a stop outside the gate, followed by a black van. She rolled down her window. "Where do you want your ark?"

Willum grinned. "Leave it there. I'll have a couple of men come get it."

Georgia hugged Astarte and they all walked to the picnic table area.

"So I have some news," Georgia said. "Ellis Kincaid's been arrested. He disappeared last night. They found him trying to cross the border into Mexico. Turns out he set the roadside bomb."

"No surprise, maggot that he is," Amanda said. "But how did they figure it out?"

"Well," Georgia hesitated, looking at Willum. "It turns out there was another mole inside the compound. He figured it out."

Willum pursed his lips. "Boonie. Has to be him," he whispered. His chin dropped to his chest. "Boonie's the only one who I didn't make take the truth serum. Probably Boonie who kidnapped Astarte also." He shook his head. "Sorry I'm a day late in figuring it all out."

Amanda touched his arm. "You've had a bit on your mind. And for what it's worth, I think Boonie really grew fond of you.

He said he's going to make sure things are set right with your son."

Willum nodded. "That's the most important thing," he breathed.

Cam turned away as he noticed the burly man tearing up. Chances were pretty good that Willum would develop some kind of cancer from the radiation. Cam hoped he'd be able to beat it, or at least spend some quality time with his boy in the meantime. "So Kincaid is facing, what, murder charges?" he asked Georgia.

Georgia nodded. "He may argue it was in the line of duty, but nobody authorized him to bomb a federal agent's car." She turned to Willum. "So with that crime solved, there's no reason for the authorities to bother you anymore."

He rubbed his eyes. "Like they need a reason. I'm sure they'll be back."

"What about Boonie?" Amanda asked. "He kidnapped Astarte."

Georgia shrugged. "That's a bit different than Kincaid. Boonie's a senior operative, on a classified case, acting in the line of duty, and nobody got hurt. I think it would be viewed as collateral damage, just the cost of doing business."

"We're talking about a little girl," Amanda said.

"We're talking about the federal government," Georgia responded.

The exchange was interrupted by a couple of men wheeling a large crate on a dolly. "Where do you want it, boss?"

Before Willum could respond, Cam interjected. "It's radioactive. So not someplace where people congregate."

Willum turned to the men. "Put it in the empty pod in the back."

"If it's okay, I'd like to examine it one more time," Cam said. "Do you have a portable microscope? I have a hunch."

Willum and Cam again donned Hazmat suits and, five minutes later, entered the empty pod. They removed the lead case surrounding the ark and set up Willum's scope. Looking through the eyepiece, Cam focused on the Levi/Lehi carving. Moving aside, he spoke. "What do you think of this carving, Willum? Does it look old to you?"

Willum leaned in. "Hard to say."

Cam moved the scope to the other side of the ark. "Let's compare it to these carvings. If the ark has been in a cave for a thousand years, even with a cover over it, I would think there would be a lot of residue, dust, sand, dirt, something in the grooves." He focused the scope. "Like this. Look in here. Lots of sand in the grooves, plus it's tarnished. On the other hand the grooves on the Levi carving are bright yellow, like new gold."

Willum peered in. "I agree. That Levi carving is much newer than these ones."

Cam nodded. "Yeah, much newer—as in this week."

They returned to the picnic area to find sandwiches and lemonade set out for them. "Not to be sexist," Amanda said, "but we ladies made lunch."

Astarte focused her cobalt eyes on Cam. "We thought it would be fair if the men cleaned up."

"I'm going to clean you up," Cam said, grabbing her and holding her upside down. "I'm going to use all this hair of yours to sweep the entire desert."

She screeched and kicked her feet for a few seconds before Cam set her down when she announced she had to go to the bathroom. Georgia offered to take her and Cam took the opportunity to tell Amanda what they had found. "I think what happened was that Kincaid's plan all along was to drive a wedge between us and Astarte. He added the Levi carving to the ark, leaving it unclear as to whether the middle letter was a Hebrew 'v' or Hebrew 'h.' He figured we would read it as 'Levi' because it fit our theory about the priestly family of French Jews carving it. And he guessed Astarte, with a little push from him, would read it as 'Lehi' since it fit the history of the Book of Mormon she had been raised with."

"Wow. That's a pretty subtle play," Amanda said.

"That's his job," Cam responded. "He figures out what motivates people, what makes them tick, how they might react."

"And he got lucky that the two names are so similar."

Cam nodded. "So basically he wormed his way into getting Astarte to trust him, figuring he might need her at some point."

"So he sent her here as a human shield, knowing we would do whatever we could to get Willum to deliver the fuel cell to protect her."

"But he didn't know Boonie was already here on the inside. That messed him up a bit. But it still would have gone his way if Willum hadn't agreed to give up the fuel cell."

Willum smiled. "Best thing I ever did. If I had thought of it six years ago, I could have saved myself a lot of heartache and headache."

They sat in silence for a few seconds, each with their own thoughts. Amanda spoke first. "You know, in some ways Ellis defacing the ark actually helps authenticate it. We now know what a modern carving looks like; anything significantly different must be significantly older."

"I'll get a team of scientists in here to study it," Willum said. "Soon. And I also want to see if the white powder can make it levitate."

Georgia and Astarte returned and they all shared lunch.

"I'm a little embarrassed to tell you," Willum said as he chewed his sandwich, "but Clarisse was drugging all of us. She was feeding us the white powder of gold."

Cam nodded. "Yeah, we figured it out also."

"I have to say, it worked," Willum said. "People around here became more … communal I guess you'd say. They were willing to sacrifice themselves for the group. Maybe you'd call it a pack mentality."

Cam nodded again. "I felt it that night I stayed over. It felt like a cult. I'm glad I only had one of the group meals—I might have become a Willum groupie myself," he said, chuckling.

Willum grinned. "Be glad to have you, Cam."

Amanda waited for the laughter to subside. "So we believe Moses fed the *mfkzt* to the Israelites to get them to accept the Ten Commandments. And we know from Willum's experiences that *mfkzt* really can be used as a kind of drug. I've been thinking about the bowl of white powder we found in our ark. What was it for?"

Cam looked at her quizzically. "We know that already. It was a fuel source."

"That made the ark levitate," Willum added.

"But perhaps it was more than that. Hear me out. The ancient Jewish commentators write that there were two things carried in the Ark in addition to the Ten Commandments tablets—the staff of Aaron and a golden bowl full of manna."

"Manna, as in the stuff they ate in the desert to stay alive?"

"Yes. Supposedly, God sent it from the heavens. And it wasn't just called manna. It was also called the Bread of Heaven."

Cam sat up. "Bread of Heaven. Isn't that the same stuff Bezaleel baked for Moses to feed to the people?"

"Yes. Bezaleel the goldsmith. Also known as an alchemist." She paused. "Someone who would know how to chemically transform the gold into *mfkzt*."

Cam smiled. "I get where you're going with this. You think manna was really white powder of gold, really *mfkzt*." He nodded. "I like your thought process; the pieces fit together."

Amanda typed into her smart phone. "It says here the word manna comes from the Hebrew, 'man-hu,' meaning 'What is it?'"

"Damn right, what is it?" Cam laughed. "Nobody knew what they were eating because the priests kept it secret."

Willum grinned. "Sort of like chef's choice in the school cafeteria."

Amanda continued. "And supposedly they ate manna every day. Not only did Moses drug his people out at Mount Sinai, but he kept drugging them for forty years as they wandered through the desert."

Georgia chimed in. "You'd have to drug me to keep me in the desert."

"And take it one step further," Amanda said. "If they kept the powder or manna in the Ark, nobody could steal it without getting zapped."

"Right," Cam said. "Only the priests could approach the Ark. And, in keeping with the Egyptian tradition, only the priests were allowed to handle the white powder."

"Spot on," Amanda said as she tapped on her smart phone again. "And guess who made the vestments the priests wore when they approached the Ark?"

Cam smiled "Our man Bezaleel?"

"None other."

"Well that explains why the name Bezaleel is carved on the ark we found. He knew the secrets of the Ark. Knew how to use it as power source, how to bake the special bread to keep the people from revolting, how to approach it without getting zapped. And somehow his knowledge got passed along to our Calalus friends in the Arizona desert."

Georgia exhaled a long breath. "I know better than to question you guys about this stuff, but you're basically rewriting the history of the Western world. This changes everything we've been taught, everything we've grown up believing. If you're right you really are calling into question one of the foundations of Judeo-Christian society."

Amanda lifted her chin. "Calling into question is an understatement. If we're right we're pretty much pissing all over the Book of Exodus." She sighed. "Moses used the Ark as some kind of high-voltage parlor trick to fool people into believing he had the power of God. Then he drugged them with the manna or *mfkzt* or white powder or whatever you want to call it to get them to follow him around the desert for forty years."

Amanda looked at each of them in turn. "I know this sounds harsh, but based on what we've learned, Moses was a huckster, not all that dissimilar to the Wizard of Oz."

A couple of days after returning to Westford, Cam received an email from Willum:

"Had a guy in here this morning looking at the ark. He says it looks really old—still needs to get final test results. I'm spending the weekend with my son. Can't wait! At least Boonie made good on that. And feds are staying away, for now at least. Thanks again to you and Amanda—not sure how this all would have come out if not for your help. I think probably this entire compound would have been turned into white powder itself!"

Cam showed it to Amanda as they sat at the kitchen table, waiting for Astarte's school bus. "Glad he's doing well. In the end, he never really deserved all the bad things that happened to him."

"Agreed. The worst you can say about him is that he's a bit paranoid. And even that seems justified, in retrospect." Cam changed the subject. "You sure you're okay with Astarte going to the Mormon church on Sunday?"

Amanda exhaled. "I am, yes. The whole thing about Moses drugging his people sort of opened my eyes. The Moses story is something I have heard my whole life—I remember watching the Charlton Heston movie with my mum as a young girl, mesmerized. I had never thought to question it. But now that I do, I see how far-fetched it all is. And it makes me realize something about religion: All religions seem like a fairy tale to people of other religions. If you're, say, Hindu, the idea of God appearing on Mount Sinai to give Moses the Ten Commandments is just plain silly. But to Jews or Christians or Muslims the thought of being reincarnated as a mosquito or something is equally ludicrous."

"And if you're not Mormon, many of their beliefs seem silly also."

"Exactly. So does it really matter whether Astarte learns one silly story over another? I guess to some degree it does, if the stories she's hearing marginalize women. But as long as we give her a strong female identity, she'll be fine no matter what she hears in church on Sunday."

Cam nodded. "I agree. And let's face it, I don't see Astarte ever suffering from a lack of self-confidence. Not with you as her mom."

Amanda looked into Cam's eyes, kissed him lightly and smiled. "No. She is the princess, after all." She paused. "And it's pronounced 'mum.'"

EPILOGUE

[April 1, Modern Day Rhode Island]

Cam, Amanda and Astarte woke up early, grabbed some fruit and made their way out of Newport's Viking Hotel.

Astarte skipped ahead. "Which way?"

"To the right," Amanda said. "A few blocks."

The girl peered at the eastern sky. "No clouds. The sun should be up soon."

"When the Newport Tower was built there were no buildings to block the sun. But we'll still get a good look at the illumination," Amanda said as she took a bite of her banana.

Astarte froze mid-stride. "Ooh," she called out. "There's a worm in your banana!"

Amanda dropped the fruit to the pavement and jumped back, spitting as she did so. "Blimey! Really?"

Astarte grinned. "Nope. April Fool's!"

Cam grinned as Amanda chased after the girl, scooped her up and spun her around. Looked like he would have competition as the family prankster.

They turned the corner onto Mill Street, the Tower rising up to greet them in the morning mist. "Hello, Beautiful," Cam whispered.

They walked along a paved path, sharing the park only with a couple of early morning dog-walkers.

"Okay, Astarte," Amanda said, "remember how on the winter solstice the sun passes through a window and illuminates the orb inside the Tower?"

The girl nodded. "It only happens once a year."

"Right. It symbolizes the rebirth of the world—the male, which is the sun, fertilizing the egg inside the womb, which is symbolized by the orb-shaped keystone inside the Tower. After that, the days begin to get longer again."

The thing that most fascinated Cam, the thing that one hundred percent convinced him that the winter solstice illumination was not some random coincidence, was the way the sun needed to pass through one of the Tower's windows before illuminating the orb. The irregularly-shaped, splayed window not only refracted the sun's beam, it shaped the beam into an ideally sized and shaped box of light that perfectly framed the orb. He had spent hours examining the window, marveling at the reverse-engineering required to produce the perfect box of light on the exact date of the winter solstice.

Astarte and Amanda were continuing their conversation. "But today's not the spring equinox," Astarte pointed out.

"Yes. And for years we could not figure out why there wasn't an exact spring equinox illumination at the Tower, similar to the winter solstice." Amanda smiled, her emerald eyes shining in the morning light. "But then we figured it out. It's not a spring equinox illumination; it's an Easter illumination."

Astarte crinkled her nose. "But Easter is a different day every year, right?"

"Precisely." Amanda led Astarte to a bench, from which they looked up at the Tower. Cam stood behind them, listening. This was Amanda's area of expertise. "This is a bit complicated, so listen carefully. You recall that Cameron and I taught you that Christmas is celebrated on the old pagan holiday that marks the rebirth of the sun, correct?"

"Yes. A few days after the winter solstice, the days began to get longer and the people celebrated."

Amanda nodded. "And that happens the same time every year, in late December. But the Easter holiday is based not only on the solar calendar but on the lunar one as well. As you said, its date changes every year. Easter is celebrated on the first Sunday after the first full moon after the spring equinox."

"That's confusing."

"Yes. But, for Christians, Easter is a very important holiday. So it is crucial that they get the date right. And even though the

Knights Templar did not agree with many teachings of the Church, they were still Christians so they did celebrate Easter."

"Okay."

"Now, can you imagine what would happen if for, say, seven or eight days, it was cloudy every day? And during that time, there was both a full moon and the spring equinox? In ancient times, how would you know which came first, the full moon or the equinox? And not knowing that, and of course not having a calendar, how would you know if you were celebrating Easter on the correct date?"

Astarte pursed her lips. "You wouldn't know for sure."

Amanda continued. "And that's why what the Tower builders did was so ingenious." She sat back. "There are 35 possible days for Easter, March 22 through April 25." She pointed. "And on each of those days, the rising sun shines through that window of the Tower. It makes a light box that passes over at least part of the niche, or alcove, on the far wall." She pointed again. "But it only happens on these 35 days—on the other days it misses the niche entirely."

Astarte sat up. "I get it. So if the light hits the alcove, you know it could be Easter. And if it doesn't, it can't be."

"Just so. This gave the Templar priests a way to check for certain that they were celebrating on the correct day, even if earlier in the month they had overcast skies."

Cam interrupted. "Here comes the sun now; you can see the light box approaching the niche."

NEWPORT TOWER EASTER LIGHTBOX

Amanda replied. "Unfortunately the sun is about to be blocked by a building." They waited ten minutes for the light box to reappear.

"There it is again," Astarte pointed.

NEWPORT TOWER EASTER LIGHTBOX

"Yes," Amanda said. "We are near the beginning of the 35-day span, so it passes close to the edge of the niche. But you can see how over the past few minutes the box would have passed over the lower left corner of the niche if the building hadn't blocked it." She paused. "That means we are in the span of eligible Easter days."

They watched in silence for a few seconds as the light box crept across the interior Tower wall. Cam wondered how many other secrets the Tower held, how many other illuminations the seemingly randomly placed windows and niches, in conjunction with the sun and moon and planets, formed to mark important dates. The Tower was an ancient stone calendar—or even an almanac.

"Uncle January would have liked seeing this," Astarte whispered. "He thought the Templars were very smart."

Amanda glanced back at Cam—this was the first time Astarte had referred to her uncle in the past tense. Amanda took her hand, while Cam squeezed her shoulder.

Amanda leaned in. "If your uncle lives in your heart, Astarte, then he sees whatever you see."

"Really?" The girl sighed, smiled and sat up. "Then I'm glad we came today. I'd like to watch for a few more minutes if that's okay."

THE END

AUTHOR'S NOTE

Inevitably, I receive this question from readers: "Are the artifacts in your stories real, or did you make them up?" The answer is: If they are in the story, they are real, actual artifacts.

It is because they are real that I have included images of many of them within these pages—I want readers to see them with their own eyes, to be able to make at least a cursory judgment as to their age, origin and meaning. Are they authentic? Do they evidence ancient exploration of this continent? I hope readers will at least consider the possibility that they do.

Just as the artifacts displayed in this book are real, so too are the works of art. Again, I display these artworks because I want readers to perform their own analysis—what hidden message, if any, is the artist trying to convey? During medieval times, artists (such as Leonardo da Vinci) who had been initiated into the secret societies often communicated ancient knowledge considered blasphemous through their art. The expression "eyes that see" applies to those who knew how and where (including inside churches themselves) to look for these messages.

It is, then, these artifacts, sites and works of art that are the raw materials for this story. From them I have crafted a narrative that offers one plausible explanation for why they exist in the form they do. The key word here is 'plausible'—to use an analogy from our system of jurisprudence, it is not essential that a fiction writer prove his or her case beyond a reasonable doubt. But the writer must present a credible, believable scenario. The writer cannot simply make things up, fabricating history to suit his or her needs. I am cognizant of that, and have made every effort to craft a story that is supported by the historical record (although I recognize that this record may sometimes be the work of alternative rather than mainstream historians). For inquisitive readers, perhaps curious about some of the specific historical assertions made and evidence presented in this story, I offer the following substantiation (in order of appearance in the story):

- The Mustang Mountain Rune Stone is an actual artifact located outside a cave in the Mustang Mountains of southeastern Arizona. The translation offered in this novel is a rough translation of the translation made by runologist Michael Carr, allowing for a degree of poetic license to advance the plot.
- The Tucson Lead Artifacts are housed at the Arizona Historical Society, Tucson, Arizona and are available for viewing by appointment. Geologist Scott F. Wolter offers an in-depth analysis of them (concluding they are authentic) in his book, *Akhenaton to the Founding Fathers: Mysteries of the Hooked X* (North Star, 2013).
- For more information on the Los Lunas stone, see this site: http://www.mysteriousarizona.com .
- Much of my information regarding the substance first discovered by David Hudson and known as white powder of gold, or *mfkzt,* comes from Laurence Gardner's, *Lost Secrets of the Sacred Ark* (Barnes and Noble, 2005). For a good summary of Gardner's research, see this article written by Stephen Robbins: http://www.gold-eagle.com/article/mfkzt-new-dimension-value-gold .
- For a discussion of the telepathic and hallucinogenic effects of ingesting white powder of gold, see http://www.halexandria.org/dward467.htm .
- For references to the Philistines suffering from hemorrhoids after capturing the Ark of the Covenant, see 1 Samuel 5:6-12.
- For the assertion that the inscription at the America's Stonehenge site is ancient Punic that translates as, "To Baal of the Canaanites," and dates back to roughly 1500 BC, see David Goudsward, *Ancient Stone Sites of New England* (McFarland & Co., 2006), at page 86.

- The research connecting the America's Stonehenge alignments to Stonehenge England and ancient Phoenicia has been conducted by Kelsey Stone, of the Stone family that owns the America's Stonehenge site in New Hampshire.

- To read about Sigmund Freud's theory that Moses may have been the Pharaoh Akhenaten, see his book, *Moses and Monotheism.*

- Regarding my assertion that Moses lived at Serabit el-Khadim while in exile, see Graham Hancock, *The Sign and the Seal* (Touchstone, 1992), at page 345. Hancock, in turn, relies on an Arab source who claims Moses spent as long as 25 years in the Sinai Peninsula. Hancock's strongest argument for Moses being near Serabit el-Khadim is that the burning bush incident occurs at Mount Sinai (or perhaps Mount Horeb)—so Moses must indeed have been residing in the immediate vicinity (within 50 miles) of Serabit el-Khadim. Midian, where Moses is believed to have lived while in exile, is usually thought of as being located across the Gulf of Acaba from Sinai, but we are talking about an exile period of 40 years so it is possible Moses lived for a time in both places.

- The *In Hoc Signo Vinces* stone is located in Newport, RI and is only visible at low tide. It is known to have existed since at least the 1930s. Concerned neighbors keep the stone covered with sand to prevent graffiti and vandalism.

- For support for the assertion that the bound figure in the upside down carving at Rosslyn Chapel is Azazel rather than Lucifer, see this site at page 155: http://www.hermetics.org/pdf/alchemy/Alchemy_Key.pdf

Out of all this, then, comes a story that hopefully both educates and entertains. Were ancient explorers secretly visiting the southwestern United States? If so, were they doing so in hopes of discovering secrets of the sacred Ark of the Covenant? These are the questions that fascinate me. Hopefully you've found both some enlightenment and some entertainment in them as well.

PHOTO CREDITS

Images used in this book are either in the public domain and/or are provided courtesy of the following individuals (images listed in order of appearance in the story):

MUSTANG MOUNTAIN CAVE ENTRANCE,
WINTER SOLSTICE SUN PATH PROJECTION
courtesy Bo Hakala

AMERICA'S STONEHENGE SUMMER SOLSTICE
SUNRISE
courtesy America's Stonehenge

AMERICA'S STONEHENGE SUMMER SOLSTICE
SUNRISE ALIGNMENT IMAGES (multiple)
courtesy Renee Brody, based on alignments first identified by
Kelsey Stone

NEWPORT TOWER EASTER LIGHTBOX
courtesy Jim Egan (multiple images)